Maureen Child writes for the Mills & Boon Desire line and can't imagine a better job. A seven-time finalist for a prestigious Romance Writers of America RITA® Award, Maureen is an author of more than one hundred romance novels. Her books regularly appear on bestseller lists and have won several awards, including a Prism Award, a National Readers' Choice Award, a Colorado Romance Writers Award of Excellence and a Golden Quill Award. She is a native Californian but has recently moved to the mountains of Utah.

Sarah M. Anderson may live east of the Mississippi River, but her heart lies out west on the Great Plains. Sarah's book *A Man of Privilege* won an RT Reviewers' Choice Best Book Award in 2012. *The Nanny Plan* was a 2016 RITA® Award winner for Contemporary Romance: Short.

Sarah spends her days having conversations with imaginary cowboys and billionaires. Find out more about Sarah's heroes at www.sarahmanderson.com and sign up for the new-release newsletter at www.eepurl.com/nv39b

A typical Piscean, *USA TODAY* bestselling author **Yvonne Lindsay** has always preferred her imagination to the real world. Married to her blind-date hero and with two adult children, she spends her days crafting the stories of her heart, and in her spare time she can be found with her nose in a book reliving the power of love, or knitting socks and daydreaming. Contact her via her website, www.yvonnelindsay.com

Little Secrets

MAUREEN CHILD
SARAH M. ANDERSON
YVONNE LINDSAY

MILLS & BOON

First Published in Great Britain 2019
by Mills & Boon, an imprint of HarperCollins*Publishers*
1 London Bridge Street, London, SE1 9GF

ISBN: 978-0-263-27004-4

0519

MIX
Paper from
responsible sources
FSC™ C007454

This book is produced from independently certified FSC™ paper to ensure responsible forest management.

For more information visit: www.harpercollins.co.uk/green

Printed and bound in Spain
by CPI, Barcelona

LITTLE SECRETS: HIS UNEXPECTED HEIR

MAUREEN CHILD

To my mom, Sallye Carberry,
because she loves romance novels
and shared that love with me.

One

Jack Buchanan listened to his interior decorator talk about swatches and color and found his mind drifting… to *anything* else.

Four months ago, he'd been in a desert, making life-and-death decisions. Today, he was in an upholstery shop in Long Beach, California, deciding between leather or fabric for the bar seats on the Buchanan Company's latest cruise ship. He didn't know whether to be depressed or amused. So he went with impatient.

"Which fabric will hold up better?" he asked, cutting into the argument between the decorator and the upholsterer.

"The leather," they both said at once, turning to look at him.

"Then use the fabric." Jack pointed at a bolt of midnight blue cloth shot through with silver threads. "We're building a fantasy bar. I'm less interested in wear and more concerned with the look of the place. If you want black leather in the mix, too, use it on the booth seats."

While the decorator and the upholsterer instantly jumped on that idea and put their heads together to plan, Jack shifted his gaze to encompass the shop. Family-owned, Dan Black and his sons, Mark and Tom, ran the place and did great work. Jack had seen that much for himself.

The shop itself was long and wide and filled with not only barstools, but also couches, chairs and tables being refinished. A chemical scent hung in the air as two men at the back of the room worked on projects. The low-pitched roar of an industrial sewing machine was like white noise in the background and the guy seated at it moved quickly, efficiently. Their work was fast and good enough that they'd also done jobs for the navy and Jack figured if they could handle *that*, they could handle his cruise ship.

But why the hell was Jack even here? He was the CEO of Buchanan Shipping. Didn't he have minions he could have sent to take care of this?

But even as he thought it, he reminded himself that being here today, in person, had all been his idea. To immerse himself in every aspect of the business. He'd been away for the last *ten* years, so he had a lot of catching up to do.

Jack, his brother, Sam, and their sister, Cass, had all interned at Buchanan growing up. They'd put in their time from the ground up, starting in janitorial, since their father had firmly believed that kids raised with all the money in the world grew up to be asses.

He'd made sure that *his* children knew what it was

to really work. To be alongside employees who would expect them to do the job and who had the ability to fire them if they didn't. Thomas Buchanan raised his kids to respect those who worked for them and to always remember that without those employees, they wouldn't have a business. So Jack, Sam and Cass had worked their way through every level at the company. They'd had to buy their own cars, pay for their own insurance and if they wanted designer clothes, they had to save up for them.

Now, looking back, Jack could see it had been the right thing to do. At the time, he hadn't loved it of course. But today, he could step into the CEO's shoes with a lot less trepidation because of his father's rules. He had the basics on running the company. But it was this stuff—the day-to-day, small but necessary decisions—that he had to get used to.

Buchanan Shipping had interests all over the world. From cruise liners to cargo ships to the fishing fleet Jack's brother, Sam, ran out of San Diego. The company had grown well beyond his great-grandfather's dreams when he'd started the business with one commercial fishing boat.

The Buchanans had been on the California coast since before the gold rush. While other men bought land and fought with the dirt to scratch out a fortune, the Buchanans had turned to the sea. They had a reputation for excellence that nothing had ever marred and Jack wanted to keep it that way.

Their latest cruise ship was top-of-the-line, state-of-the-art throughout and would, he told himself, more than live up to her name, *The Sea Queen*.

"Mr. Buchanan," the decorator said, forcing Jack out of his thoughts and back to reality.

"Yeah. What is it?"

"There are still choices to be made on height of stools, width of booths..."

Okay, details were one thing, minutiae were another.

Jack stopped her with one hand held up for silence. "You can handle that, Ms. Price." To take any sting out of his words, he added, "I trust your judgment," and watched pleasure flash in her eyes.

"Of course, of course," she said. "I'll fax you a complete record of all decisions made this afternoon."

"That's fine. Thanks." He shook hands with Daniel Black, waved a hand at the men in the back of the shop and left. Stepping outside, he was immediately slapped by a strong, cold breeze that carried the scent of the sea. The sky was a clear, bold blue and this small corner of the city hummed with an energy that pulsed inside Jack.

He wasn't ready to go back to the company. To sit in that palatial office, fielding phone calls and going over reports. Being outside, even being here, dealing with fabrics of all things, was better than being stuck behind his desk. With that thought firmly in mind, he walked to his car, got in and fired it up. Steering away from work, responsibility and the restless, itchy feeling scratching at his soul, Jack drove toward peace.

Okay, maybe *peace* was the wrong word, he told himself twenty minutes later. The crowd on Main Street in Seal Beach was thick, the noise deafening and the mingled scents from restaurants, pubs and bakeries swamped him.

Jack Buchanan fought his way through the summer crowds blocking the sidewalk. He'd been home from his last tour of duty for four months and he still wasn't used to being surrounded by so many people. Made him feel on edge, as if every nerve in his body was strung tight enough to snap.

Frowning at the thought, he sidestepped a couple of women who had stopped in the middle of the sidewalk to argue about a pair of shoes, for God's sake. Shaking his head, he walked a little faster, dodging gawking tourists, teenagers with surfboards and kids racing in and out of the crowd, peals of laughter hanging in their wake.

Summer in Southern California was always going to be packed with the tourists who flocked in from all over the world. And ordinarily Jack avoided the worst of the crowds by keeping close to his office building and the penthouse apartment he lived in. But at least once a month, Jack forced himself to go out into the throngs of people—just to prove to himself that he could.

Being surrounded by people brought out every defensive instinct he possessed. He felt on guard, watching the passing people through suspicious, wary eyes and hated himself for it. But four months home from a battlefield wasn't long enough to ease the instincts that had kept him alive in the desert. And still, he worked at forcing himself to relax those instincts because he refused to be defined by what he'd gone through. What he'd seen.

A small boy bulleted around a corner and slammed right into Jack. Every muscle in Jack's body tensed until he deliberately relaxed, caught the kid by the shoulders to keep him from falling and said, "You should watch where you're running."

"Sorry, mister." The kid jerked his head back, swinging his long blond hair out of his eyes.

"It's okay," Jack said, releasing both the boy and the sharp jolt of adrenaline still pumping inside him. "Just watch it."

"Right. Gotta go." The boy took off, headed for the beach and the pier at the end of the street.

Jack remembered, vaguely, what it had been like to be ten years old with a world of summer stretched out ahead of you. With the sun beating down on him and a sea breeze dancing past, Jack could almost recapture the sensation of complete freedom that everyone lost as they grew up. Frowning at his own thoughts, he concentrated again on the crowd and realized it had been a couple of months since he'd been in Seal Beach.

A small beach community, it lay alongside Long Beach where he lived and worked, but Jack didn't make a habit of coming here. Memories were thick and he tended to avoid them, because remembering wouldn't get him a damn thing. But against his will, images filled his mind.

Last December, he'd been on R and R. He'd had two weeks to return to his life, see his family and decompress. He'd spent the first few days visiting his father, brother and sister, then he'd drawn back, pulling into himself. He'd come to the beach then, walking the sand at night, letting the sea whisper to him. Until the night he'd met *her*.

A beautiful woman, alone on the beach, the moonlight caressing her skin, shining in her hair until he'd almost convinced himself she wasn't real. Until she turned her head and gave him a cautious smile.

She should have been cautious. A woman alone on

a dark beach. Rita Marchetti had been smart enough to be careful and strong enough to be friendly. They'd talked, he remembered, there in the moonlight and then met again the following day and the day after that. The remainder of his leave, he'd spent with her, and every damn moment of that time was etched into his brain in living, vibrant color. He could hear the sound of her voice. The music of her laughter. He saw the shine in her eyes and felt the silk of her touch.

"And you've been working for months to forget it," he reminded himself in a mutter. "No point in dredging it up now."

What they'd found together all those months ago was over now. There was no going back. He'd made a promise to himself. One he intended to keep. Never again would he put himself in the position of loss and pain and he wouldn't ever be close enough to someone else that *his* loss would bring pain.

It was a hard lesson to learn, but he had learned it in the hot, dry sands of a distant country. And that lesson haunted him to this day. Enough that just walking through this crowd made him edgy. There was an itch at the back of his neck and it took everything he had not to give in to the urge to get out. Get away.

But Jack Buchanan didn't surrender to the dregs of fear, so he kept walking, made himself notice the everyday world pulsing around him. Along the street, a pair of musicians were playing for the crowd and the dollar bills tossed into an open guitar case. Shop owners had tables set up outside their storefronts to entice customers and farther down the street, a line snaked from a bakery's doors all along the sidewalk.

He hadn't been downtown in months, so he'd never

seen the bakery before. Apparently, though, it had quite the loyal customer base. Dozens of people—from teenagers to career men and women waited patiently to get through the open bakery door. As he got closer, amazing scents wafted through the air and he understood the crowds gathering. Idly, Jack glanced through the wide, shining front window at the throng within, then stopped dead as an all too familiar laugh drifted to him.

Everything inside Jack went cold and still. He hadn't heard that laughter in months, but he'd have known it anywhere. Throaty, rich, it made him think of long, hot nights, silk sheets and big brown eyes staring up into his in the darkness.

He'd tried to forget her. Had, he'd thought, buried the memories; yet now, they came roaring back, swamping him until Jack had to fight for breath.

Even as he told himself it couldn't be her, Jack was bypassing the line and stalking into the bakery. He followed the sound of that laugh as if it were a trail of breadcrumbs. He had to know. Had to see.

"Hey, dude," a surfer with long dark hair told him, "end of the line's back a ways."

"I'm not buying anything," he growled out and sent the younger man a look icy enough to freeze blood. Must have worked because the guy went quiet and gave a half shrug.

But Jack had already moved on. He was moving through the scattering of tables and chairs, sliding through the throng of people clustered in front of a wide, tall glass display case. Conversations rose and fell all around him. The cheerful jingle of the old-fashioned cash register sounded out every purchase as if celebrating. But Jack wasn't paying attention. His sharp gaze swept across the people in the shop, looking for the woman he'd never thought to see again.

Then that laugh came again and he spun around like a wolf finding the scent of its mate. Gaze narrowed, heartbeat thundering in his ears, he spotted her—and everything else in the room dropped away.

Rita Marchetti. He took a breath and simply stared at her for what felt like forever. Her smile was wide and bright, her gaze focused on customers who laughed with her. What the hell was she doing in a bakery in Seal Beach, California, when she lived in Ogden, Utah? And why did she have to look so damn good?

He watched her, smiling and laughing with a customer as she boxed what looked like a couple dozen cookies, then deftly tied a white ribbon around the tall red box. Her hands were small and efficient. Her eyes were big and brown and shone with warmth. Her shoulder-length curly brown hair was pulled into a ponytail at the base of her neck and swung like a pendulum with her every movement.

Her skin was golden—all over, as he had reason to know—her mouth was wide and full, and though she was short, her figure was lush. His memories were clear enough that every drop of blood in his body dropped to his groin, leaving him light-headed…briefly. In an instant, though, all of that changed and a surge of differing emotions raced through him. Pleasure at seeing her again, anger at being faced with a past he'd already let go of and desire that was so hot, so thick, it grabbed him by the throat and choked off his air.

The heat of his gaze must have alerted her. She looked up and across the crowd, locking her gaze with his. Her eyes went wide, her amazing mouth dropped open and she lifted one hand to the base of her throat as if she, too, was having trouble breathing. Gaze still locked with his, she walked away from the counter, came around the display case and though Jack braced himself for facing her again—nothing could have prepared him for what he saw next.

She was pregnant.

Very pregnant.

Her belly was big, rounded and covered by a skin-tight, bright yellow T-shirt. The hem of her white capris ended just below her knees and she wore slip-on sneakers in a yellow bright enough to match her shirt.

He saw and noted all of that in a split second before he focused again on her rounded belly. Jack's heartbeat galloped in his chest as he lifted his eyes to meet hers. He had a million questions and didn't have time to nail down a single one before, in spite of the crowd watching them, Rita threw herself into his arms.

"Jack!" She hugged him hard, then seemed to notice he wasn't returning her hug, so she let him go and stepped back. Confusion filled her eyes even as her smile faded into a flat, thin line. "How can you be here? I thought you must be dead. I never heard from you and—"

He flinched and gave a quick glance around. Their little reunion was garnering way too much attention. No way was he going to have this chat with an audience listening to every word. And, he told himself, gaze dropping to that belly again, they had a *lot* to talk about.

"Not here," he ground out, giving himself points for keeping a tight rein on the emotions rushing through him. "Let's take a walk."

"I'm working," she pointed out, waving her hand at the counter and customers behind her.

"Take a break." Jack felt everyone watching them and an itch at the back of his neck urged him to get moving. But he was going nowhere without Rita. He needed some answers and he wasn't going to be denied. She was *here*. She was *pregnant*. Judging by the size of her belly, he was guessing about six months pregnant. That meant they had to talk. Now.

She frowned a little and even the downturn of her mouth was sexy. Which told Jack he was walking into some serious trouble. But there was no way to avoid any of it.

While he stared at her, he could practically see the wheels turning in her brain. She didn't like him telling her what to do, but she was so surprised to see him that she clearly wanted answers as badly as he did. She was smart, opinionated and had a temper, he recalled, that could blister paint. Just a few of the reasons that he'd once been crazy about her.

Coming to a decision, Rita called out, "Casey," and a cute redhead behind the counter looked up. "I'm taking a break. Back in fifteen."

"Right, boss," the woman said and went right back to ringing up the latest customer.

"Might take more than fifteen," he warned her even as she started past him toward the door.

"No, it won't," she said over her shoulder.

Whatever her original response to seeing him had been, she was cool and calm now, having no doubt figured out that he deliberately hadn't contacted her when he got home. They'd talk about that, too. But not here.

People were watching. The redhead looked curious,

but Jack didn't give a damn. He caught up with Rita in two steps, took hold of her upper arm and steered her past the crowd and out the door. Once they were clear of the shop, though, Rita pulled free of his grip. "I can walk on my own, Jack."

Without another word, she proved it, heading down the block toward the Seal Beach pier. The tree-lined street offered patches of shade and she moved from sunlight to shadow, her strides short, but sure.

He watched her for a couple of minutes, just to enjoy the view. She'd always had a world-class butt and damned if it wasn't good to see it again. He'd forgotten how little she was. Not delicate, he told himself. Not by a long shot. The woman was fierce, which he liked and her temper was truly something to behold. But right now, it was his own temper he had to deal with. Why was she here? Why was she *pregnant*? And why the hell hadn't he known about it?

His long legs covered the distance between them quickly, then he matched his stride to hers until they were stopped at a red light at Ocean Avenue. Across the street lay the beach, the ocean and the pier. Even from a distance, Jack could see surfers riding waves, fishermen dotting the pier and cyclists racing along the sidewalk.

While they waited for the light to change, he looked down at her, and inevitably, his gaze was drawn to the mound of her belly. His own insides jumped then fisted. Shoving one hand through his hair, he told himself he should have written to her as he'd said he would. Should have contacted her when he came home for good. But he'd been in a place where he hadn't wanted to see anyone. Talk to anyone. Hell, even his family hadn't been able to reach him.

"How long have you been home?" she asked, her voice nearly lost beneath the hum of traffic.

"Four months."

She looked up at him and he read anger and sorrow, mingled into a dark mess that dimmed the golden light in those dark brown eyes. "Good to know."

Before he could speak again the light changed and she stepped off the curb. Once again he took her arm and when she would have shaken him off, he firmly held on.

Once they crossed the street, she pulled away and he let her go, following after her as she stalked toward a small green park at the edge of a parking lot. Just beyond was a kids' playground, and beside that, the pier that snaked out into the sea.

The wind whipped her ponytail and tugged at the edges of his suit jacket. She turned to look up at him and when she spoke, he heard both pain and temper in her voice.

"I thought you were dead."

"Rita—"

"No." She shook her head and held up one hand to keep him silent. "You *let* me think it," she accused. "You told me you'd write to me. You didn't. You've been home four months and never looked for me."

Jack blew out a breath. "No, I didn't."

She rocked back on her heels as if he'd struck her. "Wow. You're not even sorry, are you?"

His gaze fixed on hers. "No, I'm not. There are reasons for what I did."

She folded her arms across her chest, unconsciously drawing his attention to her belly again. "Can't wait to hear them."

Two

Rita was shaking.

Her hands clenched, she tried to ease her galloping heartbeat and steady her breathing. But just standing beside Jack Buchanan made that almost impossible. She slid a glance at him from beneath lowered lashes and her breath caught. Even in profile, he was almost too gorgeous. That black hair, longer now than it had been when they met, those ice-blue eyes, strong jaw, firm mouth, all came together until a knot of emotion settled in her throat, nearly choking her.

For one magical week six months ago, she had been in love and she'd thought he felt the same. Then he was gone, and she was alone, waiting for a letter that never came. So the last several months, Rita had been convinced he was dead. Killed in service on his last tour of duty. When they met, she knew he was a Marine on

R and R. Knew that he would be returning to danger. But somehow, she'd convinced herself that he would be safe. That he would come back. To her.

He'd promised to write and when she didn't hear from him, Rita had mourned him. She'd had to face the stark, shattering truth that he was never coming home again. That he'd made the ultimate sacrifice and everything they'd found together so briefly was over.

And now, he was *here*.

"How did you find me?"

He shook his head. "I didn't. I was just walking down the street. Heard your laugh and it stopped me cold."

Oh, God. Just an accident. A whim of Fate. He hadn't been looking for her. Had probably forgotten all about her the moment he left her six months ago. And what had she done? *Mourned. Grieved.* The memory of that pain fueled her next words.

"I thought you were dead," she finally said, and hoped he couldn't hear the pain in her voice.

He took a breath, blew it out and said, "I wanted you to."

Another blow and this one had her reeling. He'd *wanted* her to mourn him? To go through the pain of a loss so deeply felt that it had been weeks before she'd even been able to *function*? The only thing that had kept her going, that had gotten her out of bed in the mornings, was her baby. Knowing that Jack had left her with this gift, this child, had given her strength. She'd gone on, telling herself that Jack would want her to.

Now she finds out he *wanted* her to believe he was dead?

"Who are you?" she asked, shaking her head and

blinking furiously to keep tears she wouldn't show him at bay.

"The same guy you used to know," he ground out.

"No." She stiffened her spine, lifted her chin and glared at him. "The Jack I knew would never have put me through the last six months."

For an instant, she thought she saw shame flash across his eyes, but it was gone as quickly as it had appeared, so Rita put it down to wishful thinking.

"This isn't about me," he said quietly and she heard the tight control in his voice. "You're pregnant."

"Very observant." God. She wrapped her arms around her belly protectively.

"How far along?"

Shocked, Rita bit back the words that first flew to her mouth. Temper spiked, and she had to wrestle it into submission. She knew what he was asking—*who's the father?* And she didn't know if she was more hurt than angry or if it was a tie between the two.

"Six months," she said pointedly. "So your cleverly veiled question is answered. You're the father."

Not that she was happy about that at the moment. She loved her baby, *had* loved its father. But this stranger looking down at her through icy cold eyes was someone she didn't even recognize.

"And you didn't tell me about it."

Before she could stop it, a short, sharp laugh shot from her throat. Shaking her head in complete wonder at his ridiculous statement, she countered, "How was I supposed to do that, Jack? I had no way of contacting you. You were going to write to me with your address."

A muscle in his jaw twitched and his eyes narrowed, but she didn't care.

"I don't think sending a letter addressed to Jack Buchanan, United States Marine Corps, somewhere in a desert would have found you."

"Fine. I get it." He pushed the edges of his jacket back and stuffed his hands into his pockets. The wind lifted his dark red power tie, turning it into a waving flag. His hair was ruffled, his eyes were cold and his jaw tight. "Like I said, there were reasons."

"Still haven't heard them."

"Yeah. Not important right now. What is important," he said, his gaze shifting to the mound of her belly and back up to her eyes again, "is my baby."

"You mean *my* baby," she corrected and instantly wished she hadn't come to work that day. If she'd taken the day off, she wouldn't have been in the bakery when he walked by and none of this would be happening.

"Rita, if you think I'm walking away from this, you're wrong."

"Why wouldn't I think that?" she argued, moving away from him, instinctively keeping a safe distance between him and her child. "You walked away before. Never looked back."

"That's not true," he muttered, letting his gaze slide from hers to focus on the ocean instead. "I thought about you."

Her heart twisted, but Rita wouldn't allow herself to be swayed. He'd walked away. Shut her out. Let her *mourn* him, for heaven's sake. *I thought about you* just didn't make up for the misery she'd lived through.

"And I should believe you?"

He slanted her a glance. "Believe or not, it changes nothing."

"That much is true anyway," Rita agreed. "Look, I have to get back to work."

"Your boss won't fire you if you take more than fifteen minutes."

She laughed a little, but there was no warmth in it. "I *am* the boss. It's my bakery and I have to get back to it."

"Yours?"

"Yeah," she said, turning away to head back up Main Street.

"Why did you come here?" he asked and had her pausing to look over her shoulder at him. "I mean, *here*, Seal Beach. You lived in Utah when we met."

Rita stared at him and whether she wanted to admit it to herself or not, there was a jolt of need inside her she couldn't quite ignore. With the sun pouring down on him, he looked both dangerous and appealing. He was tall and broad-shouldered and even in an elegant suit, he looked…intimidating. Was it any wonder why she'd fallen so hard for him?

That was then, she reminded herself; this was now.

"I moved here because I wanted to feel closer to you," she admitted, then added, "of course, that's when I thought you were dead. Now, the only thing that's dead is what I felt for you."

When she walked away, Rita felt his gaze fix on her. And she knew this wouldn't be the last time she'd see him.

And that was both worrying and comforting.

That afternoon, Jack went back to the bakery, took a table that allowed him to keep his back to a wall and ordered coffee. A seemingly never-ending stream of customers came and went, laughed, chatted and walked out with red bakery boxes. This was her place, Jack thought with admiration. The shop was small but it had an old-world elegance to it.

Gleaming wood floors, dark blue granite counters, brass-and-chrome cash register, glistening glass display cases boasting pastries and cookies. There were brass sconces on the walls and pots of flowers and trailing greenery in strategic spots. It looked, he thought, just as she wanted it to. Like an exclusive Italian shop.

His gaze tracked her employees as they hustled to serve their customers, then shifted to land on Rita herself. She was still ignoring him, but he didn't mind. Gave him time to think.

Jack's mind was still buzzing. Not only at news of the baby but at seeing Rita again. He'd worked for months to wipe her out of his memories and now everything came rushing back in a tidal wave of images.

He saw her standing at the water's edge, moonlight spearing down on her from a cold, black sky. December at the beach was cold and she was wearing a jacket, but she was holding her shoes in one hand and letting the icy water lick at her toes.

Her hair was a tangle of dark brown curls that lifted and swirled around her head in the ever-present wind. She heard him approaching and instantly turned her head to look at him. He should have walked on, cut away from her and headed for the pier, but something about her made him stop. He kept a safe distance between them because he didn't want to worry her, but as he looked into her big brown eyes, he felt drawn to her like nothing he'd ever experienced before.

"Don't be scared," he said. "I'm harmless."

She smiled faintly and tipped her head to one side. "Oh, I doubt that. But I'm not scared."

"Why not?" he asked, tucking his hands into the pockets of his jeans. "Empty beach, in the dark, strange guy..."

"You don't seem so strange. Plus, I'm pretty tough," she said. "And I run really fast."

He laughed, admiring the way she stood there, so calm and self-assured. "Noted."

"So," she said, "I'm a tourist. What's your excuse for being at the beach when it's this cold?"

Jack turned to look out over the spread of black water dotted with white froth as it tumbled toward shore. "I've been away for a while, so I want to appreciate this view."

"You're in the military?" she asked.

He glanced at her and smiled. "That obvious?"

"It's the haircut," she admitted, smiling.

"Yeah," he scrubbed one hand across the top of his head. "Hard to disguise I guess. Marines."

She smiled and he thought she was the most beautiful woman he'd ever seen.

"Well, thank you for your service," she said, then added, "do you get tired of people saying that?"

"Nope," he assured her. "That never gets old. So, a tourist. From where?"

"Utah," she said, smiling. "Ogden, specifically."

"It's pretty," he said. "Though it's been a few years since I've been there."

Her smile brightened, nearly blinding him with the power of it. "Thanks, it is gorgeous, and I love the mountains. Especially in fall. But—" she half turned, letting her gaze slide across the ocean "—this is hard to resist."

"Yeah, I've missed it."

"I bet," she said, tipping her head to one side to look at him. "How long have you been gone?"

He shrugged, not really wanting to bring the desert heat and the memory of gunfire into this moment. "Too long."

As if she understood what he wasn't saying, she only nodded and they fell into silence until the only sound was the pulse and beat of the sea as it surged toward shore only to rush back out again.

At last, though, she reached up to push her hair back out of her face, smiled again and said, "I should be getting back to the hotel. It was nice meeting you."

"But we didn't," he interrupted quickly, suddenly desperate to keep her from leaving. "Meet, I mean. I'm Jack."

"Rita."

"I like it."

"Thanks."

"Do you really have to get back, or could I buy you a cup of coffee?"

She studied him for a long minute or two, then nodded. "I'd like that, Jack."

"I'm glad, but you sure are trusting."

"Actually," she said quietly, "I'm really not. But for some reason..."

"Yeah," he answered. "There's something..."

He walked toward her and held out one hand. She took it and the instant he touched her, he felt a hot buzz of something bright, staggering. He looked down at their joined hands, then closed his fingers around hers. "Come with me, Rita. I know just the place."

"Excuse me."

The tone of those words told Jack that it wasn't the first time the woman standing beside his table had said them. It was the redhead. "I'm sorry, what?"

"Rita says to tell you this is on the house," she said, setting a plate with two cannoli on it in front of him.

He frowned a little.

"Yeah, she told me you wouldn't look happy about it," the woman said. "I'm Casey. Can I get you more coffee?"

"Sure, thanks." She picked up his cup and walked to the counter, but Jack stopped paying attention almost immediately. Instead, his gaze sought out Rita.

As if she was expecting it, she turned to meet his stare and even from across that crowded room, it felt to Jack as it had that first night. As if they were alone on a deserted beach.

Well, damn it.

Casey was back an instant later with a fresh cup of coffee. Never taking his eyes off Rita, Jack leaned against the wall behind him and slowly sipped at his coffee. They had a lot to talk about. Too bad it wasn't *talking* on his mind.

A couple of hours later, the customers were gone and Rita was closing up. He'd already seen the sign that advertised their hours—open at seven, closed at six. Now as twilight settled on the beach, he watched Rita turn the deadbolt and flip the closed sign. Jack had had enough coffee to float one of his cargo ships and he'd had far too long to sit by himself and watch as she moved through the life she'd built since he'd last seen her.

"Why did you stay here all day, Jack?" She walked toward him. "This is borderline stalking."

"Not stalking. Sitting. Eating cannoli."

Her lips twitched and he found himself hoping she might show him that wide smile that he'd seen the first night they met. But it didn't come, so he let it go.

"Should you be on your feet this much?" he blurted.

Both of her eyebrows lifted as she set both fists on her hips. "Really?"

"It's a reasonable question," he insisted. "You're pregnant."

Now her big brown eyes went wide with feigned surprise. "I am?"

Jack sighed at the ridiculousness of the conversation. "Funny. Look, I just found out about this, so you could cut me some slack."

She took the chair opposite him, sitting down with a sigh of relief. "Why should I? It's not my fault you didn't know about the baby. You could have been a part of this from the beginning, Jack, if you had written to me." She reached over and plucked a dry leaf off the closest potted plant. Then she looked at him again. "But you didn't. Instead, you disappeared and let me think you were dead."

Yeah, he could see this from her side, and he didn't much care for the view. But that didn't change the fact that he'd done what he thought was necessary at the time. He'd had to put her out of his mind to survive when he went back to his duty station. Thoughts of her hadn't had any place in that hot, sandy miserable piece of ground and keeping her in his mind only threatened the concentration he needed to keep himself and his men alive.

Sure, at first, he'd thought that having her to think about would get him through, remind him that there was another world outside the desperate one he was caught up in. But two weeks after returning to deployment, something had happened to convince him that images of home were only a distraction. That keeping her face in his mind was dangerous.

So, he'd pushed the memories into a dark, deep corner of his brain and closed a door on them. It hadn't been easy, but he'd been convinced that it was the right thing to do.

Now he wasn't so sure.

"Why?" she asked, folding her hands on top of the small round glass-topped table. "You could at least tell me that much. Why did you never write, Jack?"

His gaze locked on hers. "It really doesn't matter now, does it? It's done. We have to deal with *now*."

Shaking her head, Rita sat back in the chair, and tapped the fingers of her right hand against the tabletop. "There is no *we*, Jack. Not anymore."

Beside him, a wide window overlooked Main Street. Late afternoon sunlight shone on the sidewalks, illuminating the people strolling through the early evening cool. It looked so normal. So peaceful. Yet seeing even that small crowd of pedestrians had Jack's insides going on alert. He didn't like the fact that he couldn't really relax around a lot of people anymore, but he had to accept that fact. So he turned away from strangers to look at a woman he'd once known so well.

"As long as there's a baby, there's a *we*," he told her.

"If you think I'm going to walk away from my own kid, you're wrong."

Instinctively, she dropped her hands to the curve of her belly and he realized she made that move a lot. Was it something all women did, or was Rita feeling threatened by seeing him again?

"Jack—"

"We can talk about it, work it out together," he said, interrupting her to make sure she understood where he was on this. "But bottom line, I'm here now. You're going to have to deal with it."

"You don't get to give me orders, Jack." She gave him a sad smile. "I live my own life. I run my own business. I raise my own child."

"And mine."

"Since your half and mine are intertwined," she quipped, "yes."

"Not acceptable." And this conversation was veering into the repetitive. It was getting him nowhere fast and he could see the flash of stubborn determination in her eyes that told him she wasn't going to budge. Well, hell. He could out-stubborn anyone.

"I really think you should go, Jack." She stood up, rubbing her belly idly with one hand.

He followed that motion and felt his heart triphammer in his chest. His child. Inside the woman that had been his so briefly. Damned if he'd leave. Walk away. It probably would have been better for all of them, but he wouldn't be doing it.

"I'll take you home," he said, standing to look down at her.

She chuckled. "I am home. I live in the apartment upstairs."

"You're kidding." He frowned, glanced at the ceiling as if he could see through the barrier into what had to be a very small apartment. "You live over a bakery."

She stiffened at the implied insult. "It's convenient. I get up at four every morning to start the baking, so all I have to do is walk downstairs."

"You're not raising my kid above a bakery."

When her eyes flashed and one dark eyebrow winged up, he knew he'd stepped wrong. But it didn't matter how he'd said it if the end was the same. His kid was not going to live above a bakery. Period.

"And, the circle is complete," she said, walking to the front door. She unlocked it, opened it wide and waved one hand as if scooping him out the door. "I want you to leave, Jack."

"All right." He conceded on this point. For now. He started past her, then stopped when their bodies were just a breath apart. When he caught her scent and could almost feel the heat shimmering off her body. Everything in him twisted tight and squeezed. Giving in to the urge driving him, he reached out, took her chin in his hand and tipped her face up until her eyes were locked with his. "This isn't over, Rita. It's just getting started."

Sitting on her couch in her—all right, yes, tiny apartment—Rita curled her feet underneath her as her fingers tightened on her cellphone. "What am I supposed to do, Gina?"

Instead of answering, her sister called out, "Ally, do *not* pour milk on the dog again."

"But *why*?" A young, loud voice shouted in response.

In spite of everything going on in her life at the moment, Rita grinned. Ally was two years old with a hard head, a stubborn streak a mile wide and a sweet smile that usually got her out of trouble.

"Because he doesn't like it!" Gina huffed out a breath, came back on the line, and whispered, "Actually he *does* like it, idiot dog. Then he spends all night licking the milk off himself, my floor is sticky and he smells like sour milk."

It was times like these that Rita really missed her family. Her parents. Her sister. Her two older brothers. All of her nieces and nephews. They were all in Ogden, working at the family bakery, Marchetti's. Rita's family was loud, boisterous, argumentative and sometimes she missed them so much she actually *ached* to be with them.

Like now, for instance.

"Michael and Braden Franco!" Gina shouted. "If you ride your skateboards down the steps and one of you breaks another bone, I will burn those boards in the fire pit—"

The five-year-old twins were adventurous and barely containable. It's what Rita loved best about them.

Gina broke off with a satisfied sigh. "Another crisis averted. Sorry sweetie, what were you saying again?"

Back to the matter at hand. "Jack. He's alive. He's *here*." Rita bit down hard on her bottom lip and blinked wildly to keep the tears filling her eyes from falling. Though there was no one there to see her cry, she didn't want to give Jack the satisfaction.

Hadn't she already cried rivers for Jack? After two months had passed without a word from him, Rita had known that he was gone, no doubt killed in action somewhere far away. What other reason, she'd told herself, could there have been for him not to write her?

They'd had such an amazing connection. Something strong and powerful had grown between them in one short week. She'd loved him fiercely even after so short a time. But then her mother had always told her that time had nothing to do with love. If you knew someone five days or five years, the feelings didn't change.

It had taken Rita much less than five days to know that Jack was the one man she wanted. Then he was gone and the pain of loss had crippled her. Until she'd discovered she was pregnant.

"He's *there*?" Gina whispered as if somehow Jack could overhear her. "At your apartment?"

"No," she said, though she tossed a quick look toward the door at the back of the building that opened onto a staircase leading to a small parking lot. She half expected Jack to show up on her landing and knock. Shaking her head, she said, "No, he's not here, here. He's here in Seal Beach. He came into the bakery today."

"Oh. My. God." A moment or two passed before Gina continued. "What did you do? What did he say? Where the hell has he been? Why didn't he write to you? Bastard."

A short laugh shot from Rita's throat. She heard the outrage in her sister's voice and was grateful for it. How did anyone survive without a sister?

"I nearly shrieked when I saw him," Rita confessed. "Then I hugged him, damn it."

"Of course you hugged him," Gina soothed. "Then did you kick him?"

She laughed again. "No, but I wish I'd thought of it at the time."

"Well, if you need me, Jimmy can watch the kids for a few days. I'll fly out there and kick him for you."

Rita sighed and smiled all at once. "I can always count on you, Gina."

"Of course you can. So where's he been?"

"I don't know."

"Why didn't he write?"

Rita frowned. "I don't know."

"Well, what did he say?"

Rita picked up her cup of herbal tea and took a sip. "He only wanted to talk about the baby."

"Oh, boy."

"Exactly." Sighing more heavily now, Rita set the cup down on the coffee table again. "He was…surprised to find out I was pregnant and he didn't look happy about it."

"We don't need him to be happy. But why wouldn't he be? Who doesn't like babies? Hold on. I'll be right back."

While she waited, Rita's head dropped back against the couch. Her apartment wasn't tiny, it was cozy, she thought in defense as her gaze swept over the space. A small living room, an efficiency kitchen, one bedroom and a bathroom that, she had to admit, was so small she regularly smacked her elbows against the shower door. But the apartment walls were a soft, cheerful green and were dotted by framed photos of the beach, the mountains and her family.

"There," Gina said when she was back. "I took the baby to Jimmy. I have to pace when I'm mad."

Rita laughed. "Gina, I'm okay, really. I just needed to talk to you."

"Of course you did, but we're Italian and I need my hands to talk as much as I need to move around. Besides, I just finished feeding Kira. Jimmy can take her for a while."

Her sister had four gorgeous kids, the youngest only eight months old and a husband who adored her. A small pang of envy echoed in Rita's heart. Then to ease the hurt, she rubbed the mound of her baby with slow, loving strokes, and reminded herself that she had a child, too. That she wasn't alone. That it didn't matter that Jack had walked away from her only to suddenly crash back into her life.

"So," Gina said a moment later, "what're you going to do about this? How are you feeling?"

"I'm not sure, to both questions." Pushing up off the couch, Rita walked to the window overlooking Main Street and smiled, thinking Gina was right. Italians thought better when they could move around. Looking down on the street, she enjoyed the view that was so similar to the one she grew up with. Historic 25th Street in Ogden also had the old-fashioned, old-world feel to the buildings, the lampposts and the bright, jewel-toned flowers spilling out of baskets.

But as pretty as it was, it wasn't home. Not really. She was alone in the dark but for a slender thread of connection to her big sister.

"I don't know what to do," she admitted, "because I don't know what he's planning."

"Whatever it is, you can handle it." And, as if Gina had read her mind, she added, "You're not alone, Rita."

Her mouth curved slightly. "Not how it feels."

“You still love him, don’t you?”

Rita laid her hand on the glass, letting the cold seep into her skin, chilling the rush of heat Gina’s question had awakened.

“Why would I be foolish enough for that?” she whispered.

Three

"What's going on with you?"

Jack looked up. His father walked into the office that, up until four months ago, had been his. Thomas Buchanan was a tall man, with salt-and-pepper hair, sharp blue eyes and a still-trim physique. Though he'd abdicated the day-to-day running of the company to his oldest son, Thomas maintained his seat on the board and liked to keep abreast of whatever was happening. That included keeping tabs on his son.

"Nothing," Jack answered, lowering his gaze to the sheaf of papers on the desktop. "Why?"

"Well," Thomas said, strolling around the room, "you nearly bit Sean's head off when he couldn't get the shipping schedule up on the plasma fast enough."

"It's his job," Jack said, being perfectly reasonable. "He should be able to accomplish it when asked."

"Uh-huh."

Jack knew that tone. He glanced at his father, saw the wary curiosity-filled expression and looked away again. He wasn't in the mood for a chat and couldn't satisfy his father's curiosity. He knew that ever since he'd returned to civilian life, his family had been worried about him and no one more than his father. There didn't seem to be anything Jack could do about it, though. He didn't need therapy or sympathy and didn't want to talk about what he'd seen—what he wanted to do was forget about it and pick up his life where he'd left off. So far of course, that wasn't happening.

Rather than try to explain all of that to his dad, Jack chose to ignore the man's questions, even though he knew it wouldn't get him anywhere. The worry would remain, along with the questions, whether spoken or not. After a few seconds of silence from him, though, Thomas seemed to understand that it was a subject Jack wasn't going to address.

"Still don't understand why you changed the office furniture around," his father said, surprising Jack with the sudden shift of topic. "My father's the one who put that desk in front of the windows. I don't think it's been moved since then. Until now."

Jack squirmed slightly in his oversize black leather chair. He'd made a few changes since he'd stepped into his father's shoes. The main one being that he had moved the old mahogany desk across the room so that he could have his back to a wall and not be outlined in a window.

Yes, he knew it was foolish without anyone pointing it out to him. He didn't have to worry about snipers here, but it was hard to shake ingrained habits that had kept him alive.

"I like it where it is," Jack said simply.

"Yeah." His father gave a resigned sigh, then admitted, "I wish you could talk to me."

His father's voice was so quiet, so wistful, Jack's attention was caught. He looked up and found his dad watching him through concerned eyes.

He didn't enjoy knowing that his family was worried about him. In fact, it only added to the guilt and the pain that were crouched on his shoulders every day. But he couldn't ease for them what he couldn't ease for himself.

"We do talk," Jack said.

"Not about anything important," his father answered. "Not since you got back. It's like you're still too far away to reach."

"I'm right here, Dad," he said, trying to help, knowing he was failing.

"Part of you is," his father agreed, "but not all of you. I wonder every day when my son will finally come home."

So did Jack. It was as if a piece of him had been left behind in the heat of a desert and he didn't know when or if he'd find that part of himself again. Jack sat back and let a long breath slide slowly from his lungs. "I'm doing my best here, Dad."

"I know that." Thomas stuffed his hands into his pants pockets and rocked uneasily on his heels. "I just wish there was something I could do to help. That you would *let* me do. I thought that stepping down, having you take over here, would make a difference. Drop you back into the world and, all right, *force* you to find your life again. But you continue to shut yourself off. From me, from your sister and brother. Hell, you haven't even been on a date since you got back, son."

"I don't want to date." Lie. Everything in him wanted Rita, but he wouldn't give in to it. He was in no shape to be in her life and he knew it.

"Right there should tell you that there's something wrong."

"I'm fine," Jack said, hoping to head his dad off at the pass. He'd heard this before. Knew that his father had the best of intentions. But Jack couldn't give the older man what he wanted most.

Thomas shook his head, then nodded. "You're not, but you will be. I wish you could believe me on that." He walked toward his son, laid both hands on the desk and leaned in. "I know you don't. Not yet. But someday you will, Jack. Just give yourself a chance, all right?"

"I am." He looked into his father's eyes and lied again. "Everything's good. I swear."

Nodding, the older man pushed up from the desk. "Okay. We'll leave it there for now."

Thank God, Jack thought in relief.

"On another subject entirely," his father said, "I'm headed down to San Diego tomorrow. Sam and I are taking the boat out fishing for the weekend. Want to join us?"

The Buchanan Boys, as his mother used to call the three of them, had gone on hundreds of fishing weekends together. And in the old days, there had been nothing Jack liked more than getting away with his younger brother and his father. But now, the thought of being caged on a boat in the middle of the ocean with a too-curious father and brother sounded like a nightmare. They'd hammer him with questions, he'd resent being prodded and they'd all have a crappy time.

Besides, he told himself, there was Rita. Decisions to be made.

"I can't," he said. "I've got plans I can't get out of." Not that Rita knew of his plan to corner her into talking with him about their baby.

"Plans?" Thomas gave him a pleased smile. "That's good, son. Really good. To prove how happy that makes me, I won't even ask you what you're going to be doing."

"Thanks," Jack said wryly.

"All right, then." His father slapped his hands together then gave his palms a good scrub. "I've got to go by the house, pick up my fishing gear. Then I'm headed to San Diego. I'll have my phone with me if you need to contact me."

"I won't," Jack assured him. "But thanks. And say hi to Sam."

"I will."

Once his father was gone, Jack took a long, deep breath and willed the tension out of his body. It didn't work, so he got up, walked across the well-appointed office without even noticing the familiar furnishings.

Beige walls, dark red carpet, thick and plush enough to take a nap on, and twin couches facing each other across a low wood table. Windows were on two walls and Jack had moved the desk out of the line of sight of both of them.

Now, though, he walked to a far window and looked out over the sea. He didn't look at the beach below or the crowd of early-summer sun worshippers spread out on the sand. Instead, he watched the steady rise and fall of the water as wind and its own weight formed ripples and waves that seemed to go on endlessly.

It was quiet in the office and normally he treasured

that. But now, that silence tapped at the edges of his mind like a persistent knock on a closed door. As that door opened, images of Rita flooded his brain, from before, from yesterday, until he half expected her to simply appear physically in the office. But that wasn't going to happen.

Rita would never come to him, she was too angry and he couldn't blame her for it. But that wouldn't stop him from doing what he had to do. She was pregnant with *his* child and damned if he'd ignore that.

There was a knock on the office door just before it opened and his assistant stepped inside. A middle-aged woman with a brisk, no nonsense attitude, Linda Holloway said, "Excuse me, Mr. Buchanan, you've got a twelve-thirty meeting with the captain of *The Sea Queen*."

In the last four months, Linda had been responsible for Jack's seamless takeover of his father's position. She kept meticulous track of his schedule, his tasks and anything involving Buchanans. He was grateful, but right now, he didn't appreciate the interruption.

"The captain will meet you at the dock so you can take a walk-through of the areas you didn't see on your visit last month."

"Yeah," he said. "I remember." *The Sea Queen* was their latest ocean liner. And yes, he did have to meet the captain if only to go over any last-minute concerns about the ship's maiden voyage coming up in about a month. But not today.

"Cancel it," he snapped and stalked across the office.

"What?" Linda watched him, eyes wide. "But the captain has come in from his home in Arizona specifically for this meeting."

Yet one more guilt straw landed on the bale already situated on his shoulders, but he accepted it and moved on.

"It can't be helped. I've got personal business to take care of. Put the captain up in the best hotel in the city and tell him we'll meet tomorrow morning."

"But—"

"Eight o'clock on the dock. I'll be there and we can take care of this business then."

He snatched his suit jacket out of the closet and shrugged into it. What good was being the boss if you couldn't make the rules?

"But—"

"Linda," he said firmly, "I have somewhere to be and it can't wait. Make this happen."

"Yes, sir," she said, the slightest touch of defeat in her tone.

He didn't address it. "Thanks," he said and walked around her to leave without a backward glance.

"Tall, dark and dangerous is back."

Rita glanced at her friend and bakery manager, Casey. "What?"

She jerked her head toward the small cluster of tables in one corner of the bakery. "The guy who swept you out of here yesterday? He's back and looking just as edible as ever."

Rita's pulse skittered as she slowly, carefully, looked over her shoulder. Jack was sitting at the same table he'd spent hours at the day before. He wore a black suit, with a black dress shirt and a dark red tie. He looked exactly how Casey had described him. Dangerous. Edible.

As if he sensed her looking at him, he turned his

head and his gaze locked with hers. Instantly, her blood turned to a river of fire and the pit of her stomach fluttered with nerves and expectation. He'd had that same effect on her from the beginning.

The minute he took her hand that first night on the beach, she'd felt it. That something special. Magical. There was a buzz between them that was electrifying.

She hadn't been afraid when he'd walked toward her out of the darkness. Maybe she should have been, but instead, it had felt almost as if she'd been waiting for him.

They walked to a small café, took a table on the sidewalk and ordered coffee. There they sat for three hours, talking, sharing their lives, though Rita did more of that than he did. He hadn't talked about his family or where he lived, only that his name was Jack Buchanan and that he had a week to be back in the real world and how he didn't want to waste a moment of it.

And when he walked her to her nearby hotel, neither of them wanted to say goodnight. He escorted her through the lobby to the bank of elevators with mirrored doors and she looked at their reflection as they stood together. He was so tall, she so short. But they seemed to fit, she thought, as if they'd been made for each other.

He turned her in his arms and asked, "Tomorrow? Be with me tomorrow, Rita."

"Yes," she said quickly, breathlessly.

"Good, that's good." A brief smile flashed across his face and warmed his cool blue eyes. "I'll be here early. Nine okay?"

"How about eight?" Rita asked, wanting to be with him again as soon as possible.

"Even better." He cupped her face in his palm and held her there as he bent his head to kiss her.

Rita held her breath and closed her eyes. Once, twice, his mouth brushed hers, gently, as if waiting for her response to know if there should be more.

And she wanted more. She wanted it all. Never had she felt for a man what Jack made her feel. Just talking with him stirred everything inside her and now that she knew the taste of his mouth, she hungered for him.

Rita answered his unasked question by wrapping her arms around his neck and leaning in to him. Her breasts pressed against his chest and her nipples ached as her body hummed. He actually growled and that sound sent her head spinning as he grabbed hold of her and deepened the kiss. Devouring her, his tongue tangled with hers, his breath mingled with hers and Rita felt as if their souls were touching, merging. Every inch of her body lit up and awakened as if she'd been in a coma all of her life and was only now truly living.

Neither of them cared about who might be watching, they were too lost in the fire enveloping them. Lightheaded, loving the feel of his big strong hands sliding up and down her back, Rita could only think how badly she wanted him, but she wasn't a one-night stand kind of woman and didn't think she could pretend she was, even for Jack.

When finally she thought she might never breathe again, he broke the kiss and leaned his forehead against hers while they both fought to steady themselves.

"You are a dangerous woman," he whispered, a half smile curving his mouth.

"I never thought so, but okay."

His grin flashed. "Trust me."

She smiled back at him and felt her equilibrium disintegrate even further. Honestly, he didn't smile often, but when he did, it was a lethal weapon on a woman's defenses. Her mouth was still tingling from his kiss and the taste of him was flooding her system.

"Looking into those brown eyes of yours makes me feel like I'm diving into good, aged whiskey," he murmured, reaching out to smooth his fingers over her face. "Makes me a little drunk just losing myself in them."

"Your eyes remind me of the color of the sky after a mountain storm," she said, "clear, bright, with just a hint of shadow."

His smile faded then and Rita wished she could pull her words back. She hadn't meant to say anything about the darkness she saw in his eyes, but her urge to ease those shadows was nearly overwhelming.

"I've shadows enough, I guess," he admitted, letting his hand drop to his side. "But when I'm with you, I don't notice them."

"I'm glad," she said and went up on her toes to kiss him again.

Putting both hands on her shoulders, he held her in place and took a long step back. He shook his head and said, "If I kiss you again, I'm not going to be able to let you go."

That sounded pretty good to Rita, but she knew it wasn't smart to go to bed with a man she just met no matter how much she wanted to.

"So," he continued, "I'm going to leave while I still can."

"Probably a good idea," Rita said though, inside, her mind was whimpering, demanding that she beg him to stay.

"You keep looking at me with those whiskey eyes and I'm not going to be able to walk away." His voice was wry, his eyes flashing with heat.

"Then I will," she said, reaching out to punch the elevator call button.

"I do like a strong woman," he told her.

"Not so strong at the moment," Rita admitted when she looked at him again and felt a rush of heat settle and pool at her core. "But I will be. So, good night. I guess I'll see you at eight."

"Seven," he said.

"Even better," she said, throwing his own words from earlier back at him. The elevator dinged and the doors swished open. She stepped inside, then turned to look at him again. "Seven. I'll be ready."

"Good," he said as the doors slid shut on a whisper of sound, "because I'm ready now."

Alone, Rita leaned against the wall of the car, smiled to herself and lifted one hand to her mouth as if she could capture his taste and hold on to it forever. As the elevator rose to her floor, she told herself she wouldn't be getting much sleep tonight, but her morning was going to be wonderful.

"Rita?" Casey's voice and an insistent shake of her arm. "Hey, Rita? You okay?"

"What?" she tore her gaze from Jack's and looked at her friend. Coming up out of that memory that had been so filled with sensation and sound was like breaking the surface of the water when you were near drowning. You were back in reality but still too stunned to accept it easily. "Sure," she said, nodding for emphasis. "Yes. I'm fine. Really. Just…tired."

And sexually frustrated and angry and hurt and confused and far too many other emotions to even name.

"You sure?" Casey tried to steer Rita toward a stool. "Maybe you should sit down."

"No." Rita shook off all those unwelcome emotions and smiled. "I'm fine. Really. Um, will you keep an eye on the front while I go in the back to restock the cannoli tray?"

"Absolutely," Casey said, "as long as you call out if you need me."

"Don't be such a worrier," Rita told her with a pat on the arm.

Hurrying through the swinging door into the kitchen where she could get a couple of minutes to herself, Rita gave a sigh of relief to be on her own. She needed a little time to settle. Do the *ahooom* thing until she could breathe without feeling like she was going to shake apart at the seams.

"Get a grip, Rita," she mumbled as she snatched an apron off the hook by the door. Slipping it on over her head, she drew the string ties around her ever-expanding belly then tied it down. The simple, familiar task helped her get steady again.

She scrubbed her hands in the kitchen sink, dried them on a fresh towel, then turned to survey her domain. She might have chefs come in to help her, but this bakery was all hers, right down to the last cookie.

She was most comfortable in the kitchen. Rita and her brothers and sister had grown up working in their parents' Italian bakery in Ogden. From the time she was a little girl, barely tall enough to reach the mixing table, Rita had been helping the bakers. Even if it was just sprinkling flour on the cool white marble so dough could be rolled out. She loved the scent of baking cookies, cakes, pastries. She loved the feel of getting her hands into a huge bowl of dough to knead it. She'd worked off a lot of temper by working bread dough into shape.

"But there's not enough dough in the world to help me through *this*," she whispered, laying out paper doilies on a stainless steel tray. Then she moved to the end of the counter and carefully set fresh cannoli, some draped in shiny chocolate, on each doily. To her, presentation was as important as taste so before it went out to the shop, it would be perfect.

Once she was satisfied that all of her cannoli were lined up like soldiers, Rita checked on two more bowls of rising dough, punched them down, then covered them again, so they could do a second rise.

She'd be making bread before the bakery closed because her customers liked picking up a fresh loaf on the way home from work. Then she checked the meticulously aligned steel racks against one wall and made a note to have Casey get someone back there to box up the maple-nut biscotti.

"And I'm stalling," she said aloud to the empty room. "Question is, why?"

Her eyes closed on a sigh as Jack's deep voice echoed all around her. Of course he wouldn't be ignored. He was the kind of man who got exactly what he wanted *when* he wanted it. A trait that was both sexy and annoying.

"You shouldn't be back here, Jack."

"Your friend Casey said you weren't feeling well."

She rolled her eyes and told herself to have a little chat with Casey. Wouldn't do any good, of course. If a gorgeous man asked Casey to stand on her head, the girl would. And they just didn't come more gorgeous than Jack, so Casey really had been putty in his hands.

Rita surrendered to the inevitable and turned around to face him. "I don't have time for you right now, Jack. I'm working."

She walked to the tray of fresh cannoli, but before she could pick it up, Jack swooped in and snatched it from her. "You shouldn't be carrying this. It's heavy."

A thread of pleasure whipped through her at his instinctive urge to protect, even as it irritated her that he clearly thought she was either helpless or a delicate blossom.

"I carry heavy things all the time. I'm pregnant, not an invalid." He opened his mouth to argue the point, but she rushed on before he could. "I'm careful, too. I don't take chances with my baby—"

"Our baby."

"*The* baby," she corrected meaningfully. "Now, give me the tray."

"Don't be stupid," he said and turned for the door into the front of the shop.

"I'm stupid now?" she said to his retreating back.

"I said *don't* be stupid. There's a difference."

When the door swung open, snatches of conversation rushed toward her, along with Casey's prolonged sigh of "Thank you so much."

Rolling her eyes so hard it was a wonder they didn't simply pop out of her skull and skitter across the floor, Rita pulled down the decorative biscotti boxes. She'd pack them herself and that would give her yet another reason to stay back here and keep her distance from Jack. Of course she should have known that wouldn't work.

He came back through the swinging door, holding an empty tray and shook his head at her. "Do you have to do everything around here personally?"

"My business, my responsibility." She lifted a tray of biscotti off the rack and turned for the counter, dodging Jack when he would have taken it from her. "So yes, I do. I want things done a certain way and I can't expect everyone else to do all the work."

She expertly folded the box into shape, slid a dozen biscotti inside then closed the box and slapped a gold *Italia* sticker in place. Automatically, she started on the next one while Jack came closer. Rita didn't even look up from her task when she asked, "Why are you here again, Jack?"

He picked up a biscotti and took a bite, shrugging when she gave him a hard look. "I'm here because you are. Because my baby is. And I'm not leaving until we work this out between us."

"Fine." She continued boxing the biscotti in the bright red *Italia* containers, keeping her eyes on the job, rather than him. If she looked at Jack again she'd feel that torn sensation—yearning and betrayal.

He'd allowed her to mourn. Let her believe he was dead. How did you forgive someone for that when they wouldn't even explain *why* they'd done it? And how did you get past those old feelings that continually slipped in despite the pain that should have smothered them?

"You want to talk, let's talk," she said. "I'll start. I want to know why you disappeared."

"That's not on the table."

Now she did risk a quick glance at him and his features were tight, closed, his eyes cold and icy.

"So we talk, but only about what you're willing to

discuss?" Shaking her head, she sealed another box and set it aside, automatically reaching for the next.

"I'm not looking to recapture anything here, Rita."

A sharp stab of pain stole her breath at the blunt honesty. She looked into his eyes. "Wow."

He flinched slightly, but otherwise remained stoic. "I'm not saying that to hurt you."

"And yet…"

He looked down at the biscotti in his hand and then lifted his gaze to hers again. "This isn't about us, Rita. It's about the baby."

A sinking sensation opened up in the pit of her stomach. Her mouth went dry and her hands shook, so she set the box she was holding down onto the counter so he couldn't see it. How had they come to this, she wondered. Where had it all gone so terribly wrong?

What had made him shut her out when he left her to go back to his duties? What had turned him away from what they'd found, what they'd been to each other for one amazing week?

And how had he become so cold that he could stand just inches from her and look at her as if she wasn't really there?

"What is it you want, Jack?"

He set the biscotti down, planted both palms on the counter and said, "I want you to marry me."

Four

Rita actually *felt* shock slam into her like a physical blow. Whatever she'd been expecting hadn't been this. She knew she was staring. Knew she should say *something*, but for the first time in her life she was absolutely speechless. He was serious, that much she could see. But surely he didn't expect her to agree.

He laughed shortly, but it was merely a harsh scrape of sound against his throat. There was no humor in his eyes and no easing of the tightness of his mouth. "Not the usual reaction when a man proposes."

Finally she found her own voice. "It's not the *usual* situation, is it?"

"No," he admitted solemnly, "it's not."

"Jack, you don't want to be married to me." God, how it hurt to say that, because six months ago, at the end of their week together, Rita had had dreams. She'd believed that when he came home from war, they would get married, have kids, live happily ever after. All the normal fantasies that women spin when they meet a man who makes their blood burn and their heart sing.

But that dream had died with him, or so she'd believed at the time. Now he was here, but it was a different Jack who faced her asking her to marry him. It was a colder, harder man than she'd once known and the loss of that rang deep and true inside her.

He pushed one hand through his hair then scrubbed the back of his neck. "No," he admitted, looking directly into her eyes. "I don't want to be married. To anyone."

"Then what is this about?"

"I also don't want my kid born without my name."

Rita sighed heavily. "Of course you'll be on the birth certificate, listed as the father."

He frowned. "Not what I'm talking about. I want us married when the baby's born," he told her firmly. "After that, we can divorce and I won't bother you again."

Just when she thought the shocks couldn't be more earth shattering, he said something else that ripped away what was left of the earth beneath her feet. "Seriously?"

Moments ago, she'd worried about a custody battle, but in reality he wanted nothing to do with his own child? What kind of man was he?

He blew out a breath, shoved his hands into his slacks pockets and admitted, "I'm not asking you to understand—"

"Good," she interrupted. "Because I don't. If you don't want me, then fine. I get it. But how can you not want anything to do with your own child? My God, who are you?"

"Still me," he insisted, but she didn't believe him.

When she first met him, he'd been more quiet than chatty, more solemn than happy, but there hadn't been such a marked coldness about him. Now it was as if he'd submerged his old self under a layer of ice.

"Think whatever you like about me. Can't change it. But I want my kid born into the Buchanan family." His mouth tightened and the muscle in his jaw twitched as if he were grinding his teeth together. "After that, you can raise it."

It. So impersonal. So distancing. Rita hadn't wanted to know what her baby was, preferring to be surprised. But now, at her next appointment, she would ask. Because she wanted Jack to see their child as a *person*. But that was for later. "So you'll just put your baby aside like you did me and move on, is that it?"

He scrubbed one hand across his jaw. "You're putting words in my mouth."

"Because you're not explaining any of this."

"Damn it, Rita, you don't have to make this harder than it already is."

"No, I don't," she said sadly. "Because *you* did that just fine on your own."

"I'll make sure you're taken care of."

Her eyes nearly popped out of her head at that insult on top of everything else. Rita had reached her limit. She walked around the edge of the counter, leading with her belly, and didn't stop until she was standing in front of him. "You think I want *money* from you?"

He met her gaze and Rita would have given anything to be able to read what he was thinking, feeling. But there was no clue there for her. He was a blank slate. Deliberately. This new Jack had such a tight handle on his emotions, she couldn't see past the facade.

"No," he said, shaking his head. "I know you don't want money."

"That's something, anyway," she muttered, still looking up into his eyes, still looking for some shred of the man she'd loved.

"Do this, Rita," he said quietly.

"Why would I marry you knowing you don't want me?"

"Because I need it," he admitted and it looked as though it cost him to give her that much. "I need to know my kid has my name. That I did the right thing."

"The right thing." She huffed out a breath and folded her arms across her growing middle. "This isn't the '50s, Jack. Single mothers do just fine on their own and so can I." She didn't believe in what he was saying, but Jack clearly did.

Rita knew she would be fine raising her child alone. She had her family's support. She had her own business, a home and the strength to do whatever she had to do to succeed.

"It's not a matter of that," Jack argued. He picked up the biscotti again and when his hand fisted around it, let crumbs fall to the marble counter. "I know you *could* do it. I don't want you to. I get you don't owe me a damn thing and I've got no right to ask for this. Still, this is important to me, Rita. I don't want my kid knowing his parents weren't married."

"Oh, for heaven's—"

"Look, this is the best answer for all of us," Jack said quickly.

"How is a meaningless marriage the best for anyone? You're crazy."

"That's been said before," he admitted wryly. "But not about this. This is important enough to me that I'm not going to back off or give up until you agree."

She laughed shortly, turned her back on him and went back to boxing biscotti. "Good luck with that."

"I'm a rich man, Rita," he said and brought her up short.

Money again? What was he getting at? A tiny nugget of fear settled in the pit of her belly as, wary now, she asked, "How rich?"

"Very."

She took a breath. He was watching her, waiting for her reaction and she wasn't sure what that should be. Rita didn't care if he had all the money in the world or nothing at all. So what was the point of this?

"Congratulations to you," she finally said. "But why should I care?" Even as she asked that question, though, her brain was racing. A *very* rich man? She'd had no idea.

But then, there was so much she didn't know about him. He hadn't talked about himself a lot during their week together and she'd told herself that the information would come. That they could learn about each other in letters, phone calls. But that had never happened, so she was as much in the dark now as she had been then.

A very rich man, though, had power. The question was now, would he use that power to manipulate her, to take custody of her child?

"I can take care of the baby," he said.

She stiffened. "So can I."

"Rita, you live above a bakery," he snapped. "I can get you a nice place. On the beach."

"Are you trying to bribe me?" she asked, astounded at the turn this conversation was taking.

"No. Look, it's my kid, too." He took a moment to gather his thoughts and said, "We get married, I get you a house and after the baby's born, we split up."

"And if I don't want to marry you?"

"You will."

"Don't take any bets on it."

"I will bet on it." He held out one hand. "Five bucks."

"For a *very* rich man, you don't have much faith in your ability to persuade me." She shook his hand and deliberately ignored the zip of heat she felt. "Twenty dollars."

"Even better," he said and completely knocked her feet out from under her.

Even better. It reminded her of that first night, of his smile, his kiss, their eagerness to be together. And when she looked into his eyes, she saw a gleam of amusement and knew he was remembering, too. Her heart turned over at the tiny glimpse of *her* Jack. Maybe he wasn't as lost as she'd thought. Maybe he was reachable.

He let go of her hand but the heat engendered remained. The tiny moment of shared memory was over, the hint of humor gone from his eyes and she was left with this gorgeous stranger again. How could he make her feel so much while apparently feeling nothing himself? How could she allow herself to marry a man for all the wrong reasons when she once would have given anything to marry him for *love*?

"It won't work, Jack."

"We'll see, Rita."

It took her only a week to surrender.

A week of Jack coming to the bakery daily, helping out, making sure she got off her feet. He ignored his own business and showed up in jeans, scuffed cowboy boots and T-shirts, making her heart skip just looking at him. He stacked pallets of supplies, carried trays of cookies, rang up sales and won Casey over. That last part wasn't hard at all, Rita allowed. But as for the rest, he wore her down with his relentless pursuit and dogged determination.

"You owe me twenty bucks," he said when she told him she'd marry him.

"This isn't funny." Should she have held out? Refused him? Possibly. But in the last week, she'd caught repeated glimpses of the old Jack, and though they were brief, they'd given her enough hope to think that just maybe it was worth trying to get past the ice he'd packed around his heart.

"No one's laughing."

"I'll marry you, but I can't get married without my family there," she said. "They'd never understand."

They weren't going to understand a quickie wedding or a divorce so soon after that wedding, either, but one problem at a time.

"Fine. Us. Our families. Small ceremony," Jack said like he was ticking things off a to-do list.

"And I don't want anyone to know this is a…business deal," she said for lack of a better way to put it. "Also, I don't want you to buy me a house."

"Nonnegotiable," he said. "When we split, you can pick something out or I will."

It didn't make sense to argue with him now, but

Rita could be as stubborn as Jack. And she wouldn't be bought off or given a "going away gift." But this, too, was a worry for another day. God knew she had enough for today already.

"Okay, then," she said, sighing heavily. "I guess we're getting married."

He grabbed a black leather jacket off a hook by the back door and shrugged into it. "I'll take care of the details. I'll send packers to get your stuff out of your apartment. Bring it to the penthouse."

She blinked at him. "Packers?"

He stopped, looked at her. "You want this to look real, then we'll be living together at my place."

At his place? She didn't even know *where* he lived! Oh, this wasn't something she'd even thought about.

Before she could say anything to that, though, he was gone.

"It's a surprise, that's all I'm saying," Jack's sister, Cass, said for the tenth time in the last hour. "I'm glad you found someone, but it would have been nice to meet her before the wedding."

He looked at Cass and read the worry in her eyes. God, would he ever get used to seeing that emotion on his family's faces? And if not accustomed to it, could he please, God, reach a point where it wouldn't tear at him? "It was sudden. I met her six months ago—"

"Clearly," Cass said wryly.

"Right." The baby. His family had been shocked not only with the announcement that he was getting married, but that he was going to be a father. Soon.

Cass flipped her long brown hair behind her shoulder, threaded her arm through his and watched Rita with her family. "I like her already."

"Good. That's good." Jack nodded thoughtfully and kept his gaze locked on his wife. *Wife.* He swallowed hard and told himself it would be all right. The important thing here was that he'd done the right thing by his kid. He could survive three months of marriage and then his life would go back to what it had been. Quiet. Alone.

"Jack?"

He looked at his sister and nearly sighed. She was watching him so closely, trying to read every expression on his face, he might as well have been under a microscope. But judging by her own expression, she wasn't happy with what she was seeing. In fact, she was giving him the serious, concerned look he was pretty sure she gave her patients.

As a general practitioner, Cass was adept at cutting through the bull to make a diagnosis and it was clear to him she didn't like what she was seeing in him.

"Relax, Cass," he said, "I'm fine."

"Sure. It's what you've been saying for months."

"Then you should believe me," he said, patting her hand on his arm.

"No, you remind me of this one patient. He's ten. And he always insists he's fine even when his fever is spiking or his throat is sore." She shook her head. "He doesn't want me asking questions, you see. And neither do you."

"Yeah," Jack said, giving her a tired smile. "But I'm not one of your patients."

"Good thing," she told him. "We'd butt heads even

more than we do now. Jack, I have to ask you something. Will you let her in?"

"What?" He looked down at her and tried to hide his impatience. It wasn't the family's fault that he couldn't give them what they wanted. *Be* who they wanted.

Cass moved to stand in front of him and put both of her hands on his forearms. "I'm asking you. You're married now. Going to be a father. And yet I still see that distance in your eyes."

He let his head fall back and he stared unseeing at the overcast gray sky for a second or two. The steady roar of the ocean was a constant white noise in the background. The sea itself was as gray as the sky and the waves rolling to shore just a few feet away were edged with foam that looked like lace.

"Cass..."

"Don't bother to deny it. We all know it's true. You've shut down, Jack and we don't know how to reach you." She leaned in and looked up into his eyes. "Will you let Rita try?"

What no one understood was, he couldn't allow himself to be reached. Couldn't be pulled from the shadows because the darkness was where he belonged now. He felt his own helplessness rise as he watched his sister's face.

Jack wished he could reassure his whole family. Wished that this marriage was changing something. But the truth was, *nothing* had changed for him. He was who he was now and everyone would eventually accept what he already had.

The old Jack Buchanan died on his last tour.

Cass must have read the resignation on his features because she sighed, went up on her toes to kiss his cheek. "I love you, Jack. Give yourself a chance to be happy."

He nodded again, gave her a quick hug, and then sighed in relief when she walked off to join her family. Jack looked to his father and brother as they stood with Rita's parents, laughing and talking. There was no respite for Jack today. He'd dropped himself into a crowd. Yet he was still a man on the sidelines, watching as life went on around him.

Both families were gathered and they seemed to be getting along fine. His sister's family, husband and two kids and his brother Sam's group, wife and three kids, actually looked small compared to Rita's.

Her parents, her sister and two brothers with all of their kids and spouses made quite a crowd. Her sister's four kids, each brother had five and one of the wives was as pregnant as Rita. The Marchettis were clearly devoted to family and Jack was glad to see it. When this marriage ended, when he was out of her life, Rita would have their support to help her through.

Another straw of guilt dropped onto his shoulders and he nearly winced at the added weight. Had he done the right thing here? Marrying her with the promise to divorce in three months? Setting her up to have to explain what went wrong to a loving family who were assuming she was marrying for love? Wouldn't it have been better to just tell everyone the truth up front?

Easier for him, maybe, he acknowledged. But for Rita? His gaze went to her and locked on with a laser focus. Tension gripped him as every cell in his body tightened, buzzing with the kind of need only *she* had ever awakened in him. He wanted her with every breath and knew he couldn't have her because he had nothing to offer her. Not now.

All he could give her was this marriage and a house and the promise to stay the hell out of her way once this was done and over. She deserved at least the pretense of a real marriage for her family's sake, he told himself. Hell, she deserved so much more than he had.

Her curly brown hair was pulled up on top of her head to cascade down past her shoulders in a riot of wind-tossed curls. She wore a long dress of some filmy material that almost seemed otherworldly. The color was a soft lavender so pale it made him think of moonlit fog. Her eyes were bright, her mouth curved in a smile as she hugged her sister. Then those aged, whiskey eyes found his and his insides fisted. He was caught in a trap of his own making.

Married to a woman he wanted and couldn't have. Living in a shadow world, yearning for light. Wanting to bury himself inside her warmth to ease the cold that was always crouched within him. He was outside a window staring in at what he most desired, but unable to reach out and touch it.

And maybe that was his penance, he thought. The price he had to pay for living.

"You look too solemn for a man on his wedding day."

Somehow Jack's father had sneaked up on him. Damn. He'd been hyperalert for months, but looking at Rita was enough to distract him from everything but her.

"Just thinking," he said.

Thomas turned to follow Jack's gaze to Rita. "Well, I don't know how you can look at your bride and be thinking thoughts dark enough to put a scowl on your face."

Chagrined, Jack realized he hadn't been paying close enough attention. He'd let his mask slip and shown people what he was feeling and that wasn't something he wanted to happen. No point in those he loved worrying even more than they already were.

He forced a smile and hoped it looked more real than it felt. "You like her?"

Thomas smiled and slapped his back. "What's not to like? She's beautiful, kind and she's giving me another grandchild." His voice trailed off. "I only wish your mother was still here to enjoy all of these kids running around."

Jack smiled wistfully. His mother had died five years before and had only seen a few of the grandchildren she would have enjoyed so much. "She would have loved this."

"Yes, she would," his father said. "But I have a feeling she's here, somehow. I can't imagine your mother *not* being around when something big was happening to one of her kids."

True, Jack thought. And his mother never would have worried about him from afar. She would have hammered at him relentlessly until she'd dragged him kicking and screaming out of the darkness and back to where she wanted him. Carla Buchanan had been a force of nature. And Jack honestly didn't know if he was more sad or relieved that his mom wasn't there to see what he'd come to.

"Come on now," his father said. "We're all going over to *The Queen Mary* for the wedding brunch."

He had to smile. Once his father had heard about

the wedding, he'd insisted on taking care of a celebratory brunch. And of course, he'd arranged for a private dining room on *The Queen Mary.* Nothing his father liked better than ships, and in his defense, Jack was sure their out-of-town guests would enjoy visiting the historical ship.

"You go ahead," Jack said, "I'll be there in a minute."

"All right then."

Thomas walked off to join the others and Jack took a breath, steeling himself to join in, to be a part of the festivities. The stretch of beach had never looked longer to him. A cold sea wind whipped past him and tugged at the edges of his jacket. He headed for their families, but with every step he took, he felt the sand shifting beneath his feet and the sensation reminded him of too much.

Awakened too many memories that were always too close to the surface. His insides tightened and a heightened sense of awareness took over. Sounds were more defined, until he could hear shrieks from down the beach and screams that had him whirling around and crouching as if he were under fire. Then his gaze locked on a screaming girl as her boyfriend carried her into the icy water.

Heartbeat racing, hands fisting at his sides, Jack took a breath to steady himself. The wind pushed at him, but instead of scenting sea spray on the air, he smelled the stale, flat air of a desert country that had claimed too much of him. His spine stiffened, but he turned back and kept walking, determined to keep what he was feeling to himself.

To stay half in the shadows even as he pretended to be in the light.

Rita walked up to meet him and he looked into her eyes, focusing on her, only her. Staring at her, the swamping sensations nearly drowning him faded, to be replaced by a different kind of tension. She was so beautiful she stole his breath. And now she was his wife.

God help her.

Five

"I didn't let anything slip to Mom and Dad," Gina was saying. "*But*, I know there's more to this whole sudden wedding thing than you're telling."

Rita glanced past her sister to the people in the private dining room. Sure that no one could overhear, she said, "Okay, yes. There is more. Thanks for not saying anything, and I'll tell you about it at some point, I promise. Just… I can't right now and I don't want Mom and Dad worrying."

"I know how to keep a secret." Gina's eyes narrowed on her. "So I'll stay quiet. But I'm warning you, Rita, if he's a jerk, I expect you to tell me so I can kick him."

Rita laughed a little as relief trickled through her. She had enough on her mind and heart at the moment without worrying about her family worrying about *her*. Gina was always as good as her word. If she said she'd keep a secret, nothing and no one would be able to pry it out of her.

If her family knew she'd gotten married with the promise of a quickie divorce looming, there would no doubt be hell to pay. As it was, her brothers kept giving Jack a hard eye like they'd prefer to take him outside and deal with the man who'd left their sister pregnant and alone. But her parents at least were believing Rita's story of finding Jack and the two of them reigniting the love between them.

If only, Rita thought with an internal sigh.

"I promise. But, I might kick him myself before you get the chance."

"I can live with that," Gina said, sipping on a mimosa in a crystal champagne flute.

While her sister was quiet, Rita had a minute to think about her wedding day. The ceremony had been small, just hers and Jack's families on a roped-off area of the beach. The early June weather of dark skies and cool winds had kept the beach mostly deserted, so it had been intimate in spite of being so public.

When they exchanged vows, Rita remembered looking deeply into Jack's eyes and for one brief moment, she'd seen that quick glimpse of *her* Jack hidden inside him again. And that gave her hope. Maybe there was a way to reach him. To *actually* reignite what they'd shared so briefly six months ago.

Their kiss at the end of the ceremony had started off perfunctory, but after a split second, it was as if Jack had forgotten that they were putting on a show. He'd pulled her in to him and cradled her against his body as his mouth took hers in a slow, seductive kiss that had nearly blown Rita's short veil right off her head.

If there was *that* between them still, that heat, that magic, couldn't there be more? Heat didn't exist in a vacuum. Emotions, feelings, had to be there, too, right?

Was she being deliberately foolish? Probably. But if you didn't try, you couldn't win. If you didn't ask, the answer was always no.

"You're thinking."

"That's a bad thing?" she asked, a small smile curving her mouth.

"I haven't decided yet," Gina admitted. She half turned to look at Jack, across the room, standing somewhat apart from everyone else. "He's gorgeous, I give you that. But he doesn't seem the sociable type. Won't that drive you nuts?"

Rita shook her head. "No, I talk enough for both of us."

"True." Gina laughed.

"You know, he wasn't like this when we first met," Rita said quietly. "Oh, he never talked as much as I do, but he was warmer. Less…closed down. I don't know how to explain it."

"You're doing pretty well," Gina said thoughtfully, studying the man they were talking about.

"Gina, the thing is, every once in a while," Rita continued, "I see the real Jack hiding behind his eyes."

Her sister gave her a cool look. "And you think you can bring him out of hiding?"

"If not me, who?" Rita asked. "If there's a chance, I have to try."

Gina dropped one arm around her shoulders. "Sweetie, sometimes people are hiding for a reason."

She might be right, Rita acknowledged. But if she didn't find out for sure, the what-if would haunt her forever. "But what if that reason can be dealt with? Fought?"

"Oh, God," Gina murmured, shaking her head. "You're trying to save him, aren't you?"

Was she? Oh, Rita didn't like the sound of that. How many times had she seen friends fall for a guy with "issues" and then try to fix him? Get him to change. Help him deal with his demons? Is that what she was doing?

No, she argued with herself silently. This was different. *Jack* was different. Something specific had happened to him and whatever it was had affected him deeply. Even if it was because of what they'd once had, or the fact that they'd created a child together… Didn't Rita owe it to him to at least make the attempt to help him?

"Is that so wrong?" She looked at her sister, really curious to hear what she had to say.

"No, I guess not," Gina said, resignation clear in her tone. "If it's something you feel like you have to do, there's no stopping you anyway. Just make sure you don't lose yourself in the effort."

"I won't," Rita said and knew that keeping her promise wasn't going to be easy. Because in spite of everything that had happened between them, Jack was the one man in the world who could still cause her pain.

"Uh-oh," Gina said suddenly, "I've gotta go save Jimmy. Mom's just dropped Kira into his lap, so he's got all four kids and is seriously outnumbered."

Rita smiled on cue, but she wasn't thinking about her brother-in-law. Her thoughts were with Jack, standing apart and alone at his own wedding. Backlit by the light flooding in through the wall of windows he stood in front of, he looked so solitary, it broke her heart.

He'd done all he could to make this faux marriage beautiful for her. From the ceremony itself to this family reception. *The Queen Mary* was a beautiful old ship and this private dining room in its five-star restaurant was old-world elegant. Windows lined both sides of the ship and she imagined that when the old ocean liner was still sailing, the views were incredible.

Where Jack stood, there was a sweeping vista of the sea and other boats bobbing on the surface. The sun had finally broken through the clouds and slanted off the water like gold dust. But Jack was silhouetted, defining his aloneness, and that tore at Rita.

"We're staying in town for a few days," Gina was saying. "As long as we're here, figured we'd take the kids to Disneyland."

Rita glanced at her. "They'll love it."

"Yep," Gina mused. "Hope Jimmy and I survive it." She grabbed Rita's hand and squeezed. "If you need me for anything, call me. I'll be there."

"I know," she said, returning that squeeze briefly. "Thanks, Gina. I'm gonna be fine."

As Gina moved away, Rita heard her own words echo in her mind and she hoped she was right. Because at the moment, her heart was aching for the man who'd cut himself off. He'd gone to so much trouble for her, but he wasn't being a part of this at all. Even in the heart of his family, he was determinedly alone. That didn't equate with everything he'd told her about his family when they met. Back then, he'd laughed at the stories of fishing trips with his father and brother, of his sister being outwitted by her five-year-old daughter, of how devastated their family had been when they'd lost Jack's mother.

Now, though, it was as if his family wasn't even in the same room with him. She'd seen his father, brother and sister try to connect with him and eventually give up. She'd watched Jack keep to the sidelines as if punishing himself, somehow. Rita didn't have the first clue how to go about reaching him, but she knew she had to try. Because if there was even a tiny chance she could find *her* Jack, it would be worth the effort.

Smiling and nodding to her family as she passed, Rita walked to Jack. He was staring out at the ocean and Rita came up right beside him.

He didn't look at her, but he must have sensed her presence. "Everything all right?"

"It's fine," she said, staring up at his profile, waiting for some flicker of—she didn't even know what. "Are *you* okay?" she asked.

He turned his head then and looked down at her. She felt that stare sizzle in her blood. One look from him and she burned.

"Yeah," he said finally, quietly. "I'm just not good in a crowd of people."

His words, so simply stated, tugged at her heart as she realized just how important this marriage must have been to him. He'd dropped himself into a situation that would make him uncomfortable because this meant something to him. He'd stood up against what plagued him to make sure she had what she needed at the wedding. He'd brought her family in, and seen to it that everything was beautiful for her in spite of his own misgivings. Just another sign to Rita that her Jack was in there somewhere. That only strengthened her resolve to discover what had happened to change the man she'd once thought was her one and only.

But today, she only wanted to be here. With him. To let him know he wasn't alone, even if that's what he believed he wanted. Going on instinct, she slid her hand into his and was rewarded when his fingers curled around hers and held tight.

Jack lay wide awake in bed, alone on his wedding night.

Rita was down the hall in the penthouse guestroom and he couldn't tear his mind away from the image of her. His whole body ached for her, just as it had from the first moment he'd met her.

No other woman had ever affected him as she had. While he was overseas, he'd worked on convincing himself that what he'd felt with her was nothing special. He'd had to, just to survive. Clinging to the real world and the memories of a woman with a warm heart, soft body and wild, raw laugh had only made his reality that much harder to endure.

Then, when everything went to hell one afternoon, Jack had sliced every emotion out of his life because it was imperative to survival. He hadn't written to her because he couldn't lie to her about what was going on and he couldn't have told her the truth. He didn't look for her when he came back because he was in no shape to be around anyone. And because by then, he knew he could never again be the man she had once known.

"But Fate's a nasty bitch," he muttered into the darkness. His own voice seemed to echo, low and harsh in the empty room.

The gods of irony had conspired against him. He'd put so much effort into avoiding her that the gods laughed and threw her in his path, making it impossible to ignore her. And now they were married.

Shaking his head, he draped one arm across his eyes to dim the moonlight spearing into his bedroom. He had the terrace doors open, because he couldn't stand to be closed in. He needed that swirl of air, even when it was cold. Needed to smell the sea, remind himself that he was here. Home. And not in that hot, desperate situation that had nearly driven him over the edge.

His room was big, with a black-and-white-tiled gas hearth on one wall, bookcases and a television on the other walls. There were chairs, tables and a bed that was so big it felt even emptier than it actually was.

"My choice," he reminded himself and gritted his teeth against the roiling heat and tension coiled inside him.

It would be so easy to go down the hall, walk into her room and relive a few memories. Make some new ones. No guarantee she'd let him in, but then he remembered how she'd held his hand at the reception. As if she'd known, somehow sensed, that he'd needed that touch to ground himself in the moment.

She was good like that, he thought. Always had been. They'd connected so deeply in one week that it had been almost like they could read each other's minds. He hoped to hell she couldn't pick up on his thoughts now, but back then, it was different.

He was there the next morning to pick her up at seven, as agreed. She was in the lobby, waiting for him, clearly as eager as he was for them to be together again. Just seeing her in her jeans and dark green sweater had made his mouth water.

When she smiled at him, he went hard as stone and

damn near killed himself just trying to walk across the floor toward her. Then she reached out for him, took his hand and he was lost in need, heat, a fire that built with every breath.

They had breakfast on the beach, coffee and bagels shared over laughter and a breathless sense of expectation. Looking into her whiskey-brown eyes was mesmerizing. Intoxicating. On that deserted winter beach, they were alone in the world but for one or two hardy surfers out challenging the waves.

Hands linked, they walked along the beach for what felt like miles, then they hiked back to the car and drove down the coast. Music pumping, wind roaring through the open windows and the two of them, still holding hands, as if unable to bear not touching.

Two hours later they were in San Diego and stopping for lunch at a tiny inn outside La Jolla. The once-dignified old Victorian mansion clung to the cliffside and waves pounded against the rocks in a steady, rhythmic heartbeat.

"It's beautiful here," Rita said, letting her gaze slide across the water, the cliffs and the meticulously tended gardens.

"Yeah, it is," he replied, his gaze locked on her. With the wind in her hair and the winter sun shining in her eyes, Jack thought he'd never seen anything more lovely. And he knew if he didn't kiss her soon, it would kill him.

"You're not even looking at the view," she chided with a half smile.

"Depends on what you consider a great view." He snaked one hand across the small round table and cov-

ered hers. He felt her pulse pounding in time with the relentless sea and knew that beat matched his own, too.

She licked her lips and he fought to breathe. She curled her hand beneath his and the heat that blossomed between them should have set the grounds on fire.

Her gaze locked with his. "What's happening here?" she asked, her voice nearly lost in the wind and the roar of the waves.

"Whatever it is, I'm all for it," he admitted and stroked his thumb across her palm. Her eyes glazed over and her breath quickened.

"Oh, I am, too."

"You're making me crazy, Rita. Couldn't sleep last night. I kept thinking about you. About today. About..."

She pulled in a shaky breath. "I've been thinking about...too."

Oh, yeah. If he didn't have her soon, he was a walking dead man. He'd never make that two-or three-hour drive home with his body and mind so entangled with nothing but thoughts of her. All he could think of was touching her, stroking her skin, sliding his body into hers and being surrounded by her heat.

"You know, maybe we should book a room here at the inn. Neither one of us slept much last night. We could get some sleep before that long drive back up to Orange County."

Her tongue slipped out again to slide across her bottom lip and his gaze tracked that motion as if his life depended on it. Fire, he thought. It felt like he was burning up from the inside and if his body got any harder, he'd have to crawl from the table because walking would be impossible.

Nodding, she said, "That's probably a good idea. A nap, I mean. Tired drivers can be dangerous."

"Yeah," he agreed. "Safety first."

Her smile was fleeting, but brilliant, taking his breath away. "I'll see if they've got a room where we can...rest. Just wait here."

When he stood up, Rita took his hand and squeezed. "Okay, I'll wait. But hurry. I'm really tired."

That was all the encouragement Jack needed.

In ten minutes, they were entering their room on the second floor. Jack swept her up close to him, kicked the door closed and gave the dead bolt a fast turn. She laughed up into his face and he felt something inside him turn over. She was more than he'd ever had. More than he'd ever thought to find. And for now, she was all his.

"Oh," she said, tearing her gaze from his to give the room a quick look. "Isn't it lovely?"

He hadn't noticed. Now he did. White lace curtains at the windows, a brass bed with a detailed flower quilt across the mattress. There were two chairs before a tiny hearth outlined in sea-blue tiles and a table held a carafe of water and two glasses. There was a door that led to a private bath and photographs of old San Diego dotted the pale gold walls.

He supposed it was very nice, though it could have been a cave for all he cared. "Yeah," he said tightly, not caring about the room.

When she looked up at him again, she gave him a knowing smile. "Ready to nap?"

"More than you know."

"Then let's get to sleep," she said, throwing her arms

around his neck, holding on as she lifted her face for his kiss.

When their mouths met, merged, it was like the whole damn world lit up. Or maybe it was just the fire inside, blazing brighter than ever. Seconds ticked into minutes and still they stood, locked together, bodies pressed tightly to each other, heartbeats hammering in time.

Finally, he tore his mouth free, fought for enough breath to admit, "I have to touch you."

"Please, yes," she said softly, hungrily, "Now. Touch me."

In seconds, they were naked and falling onto the bed together. Afternoon light poured through the windows and winter sun painted a soft, golden slash across the polished wood floor to lie on the bed and shine in Rita's eyes.

His gaze raked over her lush curves, and everything in him stirred to a fever pitch. Jack felt as though he'd been waiting for this one moment his whole life. He bent his head to take one of her nipples into his mouth. Tasting, nibbling, working his teeth and tongue across her sensitive skin. Every whispered moan and sigh that slipped from her fed his hunger until it was like a closed fist around his throat, making breathing almost impossible. Her fingers slid through his military-short hair, nails scraping along his scalp as she arched up and into him, silently asking for more. And he had plans for a lot more.

Lifting his head, he stared down into her eyes. "This could be the longest nap on record."

"Oh, good," she said on a long sigh, "because I'm really tired."

He grinned. "And I'm really glad to hear that."

She pulled his head down to hers and this time she claimed his mouth in a kiss that seared him right to his bones. He let her lead, let her devour and gave back all that she was giving him and still, it wasn't enough.

Jack moved over her, running his hands up and down her body, discovering every curve, exploring her soft silky skin until they were both trembling with an explosive need. Her small hands moved over his chest, his shoulders and every stroke of her fingers felt like licks of flame.

They rolled across the bed, tasting, touching. Her heavy brown curls spread out beneath her head like a wild, tangled dark halo. He was lost in her, her scent, her touch, the hunger raging inside him. Body raging, mind fogging over, Jack stood poised on the brink of a cliff.

"Now," she whispered, lifting her hips, rocking into his hand as he cupped her center. "Jack, now. I can't take this anymore."

"Hold on. Just hold on." Before he lost control completely, he reached down for his jeans, dug into the pocket and pulled out the condoms he'd tucked in there only that morning.

"Boy," she said, "I really love a man who's prepared to take a nap."

He grinned at her as he sheathed himself. "Babe, ever since the moment we met, I've been prepared to nap."

"So glad to hear it." She opened her arms to him, lifted her hips again and welcomed him inside her.

That first slick, hot slide into her body stole his breath and would have finished him completely if he hadn't fought for control and held on to it. She moved into him, and the slippery threads of control fell away.

Together they climbed, staring into each other's eyes as they rode the crest of what they created. Mouths mating, breath mingling, they moved in an ancient dance as if they were born to be one. Together, they raced toward completion and together, they fell from the precipice, wrapped in each other's arms.

What could have been minutes or hours later, when breathing was easier, Rita cupped his face in her palm and whispered, "I hope you're still as sleepy as I am. Because I think I need another nap."

He turned his face into her palm, kissed it, then grinned down at her. "It's important to get enough sleep."

Jack groaned tightly as the memory faded and he was alone again in a room that suddenly felt too small, too quiet. Too empty.

He could still feel her small hand on his face, see her smile, taste her kiss. His body was tight, hard, eager. His mind raced with possibilities, before he shut them all down and accepted the cold reality.

Jack had a penance to pay and being this close to Rita without touching her was only the latest toll to be taken.

Jumping out of bed, he stalked through the open doors to the terrace and there he stood, letting the icy wind off the sea blow away the lingering heat still haunting him.

The next few days weren't easy.

Rita had to acknowledge that finding her way to the real Jack was going to be far more difficult than she'd anticipated. She was gone before he woke in the morning, heading down to the bakery where she worked to stay busy enough to keep thoughts of Jack at bay. Then in the evening, Jack did his best to avoid her completely. It was as if she was an unwanted guest he was trying to convince to leave.

Okay, yes, she'd agreed to a temporary marriage, but only because she'd caught those glimpses of *her* Jack. And now, he seemed determined to not let that happen again. He was pushing her away and expected her to simply give up and go when their time together was up.

"Well," she muttered to herself, "I'm not that easy to get rid of."

"Glad to hear it."

Rita closed her eyes, groaned quietly at being overheard—and by Jack's sister no less—then turned to face Cass. "Hi."

"Hi," the other woman said, walking farther into the kitchen. "I didn't mean to eavesdrop, but you were talking out loud so it was hard to miss."

"Sometimes," Rita admitted sheepishly, "I have to talk to myself because I'm the only one who really understands me."

Cass laughed. "Boy, I know that feeling. Between my practice, my husband and my kids, sometimes I talk to myself just to make sure I'm still there."

Rita relaxed her defenses a little. She'd liked Cass immediately when they'd met at the wedding. And listening to her now, Rita realized that with time, the two of them could be good friends. The question was, would she have that time?

"Look, I hope it's okay that I'm back here. The redhead out front said I could come in."

Casey again. "Of course it's okay. Have a seat. I'm just getting these loaves of bread ready for the ovens."

"God, it smells wonderful in here." Cass took a deep breath and sighed as she pulled a stool up to the marble work surface. Glancing around the room at the trays, the racks of cooling biscotti, bread and cannoli shells, she sighed. "Bread, cookies… I could live here."

Rita laughed and ran the blade of her knife along the elongated loaves of bread, making a few slices to give the dough room to grow while baking. "I love being in the kitchen."

"Well, clearly you have the talent for it," Cass said on a heavy sigh. "My husband has banned me from ours. He says what I call cooking, modern science calls poison."

"Oh, ouch."

Cass shrugged. "Yeah, it would be painful if it weren't true. So we have a cook and everyone's happy."

She looked at a tray of thumbprint cookies with their glossy chocolate centers and sighed again. "Can I have one?"

"Sure."

She bit in. "Wow. Just wow."

Rita laughed and said, "Thank you."

"Oh, my pleasure." Cass watched her as she readied the bread loaves and the silence spun out for several seconds before she finally blurted out the reason for her visit. "I'm really happy you married Jack."

Oh, Rita hated guilt. She'd grown up Italian Catholic and nobody did guilt better than they did. Her mother was a master at making her kids feel guilty and so Rita recognized the sensation when it slapped her. She'd lied to her family. To Jack's family.

Maybe even to herself, it was too soon to tell. "Cass..."

The other woman waved one hand and shook her head. "No, you don't have to say anything. I just mean, I wanted to let you know that we're all glad he has someone. Jack's been...sort of shut down since he came home from his last tour."

Rita watched her, unsure what to say, or even what she *could* say.

"We've all tried to get through, but it's like trying to catch fog. Every time you think you're making progress, or maybe you see a flash of the old Jack, boom. It's gone." She shook her head and unconsciously reached for another cookie. Taking a bite, she sighed a little and continued. "If our mom was still alive, she'd have pushed past whatever boundaries he's got set up inside him. She wouldn't have accepted anything less."

Rita heard the wistful tone and responded. "She was tough?"

"When it came to her family? Oh, yeah." Cass grinned. "No one could stand in her way. But she's been gone five years and it's like the rest of us can't figure out how to reach Jack." She crumbled the rest of the cookie in her fingers. "That's why we're so glad he's got you. And the baby."

Oh, that guilt was really starting to get heavy, Rita thought. What would Cass and the rest of their family think of Rita when this three-month marriage ended? Would they blame her for walking out on Jack, never knowing the real reason behind it?

"The worst part for me is I hate seeing my dad look so...helpless over this," Cass said. "He tries to talk to Jack but just can't and he's scared. Heck, we all are."

So was Rita. In the time since Jack had walked back into her life, she'd seen him withdraw not only from her but from the family who clearly loved him. Their marriage hadn't helped. If anything, he was working even harder at avoiding her.

"I don't like feeling helpless," Cass muttered. "I'm not good at it."

Rita smiled. Here, she really could bond with Cass. "Neither am I."

"Good." Cass gave her a conspiratorial smile. "I'm glad to hear it. That means you'll push him as maybe the rest of us can't."

But no pressure, Rita thought.

Six

Rita had a sister of her own and two older brothers, so she knew what it was to worry about a sibling. To want to help and not be allowed to. She could understand what Cass was feeling; Rita just didn't know if she was going to be able to do what the Buchanan family hoped she could. Bring Jack back to them.

"I don't know if Jack told you, but I'm a doctor."

She came up out of her thoughts with a jerk. "He did mention that. Family practice, right?"

"Right. Well, speaking as a doctor, not a sister," Cass said, "I can tell you that Jack's being affected by PTSD, which you've probably already guessed."

Rita nodded.

"There are so many different levels of this syndrome," Cass said with a sigh. "I've done a lot of reading and studying on it since Jack got home. And I know that the men and women affected by it are all different, so what they go through is different, as well. Naturally, treating it is a bitch. No one can find a standard type of treatment because each case is so wildly dissimilar."

Rita had come to that conclusion on her own. And it made perfect sense, really. Obviously, something horrible had happened to Jack on his last tour. When he left her six months ago, it was with a promise of a future that had been unsaid, but felt by both of them. And he'd come home for good just two months later, a completely changed man.

"I actually don't like the PTSD label—the word *disorder* bothers me. *Post-traumatic stress* I can get behind. But *disorder*? No." Cass shook her head firmly and scowled at what was left of her cookie. "That makes these men and women seem…sick, somehow. When what they are is *hurt*." She glanced up at Rita and winced. "Sorry. I didn't even realize I was climbing onto my soapbox."

Rita studied her for a minute or two. Not only was she a doctor, but she was the very concerned sister of a man suffering silently. "No apology necessary. I agree with you."

"Good. Thanks." Cass ate what was left of the cookie. "I knew at the wedding that I'd like you. And if you can help Jack through this, I'll love you forever."

Rita's heart opened up for the other woman. If one of her own brothers was in pain, she would do anything in her power, ask anyone she could think of, to get him the help he needed. Knowing that the Buchanans, in spite of all their money and power and influence, were as close as her own family made her feel more on solid ground. She could understand the driving need to save family and she liked Cass more for what she'd just confessed. "I'm going to try."

Cass smiled. "That's all we can do."

Rita walked to the wall ovens, opened the doors, then slid the bread trays inside, closed the doors and set the timers. As she wiped down the gray-streaked white marble counter, she asked, "Would you like a cup of coffee?"

"I'd *love* one," Cass said. "If you'll join me."

"No coffee for me yet," she said sadly, giving her baby bump a gentle rub. "But I'll have some herbal tea and cookies."

"That works." Cass grinned a little. "You know, if you haven't already lined up a pediatrician, I'd love to be your baby doctor."

Since she really hadn't chosen a doctor yet, this was a gift. "Who could be better than my baby's aunt?"

With Cass's beaming smile lighting her way, Rita walked to the front of the shop for the tea and coffee. Whatever else had happened today, she hoped she'd made a friend.

"Your wife is here," Linda announced over the intercom the very next afternoon.

"What?" Jack looked up from the file he was going over. "Rita?"

"Do you have another wife I don't know about yet?" Rita asked, sailing into the office with a wide smile on her face. "Thanks, Linda," she threw over her shoulder as Jack's assistant grinned, backed out of the office and shut the door.

Rita wore jeans, a white dress shirt and a black sweater over it that matched the black boots on her feet.

Her brown curly hair was loose and tumbling around her face. Her brown eyes were shining and that smile pulled him in even as he fought against the draw.

"What're you doing here?" he asked as she walked through a slant of sunlight pouring through the windows to approach his desk.

"Such a warm welcome. Thanks. I'm glad to see you, too."

He frowned at the jab and her grin widened in response.

"I brought lunch," she said simply and held up the dark green cloth bag he hadn't even noticed until that moment.

Just when he thought he'd figured out how to survive this marriage, she threw a wrench into the whole thing.

Every morning, he drove her to the bakery because damned if she was going to be driving herself through the darkness. Once she was safely inside, he drove back to the office and caught up on the dreaded paperwork that seemed to be what most of his days were made of. At the end of the day, he most often tried to just grab something for dinner and then disappear into his office or his bedroom. Jack knew the only way he was going to make it through the next three months was to keep as much distance between him and Rita as possible.

Damned hard though when she fought him at every turn. She insisted on breakfast at four in the morning. When he could, he avoided having dinner with her and simply escaped into his room or his office and stayed there until she was in bed.

He was living like a fugitive in his own damn apartment. And now, she'd hunted him down at work.

"Nice idea, but—"

"I called Linda to check," Rita said, interrupting him neatly as she began to empty that bag onto a table set between two overstuffed leather chairs. "She assured me your next appointment wasn't for two hours, so we have plenty of time for lunch."

He bit back a curse. What good would it do at this point? Sometimes, he reminded himself, surrender was your only option. "What've you got?" he asked.

She flipped her hair back, turned her head to smile at him. "I went to your favorite Chinese place. I've got beef and broccoli, chicken chow mein and shrimp fried rice."

As she opened cartons to spoon the food onto two plates she pulled from her bag, Jack took a breath and drew in the delicious scents. Well, hell, he had to eat sometime, right?

He pushed up from the desk and walked across the room, took one of the chairs and accepted the plate Rita handed him. She grinned at him and his insides rolled over. The woman had power over him, for sure. He was achy and needy most of the time now and he had her to thank for it. Her image was always in his mind. The hunger for her never eased. And having her in his house and still untouchable was harder than he even imagined it would be.

Jack was starting to think she was deliberately trying to seduce him just by acting as though nothing was going on between them. And damned if it wasn't working.

"Think you're pretty clever, don't you?"

"Absolutely," she agreed, and sat down in the chair opposite him. She dug into the bag again, and came up with two bottles of water, two sets of chopsticks and a stack of napkins.

"So," she said, "how're things in the megabusiness world?"

The food looked delicious and smelled amazing. He took a bite, savored it, then said, "Buying, selling. How's the bakery?"

She shrugged. "Measuring, mixing, baking."

Her eyes were shining, her smile was hypnotic and she smelled even better than the food. Jack was on dangerous ground already. Having her invade the office he thought of as his own personal cave wasn't helping anything. Now he'd be seeing her here, even when she wasn't. There had to be boundaries. For everyone's sake.

"Why're you really here?" he asked. "Isn't the bakery busy enough for you?"

"Oh, it really is. But Casey's a great manager." She took a sip of water. "As you said yourself, I'm the boss, I can take a break when I want to."

Tough having your own words thrown back at you and used against you.

"I can't," he said, but he kept eating the chow mein. It really was good. "Look, I appreciate this, but it's not something that should become a habit."

"Really?" She tipped her head to one side. "Why not?"

"Because we both have work," he said and knew it sounded lame. But off the cuff it was the best he had.

"Uh-huh." Thoughtfully, she took another bite of her broccoli, then asked, "Sure it's not because you're trying to avoid being around me?"

"If that were true," he countered, "why would I have married you?"

"Such a good question." She took another bite. "Have an answer?"

This was not going well. He was losing a battle he hadn't even been aware he'd entered. "You know why we got married."

"The baby."

"Exactly. This wasn't about us having lunch or dinner together," he pointed out, but hadn't stopped eating yet. "This isn't about cozy nights at home, Rita, and you know it. It's an arrangement with an expiration date."

"Hmm. And, it wasn't about you driving me to work every morning either and yet..." She shrugged again, a small smile tugging at the corner of her mouth.

Well, he'd stepped right into that one.

"That's different," he argued. "You used to live above the bakery now you have to drive to work—"

"Six miles," she threw in.

"This isn't about the distance, it's about safety." He took a drink of water. "I'm not letting you drive through the city alone in the middle of the night when it's just as easy for me to drive you."

"So you're worried about my safety. That doesn't sound disinterested to me," she mused, taking another bite.

"Being concerned doesn't mean worried." Though he was. Hell, the thought of her driving alone through the city in the middle of the night gave him chills. What if she got a flat tire? Or the car just died? Or something happened with the baby?

She took another bite and watched him as she chewed and swallowed. Sunlight filtered through the windows and made her dark hair shine with golden highlights. Just watching her chew had his body going on red alert. It was that mouth, he told himself. That full, generous, completely kissable mouth that was doing him in.

"You work so hard to pretend that you're oblivious to me and your family, but it's not working."

His frown deepened and rather than argue, he took another bite of his lunch.

"Look it up in a dictionary, Jack. *Concerned* means *worried.* And that's exactly what you are. Worried, I mean. Oh, don't say anything," she said, waving her chopsticks when he started to deny it, "I know it bothers you to be worried, so that's almost the same as not being, unless you think about it carefully and then it's exactly the same thing and you don't want to recognize that, do you?"

Jack stared at her. "What?"

Shaking her head she took a sip of water, "Nothing, never mind. Doesn't matter right now. I didn't get the chance to tell you, but your sister came to the bakery to see me yesterday."

His head snapped up. Suddenly, her conversation was taking several different paths at once and none of them were making sense. "Cass?"

"You have two sisters as well as two wives?" she asked, teasing.

"Funny." That smile was really hard to resist and he was pretty sure she knew it since she kept flashing it at him.

"A little, maybe." She shrugged again. "Anyway, Cass wanted to talk about you, big surprise."

Well, there went the appetite. He set his plate aside, reached for his water and took a long drink. "That's what this visit is about then," he said. "What Cass had to say."

"Nope." She shook her head, sending those brown curls into a wild dance that made him want to spear his fingers through them. "I was coming to surprise you anyway. This just gives us more to talk about."

"No, thanks." He took another drink, half wishing it was a beer. "I'm not interested in conversations and besides, I have to get back to work."

"No you don't," she said, setting her plate aside, too. "You're just trying to get rid of me again."

"Again?"

She sighed. "Jack, you avoid me every chance you get. The penthouse is big, but not so big that we shouldn't run into each other more often. But you see to it that we don't." She ran one hand lovingly over her baby bump, but her gaze never left his. "Even when I trap you into breakfast in the morning, you just bolt it down and dodge every attempt at conversation."

"Four thirty in the morning, not the best time for chats."

"What's your excuse then for dinner?" Still shaking her head, she said, "Usually, you grab an apple or something and disappear into your office. Or if you do sit down with me, we don't talk. Heck, you hardly look at me directly."

It was too damn hard to look at her. To want her so badly it was a constant, driving ache inside. He was paying, daily. His atonement continued and he could only hope that he survived it somehow.

"Rita…"

"Your family's worried about you."

He scraped both hands across his face, then stood up, unable to sit still any longer. "You don't have to tell me about my own family."

"Are you sure?" She stood up, too, and faced him, toe-to-toe. A part of him admired that spine of hers.

He'd liked it right off, from the moment they met and she hadn't been afraid. But right now, he wished she was more cautious, less ready for a confrontation.

"They want to help you and they don't know how," she said. "*I* don't know how."

"I didn't ask for help," he reminded her tautly. "I can deal with things my own way."

"Not so far," she countered and folded her arms across her middle.

His eyes narrowed on her. "You don't know anything about it."

"Then *tell* me," she challenged, moving closer, tipping her head back to meet his eyes. "And if not me, Jack, tell *someone*."

"Therapy?" He laughed, shook his head and shoved one hand through his hair. "Yeah, not needing a couch, or some stranger poking around in my head. No, thanks."

"Tough marine doesn't need anyone, is that it?"

He glanced at her, read frustration clearly in her eyes but there was nothing he could do about it. "Close enough."

"Well, you're wrong, Jack," she said and this time when she moved closer, she laid one hand on his chest, right over his heart. Silently, he wondered if she felt the staccato beat beneath her palm. If she had the slightest clue what she did to him.

"Even marines are human, Jack. Even marines can't fix everything solo." She stared up into his eyes and he was unable to look away. "People need each other. That's why we *have* families, Jack. Because we're stronger together. Because we can count on each other when things get hard."

He ground his teeth together and fought for patience. He knew she meant well. Hell, he knew they *all* meant well. But they couldn't help unless he talked and he wasn't going to talk about it. About any of it.

Through gritted teeth, he said softly, "I'm fine, Rita."

"Yeah, I can see that," she said. "That's why you don't have to set an alarm to get up at four a.m., because you can't sleep but you're fine."

He jerked his head back to give her a glare. "How the hell do you know I can't sleep?"

"I can hear you, moving around the apartment, going out onto the terrace..."

Apparently, he wasn't as stealthy as he liked to think. And he had to ask himself, if he'd known she was awake, too, would he have gone to her? Tried to lose himself and the dreams that dogged him in the warmth of her embrace? Would he have given in to the insistent urge to take her, to find the heat and the welcome he'd once found in her arms? He didn't know the answer and that worried him.

"Sorry," he said tightly, rubbing the back of his neck. "I'll be quieter."

"Oh, Jack, that's not what I meant at all," she said and rested her hand on his forearm. "I'm right here. Let me in. Am I so scary you can't talk to me?"

For the first time ever, he was tempted to do just that. To just start talking and in the talking, maybe the images in his head would start to fade. Looking down into those compelling eyes of hers, he could feel himself weakening, in spite of the promise he'd made to himself. That he would never talk about the past, because doing that kept it alive. Kept it vivid. But hadn't it stayed alive despite his silence?

"I'm not going to do that." He shook his head and gave a halfhearted laugh. "Besides, one thing you're not, Rita, is scary."

"I can be, when pushed. Just ask my brothers."

Gaze still locked with hers, he lifted one hand, smoothed her hair back and briefly let himself enjoy the silky feel of it against his skin. Her emotions crowded those whiskey-brown eyes of hers and her teeth tugged at her bottom lip. God, she was beautiful. He wished…

"Let it be, Rita," he said quietly. "Just let it be."

"You know I can't."

She stared up at him and he fisted his hands at his sides to keep from grabbing her, burying his face in the curve of her neck and drawing her scent deep inside him. She made him feel too much and he couldn't allow that. He was done with caring. Done with letting others care about him. It was the safest way.

Finally, she lifted both hands and cupped his face in her palms. Heat from her body poured into his and still couldn't thaw the knot of ice he carried deep inside. "Rita, just leave my secrets in the past. Where they belong."

Looking deeply into his eyes, Rita shook her head. "They're not staying in the past, Jack. They're right here, surrounding you, cutting you off from me. From everyone. So no, I won't let it be. Not a chance."

Rita couldn't sleep. Maybe it was the confrontation/lunch with Jack two days before. Maybe it was the baby, who had decided to start training as a gymnast while still in the womb. And maybe it was just the whirring sounds of her own thoughts spinning frantically in her mind. Whatever it was, though, pulled her from bed and sent her pacing the penthouse.

It was beautiful, she had to admit, though it was a little impersonal for her. Beige walls, gleaming wood floors and comfortable, if boring, furniture. There were generic paintings on the walls and in the penthouse kitchen, the appliances were top-of-the-line, but the dishware was buy-a-box-of-plates-style.

Nothing in the place spoke of Jack. It was as if some decorator had come in, put in inoffensive furniture and left it at that, expecting whoever lived there to eventually make it their own. But apparently Jack had no interest in putting his own stamp on the place. Here, like everywhere else in his life, he was simply an observer. As if he were a placeholder for the real person who hadn't arrived yet.

Rita curled up on the forest green couch, pulled a throw pillow onto her lap and wrapped her arms around it.

For two days, she'd been determined to make Jack interact with her. She refused to let him lock himself away in his office once he returned to the penthouse. She made dinner and forced him to talk to her over a meal. She told him all about what was happening at the bakery and peppered him with questions about his work.

She didn't understand half of what he was talking about—with cargo containers and shipping schedules, but at least he was talking. She asked questions about his family and listened when he told her stories from his childhood, the fishing trips, the cabin they used to have in Big Bear.

And though she was managing to keep him engaged, it was a lot of work. The man spoke grudgingly and she had to practically drag information from him. But it was better than letting him brood alone. Still, her heart hurt because she wasn't getting to him. She wasn't any closer now to finding the real Jack than she had been when she married him.

Moonlight pearled the darkness. If she'd had company, it might have been romantic. As it was, though, she felt sad and tired and frustrated all at once.

"If he doesn't care, why is he working so hard to shut me out?" she asked the empty room and her voice sounded overly loud in the quiet. Hugging the pillow a little tighter to her middle, she told herself that if he didn't care about her or their baby, he wouldn't have so much trouble being around her.

"And if that doesn't sound backward I don't know what does." But it made an odd kind of sense, too. He was throwing himself on a proverbial sword by avoiding her. Making sacrifices she didn't want for a reason he wouldn't share.

So how was she supposed to fight it?

The week she'd spent with him now seemed like a dream. Even that last morning in her hotel room had taken on the soft edges of a fantasy rather than the warm, loving reality she remembered.

"I should go," Jack said, bending his head to take her mouth in a kiss that was filled with a hunger that never seemed to ebb.

"Not yet." Rita cupped his cheek in her palm and looked into those amazing blue eyes, trying to etch everything she read there into her memory. "Stay. Just for a while."

He smiled and threaded his fingers through her hair. Rita closed her eyes briefly to completely savor the sen-

sation of his hands on her. She'd never known a week to fly by so quickly. She'd thought only to take a week at the beach. A little vacation to clear her head after the Christmas holiday rush at the bakery back home.

But she'd found so much more than she'd ever expected. A man who made her laugh, made her sigh and made her body sing in a way she'd never known before. They'd spent every waking moment together in the last few days and even asleep, they were locked together as if somehow afraid of being separated.

And now, they would be.

Her heart was breaking at goodbye. But her flight home was that night and Jack would be leaving himself first thing in the morning. Their time was up. But what did that mean for the future?

"My enlistment's nearly up," he was saying and she told herself to concentrate on the low rumble of his voice. "This time, I'm not going to re-up. I'm getting out."

She ran her hand over his chest, loving the feel of those sharply defined muscles beneath soft, golden-brown skin. "What's that mean for us?"

He slid one hand up the length of her body to cup her breast, his thumb and forefinger tugging on her hardened nipple. Electricity zipped through her entire body and set up a humming expectation at the very core of her. One touch from this man and she was a puddle of goo at his feet.

"It means I can come up to Utah as soon as I get home."

"Good," she said on a sigh. "That's very good."

"And we'll pick this up," he said, "right where we left off."

"Even better," she said and got a smile from him. "Please be careful, Jack."

She could have bitten her own tongue off. She'd promised herself she wouldn't cry. Wouldn't worry him. Wouldn't put her own worries onto his shoulders.

"I will be," he promised. "Always am. But this time, I've got even more reason for making it home in one piece."

He was smiling as he said it, but fear nearly choked her. Rita reached up, wrapped her arms around his neck and held on, as if somehow if she held him tightly enough, she could keep him safe. Keep him from going. From leaving her. Tears stung the backs of her eyes, but she blinked like a crazy person, to keep them at bay.

She didn't want to let him see her cry.

"Hey," he soothed, rubbing his hand up and down her arm for comfort. "I'll be okay. I swear it."

She nodded into his chest, but kept her face buried against him so he wouldn't read her fear on her face.

"Rita," he said, and gently moved her head back so he could look down into her eyes. "I swear to you. I'll be back. And I'll come to you."

"You'd better," she quipped, trying to take the pain out of goodbye. "I have two older brothers who will beat you up if I ask them to."

"Well, now I'm scared." He grinned, kissed her again, running his tongue over her lips until she parted them, sighing at the invasion of her mouth. When he had her completely stirred up, he pulled back again. "I never thought to find someone like you, Rita. Trust me when I say I don't want to lose you."

"I'm glad. I don't want to lose you, either, Jack."

"You won't."

Late-afternoon sunlight spilled into the room and bathed the two of them in a golden haze. A soft, cool breeze ruffled the curtains hanging at the partially opened window.

Letting his gaze sweep up and down her body, he finally met her eyes again and whispered, "You are the best thing that's ever happened to me, Rita. Never forget that."

Oh, God. That sounded too final and she couldn't accept that. He had to come home. To her. So she smiled and fought for courage.

"Don't you forget it, either," she said.

"Not a chance."

He kissed her again and she knew it was goodbye. He had to leave. See his family before shipping out in the morning. And she had a flight to Utah to catch.

When he slid off the bed and grabbed his jeans, she sat up, dragging the coverlet up to cover her breasts. Pushing her hair back out of her eyes, she watched him dress and her mouth went dry.

"You'll write to me," she said, not a question.

"I will." He patted the pocket of his shirt. "I've got your address and you'll have mine as soon as you get a letter from me. I'd give it to you now, but I can't be sure it won't change. Hell, I'm not even sure my email address will be the same."

"Doesn't matter." She shook her head, went up on her knees and reached for him. He held her close and she locked her arms around his waist, resting her head on his chest. She heard the steady beat of his heart and prayed it would remain safe and steady until she was with him again. "Just write to me, Jack. And let me know you're safe."

He tipped her chin up with the tips of his fingers. "And when I'm coming home."

"That, too." He kissed her again, looked long and deep into her eyes, then turned for the door. At the threshold, he paused, turned back and sighed. "You take my breath away."

She covered her mouth with one hand and knew she would soon lose the battle with her tears. "Be safe, Jack. And come home to me."

He gave her a sharp nod, then turned and left, the door closing quietly behind him. Alone, Rita walked to the window, the coverlet a toga of sorts, around her naked body. She pulled the edges of the curtains back, looked down into the parking lot and saw him, taking long, sure strides toward his black Jeep.

As if he could sense her watching him, he turned, looked up at her and simply held her gaze for several long seconds. Then he got in the car and drove away.

But he never wrote. He never came to her. If she hadn't moved to Long Beach to feel closer to a memory, she might never have known he was even alive. Was that Fate blessing them? Or cursing them?

"Down! Get down!"

Startled at the muffled shout, Rita jumped to her feet and whipped her head around to stare at the darkened hall leading to Jack's bedroom. Starting down the hall, the wood floor was cold against her bare feet. With every step she took, his voice came louder, more desperate.

She ran, following his shouts, his pain.

Her heart.

Seven

Jack shouted himself awake, jolted upright in bed and struggled to breathe. The dream—*nightmare*—still held him in a tightfisted grip and he had to force himself to look around the moonlit room to orient himself. He was home, yet his heart still raced and his mouth and throat were dry. A black duvet pooled in his lap, his bare chest was covered in sweat and his gaze was wild. He scrubbed one hand across his face, rubbing his eyes as if he could wipe away the fear raised by the images still stamped in his mind.

"Jack? Jack, are you okay?" Rita hurried into the room.

"I'm fine," he muttered thickly, jumping out of bed. *Perfect. Just perfect.* He'd woken her up and now she'd stare at him with either pity or fear and he didn't think he could take either.

He wore loosely tied cotton pants that dipped low on his hips and he was grateful he'd decided not to sleep naked since she'd moved in. Damn it. Jack needed a little time to get a grip. To shove those memories back into the dark corner of his mind where they were usually locked away. He needed to be clearheaded when he talked to Rita. Jack just didn't see that happening anytime soon.

He pushed one hand through his hair and looked at her as if she were a mirage. Jack had pulled himself out of a hot, dusty dream where the sound of explosions and gunfire still echoed in the stillness around him. Seeing her here, in the dark moon-washed confines of his bedroom, a world away from the scene that still haunted him, was almost too much to compute. "Sorry I woke you. Just…go back to sleep."

He turned his back on her, hoping to hell she'd leave, and walked out onto the terrace, welcoming the brisk slap of wind. Sea spray scented the air that he dragged into his lungs, to replace the dry dustiness that felt as though it was coating him in more than memories.

"Jack?"

Damn.

She'd followed him onto the terrace and the touch of her hand against his bare back had him flinching. Every nerve in his body was firing, on alert.

"What is it?" She stood right behind him, her voice soft, low, soothing. "*Talk* to me."

He whipped his head around to glare at her. "I don't want to talk. That should be clear. Just leave me alone, Rita. You don't want to be with me right now."

"Yeah," she insisted and didn't look the least bit cowed. "I do. Or I wouldn't be here."

Gritting his teeth, Jack ground out tightly, "I'm on the ragged edge here, Rita. I need some space."

"No, you don't."

He choked out a harsh laugh. "Is that right? And you're an expert on me, is that it?"

"Enough to know that you've had enough space," she countered, stepping in closer. "Too much, maybe. Everyone backs off when you tell them to, but I won't. I'm here, Jack, and I'm not going anywhere. You can't use a nasty tone and a miserable attitude to shake me off. *Talk* to me."

His skin was buzzing, his mind racing and his heartbeat was still at a fast gallop. Jack had come out of that damn dream ready to fight, but there was no enemy to face. He needed to move. To fight. To do *something*, to expel the ghosts gathered around him, shrieking for his attention.

"Damn it, Jack," Rita said, tugging at his forearm until he turned to face her again. Her whiskey eyes were hot, burning with passion and fury and he wasn't sure which had top billing.

"I'm not deaf or blind," she said. "I heard you shouting. I stepped into your room in time to see you bolt up in bed as if the hounds of hell were after you."

She'd hit that one on the head. Scraping one hand over his face, he muttered, "They were."

"Then tell me." She held on to him, the heat of her touch sliding into his arm, moving through his bloodstream. "Let me in, damn it. What does it cost you to open the door just a crack?"

He speared her with a hard look. There was no pity, no fear in her eyes. Only concern and curiosity and maybe that was worse in some ways.

"You think it's *me* I'm worried about?" He grabbed her shoulders, giving her a little shake for emphasis. "It's *you* I'm thinking about here. I'm trying to save you, don't you get it?"

"Save me? From what?"

"God, you won't let this go," he muttered thickly.

"Not a chance."

He stared into her eyes. "Fine. I'm trying to save you from me. Okay? I don't even trust myself around you right now."

"That's ridiculous."

There was a response he hadn't expected.

"You're not trying to injure me in some way, Jack," she pointed out, her voice a little louder, her eyes a little more fiery. "You've done your best to simply avoid me at all costs."

"There's a reason—"

"Did I ask you to save me?" she interrupted, breaking free of his grip. The cold ocean air lifted her hair into a cloud of dark curls around her head and with the flash in her eyes, she looked like a pagan goddess. Even the nightgown she wore that was hot-pink with the image of a cupcake on it and the words *SWEET THING* scrawled across the top couldn't diminish her. No, not a goddess, he corrected. Instead, she looked like a short, Italian Valkyrie. She was furious and her eyes were shot with sparks.

She poked her index finger into the center of his chest. "I'm a big girl. I save myself when I need it. I don't need a knight in shining armor, Jack." She shoved her hair out of her eyes impatiently. "What I need is for my *husband* to tell me what's tearing at him."

"You would have made a great warrior, Rita," he said

softly, gaze raking her up and down, from her bare toes with their purple-polished nails up to the eyes that were so incensed he was surprised she wasn't actually shooting flames from them. "You are a Fury, aren't you? Not afraid of anything."

"Not afraid of *you*, anyway," she said, whipping her head back to shake her hair free of her eyes.

How the hell was a man supposed to win an argument with a woman like this? How was he supposed to ignore her, ignore what she made him feel?

"Maybe you should be," he said, pulling her in close with one quick move. "And if I were a better man, I'd tell you to leave. Now. But I'm not—so if you want to run, now's your chance."

She reached up, cupped his face in her palms and demanded, "Does it look like I'm going anywhere?"

"No. Thank God." He bent his head, and took her mouth in a kiss that was filled with the hunger and desperation he'd felt since she reentered his life.

With the dregs of the nightmare still clinging to him, Jack held her tighter, his hands running up and down her back and down to her bottom. He pulled her against his rock-hard body and she wriggled closer in appreciation. Expectation. His blood ran hot and fast, his heartbeat raced and his mind was fogged by the want choking him. *Need* was alive and shouting inside him.

The cold ocean wind wrapped itself around them, but he didn't feel it. Nothing could vanquish the internal heat. One hand cupped the back of her head and held her still so he could completely claim her mouth. His tongue tangled with hers and her eager response fed the flames licking at his soul.

There was no time for romance, seduction. He needed to be with her. In her. Over her. Tearing his mouth from hers, he looked down into her now-glassy eyes and fought to breathe.

"What're you doing?" she managed to ask breathlessly. "Why are you stopping?"

"Not stopping. Changing location." He bent down, scooped her up and carried her back through the French doors and into his bedroom. Moonlight followed them, the wind rushed in behind them and none of that mattered. He laid her down on the mattress and, in one deft move, stripped her nightgown off, leaving her naked—just as he wanted her. She scooted back farther on the mattress and reached for him. Jack didn't keep her waiting. He yanked off the sleep pants he was wearing and joined her on the bed an instant later. His hands moved over her, exploring every curve. Every line.

He remembered this so well. Had tormented himself over the last few months, by recalling the feel of her skin, the lush fullness of her breasts and the taut, dark nipples that he loved to suckle.

And now, because of the baby, she was so much more than she had been. She was ripe, delectable and more alluring than ever. Even as he thought it, though, both of her hands went to the mound of her belly as if to hide it from him. He drew her hands away and said, "Don't. You're beautiful."

She laughed. "I'm huge."

He shook his head. "No. Curvy. Delicious. Amazing."

She sighed a little. "Wow. When you try, you really know the right things to say."

He grinned, bent his head and indulged himself in

what he'd wanted to do for weeks now. He took one nipple into his mouth and savored the taste of her. Her scent invaded him, the soft sighs and moans sliding from her throat enflamed him. He ran his tongue and teeth across the tip of her nipple and then suckled, drawing her very essence into himself.

She planted her feet on the mattress and lifted her hips. "Touch me, Jack. Touch me."

He did. Sweeping one hand down the length of her body, he cupped her center and used his thumb to brush across her most sensitive spot. She jerked beneath him and he smiled against her breast, relishing her reaction. He suckled harder, and then lifted his head to switch to her other breast and she went crazy in his arms. As if the need that had been building between them for weeks had finally reached a breaking point for both of them, she rocked her hips into his hand.

He pushed two fingers into her heat and groaned himself at the slick, tight feel of her. It had been too long. His body was ready to explode and so was hers. He couldn't wait another minute to be inside her, to feel her body surrounding his.

Lifting his head, he looked down at her then kissed her briefly. "At least we don't need a condom now."

"Points for us," she said, swallowing hard, breath coming in short, hard gasps. "Damn it, Jack, don't drag this out. I need you inside me."

"Just what I need, too," he said, and shifted position to kneel between her thighs. He spread her legs wide and looked down at her. She was wanton, wild and everything he'd ever wanted in a woman. And for this one moment at least, she was his again—as she was always meant to be.

His mind whispered that this was temporary. That this marriage wasn't real and he was nobody's idea of husband material anyway. But he shut that nagging voice down and surrendered to the mating call trumpeting through his body.

He ran his hands over her hot, slick center, watching her twist and writhe in her own desperate need.

Her response pushed his own desires beyond what he could bear. Body throbbing, heart galloping, he leaned over her and pushed himself inside her. That first, glorious slide filled him with the kind of ease he hadn't known in months. This was what had been missing in his life. This sense of rightness that claimed him when their bodies were joined.

She hooked her legs at his hips and pulled him in tighter, deeper. Tipping her head back into the mattress, she bit her lip and moved with him. Their bodies meshed, linked in the most intimate way possible, he felt the pounding of her heart. Saw the flash in her eyes, heard her gasping breaths and experienced her body quaking, quivering as he pushed her higher, faster than they'd ever gone before.

Her nails scored his back as he rocked in and out of her body, setting a rhythm she raced to meet. "Jack! Jack!"

"Come on, Rita," He urged, barely able to frame the words as his breath sawed in and out of his lungs. "Go over. Go over so I can follow."

She clung to him and shouted his name when the first tremors took her. He felt her body tighten around his in spasms of delight and when she'd reached her peak, Jack let go and found the peace that had been denied him for months.

* * *

Rita took some deep breaths and tried to ease the frantic beat of her heart at the same time. It had been six long months since he'd touched her like that. Time in which she'd almost convinced herself that her memory was making what they shared much better than it actually had been. Well, she told herself, *that* theory was just shot out of the sky.

Her whole body was so alight with sensation she thought she should glow in the dark. And even while she tried to regain control, she was thinking about doing it all again. She turned her head to look at Jack, lying beside her. One arm flung across his eyes, his chest heaved with every breath and she smiled, knowing that he was just as shaken as she. Had she finally broken through the wall he'd built around himself? Was her Jack finally back?

"You owe me twenty bucks," he said softly.

She blinked at him, then laughed. "Seriously? You want a *tip*?"

He lowered his arm and turned his gaze on her. "Nope. A bet we made. Not only did you marry me when you said you wouldn't, you just—"

She held up one hand. "I know what I just—" then she slapped both hands to her hips as if checking for a wallet "—I don't seem to have any pockets at the moment so I'll have to owe you."

One corner of his mouth quirked. "I suppose I can live with that."

Rolling to one side, he propped himself up on one elbow and looked down at her. "Rita—"

She stopped him by laying her fingers on his mouth. Disappointment welled in her chest. Looking into his eyes, she could see that her Jack was still buried behind a shutter of ice. Maybe there were a few cracks in that cold stillness, but it was a seductive stranger staring at her through Jack's eyes. Her heart hurt for it, but she wouldn't give up. Now more than ever, it was important to find a way to completely reach him.

"Don't you dare apologize for this," she said firmly. "*Or* tell me that it'll never happen again—"

He tried to speak, but she hurried on. "We both wanted this, Jack. And I want it again right now."

"Want isn't the point," he ground out as he laid one arm across her middle.

"Then what is?" She reached up and smoothed his hair back from his forehead, just because she wanted her fingers in that thick, wavy mass. Rita needed to touch him, to ground herself and hopefully *him*. To remind them both that the threads binding them were still there. They hadn't been broken, only strained. She had to believe they could strengthen them again.

"Talk to me," she said, locking her gaze on his so that he could see how much she wanted this. That when he told his story, whatever it was, he would still be safe with her. "Tell me what you were dreaming. Why were you shouting? What made you grab hold of me and hang on like I was a lifeboat in a tsunami?"

He scowled, but she was so used to that expression now, it didn't even affect her. "I don't want to talk about it."

"Just dream about it then?" she countered, refusing to give up on him. *Them*. "Don't you see that if you do tell me, maybe it will make the dreams fade?"

"Nothing can."

Then the baby kicked and his features went blank

with surprise. He glanced down to where his arm rested across her belly and then he sucked in a gulp of air when the baby kicked again, as if reminding its parents that they weren't alone. His astonished gaze snapped to hers. "That was—"

"A good kick," she finished for him. She knew what he was feeling, because she'd felt exactly the same the first time the baby'd moved. It was magic, she knew. Staggering. That tiny life making itself known. Taking his hand, she held it tightly to the mound of their child.

On cue, another kick came and Jack's eyes went wide even as an unexpected grin lit his face. "Strong baby."

That wide smile of his tugged at her heart. "Like its father."

Just like that, his smile faded into memory. Pulling away from her grasp, he asked, "What is it? The baby, I mean. Do you know?"

If he hadn't pulled away from her, Rita would have thought that she was making more progress with him. He hadn't once asked about the baby before, so normally, she would have celebrated internally that he was feeling...linked. But the look in his eyes was cool, not warm, and so she had to admit that nothing had changed.

"No," she said sadly, sorry that he was withdrawing again. "I didn't want to know ahead of time. I wanted to be surprised. There aren't many real surprises left in the world."

"*You* always surprised me," he said. "Still do." Just for a second, she saw another crack in the wall around him. Then it was gone and as if to prove it to her, he turned and pushed off the bed.

He walked naked to the open French doors and out

onto the terrace. On the twenty-fifth floor, facing the ocean, there was no one to see them. No nosy neighbors.

He stood there in the cold wind, his hair lifted off his neck and Rita wanted to touch it, feel it against her skin again. Broad shoulders, narrow hips and long, muscular legs made her mouth water, but while her blood burned, her mind mourned because he was trying to pull away from her. Again.

But Rita wasn't going to let him. Not this time. Scrambling off the bed, she went to him and pulled at his upper arm until he turned to face her. "I'm not going to quit trying to reach you, Jack."

He shook his head. "Did you ever think that maybe there's nothing to reach?"

"No." She shook her head, too, just as fiercely determined to find him as he was to hide. "There's *you*, Jack. And I'm not going to stop pestering, pushing you. I'm not going to stop asking you what happened, so you might as well give in now and tell me."

"Damn, you've got a hard head," he murmured, with the faintest of smiles.

"That's been said before." She looked at him ruefully. "By *you*, mostly. Jack, tell me. Tell me what's haunting you."

He grimaced. "*Haunting* is the right word for it."

"Talk."

A harsh laugh that held no humor scraped his throat and his gaze swung past her to lock on the dark, roiling ocean. But he looked more as though he was focusing on something only he could see. His ghosts. His past. And finally, Rita thought, he was going to bring her into the shadows with him. Maybe then, she'd be able to hold his hand and lead him back into the light.

"You want to know?" He blew out a breath. "Fine. Here it is. Two days after I left you, I was back with my unit." He glanced at her briefly before turning his gaze to the sea. "I was actually writing you a letter when my squad was sent out to do some recon on a nearby village."

Her heartbeat stuttered a little, knowing that he had been keeping his promise to write and a little fearful of what had kept him from completing that letter. Rita watched him, judging every tiny twist of his features, trying to guess at the turnings of his mind, at the nearness of his ghosts. Her gaze on his profile, she held her breath and waited.

His voice sounded far away as if he wasn't really there with her at all, but instead, he was caught in his memories. He was somehow more a part of his past than he was a part of his life, here. She had to know why.

"We were told there was sniper activity so we were careful. Well, thought we were." He shook his head, gritted his teeth and forced the words out. "I'm not going into details here, Rita. You don't need to know them anyway. Short version. One of my guys was shot. We took cover, a couple of men breaking right while my best friend and I went left, dragging the wounded man with us."

"Jack…" She put one hand on his forearm.

"There was an IED on the left."

Tears drenched her eyes. She didn't know what was coming next, but her heart ached just looking at his stony profile, the hard set of his jaw, his narrowed gaze.

"The wounded man was killed. My friend Kevin got hit hard. His legs." He blew out a breath then dragged in another gulp of the cold, sea air. Shaking his head, he swallowed hard and continued, "Somehow, we got the sniper and then I could work on Kevin's wounds. I got tourniquets on him but he fought me." He paused, to steady himself, to distance himself from the pain? She couldn't know. But he kept talking, so she stayed quiet.

"Kevin didn't want to live without his legs—kept cursing at me to leave him be. I wouldn't listen. Couldn't let him die."

"Of course not." God, to have such scenes and more in your head. To see them in your sleep. His sister, Cass, was right. These guys weren't sick. They were hurt. Right down to their souls. Rita wrapped her arms around him and held on whether he was aware of her or not.

"We called for medics and evac. One guy dead, two wounded and Kevin, half-conscious and still cursing me for saving him." Jack scrubbed one hand across his mouth as if he could somehow wipe away the taste of his own words. Then he finally shifted his gaze to hers and when she looked into his eyes, Rita felt the sympathy he'd already said he didn't want.

"I couldn't write to you after that," he said. "Couldn't even think about you. I talked to my friend's widow after they notified her and left her broken to pieces. She loved Mike so much that losing him shattered her completely. Then I went to see my best friend, Kevin, before they flew him out for surgery and he wouldn't even talk to me.

"Hell, he wouldn't *look* at me. All those curses he'd brought down on my head for saving him were still running through my head and probably his. It was like I was dead to him."

"You never talked to him again?"

"No." Jack took a breath and blew it out again. "He contacted me a couple of months ago, but I didn't get back to him."

"Why not?"

"What's the point, Rita?" He shoved both hands through his hair. "You think I want to stand there, look at him in a chair and have him ream me all over again? No, thanks."

She felt for him. He'd saved his friend, done his best for him and the man had fought him every step of the way. No wonder he was tortured by nightmares and didn't want to talk about what he remembered. But things might have changed for his friend by now. Maybe he wanted to make amends with Jack and by not allowing it, Jack kept the pain close and fresh.

"You don't know what he wanted," she told him. "Maybe he wanted to say thank you."

"I don't need to be thanked, either," he snapped. "I did what I had to do. That's it."

The emptiness in Jack's eyes was so profound, Rita didn't know how he could still be standing. He had to be the strongest man she'd ever known. And the most alone. Even with a family who loved him, a wife and a child on the way, he was so terribly alone.

Voice brisk, letting her know this little truth-telling session was now at an end, he said, "Anyway. After all that, I had nothing left for you, Rita." Shaking his head, he said softly, "Still don't. I'm not the guy you knew. Hell, I don't even recognize that man anymore."

"Well, I do," she said, going up on her toes to kiss him. "I know him. I still see him when I look into your eyes. And I know you're punishing yourself for something that wasn't your fault."

"My squad. My calls."

"And you think I have a hard head."

He glanced at her, surprise flickering in his eyes.

"Jack, you were ordered to check out that village. You all took cover. What happened, just…happened. You're not in charge of who lives and dies. Jack, you did the best you could."

"Wasn't good enough," he insisted.

"It was, because it was all you *could* do." Now that she knew, she could almost understand him cutting himself off from her, from his family, from everything that was important to him.

He'd seen too much loss. And he didn't want to risk more of it. So by shutting down his heart, he thought he was protecting himself. Instead, he'd welcomed a different kind of pain. Rita laid her head on his chest and listened to the wild thumping of his heart. He stiffened against her and for a second, she thought he was going to shove her aside, but instead, he grabbed her tight, pulled her closer. Buried his face in the curve of her neck.

"Damn it, Rita," he murmured, "you should have left it alone."

"I can't do that, Jack. I can't leave *you* alone." She wondered if he heard the love in her voice. If he understood how much she was feeling for him or that it was so much bigger than what she'd felt for him when they first met.

She held him, rubbing her hands up and down his back, wishing she could reach past the shadows inside him, wishing she could convince him that he wasn't at fault. But all she could do was *show* him. What she felt. What she saw when she looked at him.

Drawing his head up, she kissed him, pouring everything she had into the kiss and was rewarded when he groaned and took everything she offered. Her head was spinning when he fast-walked her back to the bed, when he stretched her out and claimed her in every way possible.

Rita's mind blanked out and her body took over. Sensation flooded her. Tingles of awareness swarmed through her and curls of delicious tension settled in the pit of her stomach and spread like a wildfire. His hands, his mouth, moved over her, driving her wild, until the flames he lit enveloped them both.

She touched and stroked and kissed, wanting him to experience everything she was. Wanting him to know that he wasn't alone. That she was here. With him. Wanted him to *feel* the love she couldn't bring herself to say yet.

Oh, yes, she still loved him. Yes, she still wanted the happily-ever-after with him. But she knew instinctively that he wouldn't want to hear that now. So she kept it tucked inside and told herself that they were a matched set. Each of them locking away a piece of themselves they wanted no one else to see.

Then he entered her, and all thought fled. She focused only on what he was doing to her, making her feel. His body moved within hers and the incredible friction left her breathless and she didn't care. Breathing was overrated. She didn't need air when she had Jack.

He took her higher than she'd gone before, pushing her to reach for the completion she knew was waiting. Rita kept her gaze locked on his. She couldn't have looked away if it had meant her life. Those ice-blue eyes warmed and steamed and glowed with passion. Watching him and her own reflection in his eyes, she shattered, her body simply splintering into jagged pieces of pleasure that had her screaming his name and clutching his shoulders. And only a moment later, he surrendered to her, emptying himself into her and she held him while he fell.

Eight

"Don't start thinking anything's changed," Jack warned her the next morning.

Rita bit her lip and hid a smile. She had been expecting this. She'd known that after what they'd shared the night before Jack would try to pull back again. Pretend that last night hadn't happened. And she'd come up with a way to combat it. She wasn't going to argue. She was simply going to ignore *his* arguments.

Rita had had a long night to think about this. Naturally there hadn't been any snuggling or cuddling after their amazing bout of lovemaking—and that's what it had been whether he admitted it or not. It wasn't just sex. It was making love. And though Rita had spent the rest of the night alone in the guest room, she'd been more hopeful than she had been in six months.

He might not realize it yet, but there was a chink in

the wall he was hiding behind. For one brief moment, he'd let his guard down. Let her in. Sure, he'd slammed it shut again quickly, but now that she'd made it through once, she was determined to do it again. Alone in the silence of her own room, Rita had vowed to smash those walls around Jack until nothing was left but the two of them standing in the rubble.

"Okay," she said brightly. "Got it. Nothing's changed. This ship is just gorgeous."

"What?"

She looked at him, pleased to see the confusion on his features. If she kept him off balance, it would be harder for him to plant his feet behind that damn wall.

"I said this ship is gorgeous." Rita did a fast circle on the main deck of *The Sea Queen*, taking in the gleaming wood floors, the shining windows and the sweep of sea stretching out behind it. "I've never been on a cruise ship before. For some reason I didn't realize just how *big* they are."

"Yeah," he said irritably, "it's great."

"Thanks for inviting me along to see the ship."

"I didn't invite you. *You* invited you."

"True," she said with a shrug, "but you didn't fight me on it. That was practically gracious. Congrats."

He frowned again and Rita had to fight to hide the smile tugging at her mouth. "So, do you really have to meet with the captain?"

Still frowning, he glanced around, then up at the bridge. "Just to say hello, let him know I'm doing a walk-through."

"Do you want me with you or can I wander?"

"Come with me, then wander," he said, heading toward the wide open doors that led to the main lobby and reception area.

Rita was grinning as she followed him inside, then she stopped dead, her mouth dropped open and she did a slow turn to take it all in.

The Sea Queen was palatial. A tiled floor was inlaid with a depiction of what looked like a Middle Ages golden crown. There was a staircase that was so wide she suspected trucks could pass through side by side. Copper railings lined the second and third stories that looked down onto the lobby and deep scarlet rugs climbed the stairs. The ceiling was draped with pendant lights in shades of copper and brass and the walls boasted murals of what, again, looked like the Middle Ages. There was a theme here that went toward ancient royalty, with a hint of magic.

"At night, the pendant lights glow, and starlight flickers against the black ceiling."

"Wow." She didn't even look at him. "I seriously love this. It's very...magical. I half expect to see wizards and witches walk through the doors."

"Good," he said, shoving both hands into the pockets of his black jeans. "That's what we were going for. The club rooms and bars are all done with the same kind of decor. A little mystical. A lot upscale."

Now she did look at him in time to see a flash of pride cross his face. "It's really spectacular," she said.

Nodding, he said, "Let's find the captain, then I'll show you a few of the staterooms."

She took his hand and counted it a victory when he didn't shake her off, instead holding on to her fingers as if she were a lifeline.

On the bridge, Rita was stunned. It was a huge room,

with windows giving the crew an incredibly wide view of the sea. There were enough computers to make it look like a spaceship rather than a cruise ship.

Captain McManus, a tall, gray-haired man with sharp brown eyes and an easy smile, welcomed them both then took Jack to one side to go over a few things. Rita didn't mind. It gave her a chance to look around and appreciate the nearly bird's-eye view of the ocean and the Long Beach harbor.

There were two tall command chairs that reminded her of something off the Starship *Enterprise*'s bridge and counters filled with screens, blinking lights and men and women busily going over everything. She could only imagine how busy they were when they were actually at sea.

And what would that be like, she wondered. Being on this luxurious ship, sailing off to other countries, meeting new people. She looked up at Jack. "You've been on a lot of cruises, haven't you?"

"A few," he said, looking out over the water. "When we were kids, my folks liked to pile us all on one of the ships for a couple of weeks." His features softened at the good memory. "Mom used to say it was the only way she could get all of us to stay in the same place for any length of time."

"That must have been fun," she said, a little wistfully. "I've never been on one myself. Just a little too spooky, I guess. All of that water—"

He shook his head and said, "Doesn't seem that way, though. Once you're on board, it's like you're on your own private island."

"Well," she said, glancing around, "this ship is big enough that maybe even I wouldn't be nervous."

"I can't imagine you scared of anything," Jack said.

She looked up into his eyes. If he only knew that the one thing that scared her was losing him again. She'd mourned him once and now she had him back. Rita was determined that she wouldn't let him go this time.

"You ready to see other parts of the ship?"

She half turned to look up at Jack. "Sure. I'd love to. But first let me say, the bridge is amazing. And a little disappointing, too," she added.

"Really?" The captain laughed and asked, "Why?"

"Well, it sounds silly, but I sort of expected to see a wheel up here."

Jack smiled and the captain let out a laugh that had several of his officers turning to stare at him in surprise.

"No," Captain McManus said finally. "Everything's done by computer now. Not as romantic but much more efficient."

"I suppose," she said, then held out one hand to the man. "Thank you for letting me look around."

"For the boss's wife?" He shook her hand and winked. "Anytime at all."

"Thanks, Captain," Jack said. "We'll let you get back to it."

"Excellent. We'll be ready to sail on time, Mr. Buchanan."

"Good to know."

When they left, Rita took Jack's hand again and walked beside him on the catwalk surrounding the bridge. The sea air flew fast and furious this high up and gave her a chill that was dispelled by Jack's big hand holding hers.

"We'll take the elevator down and I'll show you the

theatres, the pools and a few of the club and casino lounges."

"Okay." She whipped her hair back to look up at him. "So, you're glad you invited me along?"

His lips twitched. "I didn't invite you."

"You wish you had."

"Maybe." He glanced at her, gave her hand a squeeze, then steered her into an elevator.

There were mirrors on every surface and Rita couldn't help but look at him. The man was so gorgeous, she could have stared at him for hours. His features were strong and sharp and had been honed down over the last several months, giving him the look of a saint with a wicked side.

He met her gaze in the mirror and just for a second, the power of his stare was enough to punch her heart into a frantic beat.

"You okay?"

"Fine," she said, though she really wasn't. How could she be, when she was in love with a man who didn't want to be loved?

The elevator stopped with a ding and he announced, "First stop, Deck Three."

Just like the rest of the ship, it was elegant and luxurious, from the brass sconces on the walls to the dark ruby carpet on the floor. Then her gaze focused on the solid white surface stretching out in front of them. "There's an ice-skating rink?"

He laughed. "We've got everything."

Her imagination completed the picture, with families moving across the ice, laughing, making memories. She could almost hear them echoing in the now-empty space.

"Oh, I miss skating," she said, and rubbed one hand over her belly. "But my center of gravity's a little whacked right now, so…"

"Yeah, well, you can always skate when you're back in Utah after the baby's born."

It was a slap. A reminder. *Don't get comfortable*, he was saying. *I won't let you in. I won't let you stay. I won't let myself care.*

Rita almost swayed with the emotional impact, but she locked her knees because she couldn't let him see what he could so easily do to her. She wanted to argue with him, tell him she loved him and she wasn't going anywhere. But Rita remembered that she'd made the decision to simply not engage when he pulled back. When he tried to shut her out. So she smiled instead, though that small curve of her mouth cost her more than he would ever know.

"Yes. There's plenty of time for skating after the baby." She looked around. "Where's the theatre? What movie's playing?"

"Not a movie theatre," he said, frowning at her, as if waiting for her real reaction to what he'd said. "It's for live shows. The movies are up on Deck Eight, along with a spa and a casino and stuff for the kids and—" He broke off. "Hell, who can remember it all?"

"So, show me." She started walking in the direction he'd pointed. He was still holding her hand though and tugged her to a stop.

"Rita, last night, what I told you—"

"It's okay, Jack. Whatever you tell me is safe with me," she assured him.

"It's not that. It's…" He paused, took a breath and then released it again. "I want you to know that I made a vow to myself. You keep telling me how I'm keeping my family—and you—at a distance. You're right. But it's with a purpose. I swore I would never put anyone in the position of mourning me—and now I've got you. And the baby. And if I let my family get close again, let *you* get close, then I risk causing pain. I won't do it."

She didn't even know what to say to that.

"Rita—" His eyes were shadowed. "Bottom line, I don't want to hurt you."

Foolish man. Couldn't he see that's exactly what he was doing? Did he really believe that causing pain *now* was better than later? His family was already in pain because they couldn't reach him. And she knew just how they felt. But Rita knew he wouldn't want to hear that.

"Good." She nodded sharply. "I don't want to hurt you, either."

"Great. But my point is…"

"Oh, don't worry so much, Jack." She looked at him and the sunlight filtering through all the windows threw golden light across his face. "I get it. Nothing's changed. You're still locking yourself away from the world to save the rest of us."

He didn't want to hurt her, but he didn't want to love her, either. She had to force a smile again and he would never know how much it cost her.

He frowned. "That's—"

Rita kept her voice light, as she added, "Not important right now. I said I don't want to hurt you, but I might if you don't show me where the closest bathroom is. Honestly, this baby must be camped out on my bladder."

"Oh. Right." With the subject neatly changed, he

led her down one side of the ship and waited as she went inside.

Rita hadn't really needed the bathroom, for a change. What she'd needed was a minute or two to herself. To think. To search her heart and find the strength to keep pretending that he couldn't rip a chunk out of her soul with a word.

She gripped the edge of the black marble countertop and stared into the mirror at her own reflection. Her eyes had so many things to say and she didn't want to hear any of them. Maybe she was being foolish for loving a man who so clearly wasn't interested in making the same kind of commitment.

But how could she simply stop?

Besides, the very fact that he was trying to warn her off, save her from him, told her that he *did* care. More than he wanted to.

"And, it's not like you get a *choice* about who you love," she told her reflection. And scowled a little when her mirror image mocked her. "Fine," she admitted, "even if I *had* a choice, I'd still choose him."

Did that make her a martyr? An idiot? "Neither," she decided, staring into her own eyes. "It makes me Rita Marchetti Buchanan. I love him. It's as simple as that, really."

Nodding to herself, she shook her hair back, gave her baby belly a consoling rub, then lifted her chin and went back to face her husband with a smile.

The next few days weren't easy. Jack had expected Rita to be a little more…depressed, he guessed, about the fact that he'd brushed off their night of sex as changing nothing.

Of course, it *had*, he just couldn't admit that. Not to himself and certainly not to her. But the truth was, now that he'd been with her again, that was all he could think about.

Apparently, though, Rita was having a much easier time of it. She'd moved on as if she'd felt nothing and that he knew was a damn lie. He'd watched her, heard her, *felt* her response to their lovemaking. But she'd set it all aside and rather than being relieved, Jack was just a little ticked off. What the hell?

She wasn't talking about it and he'd fully expected her to go all female on him. Women always wanted to *talk*. To *share*. The fact that Rita wasn't bugged him. He couldn't put his finger on what was happening and that bothered him, too. Jack felt off balance somehow and he wasn't sure when that had happened.

His new reality was simply marching on as if nothing had changed at all. Every morning, since he refused to have her drive across town all by herself at four thirty in the morning, he was up and taking her to the bakery. Where she made him coffee and fresh pastries and they had breakfast together while she talked nonstop, telling him stories about her family, talking about her plans for the bakery, refusing to accept his silence.

She pushed him for his opinion and when she didn't agree with him, she goaded him into an argument. Hell, he hadn't talked this much in the four months since he'd been home.

Every night, she was right there, whether she was cooking in the penthouse kitchen or they were ordering takeout. Rita made him a part of it. She poked and prodded at him until she got him to talk about his work, about their tour of *The Sea Queen*, readying to set sail. She poked her nose into his relationship with his brother, sister and father. Nothing was sacred, Jack told himself. The woman was making herself such a presence in his life, he couldn't ignore her in spite of how hard he tried.

And every night, when she was in the guest room and he was alone in his huge, empty bed, he really tried. But her face was uppermost in his mind all the damn time. He closed his eyes to sleep and she was there. The pillow she'd used still carried her scent.

How the hell was a man supposed to do the right thing when everything in him was demanding he do the *wrong* thing?

"Hey, Jack?"

He closed his eyes and sighed a little. Even shutting himself up in his home office the minute he got home didn't work. Rita would not be stopped. "What is it?"

"Someone's here to see you."

What was she up to now? he wondered. Had she brought his whole family over? Hers? Were they all going to sit in a circle and hold hands? Frowning, he pushed up from the desk, crossed the room and stalked out into the living room, half-ready for battle.

Rita was sitting on the couch, smiling at the man opposite her. Jack stopped dead when he spotted the man's wheelchair. *Kevin.* Had to be. His chest felt tight as if something was squeezing his lungs like a lemon trying for as much juice as possible. His gaze snapped to Rita. Had she done this? No. Of course not. He hadn't even told her Kevin's last name. There was no way she could have found him and arranged to get him to the penthouse.

So what the hell was going on?

"There he is!" Rita shot him a wide, bright smile of welcome. "Jack, look who's here."

The guy in the chair turned to face him and suddenly, time did a weird shift and it was nearly five months ago. The sun felt hot, oppressive. Screams tore at the air and Kevin's curses were loud and inventive as Jack worked to stop the bleeding. He felt again the raw desperation and the sense of helplessness as he shouted for a medic.

He was standing in the penthouse and yet he had one foot firmly planted in the past and no idea how to escape it.

"Dude," Kevin said on a laugh. "You look like you just saw a ghost."

In a way, he had, Jack told himself and shook his head, trying to clear the images rising up in his mind. For just a second, he'd seen Kevin as he'd been before that last mission. Tall, strong, laughing. Now reality was back and he didn't know what to say. "Surprised to see you is all."

"Yeah. It's been a while." Kevin rested his forearms on the arms of his chair and folded his hands together. His blond hair was just a little longer than it had been in the corps and his blue eyes were sharp, shrewd and locked on Jack. He'd lost some weight, but the real difference was the pinned-up legs of the slacks he wore.

Kevin Davis had lost both legs on that mission, in spite of the medics delivering fast, heroic care. And Jack hadn't talked to him since the morning he'd been evacced to a hospital ship. Even then, it had been less of a conversation and more of Kevin damning Jack to hell for saving him. Not something he liked to think about.

"You gonna say hello anytime soon?" Kevin asked with a tilted grin.

"Yeah. Sure." Jack crossed the room, held out one hand and looked down at his friend. "Good to see you, Kev."

After shaking hands, Jack sat on the couch beside Rita and asked, "So what brings you here?"

"Cut right to the chase, no bull," Kevin said, smiling even wider. "Haven't changed much, Sarge."

For a second, Jack felt a twinge. He'd been in the military for so long that becoming a civilian again had been a stretch. Now he wasn't sure where the hell he belonged. Then he felt Rita's hand sneak into his and though he told himself not to accept the comfort she was offering, his fingers linked through hers and locked them together.

Guilt pinged around the center of his chest like a Ping-Pong ball on steroids. Here he sat. Beautiful, pregnant wife. Elegant penthouse. Successful business. His life hadn't been shattered. He'd simply stepped back into it and though it hadn't been an easy adjustment, it had been nothing compared to what Kevin had no doubt gone through. Jack's tours of duty hadn't cost him what they had Kevin. And he couldn't make himself be okay with that.

His back teeth ground together and he fought against the rising tide of regret within. This was why he hadn't answered Kevin's email. Hell, why he hadn't even opened it. His memories were thick and rich enough that he didn't need a reminder—being with Kevin in person—to make them even more so. And hell, what could he say to the man? Kevin had lost his legs. Jack had come home whole, if changed. How was that fair?

How could he look into the man's eyes, knowing that it was he who had been leading that squad? It was Jack's decisions that had eventually brought about what had happened to Kevin. If they'd zigged instead of zagged, what might have changed? A man could drive himself crazy with thoughts like that.

How could Kevin not still blame him?

Jack had spent months trying to get past the memories of that one fateful day and hadn't been able to do it. How much more difficult was it for Kevin to try to move past it when every day he was faced with a physical reminder of his own limitations?

"Jack," Kevin said quietly, as if he knew exactly what his friend was thinking, feeling, *remembering.* "You don't have to do this. Don't have to feel bad for me. I'm fine. Really."

Now, looking into his old friend's eyes, Jack couldn't find any blame there, any anger. And that alone surprised him enough that he couldn't get his head straight.

Jack felt Rita give his hand a squeeze and he appreciated it. "I can see that. I'm glad for it."

"Now all you have to do is accept it." His friend nodded, kept his eyes fixed on Jack's. "Took me a long time, I admit it. For weeks after it happened, I'd wake up and try to swing my legs out of bed." A rueful smile curved his mouth. "Could have sworn I felt them there."

"Kevin—"

"I didn't come here to make things harder for you, Jack."

"Why are you here, then?" He managed to get the question out even though he was worried about the answer.

"To see you, you damn fool," Kevin said, leaning back in his chair, shaking his head. "You never answered the email I sent you two months ago. Hell, you never even opened it."

"Yeah." Jack nodded. "Sorry about that. I just—"

"I get it," Kevin said. "You still should have read it, though. Would have saved me a drive up from San Diego."

Jack smiled at that. He and Kevin had formed a friendship at first because they were both from Southern California. Just a couple hours away from each other by freeway, so they'd had a lot of the same experiences. They'd formed a tighter bond, of course, as all military in combat did, but it had begun on the California connection.

"So," Kevin was saying, waving one hand at the chair and his missing legs, "a lot of things have changed. Obviously."

Jack watched his friend, looking for some sign of anger or bitterness or blame and couldn't find any. Instead, he looked...comfortable in his skin. In that chair.

"But, hey," Kevin added, smiling at Rita. "Looks like you've had some pretty big changes, too. You're married now, having a baby."

Jack glanced at Rita, and when she smiled at him, he felt that tug of guilt again. Kevin couldn't know that this was a temporary arrangement. And there was no way Jack would let him know. He forced himself to look back to Kevin. "I'm glad you're okay."

"I'm better than okay." Kevin shook his head and gave Jack a wry smile. "If you'd bothered to open the damn email I sent you like two months ago, you would have known that."

Jack ran his free hand across his jaw. "I know. I'm

sorry. I should have. I just didn't want to go over what happened again."

"Hey," Kevin said softly, "neither do I. Look, Jack, last time I saw you, things were a little...*tense*."

Jack laughed shortly and held on a little more tightly to Rita's hand. "You could say that."

"Why don't I go make some coffee?" Rita looked at both men. "I'll give you guys some time to talk."

"Not necessary," Kevin told her. "I can't stay long, anyway, so don't go to any trouble for me."

"Stay, Rita," Jack said, looking into her eyes. He wanted her there. It surprised him to acknowledge just how much he wanted her beside him. Seeing Kevin again, watching him maneuver that wheelchair, tore at Jack and damned if he didn't want the connection to Rita to help him get through it.

When the hell had *that* happened? When had he started counting on her?

"If you're worried I'm here to cuss you out again for saving my butt, don't be." Kevin moved the chair in closer and linked his gaze to Jack's. "I remember it all, you know?"

"Yeah. I know." So did he. Every damn night, he remembered it. He always would.

Kevin smiled, nodded. "'Course you do. Hard to forget something like that—you doing your best to save me while I'm telling you to shoot me."

"Kevin—"

"Nah, man," he said, holding up one hand to keep Jack quiet. "I'm not here to go over it all again." He grinned. "Once was enough, trust me. I just wanted to say *thank you*."

"What?" Confused now, Jack just stared at him.

"Well, that surprised you," Kevin said wryly. "Yeah. Thank you. Thanks for saving me even when I was too stupid to want to be saved." He blew out a breath, dragged his fingers through his hair. "I swear, being furious at you got me through those first few days."

Jack nodded, took a breath and held it.

"But one day I realized that I like breathing," Kevin said. "So I started being less mad at you."

"Glad to hear it."

Kevin shrugged. "I'm not saying it was easy, getting used to being shorter—"

Rita smiled and he winked at her.

"But I did. And I'm here to tell you, alive is better than dead." Kevin held his hand out to Jack. "So thanks, man. Thanks for—hell. For everything."

Jack took his hand and felt one or two of those straws of guilt fall from his shoulders. He still had plenty left of course, but there was a sigh of relief to know that at least some of the burden had been eased. And Kevin *did* look good. Yeah, he was in a chair, but he looked strong and well and, damn it, *happy.* Jack had worried about his friend, thought that maybe he'd never really find any kind of contentment again.

"You're really okay."

"I'm *better* than okay, dude." Kevin slapped Jack's shoulder. "Again, man. Read your emails."

Rita squeezed Jack's hand again and in spite of the easing of the tension within, he held on to her tightly. "So why don't you just tell me what's in the email?"

"Turns out you're not the only one settling down. I'm getting married, can you believe it?" Kevin laughed, shook his head and said, "Lisa's a nurse. Hell, she was *my* nurse at Walter Reed. I showed up there all full of myself and complaining and she just would not listen." Still smiling, he continued, "The woman refused to let me bitch. She ignored my crappy moods and pushed me to come back to life when I really didn't want to."

Well, hell. Jack felt Rita's hand in his and told himself that he and Kevin had a lot more in common than he would have guessed. Wasn't that just what Rita had been doing to *him* for the last few weeks? Prodding, pushing, refusing to give up and go away.

"Anyway, Lisa's a California girl—her folks live in Oceanside—weird, huh? Go halfway around the world to meet a girl who lived about twenty minutes from me?" Kevin laughed a little. "So I got along so well, they transferred me to a hospital out here and Lisa made the move, too. We're getting married at my folks' place."

"Congratulations," Rita said, giving Jack a nudge.

"Right, yeah. I'm happy for you, man."

"Hey, there's more. We're having a baby, too."

Surprised again, Jack blurted, "Really?"

"Hey, man," Kevin said, grinning, "I didn't lose any of the important bits over there in that hellhole."

Rita laughed and Jack just shook his head. "Damn, Kev. You really haven't changed much, have you?"

"Older, wiser, shorter," Kevin said, then his smile slowly faded away. "Look, I had to make this drive to see you in person because my wedding is this weekend."

"So soon?"

Kevin's eyebrows lifted. "When I emailed you, I gave you two months' warning."

"Right." Jack nodded. "My fault."

"Absolutely true," Kevin agreed easily. "But the point is, I drove my ass all the way up here to ask you to be my best man."

"Your—" Okay, Jack didn't know how many more surprises he could take. He never would have expected the man he'd believed hated his guts to ask him to stand up for him.

"Best man. Yeah. Because that's what you are." His features sober, serious, Kevin said, "We were buds before. Been through a lot of crap together. But what you did for me, Jack, I can never repay."

A twist of pain wrung at his heart. "You don't have to."

"Yeah, I know that. Doesn't stop the need." Kevin glanced at Rita. "Your man was always a stand-up. He kept me alive in a place that tried its best to kill me."

Rita reached out instinctively and took his hand with her free hand, somehow linking the two men even more completely than they already were. Kevin released her hand, and reached into the pocket of his black leather jacket. He drew out a cream-colored envelope that he handed to Rita.

"I'm giving this to you for two reasons," he said. "One, you're way better looking than Jack."

"You're a very astute man," Rita said, grinning. Beside her, Jack only sighed.

"And two, more important, you'll make sure he gets to the wedding. Right?" He looked at her meaningfully for a long moment.

Then Rita leaned forward, kissed Kevin's cheek and said, "You bet I will." She glanced back at Jack as if for confirmation. "We'll be there. Won't we?"

"Yeah." He looked from Rita to Kevin and back again. "We'll be there, Kev."

"Good." He clapped his hands together then scrubbed his palms. "Then my work here is done and my lovely bride-to-be is going to be picking me up outside in—" He checked his watch. "Ten minutes. We're going for dinner, then taking the long drive home."

"Do you really have to go so soon?" Rita asked, standing up as Kevin wheeled back and turned. "Why don't both of you come up and have dinner with us?"

"No, but thanks." Kevin looked knowingly at Jack. "I think we're both going to need a little time to get used to the new us, right, Jack?"

It would take time and it was good to know that Kevin not only understood but felt the same. Too many emotions were churning inside him. Waves were rocking his insides like a storm at sea and he had a lot of thinking to do. "Yeah. A little time would be a good thing."

Kevin nodded solemnly, but his gaze locked with Jack's. "We'll get there. But we'll see you Saturday?"

Just as somber, Jack promised, "I swear. We'll be there."

Nine

Once Kevin was gone, Jack gave in to the tension screaming inside him. Stalking across the room, he made for the terrace, pushing open the French doors and stepping into the icy blast of wind that rushed at him. He turned his face into that wind and wished to hell it could blow all of his churning thoughts right out of his head.

"Jack?"

Teeth gritted, he kept his gaze on the expanse of the ocean streaked with the brilliant colors of sunset rather than turn to face the woman who'd become too important to him. Until Kevin had come by tonight, Jack hadn't realized just how much he'd come to depend on Rita's presence in his life. He was already in too deep, he knew that because of just how much he'd needed her by his side when Kevin was in the house. Needed her to anchor him.

And that bothered Jack plenty.

"Are you okay?" Her voice was soft, husky, filled with concern that scraped at him. He didn't want her worried about him, caring about him, God help him, *loving* him.

He'd once vowed that he would never put anyone in the position of having to mourn him. And the more she cared, the more pain she risked. How was he supposed to stand by and let her get deeper into feelings that would only carry the promise of future pain?

Damn it, this marriage was supposed to be temporary. Supposed to be emotion-free. A bargain. Yet somehow, in spite of his best efforts it had turned into more. The question now was, what was he prepared to do about it?

"Jack?" she asked again. "Are you okay?"

"Fine." He bit the word off, hoping she'd take the damn hint for once and leave him alone. Give him enough space to get himself together again. To find the center that had slipped out of his grasp the minute he saw Kevin in that chair.

"You don't sound fine," she said and came up beside him. She shivered in the cold wind and rubbed her hands up and down her arms for warmth. She was only wearing white capris and a short-sleeved pink T-shirt. Her bare feet had to be freezing on the concrete floor. But she wasn't leaving. He knew her well enough now to expect that.

When he didn't speak, she tried another tack. "Kevin seems nice."

Nice. Yeah, he was. He was also smart. Funny. And in a damn chair for the rest of his life. Jack closed his eyes briefly. "You don't have to do this."

"What am I doing?"

"Helping." He glanced at her. "I don't need your help. And I don't need to be soothed."

"That's what you think?" she asked, leaning against the railing to look up at him. "Everybody needs help sometimes, Jack. You're not a superhero."

Silently, he laughed at the idea. He was as far from a superhero as anyone could get.

"Didn't say I was and if I want help," he added, shooting her a dark look that should have sent her skittering for cover, "I'll ask for it."

Naturally, he told himself, Rita paid no attention to his warning look. Instead, she laughed and the raw, sexy sound awakened every cell in his body.

"Sure, you'll ask for help. Jack," she said with a smile. "You wouldn't ask for water if you were on fire."

The fact that she was right only irritated him further. How much more was he expected to take tonight? Facing down a friend whose life was forever changed wasn't enough? God, he needed time alone. He needed to *think*.

"You're staring out at that ocean like you expect to find answers there."

"I don't need answers, either," he ground out. "I just need some space. Time. Some damn solitude. God, I can't even remember what it's like to be completely alone anymore."

That insult sailed right over her head. She just didn't listen to what she didn't want to hear. In a way, he admired that about her. Even when it worked against him.

"If you think you can insult me into walking away, you're wrong."

Exasperated, he blew out a breath. “Then what will it take?”

“There’s nothing you can do that will make me leave you alone right now,” Rita said. “You’ve had enough solitude, Jack. Maybe too much.”

“Fine. You won’t leave, I will.” He turned, but stopped when she laid one hand on his arm.

“I’ve got some of those answers you don’t need.” She paused and he knew she was waiting for him to look at her. Finally, he did.

“What are you talking about now?”

Shrugging, she said, “You said you didn’t need answers, but you do. And here’s one for you. You’ve been torturing yourself for months over Kevin, Jack. But there was no need. You saw him. He’s happy.”

He scraped one hand across his face. “He’s in a chair.”

“That’s not your fault.”

“Yeah, well, saying it doesn’t make that true.” He shifted his gaze back out to the water and watched that darkening surface churn with the wind. Looking out at the sky and sea was so much easier than looking into whiskey-colored eyes that saw too much. “You weren’t there. I was.”

“So was Kevin,” she pointed out, refusing to let it go. “And he doesn’t blame you.”

“He should.” His gaze narrowed on that wide, roiling water and he felt it replicated in his own soul. “Damn it, if I had made a different call, it wouldn’t have happened.”

“My God, you’re stubborn,” she said, sliding over to stand between him and the railing, so that he was forced to look at her. “Yes, you were in charge and you made the decisions, but making different ones might not have kept everyone safe. Maybe a different call would have killed Kevin. Or you. Or someone else. There's just no way to know and no point in continuing to drag yourself over the coals like this."

He shook his head. He couldn't speak. What was there to say, anyway? She couldn't get it and he didn't blame her. No one who wasn't there could ever understand what it was to hold men's lives in your hands. One wrong call and people died. Or lost their legs.

"Are you really so determined to carry the weight of the world?"

She made it sound as though he were being self-indulgent. Nothing could have been further from the truth. He had a right to feel like a damn bastard for what had happened to Kevin. To the new guy in their squad, DeSantos, who had *died* in that skirmish. Was he supposed to just close it off, pretend it hadn't happened? He couldn't do that. "Leave it alone, Rita."

"He thanked you for saving him, Jack."

"I was there," he pointed out, barely sparing her a glance. She didn't get it. Didn't know what it had been like to see his best friend lying wounded in front of him and not being able to do a damn thing about it. Didn't understand the guilt of coming home with both arms, both legs. Didn't know what it was to keep all of that locked inside you until you felt like you were going to explode.

This was why he'd never talked to his family. He couldn't share with them what they couldn't understand. Oh, they would try, but their pity for him would get tangled up in the facts and they'd only end up *more* worried about him than they already were.

She laid both hands on his chest and the heat of her slid inside him like a welcome balm, easing the harsh waves of regret and anger and frustration still roiling within. As much as he loved her touch, he almost resented it because it was temporary. She wouldn't be here for much longer and when she was gone it would be so much harder to be without her.

"Jack. If Kevin can move on, why can't you?"

He dropped his gaze to hers. Those whiskey eyes stared up at him with so many emotions rushing through them he couldn't begin to name them all. And it was probably better if he didn't try.

"Because," he said slowly, "if I move on, it's forgetting. And if I let myself forget, then I've learned nothing."

She tipped her head to one side and all those amazing dark brown curls fell off her shoulder to be lifted in the ever-present wind. "That makes zero sense, Jack."

One corner of his mouth lifted. Of course it didn't make sense to her. How could she untangle his emotions when they were so jumbled together even *he* didn't understand half of them. But right now, that didn't matter. She was there, pressed up against him, her curvy body radiating heat, the mound of their child between them and Jack let himself simply *feel*. If things were different, if he were different… But wishing wouldn't make it so.

She wrapped her arms around his middle and laid her head on his chest. Her scent enveloped him completely and he felt as if he were bathing in some soft, golden light. The tension she eased and soothed wasn't gone, just buried. It was all still inside him, twisting, writhing. But that didn't mean he had to find answers tonight.

He took a breath, drew her scent deep and let it ease every jagged corner of his soul. Closing his eyes, he held her close and told himself that just for tonight, he would take the comfort she offered.

And be grateful.

A couple of days later, they were in a backyard with a wildly spectacular garden bursting with blooms in every color imaginable. A rare June day of sunshine washed out of a clear blue sky and shone down like a blessing on the small group of people gathered.

The wedding was beautiful. Small, as Rita and Jack's had been, but instead of the beach, they were in a lush backyard with a small group of guests. There were tables, chairs and a wooden dance floor constructed just for the occasion. Music streamed from a stereo, an eclectic mix of classic rock, old standards and even a waltz or two just for tradition's sake.

Seated at a table in the shade, Rita looked at her husband, sitting beside her. Jack wore a perfectly tailored black suit with a white shirt and a dark blue tie. His black hair was a little long, his blue eyes a little too sharp, his jaw a little too tense. But he was there for Kevin, as promised.

Rita smoothed the skirt of her bright yellow dress across her thighs, and swung the loose fall of her hair back behind her shoulders. Reaching across their table, she took Jack's hand in hers.

"Look at them," she said, smiling. "They're so happy."

She watched Kevin, with Lisa in his lap, wheel around the dance floor. The newlyweds were laughing, kissing and completely caught up in each other. Maybe it was the pregnancy hormones, but Rita's eyes blurred with tears as she watched the two people so obviously in love.

"Yeah, they do look happy," Jack said and deliberately slid his hand out from under hers. He picked up his bottle of beer and took a long swig.

"But you don't." Sitting beside him, surrounded by strangers in a flower-filled garden, Rita felt a now-familiar darkness creeping closer.

There didn't seem to be anything she could do to lift the cloud that had settled on him since seeing Kevin again a few days ago. He wasn't angry or even unkind. He was…civil. He treated her as he would a stranger, with a cool politeness that chipped away at her heart and soul.

When they were first married, Jack had kept a distance between them, but Rita had still sensed that he cared for her. That there was something inside him fighting to get out. Now, it was as if he'd suddenly built the wall around his heart thicker and higher, defying her to break through. God knew she'd spent the last couple of days trying to do just that. But it was as if he was on another planet—one she couldn't reach.

He slanted her a long, thoughtful look. The dappled shade from the trees threw a pattern of dark and light across his face. His features, though, were carefully blank, as if he was determined to give her no clue at all as to what he was thinking, feeling.

"No," he said finally, "I'm not happy."

God, she got an actual chill from the ice in his voice. But she had to keep trying to get to him, to touch his heart, to make him see that he wasn't alone if he didn't want to be. "Jack, what is it? What's happening?"

"This isn't the place to talk about it," he said and

lifted his beer for another drink. His gaze shifted from her to Kevin and Lisa. His features were tighter, the glint in his eyes harder and Rita was more confused than ever.

She turned her head to watch the newlyweds, too, but what she saw made her smile. Made her heart lift. Kevin, in his chair, Lisa on his lap, looking down into his eyes with an expression of pure joy on her face. The two of them might have been alone in the world as the music played and a handful of dancers moved around them.

Why couldn't Jack see the happiness all around him and let himself revel in it? Why was he more determined than ever to wallow in misery? For the first time since finding him again, Rita was worried.

As it turned out, she had a right to be.

A few hours later, they were back in the penthouse. It had been a long, silent ride, with tension building between them until Rita had felt it alive and bristling in the car. Jack had given away nothing. She still had no idea what was bothering him but she was through guessing. Rita had waited as long as she could. There was no point in worrying over something when you could face it head-on and tackle it to the ground.

Dropping her taupe clutch bag onto the nearest chair, she stared at Jack's back and demanded, "Are you going to tell me what's bugging you?"

He was standing in the center of the living room, suit jacket tossed to the couch, hands stuffed into his slacks pockets. When he turned to look at her, Rita's heart actually dropped. If a man's face could be a sheet of ice, then that's what she was looking at.

His clear blue eyes glittered like shards of that ice as they locked on her. "What's bugging me? It's this." He pulled his hands free, lifted both arms as if to encompass the two of them and the apartment. "It's over, Rita. This marriage sham? It's done. Time for you to go."

All of the air in her lungs left her in a rush and seconds later Rita was light-headed. It felt as if the floor had opened up beneath her feet and simply swallowed her. Shock was too small a word for what she was feeling. Hurt was right up there, too, but temper was coming in a close third and quickly rising to the top. Forcing herself to breathe, she stared at him as she would have a stranger. "Just like that?"

"Just like that," he said and headed for the bar in the far corner of the room. Bending down, he opened the mini fridge and grabbed a bottle of beer. After opening it, he took a long drink and avoided looking at her.

Yep, temper was bubbling to the surface and Rita gave it free rein. Her family could have told Jack that when Rita was truly angry, it was best to run, but that was all right, she told herself. He'd find that out for himself.

"That's just not going to fly with me, Jack."

One of his eyebrows lifted in mild surprise. She could do better.

"You don't get to stand there so cool and dismissive and say 'time for you to go, Rita,' and expect me to start packing," she said, riding a cresting wave of what felt like pure fury. "You don't tell me to go and then not even bother to look at me."

He slid his gaze to hers and it was almost worse, she thought, seeing the blank emptiness in his eyes. Pain grabbed at her, but she shook it off.

"What the hell happened?" she demanded. "You've been different ever since Kevin came here. And today—" she broke off, shook her head and said, "the wedding was beautiful, but you couldn't see it. Kevin and Lisa were practically glowing and you sat there like a black hole, sucking in every bit of joy around you without it once affecting you. Where's this all coming from?"

"From Kevin," he snapped, then took a breath to visibly calm himself. When he had, he continued. "From the wedding and Kevin and Lisa and the damn hearts and flowers practically floating over their heads."

She just blinked at him. This was making no sense at all. "That's a bad thing? How does your friend's happiness equate to you being miserable?"

"I'm not miserable. I'm realistic."

"It's realistic to hate the fact that people are happy? To send me away so there's no chance of *you* being happy?"

"That's right."

God, it was like talking to a wall. Only she'd probably have gotten more out of a wall. He was bulletproof. Her words bounced off him and never left a dent.

"You don't want to be happy, is that it?" God, she was getting colder.

"You're damn right," he said, setting the beer down in a deliberately calm manner. Coming out from behind the bar, he walked toward her and stopped with a good three feet of empty space between them. "I told you going in that this was temporary, just until the baby was born."

She put both hands on her belly. "News flash. Still about two months to go."

He didn't even look at the baby. Hell, he barely looked at *her*. "Yeah, but we don't have to be living together to be married, do we?" he asked.

"Wow." She took a step toward him and he took one back. One short, sharp laugh shot from her throat. "Was I getting too close, Jack? Were you starting to care? Are you making me leave because you don't want me to go?"

"Think you've got me all figured out, do you?"

"Oh, yeah," she said, nodding. "It wasn't that hard. Answer me this. Do I scare you, Jack?"

He gritted his teeth, huffed out a breath and said flatly, "You terrify me."

Small comfort, she thought, but didn't speak again as he continued.

"I didn't sign up for this. Didn't *want* this," he muttered darkly, pushing one hand through his hair impatiently. "You're getting too close, Rita. I can see it. You're starting to believe this is all *real* and it's not. It can't be. I won't let it be."

She'd never been dismissed so completely, so casually and it hurt so much she wanted to keen, but damned if she'd let him see that. Her heart ached for them both. She'd gotten to him, reached him and because she had, he was cutting her out of his life with a single, cold stroke.

"*You* won't let it be real?" she asked. "You're the only one with a vote here?"

"That's right." His eyes were cold, empty and that one fact tore at her so deeply, Rita could hardly breathe.

"Why?" She stared at him, completely confused and hurt and even her temper was easing off to be replaced by an ache that settled around her heart and throbbed with every beat. "You at least owe me an explanation, Jack. How did Kevin showing up here and his happiness today make you so determined to throw your own chance at it away? *Our* chance."

"You want an explanation, fine. Sure, Kevin and Lisa are happy today," Jack ground out. "But what about tomorrow? What about when pain comes rolling down the track and hits them both?"

Flabbergasted, Rita stared at him. "*What?* Being happy isn't worth it because one day you might not be? What kind of logic is that?"

He shook his head grimly. "Perfect, that's what kind. I saw it happen. Too many damn times. You love someone—or worse yet, let someone love you—and things go wrong, lives are shattered. I heard a guy's widow sobbing. I watched parents grieving." He wasn't cool and detached now. His voice was hot, words tumbling over each other. "I saw the strongest men I've ever known break under the agony of loss. Why the hell would anyone risk that? No, Rita. There's no way I'm setting either one of us up for that."

Her own breath came short and fast, because she knew he believed what he was saying. None of it made sense but that didn't keep him from having faith in every word. "So screw ever smiling or being joyful because of what *might* happen."

He didn't even flinch.

"It will happen," he insisted. "You think anybody gets through life unscathed? They don't. The best you can do is protect yourself from misery."

"By *being* miserable?" she demanded.

"Think what you like." Shaking his head, he ignored that and said, "I'm not letting you get any deeper into this marriage, Rita." His voice was tight, hard. "You're getting too damn close, pulling me along with you, and I can't go any further. I won't let myself start coming back to life only to risk more grief. Trust me, it's not worth it. I *know*."

God, he'd already cut her off. He'd made that call a couple of days ago when Kevin visited and since then it had been solidifying in his mind until now; it was a done deal. Without talking to her about any of it, he'd made the decision to end what was between them.

"You're wrong," she whispered, and to her fury, felt tears fill her eyes. She *hated* that. Rita always ended up crying when she was at her angriest. Too much emotion had to eventually spill from her eyes and the tears were lowering. Viciously, she swiped at her eyes. "You're so wrong it's sad, Jack. Caring about people? That's worth *everything*."

"Don't cry." He scrubbed one hand across the back of his neck. "Just don't. It'll rip at me because I…*care* about you."

"You don't just care, Jack," she told him flatly. "You love me."

His gaze snapped to hers. "See? That's another reason you have to leave."

"What?"

"Love's coming, and I know that, too. So I need you gone before I love you."

Rita laughed shortly then actually reached up and tugged at her hair in frustration. This had to be the weirdest and most heartbreaking conversation she'd ever had. "Right. Don't want to take a chance on actually *loving* someone."

"I'm doing what I have to do."

"No, you're not, Jack," she said, lifting her chin and meeting that cold stare with all the heat she could muster. "You're doing what's easiest."

"You think this is *easy*?" he demanded.

"I think it's unnecessary," she snapped. "But no worries. I'm leaving. I'll be out of here tonight." Damned if she'd stay with a man who was so determined not to love her. To cut himself off from any feeling at all.

"You don't have to go tonight," he said. "Tomorrow's soon enough."

Her gaze locked on his. "No, it's really not."

A couple of hours later, Jack was alone in the apartment.

As good as her word, Rita was gone so fast, she'd been nothing but a blur. She hadn't said another word to him, but her silence came across loud and clear. He hadn't wanted to hurt her and someday soon, Rita would realize that he'd done all of this to protect her. He didn't want her hurt. Mourning him as he'd seen others mourn the fallen.

She'd cried.

He slapped one hand to the center of his chest in a futile attempt to ease the ache centered there. Jack had never seen Rita cry before. Not even the day he'd left her in that hotel to go back to his tour of duty. She'd sent him off with a smile that had no doubt cost her. But today, she'd cried.

If he could have changed it, he would have. But this was the only way and Jack knew it. He stepped out onto the terrace and let that cold wind slap at him. He finally had what he'd wanted—*craved*—most. Solitude. There was no one here talking to him, trying to make him laugh, drawing him back into a world he'd deliberately turned his back on.

"This is for the best. For both of us. Hell," he added, thinking of the baby, "for all three of us."

Didn't feel like it at the moment, but he was sure it would. One day. Rita would see it, too. Eventually.

"Damn it," he said when the doorbell rang. He thought about not answering it, but even as he considered it, the damn thing rang again.

"Rita probably forgot something," he told himself as he headed back inside. He took a peek through the judas hole and sighed heavily. So much for solitude.

Reluctantly, he opened the door and said, "Hi, Cass."

"Don't you 'hi' me," his sister said as she pushed past him into the apartment. She threw her purse onto the couch, then turned around, hands at her hips and glared at him. "What the hell is wrong with you?"

Calmly, Jack closed the door and faced his sister. She was practically vibrating with anger. Her eyes, so much like his own, were flashing dangerously and her features were set like stone in an expression of indignation. "What're you talking about?"

"Rita called me from the airport."

That threw him. "The *airport*?"

"Yeah, she found a flight to Utah and she went back to see her family."

Okay, he'd wanted her to leave the apartment—not the state. He wasn't sure how he felt about her being so far away. Was she planning on staying there? Giving up her bakery? Her friends?

"Are you out of your mind for real?" she asked.

"This is none of your business, Cass."

"Since we're family, it *is* my business," she countered grimly. "Rita asked me to come and check on you," Cass added, not bothering to hide the disgust in her tone. "She was worried about *you*."

"Which is just one of the reasons I asked her to go," Jack said calmly. "I don't want her worrying about me."

She jerked her head back and gave him a look of pure astonishment. "Y'know," she said, "that's what people on Earth do. We worry for the people we care about."

"I don't *want* her to care about me, that's the whole point."

"Right." Cass nodded sharply, paced a little frantically for a few minutes, then came to a stop and glared at him again. "And it's all about what you want, isn't it, Jack?"

"I didn't say that."

"Oh, please," his sister countered, waving one hand at him in dismissal. "You've been saying it in every way but words for *months*."

"I'm not doing this with you, Cass," he said. "Not going to talk about it."

"Good. Because I don't care what you have to say. Not anymore. All you have to do is listen." She came closer and he saw sparks dazzling her eyes. "I've tried to be patient with you. I'm a doctor, Jack. I know what's going on with you."

"I don't need a damn doctor and if I did," he told her hotly, "I wouldn't go to my little sister."

Damned if he needed *everyone* telling him what he should do and when he should do it. And he *really* didn't want his younger sister standing there like the voice of God telling him to shape up.

"Yes, you've made that abundantly clear and I've really tried to keep quiet, give you room to deal."

"There's nothing going on with me."

"You denying PTSD doesn't make it go away. My God, you're practically a textbook case." She walked to the couch, dropped onto it, then just as quickly jumped to her feet again, apparently unable to sit still. "I told Sam and Dad they had to give you time. Let you get used to being back in the world. That you'd come around eventually."

"I'm fine," he insisted but saw that his sister wasn't buying it.

"Sure you are." She snorted. "You notice Sam doesn't come up from San Diego much anymore? Or have you paid any attention to the fact that Dad almost never comes into the office these days even though he used to love it?"

He thought about that for a minute or two. She had a point though he'd never really considered it before. His brother, Sam, was a busy guy. And his father had recently taken up golf, so why would he be coming around an office he'd retired from. "Yeah, but—"

"Sam got tired of you shooting him down every time he tried to spend time with you."

"I didn't—"

"Yeah, you did. You've shot me down often enough for me to know that and I can tell you it's no fun having a proverbial door slammed in your face every time you try to talk to someone." She took a long breath. "Damn it, Jack, we're your *family* and we deserve better."

"I just needed—"

But she kept talking. "Dad gets his heart broken just a little more whenever he's with you and can't reach you, so he stays away."

Guilt dropped onto his shoulders, but he was so used

to the burden he hardly noticed. Remembering the last time he'd seen his father, Jack could admit to the sorrow he'd seen in the older man's eyes. And still… "He doesn't—"

"Not finished," she snapped. "Honestly, Jack, you make me so furious. Do you know how many men and women come home from dangerous duties and have *no one* to talk to? To count on? Do you know how lucky you are to have people who love you? Who are willing to put up with your bullshit?"

"I—"

"Does it look like I'm done?" She inhaled sharply, blew the air out in a huff and stared up at him. "You're my brother and I love you. You're Rita's husband and *she* loves you."

There was that pang around his heart again. He rubbed the spot idly, almost unconsciously. She loved him. He'd been pretty sure she did, but *knowing* it was something else again. He swallowed hard against that pounding ache in his heart and told himself that even if she did love him, he'd done the right thing.

"You don't get it, Cass." He sighed. "I don't want to be loved. Whoever loves me is just setting themselves up for a letdown later. Why do that to anybody?"

"Well, good God," Cass said, clearly stunned. "It's worse than I thought. It's not just your memories haunting you that's kept you tucked away up here in your fortress of solitude. It's something else. You're an idiot." Shaking her head, she said, "I'm so glad Mom can't see you like this, although she'd probably have kicked you into shape by now. You don't want to be loved? You don't want to feel anything for anyone? Too damn bad. Boo the hell hoo."

"What?" A choked off, surprised laugh shot from his throat. It seemed he was destined to have the women in his life constantly surprising him.

"You have a chance at something amazing, Jack, and you're letting it get away. You told the woman who loves you, the mother of your *child*," she added with emphasis, "to leave because you're scared to be hurt again. To know pain again."

"Careful, Cass," he said, voice soft. Even for his sister, he was only willing to put up with so much. He was doing the hard thing here. Why could no one see it, appreciate what it cost him?

"No, I'm done being careful. I should never have given you time to adjust, Jack," she said sadly. "That was my mistake. I should have done just what Rita did, grab hold and drag you, kicking and screaming back into life."

"It wouldn't have worked."

"We'll never know, will we?" she asked. Still shaking her head, she walked over, picked up her purse and slung it over her shoulder. "Look around Jack," she said. "You got what you wanted. You're alone. I hope you enjoy it. Because if you keep acting like a jackass—this is all you'll ever have."

He watched her go and the slam of the door behind her echoed in the stillness.

Ten

The Marchetti bakery on historic 25th Street in Ogden was in an antique brick building with sloping wood floors that creaked musically with every step. On one side of the shop was a handmade-chocolate shop and on the other, an artisan boutique that sold local artists' work.

The bakery drew customers from all over northern Utah, so they were constantly busy, which meant the entire family—except for the younger kids—were there when Rita arrived. Her mom and sister were in the kitchen while her father and brothers ran the front of the shop and handled any deliveries. This didn't change, she thought with a smile as she glanced around at the shining display cases and the customers wandering, looking, sitting at tables and sipping lattes.

Just walking into the bakery soothed the ball of

ice in the pit of her stomach. It had been the longest hour-and-a-half flight of her life to make it here from Long Beach. She hadn't told the family she was coming; there hadn't been time. She'd simply packed her things, told Casey to close up the bakery for a few days and then raced to the airport. All Rita had been able to think of was getting here, where she knew her heart was safe.

The long drive from the Salt Lake City airport had given her more time to think and she still had no answers. Hadn't she done everything she could to reach Jack? Hadn't she given him every reason to come out of the darkness? To live again?

Tears were close so she blinked furiously to keep them at bay and smiled at a woman she knew who was busily wiping chocolate off her child's mouth. Here was safety. Love. Understanding.

The joy on her father's face when he spotted her was like pouring oil on the churning waters inside her. Rita's brothers, Anthony and Marco, called out to her as she threaded her way through the crowd toward the kitchen to find her mom. Of course she had to stop along the way to say hello to people she knew and try to make small talk, while inside she was screaming.

Behind the counter, Rita was hugged hard by her dad, then passed from brother to brother before they released her.

"This is a nice surprise," her father said, then took a closer look at her face and frowned. "It *is* nice, isn't it?"

Nick Marchetti was in his sixties, with graying black hair, sharp brown eyes and a belly that was a little fuller than it used to be. Both of his sons were several inches taller than him, but it didn't matter because

Nick was, just as he always had been, a force to be reckoned with.

"It's good to see you, Daddy," Rita whispered, relaxing into his familiar hug.

He kissed her cheek and said, "Go on now, go sit down and talk to your mother. She'll be happy you're here."

"Okay." Rita nodded, slipped through the swinging door and never saw the worried frowns on the faces of the men in her family.

Stepping into the kitchen with the familiar scents and the heat from the ovens was like walking into the comfort of her childhood. Growing up, she and her siblings had spent most of their free time working in the bakery, so the memories were thick and reassuring.

Rita had gone home to Ogden hoping for a little peace and quiet and maybe some understanding. A half hour later, she told herself she'd clearly come to the wrong place for that.

"I can't believe you left," her mother said hotly. Teresa Marchetti had short black hair, carefully touched up to hide the gray every five weeks. She was a tiny woman but ruled her family like a four-star general.

Rita took a sip of the herbal tea she wasn't interested in. "Jack didn't want me there. He told me to leave."

"And so you do it?" Teresa shook her head and scowled. "I don't remember you being so obedient as a child."

Rita stiffened at the accusation. "I wasn't being obedient." God, that made her sound like some subservient fifties' housewife asking her husband for an allowance.

"Yet here you are." Her mother huffed a little, muttered something Rita didn't quite catch, then slid two trays of bread loaves into the oven. Turning back around, she reached for a bottle of water and took a drink.

It was hot in the kitchen with four ovens going constantly. Rita's father and brothers had deliberately stayed out front, leaving her mother and sister to do the heavy emotional lifting.

Gina looked up from the counter where she was rolling out cookie dough. "So Jack says go and you say okeydoke? What the hell is that, Rita?"

"Language," their mother said automatically, then added, "your sister has a point. Do you love this man?"

"Of course she does it's all over her face," Gina said before Rita could open her mouth.

"Thanks, I can talk for myself," Rita said.

"Just not to Jack, is that it?" Gina rolled her eyes as fiercely as she rolled the dough.

"I did talk to Jack." Rita broke a cookie in half and popped it into her mouth. She should have known that no one in her family would pat her on the head and simply accept what she said. They all had opinions and loved nothing better than sharing them. "I talked till my throat was dry. He doesn't listen to what he doesn't want to hear."

"Hmm," Teresa mused with a snort of amusement. "Sounds like someone else I know."

Fine, she was stubborn. Rita knew that. But this wasn't about *her*, was it?

"Mom, how could I stay if he didn't want me?"

"Oh, for God's sake," Gina blurted. "He does want you. You told us already he admitted that."

"Yes, but he doesn't *want* to want me."

"That's female logic," Anthony said when he hustled in to restock a tray of cannoli.

"Jack's the one who said it," Rita pointed out, finishing off the rest of her cookie.

Anthony countered, "He only said it because that's how men think women think."

"What?" Gina asked, clearly as confused as Rita. "That must be more male logic because it makes *no* sense."

"It does to men," Anthony argued before picking up the tray to head out front.

Rita propped her elbows on the counter and propped her head in her hands. A circus, she thought. It was a circus at Marchetti's.

"Go on, back to work," Teresa ordered, waving at her son to hurry him along. When it was just the three women in the kitchen again, Teresa sat down on a stool opposite Rita. "Don't think about what he said or what he did or even what your family thinks about all of this. There's just one thing to consider, Rita." She paused, shot her other daughter a don't-open-your-mouth look and asked Rita, "Do you love him?"

"Of course I love him, Mom. That's not the point."

"It's the only point," her mother said.

Gina kept quiet for as long as she could, then blurted out, "For God's sake, Rita, *all* men are impossible to deal with—"

"We can hear you!" their father shouted from the front.

Rita chuckled and shook her head. The heck with peace and quiet. *This* is just what she had needed.

"Am I wrong?" Gina shouted to her father. Then turning back to her mother and sister, she demanded, "See? Brothers, fathers, husbands, sons, they're all crazy. But giving up is never the answer, Rita. You have to dig in and fight back. Never give an inch."

"Your sister's right." Teresa nodded.

"It's a miracle!" Gina looked up at the ceiling to Heaven beyond and got a dark look from Teresa for her trouble.

Then, ignoring one daughter, Teresa reached out and took both of Rita's hands in hers. "I'm ashamed that you didn't fight for what you want, for what you need. Rita, we didn't raise you to walk away."

Her heart gave a sharp tug at the realization that that's exactly what she had done. In her own hurt and grief, she'd tucked tail and run away. But how could she not have?

"So I'm supposed to stay with a man who doesn't want me there?"

Gina opened her mouth and shut it again when her mother held up one hand.

"He does want you there. He told you so," Teresa said. "He wants you to leave before he loves you? What kind of statement is that? He already loves you and it scares him."

Rita laughed shortly and shook her head, denying the possibility. "Nothing scares Jack."

Although, the minute those words left her mouth she remembered Jack saying "You terrify me." Maybe her mother was on to something.

"Oh, honey," her mother said, "nothing scares a man more than *love* when it finally shows up." She gave Rita's hands a pat, then picked up a cookie and took a bite. "It's especially difficult for a strong man, because being out of control is a hard thing to accept."

"Jimmy wasn't scared," Gina muttered.

"Sure he was," her mother said on a laugh. "You just didn't give him time to think about it."

Shrugging, Gina admitted with a grin, "Okay, fair point."

"And your brothers?" Teresa laughed. "They were terrified."

"We can *still* hear you," Marco yelled.

Ignoring her son, Teresa looked at Rita. "Even your dad fought tooth and nail to keep from loving me."

"As if I stood a chance at that," Nick called out.

"Why do we have a door," Teresa wondered, "when everyone hears everything anyway?" Shaking her head again, she continued, "What I'm saying is, everything worth having, is worth fighting for."

Rita just didn't know. She'd left the penthouse in a rush, hurt beyond belief, angry beyond anything she'd ever experienced before. Heart aching, she'd had only one thought. Come home. To the family that was always there for her.

"So what're you going to do?" Gina spread a cinnamon-and-sugar mixture on the rectangle of dough then carefully rolled it up for slicing and baking. "You going to stay here? Or go back and reclaim your life?"

Well, that was the question, wasn't it? Being here with her family, she was starting to think and as she did, she was embarrassed to admit that running away from her problems, from the man she loved, just didn't feel right. She'd pulled back from him and hid away—the very thing she'd accused Jack of doing.

"Why should I leave?" she murmured, hardly realizing she was speaking aloud.

"Exactly," Gina agreed, slicing cookies and laying them on sheets to bake.

"I have a business there. And a home—okay, not the penthouse, but I was happy there and I can be again."

Rita ate another cookie while her brain raced and the pain in her heart began to ease.

"Sure you can," her mother said.

"Jack doesn't make decisions for me."

"'Course not," Gina agreed.

"He doesn't get to tell me when to go. When to stay. Sit. Heel."

"That's my girl," Teresa cheered.

"Why should I make this easy on Jack?" Rita demanded of no one in particular.

"You never made it easy on any of us," Marco quipped when he brought an empty tray into the kitchen.

"Oh, please," Gina sneered. "And you were the angel child? Do you remember shaving my Barbie dolls bald?"

"A fond memory," Marco assured her, dodging when she took a swing at him.

"I'm going back," Rita announced. "And I'm going to look Jack in the eye and tell him that he can't dictate my life."

"I feel like I should have pom-poms," Gina murmured.

"He's not chasing me away," Rita proclaimed, scooting off the stool to stand on her own two feet. "I'm going back. I'm going to tell him he's in love with me and when he's done being scared of it, he can come and find me. I'm building a life there and I'm not giving it up."

"Good for you." Her father came into the kitchen and gave her a quick hug before grabbing another cookie. "But you can stay for a couple of days, right? Have a nice visit before you go back?"

"I sure can, Daddy," she said and leaned in to the most wonderful man she'd ever known. "Let Jack miss me. It'll be good for him."

"You women are devious, wonderful creatures," her father said.

"And don't you forget it," his wife warned.

Solitude was overrated.

Three days of it and Jack felt like he was suffocating. Quiet. Too much damn quiet. He kept seeing Rita's ghost in the penthouse. He heard her laugh. He caught her scent in the guest room she'd used and ached for her in a way he wouldn't have thought possible.

It was worse somehow, knowing that she was in Utah. Jack hadn't really believed Cass when she told him that Rita had left the damn state. So he'd driven to Seal Beach, walked past the bakery and got a chill when he saw the closed sign on the door.

He'd driven her off and she'd actually left. He should be happy. Instead, he felt…hollowed out. Like a shell of the man he used to be. At that thought, he imagined what Rita would say to it and he could almost hear her. *Whose fault is that, Jack? Who keeps running away from life?*

Shaking his head free of irritating thoughts and reminders of all he'd lost, Jack turned his attention back to the stack of papers waiting for his signature. He'd been spending more time than usual in the office because it beat the hell out of being alone in the penthouse with too many memories.

"I'll get over it. Hell," he murmured, scrawling his name along the bottom of a contract, "*she'll* get over it."

"Mr. Buchanan?" Linda stood just inside the open door to his office.

"What is it?"

"Marketing reports *The Sea Queen* is now sold-out."

"Good. Great." The cruise liner would be a huge success, one more feather in the Buchanan family cap and Jack couldn't have cared less. "Is there anything else?"

"Just one thing." Linda stepped back, a smirk on her face and Rita sailed past her into the room.

The door closed behind her, but Jack hardly noticed. All he could see was her. That amazing hair of hers was a tumble of dark curls. Her eyes were sizzling. She wore black slacks, a lime-green shirt that clung to the mound of her belly and a white linen jacket over the shirt. Black sandals were on her feet and her toenails were a bright purple.

He'd never seen anything more gorgeous in his life.

Standing up behind his desk, he curbed the urge to go to her and grab hold of her. He'd done the right thing and he wasn't going to backtrack now. "Rita. I thought you were in Utah."

She tipped her head to one side and gave him a cool glare. "Hoping I'd stay so far away you'd never have to think about me again?"

"No." There was nothing on this earth that could keep him from thinking about her. "I just—"

"I didn't come to chat, Jack," she said, cutting him off as she dug into the oversize black tote slung over her shoulder. She pulled out a large manila envelope and handed it to him.

"What's this?"

"It's an ultrasound picture of your daughter."

His eyes widened, his jaw dropped and his fingers tightened on the envelope. "I thought you didn't want to know what the baby is."

"Turns out," she said, "surprises aren't as much fun as I used to think they were."

Okay, he knew that was a dig for the way he'd ended things between them. And fine, she was due a fair share of hits. He could take it. Then what she'd said suddenly hit him.

"A daughter?"

"Yes," she said, and clutched her fingers around the handle of her bag. "It's a girl. And I wanted you to know."

"Thanks for that..."

"I didn't do it to be nice, Jack," she said, interrupting him. "I came here to tell you that I'm not running away. I'm not *you*. I don't hide."

"I'm not hiding."

"Call it whatever you want to," she said, voice tight. "It amounts to the same thing."

Sunlight spilled into the office through the wide windows, lying in long, golden rectangles across the floor. Rita stood in one of those slices of light and it was as if she were glowing from the inside. Even the ends of her hair shone, and the sunlight was reflected in her whiskey eyes, making them look as if they were on fire.

"You're upset, I know," he started.

"Damn right I'm upset, Jack." She stopped, took a long breath and steadied herself. "But I didn't come here to get into another futile argument, either."

Still holding the envelope he wanted very badly to open, he asked, "Why are you here, then?"

"To tell you that I'm staying. Our daughter will be raised by *me*, in the apartment over the bakery. I'll tell her all about you, but you're not going to be a part of our lives, Jack."

"You can't keep her from me."

"Watch me," Rita countered. "You don't want *her*

or me. You just want to do what you think is the 'right' thing. Well, I don't care about that. My daughter's going to grow up loved. Happy. And if her father isn't willing to give up his self-pity party long enough to be grateful to be alive, then he just won't be a part of our lives."

"Self-pity?" He repeated the words because they'd slapped him hard enough to make an impact. Was that who he was? Who he'd become? Was she right? "That's what you think?"

"Jack," she sighed out his name. "If you ever manage to work your way out of that cocoon you've wrapped yourself in long enough to realize you love me, let me know. Until then? Goodbye, Jack."

He looked up as Rita turned around, stormed across the room and out the door, slamming it behind her.

Jack fell asleep that night, still holding the ultrasound picture he couldn't get out of his head. A daughter. A little girl. Torn between desire and caution, he wasn't sure which move to make. And then the dream came.

It was hot. So hot every breath seared his lungs. He squinted into the too-bright sunlight and signaled to his men for quiet as they approached the village.

Shots were fired. Explosions rocked all around them, making his ears ring. Someone screamed and another shot fired and Jack was down. Pain burst in a hot ball in the center of his chest. Air caught in his lungs, refusing to move in or out. Jack stared up at a brassy sky, the sun beating down mercilessly and he knew he was dying.

But this wasn't how it happened. The dream was wrong.

Then Kevin was there, leaning over him. Jack looked up at his friend. "I'm hit. I'm hit bad."

"Yeah, dude. It doesn't look good."

"But this is wrong. You were wounded, not me." Jack breathed past the pain, felt it sliding through his body. "Help me, Kev. Do something. I did it for you."

"Yeah, you did." Kevin grinned and was suddenly in a wheelchair. "And I appreciate it. Wish I could help you now, bro. But it's all on you."

None of this made sense. Jack looked around. The sand. The sun. The men. Everything was the way it always was in his dream. Well, except for Kevin, grinning like a moron at him from a chair.

"What's so funny? Do something, damn it!"

"Nothing I can do, dude," Kevin assured him. "It's a heart shot. You're done for. There's no hope."

Panic roared through him followed by fury. Damned if he'd end like this. "What the hell kind of help is that? Call a medic. Slap a bandage on my chest."

"Hearts can't be healed with a damn bandage, man. You're way past that."

Fear and fury were a tangled knot inside him. "Then what do I do?"

"You already know that, Jack," Kevin said. "You're not shot, man. Your heart's broken and the only way to fix it is to find Rita and make this right. It's as good as over for you."

Reaching down, he held out one hand and waited for Jack to take it. Then Kevin pulled him to his feet and slapped Jack on the back. "The only way out is Rita."

"Rita." Jack looked down at his chest. He wasn't bleeding. He was healthy enough. He was just...lost. Lifting his head, he glanced around. The dream had changed. The desert was gone.

He was on the beach, the roar of the sea pounding in his brain. And there was Rita, standing at the shoreline as she had been on the first night he'd seen her. And just like that, Jack knew Kevin was right. He felt as if his heart had been ripped out of his chest. It was over for him.

It had been over from the first moment he'd seen her.

Just the memory of her was strong enough to tear down the dream that had been haunting him for months. Rita had drawn him out, with the help of an old friend.

But when he turned to thank Kevin, the man was gone. Looking back down the beach, he saw Rita, holding a baby girl with dark brown curls and bright eyes. He started toward them just as Rita smiled. Then slowly, she and the baby faded until they finally disappeared completely. When he stood alone on the darkened beach, pain hit him like a fist.

Fix this, *he told himself,* or lose everything.

Jack woke with a start and sat straight up in bed. His mind racing, heart pounding, he realized so many truths at once, he was breathless. Maybe it made sense that the lesson he needed to learn had come from Kevin. He'd think about that later. Right now, he knew what he had to do, so he lunged for his cell phone on the bedside table. He punched in a familiar number and waited interminably as it rang on the other end.

"Dad? Yeah, it's me, Jack." He walked out onto the terrace, into the teeth of the wind and had never felt warmer in his life.

"Jack? Are you all right?" his father asked. "What time is it?"

He winced and glanced at the clock. Two o'clock. He rubbed his eyes and laughed shortly. Taking a deep breath, Jack realized that for the first time in months, he didn't have a cold stone in his belly. In fact, he felt pretty good.

"Weirdly enough," he said, "I think I am all right. Or I will be. I'm sorry it's so late, but look. I need you to do something for me."

Eleven

"So have you thought of a name for her yet?"

Rita looked at her bakery manager and shook her head. "No, but I have plenty of time."

"Yeah, you do. But just remember, Casey's a great name for a girl."

Laughing, Rita slid the tray of cookies into the oven. It was good to be home. She'd needed that visit to her family, but being here was what felt right. Back in her apartment over the bakery, doing familiar work with people she loved, it was all good.

Sure, she missed Jack desperately, and there was an ache around her heart that she was really afraid would be permanent. But she would learn to live with it. Learn to live without him, because she had to.

"Thanks, Casey, I'll keep that in mind."

When her phone rang, Rita answered, still laughing. "Hello?"

"Rita, this is Thomas."

Jack's father? For a second a thread of fear wound through her. Was Jack okay? Had something happened? Would she always be wondering about him? The answer was of course, yes.

Sighing, she said, "Hi, Thomas, everything all right?"

"Oh, yes, yes. Everything is great, really. I was just wondering, though, if you might do an old man a favor."

Setting the timer on the oven, Rita wandered to the refrigerator and pulled out a bottle of water. She uncapped it, took a long drink and said, "Of course. What can I do?"

She heard the smile in his voice when he said, "I hoped you could come down to *The Sea Queen* to see me."

"You're on the ship?"

"Yes," he said. "I'm taking the first cruise. Thought I'd get a little golf in on the islands. But there's something I'd like to give you before I go."

Rita did some fast thinking. She really liked Jack's father and just because the man's son was behaving like a loon didn't mean she couldn't be close to his family. Thomas was, after all, her daughter's grandfather. And Jack's sister was going to be the baby's doctor. Family mattered, whether Jack could see that or not. "Of course I can. What time do you want me there?"

"Wonderful," he said, pleasure ringing in his voice. "As for what time, the sooner the better."

Now she was curious. Jack hadn't said anything to her about his dad going on the first cruise. But then, she told herself, maybe he didn't know. What could Thomas possibly have to give her that was important enough for her to go scurrying down to the harbor just before the ship sailed? "Okay, I'll just arrange for my manager to take over and I'll come right down."

"Thank you, Rita. I'll leave word at the dock and they'll bring you to my suite."

"Okay, then," she said, still baffled, "I'll see you soon."

She hung up and just stared at the phone for a second or two. Rita had no idea what was going on, but the sooner she got to the harbor, the quicker she'd find out.

Half an hour later, she was boarding the ship and being met by a young man in a navy shirt and sharply creased white slacks. *The Sea Queen* was stitched onto the breast pocket of his shirt and just below, he wore a name tag that read "Darren."

"Mrs. Buchanan?" he asked and when she nodded, he said, "If you'll come with me, Mr. Buchanan is waiting in the owner's suite."

The crowds were frantic. People rushing around, having their pictures taken, waving to people on the dock. Children ran past her, their laughter hanging in their wake. The scent of the sea flavored the air and Rita lifted her face into the wind briefly before boarding an elevator with Darren.

"Everyone seems really excited," she said.

"They are," Darren assured her. "It's a great ship and it's always fun to go out on the first cruise."

Probably would be, she thought and told herself that one day she'd have to try it. Right now, sitting on an island beach with nothing to do sounded pretty good.

She had no idea what deck they were on when the

elevator stopped and they stepped off into a luxurious hallway. But it was quiet with none of the eager abandon down on the main decks. Darren led her to a door at the end of the hall, then opened it for her.

"Mr. Buchanan said you should just go on inside, ma'am," he said, then strode quickly away, back to the elevator.

Rita walked into the massive suite, closed the door behind her and for a second, all she could do was stare with her mouth open. It was more than elegant. It was opulent.

Midnight blue carpeting was so plush her feet sank into it. There was a huge living area, with a flat-screen TV, an electric fireplace and several couches and chairs all done in cream-colored fabric. There was a bar, and out on the private balcony, she could see a table and chairs as well as lounges.

She'd love to get a look at the rest of the suite before she left, but for right now… "Thomas?"

Someone stepped into the room from the terrace, but it wasn't Thomas. Even before he spoke, she knew it was Jack because her blood started bubbling and her heart leaped into a gallop.

"Thanks for coming, Rita," Jack said.

She backed up. Cowardly, yes; she'd be embarrassed later. "What're you doing here? Where's your father?"

"That's the thing. He's not here. I asked him to call you for me, since I figured you wouldn't speak to me anyway."

"You were right about that," she snapped and turned for the door. She had to get out of there. Off the ship, back to the bakery.

But Jack was too fast and his legs were much longer

than hers. He beat her to the door and stood with his back against it, blocking her way.

"Move, Jack."

"Not yet."

"You really don't want to push me right now," she warned, though she didn't know what she could do to move him if he didn't want to be moved. Gina would kick him, but Rita just wasn't the kicking kind. Too bad.

"Just hear me out. Then if you want to leave, I won't stop you."

"Why should I?"

One corner of his mouth quirked up and her heart thudded painfully in her chest. "Because you're curious. Admit it."

She hated that he was right. Hated that he could make her body burn with a half smile and hated that just standing this close to him made her want to lean in and take a bite of his lower lip. "Fine. Talk."

He shook his head. "Not here. Come in. Sit down."

When he took her arm, she pulled free of his grasp. She didn't trust herself to stay mad if he was touching her and she really wanted to stay mad. She'd earned it, hadn't she?

"No," she said. "I'm not sitting down. I'm not staying. Just say whatever it is you want said and get it over with." She felt a little wobbly. Too many emotions churning inside at the same time. Didn't he know how hard this was for her? Didn't he care at all? Shaking her hair back, she said, "Unless you've brought me here to declare undying love, then just let me go, okay?"

"That's why you're here," he said softly.

"What?" She couldn't have heard him right, Rita told

herself. Jack wouldn't have said that unless he had another agenda. "What're you saying, Jack?"

"I love you."

She swayed in place and he instinctively reached out one hand to steady her. Tears blurring her vision, Rita slapped at his hand. "No, you don't. You're just telling me what you think I want to hear."

Irritation bloomed on his face. "I should have known you wouldn't react the way I expected you to. You've always surprised me, so why should now be any different?"

"What are you talking about?"

"I'm trying to tell you that I was wrong. That I love you. That I want you—but if you're not going to believe me why bother?"

"I didn't say I didn't believe you—" She broke off, stared up into his eyes and saw, along with sparks of exasperation, the love she'd always hoped to see. "You love me?"

"Now will you sit down?" he asked.

"I think I have to," she said. She was shaking all over and her heart was pounding so quickly it sounded like a frantic drumbeat in her ears.

Once she was perched on the couch, Jack started pacing. He glanced at her and said, "You were right."

"Always a good start," she said. "Right about what?"

"Pretty much everything." He paced away from her, then whirled around and came back. "I was hiding. Not just from pain, but from life. I didn't really see that despite how many of you kept trying to tell me. I guess it's not easy for a man to admit he's been a damn coward."

"I didn't say you were a coward."

"No," he agreed, "that's one thing you didn't say.

But it's true anyway. Hell, Rita, seeing Kevin again, it shook me. Then the wedding, him and Lisa, you and me… It was like an overload or something. My brain just exploded."

"So you told me to leave."

"It seemed like the right thing to do at the time—"

She started to speak but he cut her off for a change.

"—but it wasn't. Damn it Rita, I've *missed* you. Your voice, your scent, the taste of you. Hell, I miss that loud laugh of yours so much I keep thinking I hear it echo around me."

"Loud?" she repeated.

He grinned. "Loud. And sexy as hell."

Rita took a breath and held it, really hoping this was going to keep going the way she wanted it to.

"That day in the desert almost finished me and did a hell of a lot more to Kevin." Jack stopped pacing, stared into her eyes and said, "But he got past it. Moved the hell on, found a life, while I was still stuck in the past, trying to rewrite history."

"Oh, Jack." She was glad to hear that he had done some thinking, but she hated hearing him put himself down like this, too. It was, she thought, the way of family. *I can call my sister names but if you do it, we go to war.* Well, that's how she felt here, too.

"Just let me get all of this out, okay?" He pushed one hand through his hair. "I've been doing a lot of thinking the last few days and last night, it all sort of came together."

"How?" She needed to know. Needed to believe that this was all real and that somehow he wouldn't go back down that dark road he'd been so determined to stay on.

"The dream came again."

And she hadn't been there to help him through it. Pain for what he'd been through chimed inside her as she pushed off the couch to go to him. "Jack…"

"No," he said, smiling. "It wasn't the same at all this time. In lots of ways. And it doesn't matter right now. All that *does* matter is that I finally figured something out."

She looked up into his eyes and for the first time, noticed that he seemed different somehow. There weren't as many shadows in his eyes. He looked…lighter. As if at least a part of the burden he carried with him had slipped off. And that gave her hope.

"What, Jack? What did you figure out?"

"That I was an idiot. Telling you to go when I should have been begging you to stay." His gaze moved over her face like a touch. "Hell, Rita, I should have been thanking the Fates for bringing you back to me and instead, all I could think about was if I loved you and lost you it would kill me."

Tears blurred her vision but she blinked them back. She didn't want to miss a moment of this. "So," she said wryly, "to keep from losing me, you lost me."

"Yeah." He sighed. "Like I said. Idiot."

"Agreed."

He laughed shortly. "Well, thanks."

"Hey, who knows you better than me?" She asked and reached up to smooth his hair back from his forehead.

"Nobody," he said, voice hardly more than a whisper. He laid both hands on her shoulders and stared directly into her eyes when he said, "Forgive me, Rita.

I was too messed up to see what I had. What I lost. I told you once that you had to leave before I loved you."

"Yeah," she said, the memory of that pain filling her. "I remember."

"That was a lie, too." He rested his forehead against hers. "I loved you the minute I saw you on that beach. When you smiled at me, my heart dropped at your feet. I didn't want to acknowledge it and that's the idiot part." He slid his hands up to cup her face and wiped away a single tear with his thumb. "But my heart is yours, Rita. Always has been. I love you."

She sucked in a gulp of air and held it. "Say it again."

He grinned. "I love you. More than I ever thought possible to love anyone."

"Jack…"

He frowned a little. "Is that an irritated sigh, or a dreamy one?"

Rita smiled up at him. "Dreamy. With just a little bit of irritation tacked on to the end for what you put us all through."

"That's fair," he said, nodding. "Rita, I want to stay married to you. I want to raise our daughter and however many more kids we have together. I love you. Always will. I'm sorry I hurt you. Sorry I hurt my family. My friends."

She reached up to cover his hands with hers. "I love you, Jack."

"Thank God." He sighed in relief. "You'll never be sorry, Rita. I swear it."

"I never was sorry, you dummy," she said and went up on her toes to kiss him.

Jack took her mouth like a drowning man taking his first clear breath. She leaned in to him, wrapped her arms around his neck and held on as he picked her up and swung her in a circle, their mouths still fused together.

Finally though, breathless, he broke off and grinned down at her. "I love you."

"Keep saying it," Rita told him. "I want to hear it. A lot. In fact, I'm going to send Kevin and Lisa a thank-you card for inviting us to their wedding."

"Oh!" Jack let her go long enough to walk to a table, pick something up and come back to her. "Hey, that reminds me. I brought this along for you to see. Kevin sent me an email this morning. I learned my lesson there, too, and opened it right away. Then I printed it."

Rita's eyes blurred again as she looked down at the picture of Kevin and Lisa, standing side by side. The picture was captioned "Got my new legs. I'm an inch taller than I used to be. Thanks again, Jack. For everything. Give us a call sometime."

She looked up at Jack. "That's so great."

"Yeah, it is." He took the picture, tossed it to the table again, then held her hands in his. "And one of these days, I'll thank him for waking me the hell up in time to save the only thing that matters to me." He cupped her cheek with one hand. "You, Rita. I love you."

"I love you back," she said and felt her world completely right itself and steady out. He'd been worth the fight. Worth the pain. Worth everything to get to where they were now.

Bending down, he kissed her baby belly and then stood up to face her. "You know I told you I've been doing a lot of thinking the last couple of days and I wanted to ask you something. How do you feel about naming our daughter Carla? After my mom."

Rita's heart melted. It was perfect. It was all so perfect. She stepped into his embrace. "I think I love it. You're back, Jack. Really back, aren't you?"

"Yeah." He gave her a smile. "I'm finally home. *You're* my home, Rita. I know that now." His arms closed around her and she felt the steady thump of his heart beneath her ear. She had Jack. She had her daughter. She had everything.

The ship's horn sounded and Rita jumped. "Hey, we've got to get off the ship before it sails."

He only tightened his hold on her and laughed. "No, we're not getting off."

Confused, she stared up at him. "What do you mean?"

"Just in case you didn't kill me," Jack said, grinning, "I arranged for Gina to come to town to run the bakery for two weeks. My dad's coming out of retirement to run the company and you and I are sailing to St. Thomas."

"You can't be serious," she whispered, a little panicked, a little excited.

"Absolutely serious."

"But, I don't have any clothes..."

"We'll buy whatever we need." Then he kissed her and admitted, "But I'll say I'm going to want you naked most of the time."

Oh, boy. A tingle of anticipation set up shop low down inside her. But could she really just leave? On the spur of the moment?

"But—" Was this happening? When she woke up that morning, she'd been alone and afraid she would stay that way. Now, she had Jack, a dream vacation and the life she'd always wanted being handed to her. How could she keep up?

"Oh," he said, that tempting smile curving his mouth again, "Gina said to tell you she had lots of ideas on how to 'fix' your bakery."

Rita's eyes narrowed on him. "Oh, you're going to pay for that," she promised.

"Can't wait," Jack said and bent to kiss her again. "You brought me back to the world, Rita. Let me show you some of it."

And just like that, it was all right. She'd go with him anywhere.

"Show me, Jack. Show me everything." Love shone so brightly all around them it was blinding, and Rita would never stop thanking whatever Fates had brought them back together.

"Come with me," he said and dropped one arm around her shoulders, pulling her in close to his side as he led her out to the balcony. And there they stood, wrapped in each other's arms, looking ahead as they sailed into the future. Together.

* * * * *

LITTLE SECRETS: CLAIMING HIS PREGNANT BRIDE

SARAH M. ANDERSON

To everyone who stood up for what they believed.
You continue to inspire me!

One

Of all the things Seth Bolton wanted to be doing today, attending the wedding of a guy he went to college with was pretty low on the list.

Besides, he hadn't even liked Roger Caputo. Seth had been forced to live with Roger for three hellish months in college when Seth's roommate had backed out and Seth had been desperate to cover the rent without asking his family for help. That Roger had been a senior and unable to get any roommate but a freshman should have been the first clue to how Seth's three months were going to go.

It wasn't that Roger was a bad guy—he was just a jerk. Entitled, spoiled, inconsiderate—every privileged white-guy stereotype rolled into one. That was Roger.

Seth couldn't imagine who was foolish enough to marry Roger, but clearly someone was. Seth had no idea if he should pity this woman or not.

He gunned the engine up the incline, following the road as it snaked through the Black Hills. The wedding was supposed to start at five thirty—Seth was running late. It was already five forty and he had at least fifteen miles to go.

For some reason, the wedding was being held at a resort deep in the Black Hills, forty minutes away from Rapid City.

Why did people have destination weddings? Well, he knew why. The late-summer sun was already lower in the sky, casting a shimmering glow over the hills. They weren't black right now, not with the sun turning them golden shades of orange and red and pink at the edges.

It was *pretty*—not that he was looking as he took the next curve even faster. Roger must've found one hell of a woman if she wanted to tie herself to him with all this beauty around her.

Or maybe the jerk had changed. It was possible. After all, Seth himself had once been the kind of impulsive, restless kid who'd stolen a car and punched a grown man in the face because the man had dared to break Seth's mother's heart. Sure, that man—Billy Bolton—had married his mother and adopted Seth, despite the punch. But still, that was the sort of thing Seth used to be capable of.

Maybe he was still a little impulsive, he thought as he flew down the road well over the speed limit. And yeah, he was definitely still restless. The last year living in Los Angeles had proved that. But he'd gotten good at controlling his more destructive tendencies.

So people could change. Maybe Roger had become a fine, upstanding citizen.

The road bent around an outcropping, and Seth

leaned into the curve, the Crazy Horse chopper rumbling between his legs. This was a brand-new model, in the final stages of testing, and he was putting it through its paces. The new engine had throwback styling combined with modern power and a wider wheelbase. The machine handled beautifully as he took another curve and leaned in hard. Seth felt a surge of pride—he'd helped design this one.

Damn, he'd missed these hills, the freedom to open up the throttle and ride it hard. LA traffic made actually riding a chopper a challenge. And palm trees had nothing on the Black Hills.

His father and his uncles, Ben and Bobby Bolton, owned and operated Crazy Horse Choppers, a custom chop shop in Rapid City, South Dakota. Crazy Horse had been founded by their father, Bruce Bolton, but the Bolton brothers had taken the company from a one-man shop in Bruce's garage in the early eighties to a company with sixty employees and a quarter of a billion in sales every year.

Seth had never had a father growing up, never expected that he would be a part of any family business. But when Billy adopted Seth ten years ago, the Bolton men had embraced him with open arms.

And now? Seth was a full partner in Crazy Horse Choppers.

He still couldn't get his head around the meeting yesterday. His dad and uncles had called him into the office and offered him an equal share in Crazy Horse. And Seth was no idiot. Of course he'd said yes.

At the age of twenty-five, he was suddenly a millionaire. A *multimillionaire*. Considering how he and his mom had sometimes been on welfare when he was a little kid, it was a hell of a shock.

But Seth knew it wasn't straight nepotism—he worked hard at making Crazy Horse Choppers a successful business. He'd just gotten back from living in Los Angeles for a year, managing the Crazy Horse showroom and convincing every A-to D-list celebrity that a Crazy Horse chopper was good for their image. And he'd excelled at the job, too. Getting Rich McClaren to ride up the red carpet at the Oscars on a Crazy Horse chopper—right before he won the award? Seth's idea. The free advertising from that had boosted sales by eight percent overnight.

The McClaren stunt was the kind of strategic thinking that Seth did now. He didn't just react—and react poorly. He planned. The best defense was a good offense.

Even now—he wasn't just going to a former friend's wedding. A quick internet search had revealed that Roger was a real estate agent now, part owner in his own agency. He was up-and-coming in the civic world of Rapid City. And after a year in LA, Seth was back in Rapid City. Maybe even permanently.

Seth was not going to this wedding to wish Roger and his new bride happiness, although he would. Seth was going to the wedding because he planned to be an up-and-comer himself. God knew that he had the money now.

The Bolton men might have given him a place at the table, but Seth was going to damn well keep it.

He screamed around a curve but saw something that made him ease off the throttle. There was a limo at a scenic overlook—but something wasn't right. Seth couldn't brake fast enough to stop without crashing, but he slowed enough to get a better look.

Something was definitely wrong. The limo was parked at a crazy angle, its bumper hanging in the roadway. Was there someone behind the wheel? He didn't see anyone enjoying the view.

He was late—but he couldn't in good conscience ride on. Seth pulled a U-turn on the road and headed back to the overlook. Did his phone even have service out here? Because if this wasn't some crazy wedding photographer stunt and the driver was having an emergency…

The limo was still running when Seth pulled up alongside it. His heart leaped in his throat when he realized that the front wheel on the passenger side wasn't exactly on solid ground. The driver had stopped just before the wheel went off the edge of the overlook completely. Hitting the gas would mean certain death.

He hopped off the bike and hurried to the driver's side. He hadn't been wrong—there *was* someone behind the wheel. A woman. Wearing a wedding dress and a…tiara?

Definitely not the limo driver.

She wasn't crying, but her eyes were wide as she stared at nothing in particular. Her color was terrible, a bluish shade of gray, and she had what appeared to be a death grip on the steering wheel. Basically, she looked like someone had shot her dog. Or ruined her wedding.

For all of that, she was quite possibly the most beautiful woman he'd ever seen.

How many brides were wandering around this part of South Dakota? Was this Roger's bride? If so, what was she doing *here*? Where was Roger?

He knocked on the glass of the driver's-side door.

"Ma'am?" he said in what he hoped was a comforting voice. "Could you roll down the window?"

She didn't move.

"Excuse me? Ma'am?" This time, he tried the handle. Miracle of miracles, the door was not locked. When he opened it, she startled and swung her head around to look at him. As she did so, the limo shuddered. "Where did you come from?"

"Hi," Seth said in a soothing voice, hanging on to the door as if that could keep the car from plummeting off the side of the hill. "I'm going to turn this off, okay?"

Her eyes blinked at different speeds. "What?"

Seth leaned into the limo, keeping an eye on her in case she started to freak out. The limo was actually in Park, thank God. She must have taken her foot off the brake when he startled her. "I'm Seth," he told her, pulling the key from the ignition. "What's your name?"

Seth didn't expect her to burst out laughing as if he had told a joke. Clearly, this was a woman whose actions could not be predicted. Then, as quickly as she'd started laughing, the sound died in the back of her throat and she made a strangled-sounding sob. "I'm not sure."

Bad sign. He had to get her out of the limo. "Can you come talk to me? There's a bench over there with a great view of the sunset." He tried to make it sound like he was just here for the vista.

"You not going to tell me to get married, are you?"

Seth shook his head. "You're here for reasons. All of those reasons—I bet they're good ones."

She blinked at him again, her brow furrowed. He could see that she was coming back to herself now. "Are you here for a reason, too?"

He gave her a reassuring smile. "Everything happens for a reason."

This time, when she started laughing, he was ready for it. He chuckled along with her as if they were at a comedy club in downtown LA as opposed to on the edge of a scenic overlook in the Black Hills. He held out a hand to her and bowed at the waist. "Seth Bolton, at your disposal."

For the longest second, she just stared at him, as if he were a *Tyrannosaurus rex* that had emerged from the undergrowth and was roaring at her. "I'm not imagining you, right? Because you're kind of perfect and I made a mess of everything."

"I'm very real—the last time I checked, anyway," he joked, which got a small, quick smile out of her. He kept his hand out, the picture of a chivalrous gentleman. *Take it*, he thought. He would feel so much better if she were on solid ground next to him.

She placed her hand in his and it took everything he had not to close his fingers around hers and yank her out of the driver's seat—and into his arms. Instead, he tightened his grip on her ever so slightly and waited as she swung her feet out and stood. Her layers of dress settled around her—silk and satin and chiffon and all of those fabrics that his aunt Stella made dresses out of for her fashion line.

He didn't think this was one of Stella's dresses. Stella designed classic gowns that looked deceptively simple. This gown?

There wasn't anything simple about it. The bride looked a little bit like an overdone cupcake, with sparkles and sprinkles. The skirt was huge, with tiers and layers of ruffles and lace. How had she even fit behind the wheel in that monstrosity?

Her golden-brown hair was swept up into some elaborate confection that matched the dress, but at some point it had tilted off its bearings and now listed dangerously to the left. Pearls dripped off her ears and around her neck, but her ring finger was bare.

What did she look like when she wasn't dressed up like a bride? All he could see of her was her face and her bare shoulders. And her cleavage, which was kind of amazing—not that he was looking. His body tightened with awareness even as he tried to focus on her eyes. It didn't help, staring down into her face. Everything tugged him toward her with an instinctive pull that wasn't something he'd planned on, much less could control.

His first instinct had been right—she was gorgeous, he realized as she lifted her gaze to his. A sweetheart face, wide-set eyes that were the deepest shade of green he'd ever seen. The kind of eyes a man could get lost in, if he weren't careful.

Seth was careful. *Always.*

He knew exactly what happened when a man lost his head around a woman. So it was final—no losing himself in her eyes. Or any other of her body parts. She might be a goddess, but she was obviously having a very bad day and he wasn't about to do a single damn thing that would make it worse.

So he locked down this intense awareness of her.

She wasn't for him. All he could—and should—do was offer her a helping hand.

"Hi." He launched another smile, one that had broken a few hearts, in her direction. "I'm Seth," he repeated because he honestly wasn't sure if she'd processed it the first time.

"Kate," she replied in a shaky voice. She hadn't pulled her hand away from his yet. Seth took an experimental step back—away from the limo—and was pleased when she followed. "I…I'm not sure what my last name is right now. I don't think I got married. I'm pretty sure I left before that part."

In his time, Seth had seen people involved in accidents still walking and talking and functioning almost normally because they were in a complete state of shock. Big dudes thrown from choppers and yet walking around and cracking jokes with one of their arms hanging out of the socket. Later, when the adrenaline had worn off, they'd felt the pain. But not at first.

Was this what this was? Had she been hurt? He looked her over as surreptitiously as he could, but he didn't see any injuries—so this was just a mental shock, then.

"Kate," he said, his voice warm and friendly. "That's a pretty name. What would you like your last name to be?

"Burroughs," she said firmly. "I don't want to be Kate Caputo. I can't be."

Seth let out a careful breath. That answered that question.

He had found Roger's runaway bride.

Two

Kate felt like she was moving in a dream. Everything was blurry at the edges—but getting sharper. How much time had she lost? A couple of hours? A couple of days? The last thing she remembered was…

She had been sitting in the little room set aside for the bride to get ready, staring at the mirror and fighting back the rising tide of nausea. Because she was pregnant and she was supposed to be marrying Roger and—and—

"Easy," a strong, confident male voice said.

She looked down to see that her hand was being held by a man who was *not* Roger and they were *not* at the lodge she had especially selected for the beautiful sunset. She looked around, startling again. None of this looked familiar. Especially not him. She'd remember him. "I don't…"

The man's arm went around her waist and even

though she didn't know who he was or what was going on, she leaned into his touch. It felt right—comforting. *Safe.* Whoever he was, he was safe. Maybe it was all going to be okay. She could have cried with relief.

"I've got you," he said, sounding so very calm when there was nothing to be calm about. "It's all right."

She laughed at that. "No, it's not."

"It's not as bad as you think, I promise. Roger will get over this, and so will you."

She wasn't sure she believed that, but his arm tightened around her waist. Kate couldn't have said if she leaned on him or if he picked her up or how, exactly, she got to the bench. All she could focus on was this man—with dark hair and dark eyes and tanned skin, wearing a motorcycle jacket over what looked like a pair of suit trousers. He sat her down on the bench and then took a seat next to her. "You're cold," he said, picking up her hand and rubbing it between his.

"Am I?" Yes, now that she thought about it, she could feel a chill in the air. The way he spoke to her called to mind someone trying to capture a bird with a broken wing.

Then something he'd said sank in. "You…you know Roger?"

The man—Seth? Had he said that was his name? Seth nodded. "I lived with him in college." He stood and peeled off his leather jacket and even though Kate was having a terrible day, she was struck by how nicely this strange, sympathetic man filled out a button-up shirt. He even had on a tie—but somehow, it didn't look stuffy. It looked dangerous, almost. "Frankly, I think you're doing the right thing," he went on as he settled his jacket around her shoulders. "Assuming he hasn't seen the light and become a better human, that is."

"No, I don't think he has," she said slowly. His jacket was warm and soft, and she immediately felt a hundred times better. She had been cold for far too long. It was good to realize there could still be warmth in the world.

Then she realized what she'd said. "I didn't mean that," she quickly corrected, feeling the heat rise in her face. She blinked. Seth was staring at her with a level of focus that she wasn't used to. Roger certainly didn't listen to her like this.

But even thinking that made her feel terrible. She was supposed to be marrying Roger and she wasn't. She didn't have to add insult to injury by—well, by insulting him. "I mean, he's not a bad guy. He's a great catch." On paper.

On paper, Roger was handsome and educated, a successful small-business man. On paper he was perfect.

She couldn't marry a piece of paper.

She was supposed to be marrying a flesh-and-blood man who didn't love her. She was fairly certain about that.

"Even if he somehow magically turned into a great catch—which I doubt," Seth said, fishing something out of his pants pockets and sitting next to her, "that doesn't mean he's a great catch for you."

Her breath caught in her throat as he closed the distance between them. As he lifted her chin and stared into her eyes, Kate knew she should pull away. She couldn't let this stranger kiss her. That wasn't who she was.

She was Kate Burroughs. Only child to Joe and Kathleen Burroughs. A real estate agent who worked for her parents at Burroughs Realty—which was now Burroughs and Caputo Realty.

She didn't make waves. She did the right thing, always. She got good grades and sold houses. She didn't get unexpectedly pregnant. She most definitely didn't leave her groom at the altar, and under no circumstances could she be attracted to a man who wasn't her fiancé.

At least, that was who she'd been yesterday. It seemed pretty obvious that she wasn't that same woman today.

He had such nice eyes. A deep brown, soft and kind and yet still with an air of danger to him. He was dangerous to her, that much was clear, because he was going to kiss her and she was going let him and that was something the woman she'd been yesterday never would have allowed, much less entertained.

"It's going to be okay," he said softly. Then he touched her cheeks. With a handkerchief.

Kate hadn't realized she was crying until Seth dabbed at her cheeks.

When he was done, Seth pressed the handkerchief into her hand and leaned back. She wouldn't have thought it possible, but she got even more embarrassed. *Really, Kate? Really?* She wasn't even close to holding it together and she wanted to kiss this complete stranger?

She'd lost her mind. It was the only rational explanation.

She was relieved when Seth turned his gaze back out to the landscape. The sun was getting lower and the world was crimson and red. "Bolting on a wedding," he said slowly, "may not be cheap and it may not be easy. You may feel…"

"Like an idiot," she said bitterly.

"Confused," Seth corrected. "You're trying to talk

yourself into going back, but your instincts made you leave. And it's a good idea to listen to your instincts."

"That's easy for you to say. Your parents didn't shell out thousands of dollars on a fairy-tale wedding and invite hundreds of guests, all of whom are probably wondering where the hell you are and what's wrong with you."

He made a huffing noise, as if she'd said something idiotic instead of stating the facts of the matter. "Correct me if I'm wrong, but your parents aren't marrying Roger. None of the guests are, either. You can put on a good show for them because of the sunk cost of the reception, but at the end of the day you're the one who has to go home with him. For the rest of your life." She shuddered involuntarily. Seth put his arm around her shoulders and, weak as she was, she leaned into his chest. He went on, "If he hasn't changed, then you don't want to be stuck with him."

She sniffed. She knew she was crying again, but she was powerless to stop. Seth was warm and he smelled good and it was okay if she cried. "I don't. I really don't."

"Leaving him at the altar is cheaper and easier than getting a divorce," he said with finality. "Better to feel foolish now than to wake up tomorrow knowing you've made a huge mistake. Besides, if you realize you should have married him, you can still do that. If he really loves you, he'll understand."

That was what she needed to hear, because that was the truth that she felt in her heart. She was making a horrible mess for Roger and her parents, and she didn't want to humiliate him or their families and friends.

But at the end of the day, she was the one who had to

live with him. With herself. And she *knew* she wouldn't be able to make the marriage last the rest of her life. How far would she and Roger get before she couldn't take it anymore? A year? Three? The divorce—because there would be one. Seth was right—would be ugly. Especially because of the baby.

She lost track of time, quietly crying into Seth's shoulder and his handkerchief as the sun got lower in the sky. Purple joined the reds and oranges. It was truly a beautiful late-summer day. Perfect for a wedding.

And where was she? Marrying her Prince Charming? Celebrating? No.

She was sitting on a bench with a man who had been Roger's roommate. A man who understood that Roger was better on paper than he was in real life.

A man who didn't think she was insane for running away from her own wedding.

"I'm pregnant," she announced because she hadn't been able to tell anyone yet and that single fact—those two little words—had completely altered the trajectory of her life.

Seth stiffened and then said, "Oh?" in a far too casual voice.

"Roger is the father," she went on in a rush of words. "I'm not the kind of person who would cheat on my fiancé." Ironically, though, she was the kind of person who'd abandon her fiancé. What did that say about her? "It's his child and I should probably go back and marry him because we're going to have a baby. Together."

Seth didn't say anything, nor did he spring to his feet to lead her back to the limo. Back to her doom.

Wait—how did the limo get here? Had she stolen it?

And was it stealing if she'd rented it for the whole evening?

"Easy," Seth said again in that soothing voice of his. She could feel it in her chest, warm and comforting. "You might not believe this, but people have babies without being married all the time. It doesn't mean you've doomed your kid from the beginning."

"How can you say that?" And how was he reading her mind?

His arm tightened around her shoulders. "Because I've lived it, Kate. I won't let anything happen to you—I promise. Now," he went on even as she gasped at that honest promise—something she'd never heard cross Roger's lips, "do you remember where the limo came from?"

"Um..." She sat up and dabbed at her eyes again. The waterproof mascara was doing its best, but it was no match for this day and his handkerchief was paying the price. She tried to focus on the limo. "Stein, maybe?" It felt right—Stein Limo. That was a thing, she was pretty sure.

"Ron Stein? He's a great guy."

She stared at him in confusion. "You know the limo guy?" She didn't even know Seth's last name, but he knew Roger and now the limo guy. Was there anyone Seth didn't know?

"He rides," Seth said, as if that explained everything. "I'll see if I can make a call and let him know where his limo is. But I need you to stay right here, okay?"

"I don't know where you think I'd go. I'm not walking home." She wiggled her toes and realized she wasn't wearing her shoes. Where the hell were they?

But even the thought of going home made her wince.

She had a home—with Roger. They'd bought it last year, after finally setting a date for the wedding. It'd been a big sign of their commitment to each other.

No, that wasn't right. She didn't have a home with Roger. She owned part of a house. She shared a property with him. They split the bills right down the middle. They'd maintained separate bank accounts, even.

She'd lived with Roger, but it'd never felt like home.

"Promise me, Kate." His eyes were intense and serious. "You're not going anywhere without me."

"I promise." It wasn't like she'd sworn to love, honor or obey—but there was something to that promise that resonated in her mind.

Why could she make such a promise to this man she didn't know but couldn't to the one she did?

He gave her a satisfied nod of his head, leaned over and slid his hand inside his jacket, right over her left breast. She stiffened and he paused. "Just getting my phone," he said, purposefully not touching her. "Don't move." He stood and walked off to the side, far enough away that she couldn't hear what he was saying. But he turned back to her and gave her a little smile that set off butterflies in her stomach.

She ignored them and settled back on the bench, trying to get a handle on everything that happened.

It was a lot. But she'd had a good cry and Seth's jacket was warm and she felt better. Her mind was clearer and she could look past the next five minutes without having a panic attack.

She hoped.

She tried to rationally go over the facts. She was pregnant. She wasn't marrying Roger. She couldn't go back to the house she shared with him and she didn't think she could go to work on Monday. Her parents had sold half of Burroughs Realty to Roger in anticipation of the wedding. He owned it now.

She'd worked for Burroughs Realty her whole life, starting when they had her making copies and greeting clients as a little kid.

But they hadn't seen fit to give or even sell her part of the agency. Instead, they'd used it almost like a dowry, rewarding Roger for taking her off their hands.

Why hadn't she realized that before? She was a good real estate agent. She sold her market well. She was more than capable of being a full partner in the family business and running the office.

But it was Roger Caputo who was being rewarded with his name on the front door. Because why? Because he was marrying her?

She was their daughter. Wasn't she good enough on her own?

Oh, what would her parents say about all this? Especially once they found out she was pregnant? Her mother would try to be supportive—Kate hoped. The prospect of a grandbaby would be exciting, once the humiliation of a broken wedding passed.

But her father? Joe Burroughs was a dyed-in-the-wool workaholic who demanded perfection—or at the very least, that everything be done his way, and in his mind, those two things were the same.

She had to face the facts—her father might disown her for this, and if he did, he might forbid Mom from seeing Kate. Hadn't he already chosen Roger over her?

Just as she began to panic at the thought, Seth looked up at her again and smiled. It was a very nice smile, seemingly real and not the kind of expression one directed at a crazy person. He hadn't treated her like she was nuts at all, actually—even though the situation certainly did seem to warrant a little concern.

Instead of telling her she was insane to walk away from Roger, he'd agreed that tying herself to him was a bad idea. Anyone could have said the words, but Seth wasn't just saying them because she was having a really bad day. He was saying them because he actually *knew* Roger. Maybe not well, but he'd lived with Roger. He understood what that was like in a way that her friends and even her parents might not. Seth was speaking from a place of wisdom, and that counted for a lot.

It didn't make any sense that she felt safer with a strange man who rode a motorcycle than she did with the man she'd been with for four years, but there it was. Seth didn't know her at all, but he was more concerned with her well-being than anyone else. After all, how long had she been here? At least half an hour, maybe much longer. And had anyone come looking for her? Roger? Her parents? Any of the wedding guests?

No. Seth had stumbled upon her, noticed something was wrong, and he was actively making sure she was okay. He'd given her his leather jacket and dried her tears.

He glanced at her again, another smile on his lips—which set off another round of butterflies in her stomach. Now that her mind had cleared, it was hard to miss the fact that her Good Samaritan was also intensely handsome.

No, no—she was not going to be the kind of woman who defined herself by her attractions to men. It was blatantly obvious that she couldn't run from Roger's arms straight into a stranger's. She was pregnant, for God's sake. Romance should be the last thing on her mind.

She needed a place to stay tonight. Maybe tomorrow. She needed a job that didn't involve Roger or her father. She needed…

A plan. She couldn't sit here at a scenic overlook forever.

Had she managed to bring anything important with her—her wallet, money, credit cards, her license—*anything* that could help her out tonight? She rather doubted it—she didn't even know where her shoes were.

Seth ended his call and began to walk back toward her, and Kate realized something.

She needed him.

Three

"Come on," Seth said, pulling her to her feet. She was not a tiny thing—she was only a few inches shorter than he was—but there was still something delicate about her. "I'm going to take you to a hotel." Her eyes widened in surprise but she didn't lean away from him. Not that that mattered. "And I'm going to leave you there," he added with a smile.

"Oh. Of course," she said, her cheeks blushing a soft pink. "Thank you. I don't think I can go back to the house I shared with Roger." She cleared her throat. "Are we taking the limo?"

"No. I talked to Ron—he's going to send someone out to pick it up. They did have cops looking for it but he's reported it not stolen. He's not going to press charges."

She blinked at him. "Is that because of you?"

The short answer was *yes*. Ron had been furious that

Kate had driven off with his limo—apparently it was his most expensive ride. He'd already fired the driver for dereliction of duties.

Ron's temper burned hot, but it always fizzled out quickly. Ron had been buddies with Billy Bolton for years and Seth had seen him in action plenty of times. He had to blow his top, and then he could be reasoned with.

Seth had waited until Ron finished blustering and then had convinced the man not to fire his driver—who had reasonably thought he'd had another hour before anyone would care about the whereabouts of the limo—and to inform the police that no theft had been committed.

But that's not what he told her. Instead, Seth said, "Ron's a great guy. He understood." Kate notched an eyebrow at him—clearly she wasn't buying that line.

But that was his story and he was sticking to it. Kate had already had a terrible day. The prospect of being arrested and booked for grand theft auto would only make everything a thousand times worse and he didn't want that, especially now that she'd calmed down.

He hadn't lied when he'd told her he'd keep her safe. This pull he felt to protect her—from the consequences of taking a limo, from Roger, from her thoughtless parents, from the harsh realities of life as a single mother—it wasn't something that made sense on a rational level. He didn't know her. He had no claim to her.

But by God, he wasn't going to cast her to the winds of fate and call it a day.

"Okay," she finally said, exhaling heavily. Which did some very interesting things to her chest. "Then what do we do next?"

"We ride." The color drained out of her cheeks. "Have you ever been on a motorcycle before?"

She shook her head, her tilting hair bobbing dangerously near her left ear. He reached up and tucked it back in place as best he could. He managed to do so without letting his fingers linger, so there was that.

"I've been riding for years," he assured her. "All you have to do is hold on. Can you do that?"

"I…" She looked down at her dress. "Um…"

She had a point. He eyed the confection suspiciously. The skirt was a full ball-gown style, layered with ruffles and lace. It spread out from Kate's waist in a circle that was easily five feet in diameter.

Ron had made it clear—Seth wasn't driving the limo. But Kate in that dress on the back of the chopper was a recipe for disaster. He could just imagine the wind getting underneath her skirts and blowing that dress up like a balloon.

"Is there any way to reduce the volume?" He tried to think back to what his aunt Stella had taught him about women's fashion. "An underskirt of some kind that we can remove?

Her face got redder. "I have on a structured petticoat. It's separate from the dress."

"Can you get it off?"

Kate's hands went to her waist. "I'm…I'm wearing a corset. I can't bend at the waist very well. And the skirt is tied on behind." She sounded unsure about the whole thing.

Seth mentally snorted to himself. Because if there was one thing a groom enjoyed on his wedding night, it was fighting through complicated layers of women's clothing. Petticoats and corsets—what was this, the 1800s? "How did you get into it?"

"I had help. My bridesmaids..."

Seth realized that if he wanted to get her on the bike anytime soon, he was going to have to play lady's maid. Which was not, he mentally reminded himself, the same as undressing her. At no point was he getting her naked.

No. Definitely not undressing a beautiful woman he wanted to pull into his arms and hold tight. Just... removing a few unnecessary layers of clothing. So that she could safely sit on his bike. That was all.

Trying to keep his mind focused on the task at hand, he eyed the bodice of her dress. "Do you need to take the corset off?" he asked reluctantly, because that seemed less like removing layers and more like just stripping her completely bare.

She shook her head quickly. "I was able to drive in it, apparently. If we can get the petticoat off, it should be fine."

Of all the things Seth thought he'd be doing today, falling to his knees in front of a runaway bride and lifting the hem of her skirt over the voluminous petticoat was not something that had made the top ten. Or even the top one hundred. But that's what he was doing. He lifted the satin of her dress, rising as he moved the fabric up.

There should have been nothing sensual about this, lifting her skirts. She was still completely dressed. The petticoat stood between him and her body. God only knew how many layers were built into it, because she was still shaped like an inverted top. So this should have been nothing.

But there was something erotic about it.

Focus, Bolton, he scolded himself. This was just an action born of necessity. He had to get her someplace safe, where people she knew could step up and take over. Taking care of a pregnant runaway bride was not in his skill set, and besides, it wasn't like he was attracted to her anyway.

Sure, she was beautiful—more so now that she'd calmed down. And yes, he was curious about what she looked like without the overdone hair, makeup and dress. And fine, he did feel a protective pull toward her. But that didn't add up to attraction any more than helping her adjust her outfit to ride on the bike was undressing her.

And that was final.

After a few snags—the petticoat was *huge*—he succeeded in getting the skirt up to her waist. He handed the bunched-up fabric to her and eyed the next layer. He could just see the bottom edge of her corset—white satin trimmed in baby blue. It appeared the waistband of the petticoat was underneath the corset.

This just kept getting better, because if he had to undo the corset, he'd have to remove the dress completely. He hoped it wouldn't come to that. If he were going to properly undress this woman, it sure as hell wouldn't be at a roadside pull-off.

He could see her chest rising and falling quickly. Did she feel the tension, too? Or was there something else?

He managed to pull his gaze away from her chest and found himself lost in her eyes. Her pupils were wide and dark and damn if she didn't look like a woman who was being undressed by a lover.

He put his hands on her waist, just below the bunched

fabric of her skirt. Her waist felt right under his hands, warm and soft—and a little hard, thanks to the corset.

Who was he to talk about instincts? Yeah, she shouldn't get married when her instincts told her to run. But his were telling him to pull her against his chest and tuck her into his arms and not let go. And fighting that instinct only got harder when she lifted her gaze to his because she took his breath away.

"Turn around," he told her because he needed not to get lost in her eyes.

He needed to keep a cool head here—among other body parts. She was not for him. Only a complete asshole would take advantage of a woman in this situation. Seth was many things, but he didn't think he was an asshole, complete or otherwise.

She turned in his arms, and Seth forced himself to step back and assess the situation. Luckily, the corset didn't ride as low in the back as it did in the front. He could see where the petticoat was tied—in a knot.

Of course it was knotted.

He was tempted to just cut the damn thing off her body, but then a shiver raced over her skin. Brandishing a blade wasn't the best way to keep her calm, so Seth gritted his teeth and got on with it. It felt like it took forever, but after only a minute or so, the knot finally gave. "Now what?" he asked as the waistband sagged down around her hips.

She didn't answer for a moment. "I had to step into it and they pulled it up because..." She swallowed. "Because it's so structured, it won't fall on its own. So I guess you'll have to push it down and I'll step out of it." Her voice shook.

Just for the ride, Seth repeated as he grabbed the

waistband of the petticoat and worked it over her hips. *Structured* must mean *able to stand upright on its own*, because the damned fabric had no give in it at all. What kind of fresh hell was this, anyway?

The petticoat slipped over her skin, and he had to bite back his groan. He barely knew this woman and he wasn't even sure he liked her. But as he revealed the frilly lace of the white thong and the bare cheeks of her bottom, *liking* had nothing to do with it. His mouth went dry and his hands started to shake.

His instincts—they were pushing him past protective and into raw lust. He was strong, but how strong did one man have to be? Because he wasn't sure he could handle the way that thong left her bottom completely exposed.

Then it only got worse as he wrestled the petticoat down and revealed inch by creamy inch of her legs and bare skin. Why couldn't she be wearing those supportive bike shorts that some women wore instead of this scrap of lace? Why couldn't she be wearing a simpler outfit? Why couldn't she be someone who didn't inspire this reaction in him?

It only got worse when he hit the top of her thigh-high stockings and the blue garter on her right leg. Of course it matched the blue trim on her corset.

Roger, Seth concluded, was an idiot to let this woman go. Because Seth was pretty sure that he was going to have fantasies about this moment for the rest of his natural life.

He struggled not to touch her skin—but his hands shook even harder with the effort of it. Although he had to fight all that "structure" for every damned inch, he managed to get the petticoat pushed down to the ground, which meant that he was at eye level with her bottom. And it was perhaps one of the nicer bottoms he had ever seen. Firm and rounded and begging to be touched.

Except it wasn't. This was not a seduction. This was an action born of necessity. He would not touch her. She'd already had a bad day, and being groped by a biker wouldn't make anything better.

"Now what?" His voice cracked with the strain of trying to sound normal. "Do you just step out?" That was when he realized she didn't have on shoes. They were standing on gravel. Had she been missing her shoes the entire time?

"I…I don't want to lose my balance," she said in a strangled-sounding voice. Before Seth could process what she meant by that, she turned. Which was good due to the fact that he was no longer staring at her ass.

But now he was staring at her front. The thin lace of her virginal white thong covered the vee of her sex and everything about Seth came to a screeching halt. His blood, his breath—nothing worked. He couldn't even blink as he stared at her body.

It only got worse when she placed one hand on his shoulder for balance. Seth squeezed his eyes shut because there was no point in looking if he couldn't have her, and he *couldn't* have her. Offering anything beyond assistance would be a mistake. She'd run away from a wedding today. She was pregnant with another man's baby. None of her was for him.

Even though his eyes were closed, the scent of her body surrounded him, torturing him. It wasn't the scent of arousal, but there was no missing the sweet notes of flowers—maybe lilacs, and a hint of vanilla that had been buried underneath the layers. Her smell reached out and stroked him, making him shake with need.

She stepped out of the petticoat and—thankfully—let go of the skirt. It fell, covering her legs and hiding that lacy thong and those white thigh-highs and that garter belt from his eyes. Seth gave himself another few moments to make sure he had himself under control.

Then she let out a little cry and stumbled. He moved without thinking, catching her before she fell. His arms folded around her body and finally, he was able to pull him to her.

But despite his awareness of her body—and the fact that her arms went around his neck so that he could feel her breasts pressing against his chest—he didn't miss the way she shivered or how her breathing was ragged.

"Easy," he said, coming to his feet with her in his arms.

"I stepped on a rock," she said, her voice wavering. She sounded like she was on the verge of tears again, and that hurt him in a way he hadn't expected.

He wanted to make sure she didn't hurt. He'd wanted that from the very beginning. But now, it felt more personal.

He didn't understand this strange drive to take care of her. He could've called her a ride. Surely someone could've come to get her. Rapid City had taxis, and for a price they could've made it out this far.

But he hadn't. He hadn't done anything except hold her close and make sure she was okay.

He didn't want to think too much about why.

He carried her over to his bike and sat her on the back. He gave thanks that his father had built this prototype with the passenger seat behind the driver's seat.

Part of Billy Bolton's rigorous testing was to make sure that he took Seth's mom, Jenny, out for rides with him. Billy claimed that sometimes, the additional weight of a passenger would reveal design flaws that needed to be tweaked. Because Seth didn't want to consider any other options about what happened when his parents went out riding, he accepted that explanation at face value.

"I'll put the petticoat in the car and then we'll go, okay?" he said. "But you're going to have to straddle the bike. See if you can figure that out with your skirts." He waved a hand over her dress and hoped like hell he wouldn't have to take the whole thing off to get her corset removed.

But even as he thought that, his brain decided it would be a really great idea. He would kill to see Kate Burroughs in nothing but a corset and some stockings and a garter. Splayed out on the bed, a package that Seth was almost done unwrapping.

He slammed the brakes on that line of thought. *Nope.* She had too many bags to carry, and he was a single twenty-five-year-old man. He had no interest in tangling with someone whose personal life was as messy as Kate Burroughs's was. No matter how good she looked, no matter how sweet she smelled, no matter how much she'd clung to his neck.

No matter how right she'd felt in his arms.

She nodded and he went back to get the petticoat. It was all dirty with rocks and bits of grass stuck in it. He shoved it into the back of the limo and glanced around, hoping against hope that there would be a purse with a wallet, but nothing. There was some champagne that was probably warm, though. But he didn't think that'd help anything right now.

He locked the limo and left the keys on the ground on the inside of the front driver's-side wheel, where Stein had told him to leave them. True dark was settling now and it was going to be a long, cold ride back to Rapid City. It wouldn't be so bad if he had his jacket, but he couldn't let her freeze to death behind him.

The other logistical problem was that he only had one helmet. He had no idea if it would fit over her hair.

He went back to the bike and picked up the helmet. "Let's see if this works," he said. At the very least, she had managed to straddle the bike. The skirt had hiked up over her calves, and her legs were going to be cold by the time they got out of the hills, but there was no way he could risk having her fall off if she was riding side-saddle. Maybe if she pressed herself against him, his body could take the worst of the wind. He'd be a Popsicle by the time they made town, but he'd take it for her.

But even that noble sentiment was almost completely overridden by the image of her arms around his waist, her chest pressed to his back, her legs tucked behind his. Of that lacy little thong and the corset.

Of a wedding night that ended differently.

He pulled at the collar of his shirt. Yeah, maybe he wouldn't freeze.

She looked up at him, her eyes wide. "I can't thank you enough, Seth," she said, her voice soft. "I'm having a really bad day, but you're making it better."

If she were anyone else, he'd cup her cheek and stroke her skin with his thumb. He'd tilt her head back and brush his lips over hers. He'd offer comfort in a completely different way.

But she wasn't anyone else. She was Roger's pregnant runaway bride. So instead of kissing her, he settled the helmet over her hair. It didn't work. He pulled it off. "Let me see what I can do here." She tilted her head so he could get at the elaborate updo—it probably had some sort of name, but he didn't have any idea about women's hair. He could see the pins and clips—sparkly stuff in her hair. And hairspray. Lots of hairspray. He began pulling them out and shoving them into his pants pocket. What would her hair feel like without all this crap in it? Soft and silky—the kind of hair he could bury his hands in.

He really had to get a grip. The whole mass of hair sagged and then fell. It looked awkward and painful, but he was sure he could fit the helmet on now. "There."

She looked back at him as he settled the helmet on her head and strapped it under her chin. She looked worried. "This will be fun," he promised. Cold, but fun. "Just hold on to me, okay?"

She nodded. Seth took his seat and fired up the engine. It rumbled beneath him. He loved this part of riding. Bringing the machine to life and knowing that a journey was ahead of him.

After a moment's hesitation, Kate's arms came around his waist. His brain chose that exact moment to wonder—when was the last time he'd had a woman on the back of a motorcycle?

Of course he'd ridden with women before. That was one of the reasons to ride a bike—women loved a bad boy, and Seth was more than happy to help them act out their fantasies. Motorcycles were good seduction and he was a red-blooded American man. He wasn't above doing a little seducing.

But there was something different about this—about Kate. This wasn't a seduction, leaving aside the fact that he knew what her thong looked like. This was something else, and he couldn't put a name to it.

Then he felt more than heard her sigh against the back of his neck as the helmet banged his shoulder. He winced but didn't flinch as she settled her cheek against his back, her arms tightening around him even more. Her body relaxed into his. Which was good. Great. Wonderful. The tighter she held on, the safer this ride would be.

Except his body was anything but relaxed. He was rock hard and she'd know it if her grip slipped south in any way.

He needed to get her to a hotel and then he needed to get on his way. He had a future as a partner of Crazy Horse Choppers. He had plans for the business. He had motorcycles to sell.

None of those things involved a pregnant runaway bride.

He rolled away from the scenic overlook and hit the road back to Rapid City.

Kate Burroughs wasn't in his plans. After today, he wasn't going to see her or her stockings ever again.

That was final.

Four

"Good morning, Katie," Harold Zanger said, strolling into Zanger Realty with a smile on his face and a bow tie around his neck. "It's a zinger of a day at Zanger, isn't it?"

As cheesy as the line was—and it had been cheesy every single day for the last month and a half—Kate still smiled. She smiled every day now. "It is indeed, Harold," she said.

Harold Zanger was one of her father's oldest friends. They'd been playing poker together for a good forty years—longer than Kate had been alive. Harold was almost an uncle to her.

Kate had not gone back to Burroughs and Caputo Realty. She just couldn't—especially when her parents had made it clear that splitting Roger off from the business was going to be quite complicated, which was one way to say that her father wasn't going to do it because he was beyond furious with her.

So it had been Kate to decide that, rather than grovel before her father and Roger, she'd start over. She was the one who put distance between them.

It had hurt more than she wanted it to, to be honest. Although she'd known it wasn't likely, she'd wanted her parents to put her first. She'd wanted them to take her side and tell her it'd all work out. She'd wanted her mom to get excited about the pregnancy.

She'd wanted the impossible. Oh, Mom was excited—to the extent that she'd underlined the word *excited* three times in the congratulations card she'd sent. Other than that, there'd been no discussion of pregnancies, no trips down memory lane, no planning for the baby's room.

There hadn't been anything, really, since Kate had walked out of their house and driven back to the hotel where she'd been staying since Seth had dropped her off and paid for three nights.

And the hell of it was, it wasn't like they had put Roger first. No, Joe and Kathleen Burroughs had done what they always did—they'd put their business first. Burroughs Realty—Burroughs and Caputo Realty now—had always been the most important thing. Her father hadn't disowned her outright, but it was clear that, for the time being, there was no point in pursuing a family relationship. Joe Burroughs was a workaholic and Kathleen refused to go against her husband's wishes.

No, the business came first, and Roger was now part owner of the business, which meant that Roger came first. So Kate had left because she hadn't wanted to make things difficult for her mother.

Harold Zanger, gregarious and happy, had offered her a job. Kate strongly suspected it had put a strain on his friendship with Joe Burroughs, but Harold insisted everything was fine. Of course, he was an eternal optimist, so perhaps everything was. Harold had given her a desk and a blazer and some business cards and told her to "get out there and sell some houses, sweetheart."

If anyone else had called Kate *sweetheart*, she would've walked, but Harold had been calling her sweetheart since she was old enough to crawl—probably even before that.

So here she was. Ready to get out there and sell some houses for Zanger Realty.

"Today's the day," Harold said, snapping the suspenders underneath his Zanger Realty blazer, which was a delightful shade of goldenrod. "Something big is going to happen today, Katie my girl. I can feel it."

There was comfort in familiarity and Harold said this to her every morning. She hadn't believed it at first—she still didn't really believe it—but Harold's optimism was infectious.

"Today's the day," she agreed.

"Your big sale," Harold all but crowed, "is going to walk through that door. I just know it."

"I'm sure it will," she said with an indulgent smile. Really, it was sweet that Harold believed what he said, because that was just the kind of man he was and had always been. If opposites attract, then that held true for friendships, too. Joe Burroughs had been a pessimist, convinced that tomorrow the bottom would fall out and the world would end and so he'd better sell a house today so that his family would have something to live on. Disaster was always lurking right around the corner for Joe Burroughs, so he had to miss his daughter's concerts and plays because there was work to be done.

Harold was the opposite. Today was a good day. Tomorrow would be even better. It would all work out in Harold's world, and Kate would be lying to herself if she said she didn't need that in her life right now.

Because she was three months pregnant. She'd sold exactly two houses—but they hadn't been big sales. She'd earned enough on commission to rent a two-bedroom apartment and buy some secondhand furniture. But she had to sell a lot of houses in the next six months if she wanted to be able to take time off when she had her baby.

Roger would pay child support. Just because he didn't love her and she didn't love him didn't mean that he would leave her out to dry. Roger wasn't a bad guy, really.

But when they had sat down face-to-face and confronted the aftermath of their relationship and the baby that would always tie them together, it had been clear—he'd been relieved that she'd walked away. And he hadn't even tried to hide it. He'd gone on their honeymoon trip to Hawaii without her and he hadn't missed her at all.

Even more than that, Roger had been relieved when her father had not asked him to give up his stake in the real estate business. Which really had Kate wondering—had he been marrying her because of her or for the business?

She knew the answer—the business—but she couldn't think about that.

If she ever had another wedding, she would be damned sure she was marrying someone who wanted her. Not her family's business. Not her name.

Her. Kate Burroughs. Future single mom and semi-professional hot mess.

Aside from child support, Roger made something else clear—they were done. He wasn't going to be an active part of raising his child. It was painful, it really was. But at the same time, it was also a relief. She wouldn't have to worry about navigating around Roger at the same school plays and concerts that her own father had skipped. She wouldn't have to negotiate who would get the baby for Christmas and birthdays. It would be simpler without Roger.

It would be harder—she was under no illusions that being the single mother of a newborn wouldn't be the hardest thing she'd ever done. But she only had to negotiate with herself.

She was on her own. For the first time in her life, she didn't have to answer to anyone. Not her father, not Roger, not her mother. There was something freeing about that. Terrifying, but freeing.

Harold went back to his office and Kate turned to her listings. She had been a real estate agent for years, so it wasn't like she was learning on the job. She knew what to do. She had grown up at Burroughs Realty, copying things for her parents and then going with them when they looked at houses. She'd learned how to stage a house when she was in high school. Her parents had paid her for her help, although not a lot.

She could sell a home in her sleep. But she needed buyers and sellers. She needed someone to walk through that door and instead of asking for Harold, to ask for

Kate. That was what she'd had at Burroughs Realty. She had been a Burroughs, and any Burroughs would do for some people. The name was the important thing.

As her thoughts often did when she was faced with the weight of her future, she imagined that one person in particular walking through the door—a tall, dark, mysterious biker. A man who looked dangerous and yet treated her as if she were worth protecting.

Seth Bolton.

She had not seen him since he had taken her to a local hotel and shaken her hand in the lobby. He hadn't even suggested that he come up to the room and make sure she got settled. He was too good a guy for that.

That had to be why she couldn't stop thinking about him. It had felt like…like there was unfinished business between them. Which was ridiculous. They didn't have any business together to begin with. She'd had the worst day of her life and he'd taken pity on her. That was all there was—a Good Samaritan doing a kind deed for a woman having a really terrible day. Because there was no way a man like that was single or available. And even if he were—why would he be interested in her? She had not made the best of first impressions.

Looking back at what had happened over six weeks ago, she could see with a little objective distance that she had been in a state of complete and total shock. Discovering she was pregnant had left her stunned. Deciding she couldn't marry Roger had been a realization that sent her reeling. Each shock mounted upon the next. She still didn't remember stealing the limo, but at least she hadn't been arrested. Whatever Seth had done or said to the limo owner had worked. The cops hadn't gotten involved, and she was beyond grateful for that. He had helped her see that her reasons for running were valid, made sure she was okay and let her cry it out.

But gratitude wasn't the only reason she kept thinking about him. There'd been the way he'd untied her petticoat and slid it down her legs. And the way she'd wrapped her arms around his waist and leaned into him on the long, cold ride back to Rapid City. Hell, even just the way his jacket had smelled—leather and something lighter, maybe sandalwood. He'd smelled good.

She was not fantasizing about the man. Oh, sure, he drifted through her dreams every so often, but that didn't mean she was fantasizing about him, specifically.

It was the fact that he had taken care of her. And she had needed to be taken care of. That was all.

She didn't need to be coddled anymore. She'd gotten back on her feet. Her parents and Roger had handled the entire disaster with a surprising amount of good humor—for them, anyway. But that didn't change the fact that, moving forward, she needed to sell a house. A lot of houses. Heck, even one big sale would get her through the winter.

While she was wishing for the impossible, she might as well ask for a pony. Sadly, Santa had never delivered on that one, either.

As she mused, she worked on assembling a potential list of houses. A family from out of town had called and said that the husband might be relocating to Rapid City. Nothing was definite yet, but there was a good chance that they'd move and if so, Kate was going to be the one to sell them a house. Harold had gifted her with this opportunity, rather than keep it for himself.

The Murray family had given her their standard list of requirements—three bedrooms, two baths, a fenced backyard, a two-car garage. She was putting together a list of potential homes and praying that Mr. Murray decided to take a job in Rapid City when the door jingled.

On reflex, Kate said, "It's a zinger of a day at Zanger. Can I help you?"

Then she looked up at the same moment a hearty chuckle reached her ears. There was something familiar about that chuckle, warm and comforting.

She froze. There was something familiar about the man standing in the entryway. Tall, dark. Black hair, dark eyes—that motorcycle jacket settled over his shoulders like a second skin.

And that smile. She didn't remember everything from her wedding day. But that smile? She'd been dreaming about that smile for a month. She was helpless to *stop* dreaming about it.

It was entirely possible, she decided as she stared at him, that she was still asleep because her fantasy had just walked into her office and into her life, hotter than ever. This was the man who'd talked her off the ledge. Who'd supported her when she'd admitted that marrying Roger would've been the biggest mistake of her life.

Who'd practically stripped her bare at a roadside overlook.

"Kate," he said, his voice stroking over her name in a way that made her toes curl. "I was hoping I'd find you."

Okay, that did it. She was definitely dreaming. "Seth? What are you doing here?"

If she were dreaming, the answer would be *I have come to sweep you off your feet, my darling. Let me take you away from all of this and solve all your problems.*

"I looked you up."

She blinked. "You did? Why?"

"I wanted to see how you were doing." He took another step into the office. "How are you doing?"

Her breath caught in her throat. As odd as it seemed, not many people asked that question. The fallout from leaving Roger at the altar had shown her who her true friends were—and the number was few and far between. Really, her mother was the only one who asked that question and was actually interested in the answer.

Except for Seth Bolton, a stranger who had seen her at her lowest moment. Instead of running, he'd stood by her side. He'd taken care of her. He'd made everything better.

Was it any wonder she'd been dreaming of him nearly every night?

This wasn't possible. She could not be watching Seth walk into her office, that sexy smile on his face, asking about how she was. It simply wasn't possible.

"I…I'm fine," she told him. "I mean, I'm all right."

"Good." His smile deepened and she was stunned to realize that he had dimples. What a difference. That made him hot and sweet and more than everything she dreamed of. "I meant to check in on you earlier, but I had some business to deal with first."

She lifted her eyebrows at that. Was he serious? She was nothing to him, other than a strange afternoon that had probably become an amusing anecdote. *Did I ever tell you about the time I found a runaway bride in the middle of the Black Hills?*

She would expect that if he remembered her at all, he'd remember the crazy woman who stole a limo and refused to marry the father of her child. Nobody should've found her desirable. Memorable, maybe. Definitely not someone worth worrying about.

"Well, as you can see, everything's okay." That was a gross generalization. She was exhausted and hormonal and worried sick about how she was going to make everything work out.

But she wasn't the same lost woman he'd found by the side of the road, either. She held her head high and faced every challenge she met with open eyes. She had a job and a purpose. She didn't need to be coddled anymore.

Not even by someone as attractive as Seth Bolton. Was it possible that he was even more gorgeous now? He took another step closer and she swore she could feel the tension between them hum, like he'd plucked the string of a violin.

The jacket was the same, but he had on a gray T-shirt with some sort of logo on it and a pair of well-worn jeans that were black. They hung low on his hips and she realized she was staring at the vee of his waist as if she'd never noticed that part of a man before.

She jerked her gaze back up, her cheeks hot. His lips quirked into a smile that did things to her. Things she hadn't felt in over a month.

No, she scolded herself. It was one thing to fantasize about a great guy she'd never have to face again. It was a completely different affair to lust after a flesh-and-blood man standing in a real estate office.

Why was he standing in a real estate office? She cleared her throat and tried to relocate her lost sense of professionalism. "Was there something I could help you with?" Or had he just come here to make sure she hadn't completely fallen apart? She hoped not. She didn't want him to think of her as this pitiful creature who couldn't function.

That string of tension that had been humming between them tightened as his eyes darkened. His gaze swept over her face, her body. Was he checking her out? Or just checking for signs of her pregnancy? It was still pretty early. Her clothes still mostly fit, although she'd already gone up a cup size in bras.

"Actually, there is," he said. "As crazy as it sounds, I'm settling down."

Oh. That sounded like…like he was setting up house with a girlfriend. Or a wife. Well. So much for that fantasy. She was not about to poach anyone's man. At least now he'd stay safely in her dreams and she wouldn't make a fool of herself over him.

She stood from the desk, straightening her tacky Zanger jacket. "I can handle all your needs. Your *real estate* needs," she added, her face burning.

Well. So much for not making a fool of herself over him.

For a second, she wished she were someone different—someone more together and charming and…

Well, someone who wasn't pregnant and coming out of a long-term relationship.

He didn't laugh. Or even snort. Instead, something in his eyes changed—deepened—and warmth spread through her body. She recognized that warmth—*desire*. It was like running into an old friend from high school she hadn't seen in a few years. She hadn't realized how much she'd missed it—until here it was.

When was the last time she had felt desire? At one point she was sure she had enjoyed sleeping with Roger, but she couldn't remember when it stopped being fun and started being routine. It hadn't been bad. It just hadn't been good.

Kind of like Roger himself.

Seth was still smiling. It would be great if she could get her act together today. Within the hour, even though that was probably too much to ask.

Still, she had to give it a try. "What sort of properties are you looking for? Because a home is very different from a condo." There. That was a viable thing to say that didn't make her sound like an idiot.

And if she wasn't making any sense, she was blaming that on the pregnancy, which went right back to Roger. So if she was flabbergasted before Seth for the second time in a few short weeks, it would be entirely Roger's fault.

She motioned for Seth to sit because standing was getting more awkward by the second. Seth took the chair in front of her desk and crossed one of his legs, bringing his heavy leather boots into view. Up closer, Kate could see that the T-shirt was for Crazy Horse Choppers, which fit with the leather jacket and the motorcycle.

In other words, he looked like a badass biker dude.

Except for those dangerous dimples. Because it took everything hard about him and made it something else. Something that had her pulse pounding in her veins, heating her from the inside out. "Tell me what you're looking for."

He held her gaze for a beat too long before he spoke. "Well, I've been back in Rapid City for about a month and a half."

Wait—did that mean he'd been living somewhere else until…until when? Had he come back for the wedding that wasn't? "Where were you before?"

"I'm not sure if you recognize my name or not but my family owns Crazy Horse Choppers."

"Um…no? I'm sorry," she quickly added. "I mean, of course I've heard of Crazy Horse Choppers."

They were one of Rapid City's most famous local businesses, started twenty or thirty years ago by a local boy made good and now run by his three sons, whose names hadn't ever really registered for Kate. She thought there'd been a reality show featuring the three unruly biker brothers a number of years ago. Kate had been in high school when it'd been on the air—and it hadn't been interesting to her then.

Clearly, she'd underestimated the power of a bad boy in a leather jacket.

She shook her head, trying to push that thought away. She was definitely going to blame that line of thinking on the pregnancy hormones. "I just didn't make the connection between you and the company," she explained. "I'm not up-to-date on motorcycles. I'd never even been on one until…"

Until he'd stripped her petticoat off her and set her on the back of his bike and she'd wrapped her arms around his waist and held on to him.

She wouldn't have thought it possible, but her face got even hotter.

"I lived in LA for a year while managing the Crazy Horse showroom we operate there," Seth said, ignoring her red face. "My father and my uncles recently made me partner in the company, so I'm thinking I need to set up a permanent base."

She eyed him. She had no idea how old Seth was, but he seemed young to be a partner in such a successful company. Was that just because it was the family business and he was family? Or was he really good at what he did?

Of course it was because he was good at what he did. He'd talked her down from the ledge, hadn't he? The man could probably sell motorcycles to anyone.

"'Permanent base'? That's not how most people describe buying a house." In fact, it sounded more like he was setting up a strategic military outpost or something.

He shrugged. "My uncle Bobby has wild expansion plans. He expects me to travel and represent the brand. But the company is based here, so I need to maintain a residence. I anticipate that I'll only be in Rapid City maybe half the year. The other thing—"

"The other thing?" A house would be a great sale. As partner to a successful and growing business, he'd want something that spoke of his power and, one assumed, wealth. Or at the very least, a condo with all the bells and whistles.

"I'm in the planning phase for a new project for Crazy Horse," he went on, ignoring her interruption. "We're going to need an industrial space for a museum."

Her mouth fell open. A house was terrific. A house *and* an industrial space?

She'd be able to live off that commission for months. She could take time off to be with her baby without having to worry about money.

Seth Bolton was her guardian angel. It was really that simple.

He was staring at her expectantly. "Kate? You okay?"

"What? Oh. Yes. Yes! I'm just…a museum?"

That grin made it plenty clear that she wasn't fooling him. "My granddad and my dad have been building choppers for thirty years. My dad's kept one of everything he's ever built, including a lot of prototypes that never saw production. He's got close to four hundred motorcycles stored in the original Crazy Horse factory. I think we can build the brand loyalty if we take those bikes out of storage and put them on display. Harley-Davidson did something similar and they've had a great response."

"Wow..." she said, which was lame and stupid but really, how was she supposed to react here? Seth Bolton was hot, kind, supportive...hot—and now also an amazing salesman and a whip-smart business owner?

Her fantasies weren't this good. They just weren't. If he also loved babies and puppies and was single, then she'd know for certain that she was having the best dream of her life.

Nothing about this made the least bit of sense. Not only was the man of her dreams—literally—sitting in front of her, suddenly in the market for a great deal of real estate, the commissions of which could carry her through the next several months, but he was part of Rapid City's most famous local family.

Underneath the desk, she pinched her leg. But nothing changed. Seth was still sitting in front of her, dimples in full force, ready to discuss all his real estate needs while also giving her those searing looks.

She was in trouble. The very best kind of trouble.

Five

One thing was clear, Seth realized as he sat across from Kate while she called up listings to give him an idea of what was on the market.

He should have checked on her sooner.

He remembered a hot woman. Okay, that had been more her body than her face because she'd had a very bad day and had looked like hell. But it was hard to forget skimming that petticoat down her legs, revealing her gorgeous ass in that little scrap of fabric—not to mention the stockings and garter.

He shifted in his seat. The woman sitting across from him in a tacky yellow blazer with Zanger embroidered on the chest wasn't *hot*.

Kate Burroughs was beautiful.

Without the false eyelashes and lopsided hair—and without the lost look in her eyes—Kate was simply stunning. Even more so because today, while it was clear that she was shocked to see him, she wasn't in a state of shock. And what a difference that made.

He might be imagining things, but she even seemed happy to see him. Surprised, sure. Excited about the business he was throwing her way, yes. But Seth saw the way she looked at him—especially the way her whole face had softened when he'd asked how she was doing.

He should've come sooner. But he'd had to represent Crazy Horse Choppers at two trade shows and Julie's soccer season had started, and although it wasn't good for his image as a tough biker, Seth was the kind of guy who went to his baby sister's games and cheered her on from the sidelines. Then there'd been a pow-wow on the reservation and career day at the school where his mom taught and moving out of his folks' house into the hotel and putting his stuff in storage and…life happened.

But he hadn't forgotten Kate Burroughs. That wasn't possible, not after their memorable introduction. But it wasn't until he'd come to the belated realization that at the age of twenty-five, he couldn't continue to live in a hotel that he had decided to seek her out.

It'd taken a lot of digging. She had apparently been the Burroughs in Burroughs and Caputo Realty for some years. Seth wasn't entirely sure what the deal was, since she was now at Zanger Realty and Roger was still at Burroughs and Caputo Realty. The whole situation was messy and Seth was not interested in messy.

Which did not explain why he was currently sitting across from the messiest woman he'd ever met.

That wasn't fair, though. She'd been a mess the day of her failed wedding, yeah. But the woman before him now? If he hadn't known she was pregnant, he never would've guessed. She looked amazing. Her golden-brown hair was free of the shellacked mass of curls that had overwhelmed her delicate features. Her hair was away from her face, but the rest of it fell in gentle waves down her back. Her eyes were the same startlingly bright green he remembered and today, they were clear and hopeful instead of lost and afraid. Without the heavy layer of makeup, he felt like he was seeing her for the first time.

Seth had seen a lot of attractive women in his time. Los Angeles was overflowing with them. But that was hotness for public display and public consumption.

Kate was more of a quiet beauty. There was just something about her.

Which was the only possible explanation as to why he was here. He couldn't stop thinking about that something and it went way beyond thongs and garter belts.

"So if you'll be traveling a lot, a condo would probably be the best property for you. The exterior maintenance is…" Seth scowled at her. Anyone else would have been terrified. But Kate merely lifted her eyebrows and…smiled? "No?"

"Don't condos—by definition—have other people living in close proximity?"

She tilted her head to one side, studying him. "Yes. It's not a stand-alone building. You would have neighbors with whom you'd share walls."

He shook his head. "No. LA was full of people who talked all the time because they were afraid if they didn't, no one would notice how important they were. I couldn't stand it." Among other things. He'd hoped that getting the hell out of South Dakota would be the answer for this restlessness.

It hadn't been. Traveling the world and selling motorcycles was probably the cure for what ailed him.

Yet here he was, buying a damned house while planning on barely living in it. He went on, "I want peace and quiet. No neighbors."

"You're talking to me," she pointed out, pinning him to his chair with her gaze.

"You're different," he said and the funny thing was, it wasn't a line he was feeding her. He meant it. He couldn't have said why, but she was. "So I need a house."

"With enough land to protect you from nosy neighbors. What else do you need? I'm assuming a garage is important—or room to build your own?"

He had to hand it to her as she grilled him on the number of bathrooms and bedrooms he required or if he wanted a finished basement or would he consider building from scratch—the woman knew what she was doing. He'd had some vague notion of a house that he now realized didn't look all that different from his parents' home.

But his parents' home was built for a family. And Billy's bikes, but it'd been sprawling enough to house the fourteen-year-old boy Seth had been when Billy had married Jenny Wawausuck and adopted Seth and big enough to hold them all when Julie had been born the next year.

It'd been a family home. And that was not what Seth wanted, as he had no plans to start a family anytime soon. Not even by accident. He was careful.

So he wasn't settling down. Not even a possibility. Billy Bolton—hell, all the Bolton men—might be dyed-in-the-wool family men, but Seth was a Bolton in name only.

Still, he needed a place to keep his stuff and the freedom to come and go—and have guests over—without his parents keeping tabs on him.

He looked at the photos of the four or five houses she'd pulled up, but nothing jumped out at him. "I need to walk through them," he said.

"Absolutely," she agreed. "Pictures can tell us a lot, but they can't give you a real sense of how the house will work for you. I'll need to schedule tours, if that's all right. Only a few of these houses are empty. Unless you are looking to buy today?"

Seth snorted. "This isn't a snap decision. I want to make sure I find the right place. Even if I don't live there full-time, I still want it to be home." He didn't know if that was possible or not, but at the very least, he wanted something he could be proud of.

Besides, owning and caring for his own home would just further prove to his father and his uncles that they'd made the right decision in making Seth a partner in Crazy Horse Choppers, and he couldn't let the Bolton men down. Not after everything they'd done for him.

His parents hadn't been huge fans of Seth relocating to a hotel and, aside from room service, neither was Seth. But as much as he loved his family, he hadn't been able to move back in with them after a year in LA. So if he had to pay for a hotel, then he paid for the hotel. He had the money to spare.

Kate nodded eagerly. "And if none of these houses are right, there are always more houses coming on the market. Sometimes we get notice before properties are officially listed—as long as you've got the time, the right house for you is out there."

She made it sound like it was only a matter of patience. Seth was not always the most patient of people. His dad said it was because he was still young and stupid—although Seth didn't feel particularly young or particularly stupid.

Seth was afraid it was something else. Billy was a good father—but it wasn't his blood that ran through Seth's veins. What if this restlessness wasn't just youth?

What if it was something he'd inherited from his birth father, the sperm donor?

Seth pushed that question away. He didn't like to compare himself to the man who'd abandoned Jenny Wawausuck when she'd been pregnant, never to show his face again. Seth was a Bolton now. The past didn't matter. Only the future.

A future where he owned a sizable chunk of a family business as well as his own home. "That's fine. Saturday? We can make a day of it. Unless you have other plans?"

Because he had no idea. It was a fair assumption that, since she was no longer at the office where Roger worked and—he glanced down at her hand—she wasn't wearing any ring, she wasn't actively involved with anyone. Kate didn't strike him as the kind who rebounded indiscriminately.

But that didn't mean she might not have something to do on a Saturday.

Kate smiled and damn if Seth wasn't dazzled by it. "Saturday would be perfect. Now tell me about this museum you're planning. Does it need to be close to the production facility? Do you want to build to suit or adapt a preexisting space? Do you have a handle on how much square footage you're looking at?"

Seth took a deep breath. The museum was his idea—he'd toured the Harley-Davidson museum in Milwaukee a while back and had been damned impressed. He didn't want to replicate that facility, because the Crazy Horse collection was vastly different from the Harley collection.

Seth still remembered the first time Billy had taken him to see all the choppers that he'd built. Seth had been like a kid in a candy store. The original choppers were impressive, but what had blown his teenaged mind had been the wild prototypes Billy had created over the years.

That was what he wanted to capture—that feeling of shock and awe that only a Crazy Horse chopper could inspire. And he wanted to capitalize on that experience. The motorcycle business had its ups and downs and having a secondary stream of income—or even tertiary stream—to help even out the lows was a good business decision. After several interesting discussions—and only one fistfight—the Boltons had agreed to spot him the capital. He just needed a property.

Besides, it wasn't like he was making it up as he went along. He had a master's in business administration. He hadn't needed a college degree to build choppers—he'd been doing that by Billy's side since he'd been thirteen.

But running a business was not the same thing as welding a frame. And the Bolton men had been good to Seth for last ten years of his life. His father and his uncles were demonstrating a great deal of faith in Seth. He couldn't screw this up and run the family legacy into the ground. His adopted last name meant he had to make sure the family business stayed relevant and important.

"We're still in the idea phase," he finally said. Which really meant it was all still in his head. "At least sixty thousand square feet. I'm envisioning the museum, a gift store, a café—maybe an area where we can have special exhibits. And possibly a showroom. We're still selling bikes out of the factory, but I don't think that's sustainable. If it's closer to the original factory, that'd be ideal, but it doesn't have to be. I hope that makes sense," he added.

Her eyes lit up. He couldn't tell if she was excited by the vision or the commission it would generate. Which was fine. He didn't need her to be excited about his big plans. Once he'd realized she was in real estate, the whole reason he'd come looking for her at work was to give her the commission. It'd been important to him.

He honestly wasn't sure why—she wasn't his responsibility. But he needed several properties, and he wasn't on a first-name basis with any other real estate agents. So why shouldn't he help out a soon-to-be single mom? God knew that Seth's mom could've used a hand up before Billy came into their lives.

He was paying forward the good fortune Billy Bolton had brought into Seth's life. It was that simple.

But it didn't feel simple when Kate leaned forward, her gaze locked on his. It felt messy and complicated and…right.

"It makes perfect sense," she told him. "But I'm going to need to do some research as to what's available. Do you have a budget in mind?"

Seth shifted nervously. The budget was, predictably, the part Ben and Billy objected to the most. "I'd like to get a list of potential properties and the associated costs first so we can budget for design and building after that." Billy was not in the mood to spend millions and millions of dollars on this. The only reason he'd agreed to the museum in the end was because Seth had promised that he'd take care of everything and Billy could just keep right on building bikes.

Kate nodded and took a few notes. "This will be a process," she warned him. "We could have a house under contract in a matter of weeks. The commercial property is much more involved—months of looking at properties, negotiating with sellers and dealing with architects."

Months of riding around with Kate, spending time with her when neither of them were under extreme duress. Months of getting to know her. Months of seeing that particular smile.

"Are you trying to talk me out of this?" God knew Billy had. He hated anything that distracted from building bikes.

And yeah, it was true that they didn't have a company without the bikes. But no one could compete in today's market without having a plan for the future.

So this was Seth's plan. He'd buy a house so he could be on hand to manage the museum project and the Bolton brothers. He'd prove that he had what it took to help the company and the family prosper.

That he had what it took to be a Bolton.

Kate's cheeks flushed as she dropped her gaze to the desktop. "No," she said quickly. "I just want you to go into this with realistic expectations." She looked up at him through her lashes. "It means we'll have to work together. A lot," she emphasized, as if the idea of spending more time with her was a deal breaker instead of one of the main reasons he was here in the first place.

Seth fought the urge to reach across her desk and cup her cheek in his hand. “Kate,” he said in all seriousness, “why do you think I looked you up?”

Six

Kate was always polished and professional when she showed houses. Nobody wanted a real estate agent who was slovenly. That was just a fact. She was careful with her hair and makeup and put forth her best appearance.

But for this afternoon with Seth? She had gone above and beyond her normal preparations. She hadn't just carefully applied mascara—she'd primed and preened, showered and shaved until she was as glamorous as she could possibly be on her budget. If she'd had the cash, she would have gotten her hair blown out. As it was, she'd used hot rollers to tease her hair into a delicate half twist that she'd seen on Pinterest. It'd taken her a good half hour, which was a solid twenty-five minutes longer than she normally spent on her hair.

She was also thankful her best pair of trousers had buttoned. True, that button was straining as she drove her car toward the first house on the schedule for the day. If she were alone in the car, she'd undo the button and let her stomach relax.

But she wasn't alone. Seth Bolton was in her passenger seat, filling the space with his raw masculinity and leather jacket, tapping his fingers on his jeans. They were a dark-wash denim today, not nearly as scuffed as the black ones he'd worn the last time she'd seen him. And instead of a distressed T-shirt, he had on a gray flannel shirt. She'd never thought of gray flannel as a particularly attractive fabric before, but on him?

Yup. Keeping her button fastened and her baby bump sucked in.

Every day it seemed her clothing shrank just that much more. And for a woman who'd maintained a steady weight since she'd lost the freshman fifteen during her sophomore year, to suddenly be faced with a wardrobe that might not fit today and most definitely wouldn't fit tomorrow was more than a little daunting. Not to mention that she had to buy replacement clothes on a supertight budget.

She could tell by the way Seth fidgeted that he wasn't used to being a passenger but despite that, he hadn't changed the radio station or adjusted the mirrors or any of the other things Roger had always done every time she'd had to drive him home after he'd had too much to drink.

After all, Seth had arrived at Zanger Realty this morning on a motorcycle that didn't look familiar. Not that she remembered much about her wedding day fiasco, but she was certain that the bike hadn't been candy-apple red.

She'd never been into bikers before, but looking at

that beautiful machine this morning as Seth straddled it, his hair tousled from the wind, those dimples in full force…

She shivered and pushed those thoughts aside. She really needed Seth to buy a house. Even if his big ideas about the museum of motorcycles fell through, as long as he bought a nice house with a big piece of land attached, it'd be enough. But if there was something more…

She was being absolutely ridiculous as she turned onto the street of the first house. "We've got thirteen houses today," she warned him.

"Is that a lot? It seems like a lot," he said in a thoughtful voice before he turned that winning smile on her.

It was a good thing she was sitting because that smile was dangerous to her balance. "I've done more in a day. I don't anticipate you'll love them all."

"You mean, we might have to do this again sometime?"

Was she imagining things or did he sound happy about that prospect? "If you don't find something you like, we might."

"That would be too bad, wouldn't it?"

He was just a Good Samaritan, she reminded herself. A hot, kind, wealthy Good Samaritan. He'd probably been a Boy Scout or something and this house-hunting expedition was the adult equivalent of helping an old lady across the street.

He'd comforted her on the day of her not-wedding. He'd made sure that she was safe and secure in a hotel that night. He hadn't taken advantage of her confusion or vulnerability.

Seth Bolton was a hell of a good guy. Maybe the best she'd ever known.

"Saturdays are usually free for me—after about eleven," he added. "We could have a standing date."

Oh, Lord—how was she supposed to react to that? "We might have to do that," she said, keeping her voice carefully professional. "Even if you love a house today, there are still the commercial properties to deal with."

A standing date didn't mean anything. Hell, it wasn't even a date. For all she knew, he always looked at women with that intensity. He probably wasn't flirting on purpose and besides—why would he flirt with *her*? She was pregnant and had not demonstrated the best of judgment. He might not hold abandoning Roger against her, but he'd be well within his rights to blame her for settling on Roger in the first place. Frankly, who could blame him?

So there wasn't anything here. He was using her as his real estate agent out of the kindness of his heart. It was a generous thing to do, but that was it.

She absolutely should not be thinking about Seth and dating in the same breath. No dating. He was a client. That was final.

How many times would she have to repeat that before she believed it?

"This property," she said as she pulled up in front of the split-level ranch in the Rapid Valley neighborhood because she was a professional and would not ask if his Saturdays were free because he was single, by God, "has a three-car garage." It was the only redeeming feature of the property, but she wasn't going to say that out loud. It was an ugly house. The shrubs were overgrown, the paint was peeling—absolutely no curb appeal, and she could tell from the pictures that the inside was in no better shape.

If it were up to her, it would be a complete teardown. But it wasn't. All she could do was sell the positives of any home. She almost hadn't put this house on the list, but sometimes seeing a house a client definitely didn't want helped clarify what they did, and since Seth had been vague about what he wanted—beyond no neighbors—she had to work from the process of elimination.

"So there would be plenty of room for a workshop and multiple motorcycles. Or a car, assuming you have one?"

"I own a car." He chuckled. "And a truck. Don't forget that I grew up in Rapid City. We have this thing called winter—maybe you've heard of it?"

She shot him a look. "I'm familiar with the concept."

Oh, there were those dimples again. She really needed to stop making him smile. "I also have three personal motorcycles, but I've been known to test out prototypes. It'd be great to have space for all of them."

In the week and a half since Seth Bolton had walked into Zanger Realty, Kate's dreams had gotten a lot more vivid. It wasn't like she hadn't dreamed of him before—she had.

Maybe it was the pregnancy hormones—that was her answer to every strange new change in her mind and body. Because her dreams now weren't just nonsensical images all jumbled together. Her dreams of Seth stripping her down—again—and this time instead of shaking her hand and riding off into the night, he laid her out on a bed and spent the evening feasting on her body.

She always woke up unsatisfied, with an edge of longing that no dream could fully erase.

Seth looked at the property. “It’s kind of ugly.”

“But there’s a lot of potential,” she pointed out. He slanted a side-eye look at her and she realized that she had said that with a little too much fake enthusiasm. “Okay, it’s a little ugly. But there are things you can do to make it less hideous.”

“You’re really selling it,” he said drily. “I guess we should look inside?”

“Never judge a book by its cover,” she agreed.

He snorted. “The Boltons are a family of bikers. They look like mercenary criminals but underneath, they’re all great big teddy bears.” He paused, hand on the handle. “Don’t tell my dad I called him a teddy bear.”

She laughed as they got out of the car. “It’s all confidential,” she reminded him.

The split-level ranch did not improve in appearance outside the car. “It better have one hell of a kitchen,” Seth commented, kicking at the unmowed grass.

Kate winced. Well, now she knew that a good kitchen was important. “Don’t see what it is. See what it can be.”

Seth scowled at her. “The other twelve aren’t this ugly, are they?”

“No. I don’t normally tell people this, but we’re going in order from what I think you’re least likely to buy. But,” she added before he could suggest skipping half the list, “I’ve been wrong before. People can be surprising in what they want, and I don’t know you well enough yet to be able to say definitively what you’ll like and what you won’t.”

Seth’s gaze snapped to hers and there it was again, that tension between them that hummed like a string, and Kate's brain took that moment to remind her this was the man who'd stripped her skirts off her and gotten a full view of her wedding thong.

He took a step closer. "I imagine," he said, his voice low, "that if we make this a standing date, you'll figure out what I'm looking for real quick."

She could feel the heat in her cheeks, but she couldn't look away, couldn't put any distance between them. "I imagine I will," she murmured.

His eyes darkened, and he looked dangerous in the very best sort of way.

Against her will, her body pitched toward his. His lips parted—he had nice lips, full and warm and…

"Kate." His voice stroked over her name like a lover's kiss as he took another step closer.

"Seth," she replied. It came out high and breathy.

Good God, what the hell was she doing? She couldn't—really, she *couldn't*. She was pregnant and coming off a failed long-term relationship and he was a client and…and…well, there were just a lot of really good reasons why she couldn't act on any of her fantasies right now.

She pulled away before she did something idiotic, like throw herself at him. "We…" She cleared her throat and tried again in her real estate agent voice. "We should go inside."

Some of the heat in his gaze cooled. "We should," he agreed. But he didn't sound happy about it.

And he didn't get any happier as they toured the house. The place was just as hideous on the inside as it was on the outside. The kitchen still had original appliances, the carpet was probably early 1980s—a cream color that had dimmed to a dull gray with grime. The wallpaper was peeling in the bathroom, and the tub was the stuff of horrors.

Kate cleared her throat. “As you can see, there is room to grow.”

Seth snorted again. “But what? Is that mold, do you think? You shouldn’t be breathing this air.” He ushered her out of the bathroom, his hand on the small of her back. When they were in the hallway, he didn’t remove it.

“You have to look into the future. Do you want room for a girlfriend or a wife?” She swallowed. “A family?”

His hand dropped away from her waist. “I don’t have any plans for family anytime soon and I’m not seeing anyone,” he told her. He stopped in the middle of peeking into the linen closet. “How are things going? With the pregnancy, I mean.”

Kate blushed from the tips of her ears to her toes. “Good.” Aside from her parents and Roger and Harold, few people knew she was pregnant. It had been hard enough to explain to everyone why the wedding was off without the added complication of an unplanned pregnancy. She had wanted to keep it quiet for long as long as possible.

Which meant she wasn’t very good at talking about it yet.

Seth peeked into the third bedroom and winced in horror at the walls. “Is Roger going to step up?”

“In his way,” she admitted. “He’s been willing to provide child support.”

Seth heard what she didn’t say. “But nothing else?”

The concern in his eyes did things to her that had nothing to do with his dimples or her inability to stop blushing. He cared, damn his hide. He cared about her and her pregnancy, and she had the urge to tell him about all the strange things happening to her because he was the only person who'd asked. "No. We should look at the basement."

They went downstairs. The heart-of-pine paneling had seen better days, just like everything else in this house. "So he's not going to be a father to his child. Typical."

Kate was surprised by the bitterness in Seth's voice. "That's an accurate assessment of the situation," she said. When he gave her a hard look, she added, "Which is for the best, honestly."

"If you say so." He surveyed the rest of the basement room, his hands on his hips. "I think we're done here. We can cross this off the list."

"Done." They headed outside. "No more split-level ranches?"

"Good Lord, no," he said, getting back into the car. "I like the idea of having room to grow, though. There's always the possibility of houseguests, at the very least. Julie might come over."

She nodded and tried not to imagine what sort of houseguest this Julie would be. Young, pretty and not pregnant, most likely. Kate shook her head trying to get images out of her mind and focused on her job—the job she desperately needed.

She wished she could show him her favorite house—the one in the Colonial Pines neighborhood that had been on the market for almost a year. If she'd been able to afford it, she would have snapped that home up in a heartbeat. But even with combining her and Roger's incomes, the house on Bitter Root was out of reach—it was over twice the price of homes like this one and she didn't want to push Seth into more house than he wanted.

So she put that house out of her mind and focused on her job. "We have other options. One down, twelve more to go."

Seth groaned.

Seven

"I take it from the expression on your face that this one's a no, too?"

Seth was all for wood-burning stoves, but not ones that left scorch marks up a wall and dark shadows on the ceiling. "How is it possible that the house hasn't burned down?" Even as he said, his foot hit a particularly creaky board and he hoped like hell he wasn't about to fall through.

Kate sighed and put a hand to her lower back. "These are the houses at this price range," she began, closing her eyes and stretching.

"Then we go up." He had the money.

Even though Seth and his mom had lived comfortably—more than comfortably—for ten years with Billy Bolton, old habits died mighty hard. Seth had been looking at the cheaper end of homes simply because there was a part of his brain convinced that was all he should spend on a house.

That part of his brain was wrong. He could afford homes that cost four times the ones they'd spent the day staring at.

He was a partner in a wildly successful business. He had to start thinking like one. And living like one, too. Which would be good for Kate, too. A more expensive house for him would be a bigger commission for her.

He watched Kate sway as she massaged her lower back. They had walked through thirteen houses—only three of which were even remotely habitable. And she was pregnant. He had kept her on her feet all afternoon and clearly, she was tiring.

God, he was a cad. He wished he could make this easier on her. But he wasn't going to buy a mediocre house just so she wasn't on her feet as much.

Not that she looked pregnant. Instead, she looked *lush* and it took most of his willpower to keep from touching her. Her hair shone and her figure—she was a perfect hourglass. A voluptuous, decadent hourglass figure that he wanted to appreciate properly.

But he didn't. He was a gentleman, by God. But then she made a moaning noise and what was left of his willpower went up in smoke.

He stepped in close and pushed her hands aside. This was a bad idea, and yet he settled his hands on her hips, rubbing his thumbs in circles along the small of her back, and damned if she didn't feel right under his touch.

"Would you buy any of these houses?" he asked, trying to focus on relieving her tension instead of the way her body filled his hands.

For a long second, she didn't respond. She held her back straight, and her arms awkwardly hung at her sides. But then he must've found the right spot because all of a sudden, she sighed heavily and leaned back into his touch. "I would not," she admitted. "But my housing needs are different than yours. If I were to buy a home, it'd need to be a family home."

"Where are you living now? Not with Roger, right?" When Seth had found her at the scenic overlook, she had made it very clear that she couldn't go back to the place she'd shared with Roger. Seth knew that she had been at the hotel for a week—because the room had been charged to his credit card. But where she'd gone after she'd checked out, he didn't know.

"No, not with Roger." She sighed again, leaning back into him some more. "We… You shouldn't…"

"Hush," he said, closer to her ear than he should've been. She was right—he shouldn't be touching her like this and certainly not in a crappy house he wasn't going to buy. Funny how that wasn't stopping him. "Was this the last house?"

She nodded, not pulling away as he worked at her tired muscles.

"I'm taking you to dinner. No argument," he said quickly when she jolted. "We'll discuss real estate things. But I'm hungry and you need to get off your feet."

He could feel the tension in her body and there was a moment when he knew she was going to say no. And really, why had he asked? He was tired, too. He'd been sociable and chatty all afternoon and he should've been absolutely done with other people.

Instead, he was kneading her tired muscles and hoping she'd say yes. To dinner, that was. Nothing else.

But she wasn't going to. He let go of her hips as she stepped away from him. When she turned, her eyes were in shadows. "Dinner?"

It wasn't a no. He wanted to take her to an expensive place, with haute cuisine and complicated wine lists. He wanted to show her he was more than a biker, more mature than any other twenty-five-year-old. God knew he had the money now to wine and dine her. Hell, he could buy a restaurant for her if she wanted.

Suddenly, he realized he didn't want to take her to a fancy place. Yeah, he wanted to impress her—but for some reason, it also felt important that he show her who he really was.

And who he really was, was a biker. A multimillionaire business owner, yeah—but choppers were his life. "Sure. There's a great burger place not too far from here, but it's whatever you want."

She tucked her lower lip under her teeth and worried at it. The effort it took not to stare was surprising. "I should buy you dinner," she announced. "You paid for the hotel."

No way was that happening. "The hotel was a wedding gift. A not-wedding gift," he corrected with a smile when she opened her mouth to argue. "Dinner's on me. What are you in the mood for?"

He hadn't heard a no yet—but he still hadn't gotten a yes, either. "I'm sure you have someone you'd rather have dinner with."

Well, wasn't *that* an interesting statement? Was it possible that Kate Burroughs was jealous? It was, of course. But—jealous of who?

Then she answered the question for him. "This Julie—she's probably waiting on you?"

Seth knew it was not a good idea to laugh at an expectant mother. He fought it as hard as he could, but he lost ground little by little. His lips twitched up and then they broke open into a wild grin and the next thing he knew, he was chuckling.

Kate looked indignant. "What's so funny?" she demanded, crossing her arms in front of her chest.

The sight of that had Seth standing straighter at attention. "Julie's my little sister. She just turned ten. She's a year younger than Clara, and almost the same age as Eliza. We're all cousins." At this point, he couldn't explain his family tree without a whiteboard and color-coded markers. The all-purpose designation of "cousins" would have to do. "They are a tough pack of middle-school girls. You should see them play soccer sometime—they're brutal."

He didn't know what she had expected him to say, but it was pretty clear that wasn't it. Kate's mouth opened and then shut, her brow furrowed, then her mouth opened and shut again.

Seth smirked and took her by the elbow, leading her out of the house that might well burn down tomorrow. Gallantly, he opened the driver's-side door and bowed her into her seat. "You have two minutes to decide if you want burgers or not. I'm hungry."

It took less than two seconds before Kate said, "I would kill for some french fries," in a tone of voice that made it sound like french fry cravings were a crime. "Does this place have ice cream?" she asked hopefully.

"Malts *and* milkshakes."

She sighed, a noise that shot straight through him. "Burgers it is."

In short order, they were sitting in Seth's favorite booth at Mike's All Night Diner. Kate looked around nervously because Mike's was not quite a bar, but it was popular with a certain clientele. In fact, her car had been the only car in a parking lot full of bikes. But this was a family restaurant. People came here to eat. If they wanted to get drunk and brawl, there were bars for that.

"You come here often?" she asked as a guy in motorcycle leathers walked past them.

Seth shrugged. "Often enough. Don't forget, I own part of a motorcycle company. This was normal when I was growing up."

In fact, now that he had her here, he wasn't sure that this was a good idea. The odds of him being recognized by one of his dad's buddies were pretty decent and this could be an intimidating crowd. Kate stuck out worse than a thumb, sore or not, and word would probably get back to his dad.

Damn.

She really didn't belong in a place like this. He should've taken her to a classy place, with linen tablecloths and snooty waiters and artistically displayed food on oddly shaped plates.

Then again, he'd been so busy since he'd officially returned to Rapid City that he hadn't had time to catch up with the old gang. It just wasn't a priority—not right now, anyway.

Not that he would ever admit it out loud and certainly not in a joint like this, but Seth had missed his sister and even his parents. However, the phrase "you can't go home again" turned out not just to be a tired cliché but an absolute truth. Seth loved his family, but he didn't fit in their household anymore.

Still, he hadn't seen a single home today that made him want to give up his suite of rooms at the Mason Hotel. There, at least, he could come and go as he pleased, the bed was always freshly made and if he ate out too much, well, it wasn't that different from how he'd lived in LA.

The waitress took their orders—Kate went with a chocolate shake and Seth ordered an extra side of fries. Once they were alone again, he waited.

She didn't make him wait long. "Can I ask you a question?"

God only knew where this would go. "Of course."

"How old are you?"

Seth notched an eyebrow at her. "Does it matter?"

He had the feeling she was older than he was—not much older, but she might be anywhere from twenty-five to her early thirties. And really, was that such a big leap from twenty-five? No. It wasn't. It wasn't like he was thinking improper thoughts about a grandmother, for crying out loud.

He cleared his throat and shifted in his seat. It wasn't like he was thinking improper thoughts about her at all. She was his real estate agent. The only thing that mattered between them was that she helped him find the right properties.

Yeah, right.

"No, no," she defended weakly. "It's just that you seem a little…old to have a sister who's only ten."

He couldn't stop the smirk if he wanted to. "Technically, she's my half sister. My mom married into the Bolton family when I was fourteen."

He could see her doing the math in her head. It really wasn't complicated—except, of course it was. And he still didn't have a whiteboard to help explain the ways the Bolton half of his family overlapped with the Lakota half.

"Oh. I just assumed..."

"That I'm really a Bolton? I am—Dad adopted me. But I'm also a full-blooded member of the Pine Ridge Lakota tribe." He hoped that was enough of an answer for her, because he didn't want to get into his birth father, the sperm donor. Not at Mike's, not ever.

She dropped her gaze to the table, and he saw that she was nervously twisting the straw wrapper around her fingers. Seth had a moment of panic—his heritage wasn't going to be an issue, was it? He'd grown up on the reservation with his tribe, where he'd been loved and protected and then, when Billy had adopted him, the Bolton name—and reputation of his dad—had shielded him from the worst of the bullying off the reservation.

But that didn't mean he didn't know racism existed, in both subtle and overt ways. Once he'd left the rez, he'd seen how kids at his new high school had talked about other Native kids. He heard stories from his friends on the rez. And his dad had made damn sure he knew how to defend himself.

Part of that defense mechanism was not announcing his heritage until he was sure of his reception. And sometimes, that meant he never found the right time to tell a paramour before the relationship drifted away.

Within his family, his ethnicity wasn't just accepted, it was normal. *Welcomed.* His dad and his uncles came to powwows and helped out at the school on the rez and had married into the tribe. They hired Seth's uncles and cousins and friends from the rez to work in the factory. It all overlapped and blended together. Just like it had in Seth.

They'd never demanded that to be a Bolton, he had to give up being a Wawausuck. His legal name was Seth James Wawausuck Bolton. He was safe to be both, and that freedom was not something he took lightly.

It shouldn't matter what Kate believed, really it shouldn't. Because there was nothing more than a professional business relationship between them.

Except…

Except for the way she'd leaned into his touch as he'd rubbed circles on the small of her back. And the way she'd looked when he'd stripped the petticoat off her. And the way her entire face had lit up when he'd walked into her office—and that was before he'd told her why he was there.

Okay, it mattered, what she thought. It mattered a lot.

Kate opened her mouth just as the waitress arrived with their food and said, "Anything else?" as she unloaded enough french fries to feed an army.

Seth eyed the plates of food. Mike didn't mess around with his burgers, and the malt was huge. There was easily enough food for five on the table, but Kate was staring at it with something that looked like devotion. "I think we're good," he said.

The waitress left and Seth turned his attention back to Kate. She was staring at him openly. "Is it a problem?" He wasn't talking about the food.

"Of course not," she said easily. But she looked worried. "It's just…"

She picked up a fry and slid it slowly between her lips as she nibbled at the tip.

Who knew that eating french fries could be so erotic?

"You obviously have a really complex family history," she finally said.

Seth snorted. "That doesn't begin to cover it." Which was not an observation that let him relax. Crap, why had he brought it up at all? Oh, right—because Kate had thought Julie was a girlfriend and it had been important to make sure Kate knew that wasn't true.

He sighed and picked up his burger. Deep thoughts about identity and fathers could wait. "Eat, Kate. I know you're starving." And one fry at a time wasn't going to make much of a dent in this meal.

They made good headway into the food. Kate ate delicately—but she ate, thank God. Finally, she said, "I'm glad you came for me at Zanger, Seth."

"Are you?" Because there were several different ways he could interpret that statement. She might be happy about the commission, the chance to say thank you for the hotel room or…

"I'd been wondering about you," she replied, not quite meeting his gaze.

He let that statement settle around the table as he scooted the extra fries toward her. She'd cleared her plate. "In a good way?"

She nodded. "I…" She took an especially deep breath. "Most people wouldn't have done what you did for me."

Which part? Depositing her safely at a hotel? Or stripping off her petticoat? "I think you underestimate people."

That got a rueful chuckle out of her. "No, I don't. I

almost married Roger. And you haven't even met my father. People like you are rare, Seth." She looked at him through thick eyelashes. "You're special. You just don't realize it."

That sure as hell seemed to answer at least one question. A question that set his blood to pounding in his veins.

His hands itched to settle around her waist again. She wanted special? Hell, he could show her special. Slow and tender and hot and very, very *special*.

He put the brakes on those thoughts—something he was doing a lot around her. She was not technically available. She was expecting and they were working together and he didn't have any interest in being a rebound.

Well, not a lot of interest, anyway. But when she looked at him like that he had to admit that yeah, maybe he was a little interested.

"You know what I think?" he said, snagging a few more fries.

"Split-level ranches are the work of the devil?"

He snorted and damn near choked on a fry. "That, too. But seriously—I think you don't realize how special *you* are."

Her cheeks shot past a delicate blush and straight on over into red. "I'm not special. I'm a mess. You know that."

He considered that statement. "The situation is messy, maybe. But," he went on as she gave him an arch look, "that doesn't make you a mess. You believe leaving Roger at the altar makes you an utter failure, and when I look at you, all I see is one of the strongest, bravest women I've ever met."

She gasped, a hand covering her chest, right over her heart. "Seth…"

"No, I'm serious." He wasn't going to let her undermine her worth. "You walked away from a crap marriage and gave up your family business, right?"

She nodded, her eyes getting suspiciously bright.

"You know why? Because you're going to have a baby and you'd do anything—*anything*—to give that child the very best life possible. To walk away from everything you know, even though you know it's going to be hard—because it's the right thing to do? You amaze me, Kate. You simply amaze me."

Aw, hell. Sincere compliments were a bad idea, because now she was crying. Quiet tears slipped down her cheeks, and he couldn't stand that.

He leaned over the table and cupped her face in his hand, swiping at her tears.

"I'm sorry," he said softly. "I didn't mean to make you cry."

"Don't you dare take that back." She sniffed, grabbing a napkin and dabbing at her eyes. "That's the nicest thing anyone's ever said to me."

Wasn't that a shame? Her former fiancé, her father—had anyone ever noticed who Kate really was?

He sat back as she took a bunch of deep breaths and got herself under control. "Sorry—hormones," she said, giving him a watery smile.

"Don't apologize. It was rude of me to ambush you with compliments."

That got him a slightly less watery smile. "It was, wasn't it?"

A strange silence settled over the table and then a movement behind Kate caught Seth's eye. Oh, hell—it was Jack Roy, one of Billy Bolton's oldest friends. Seth gave a friendly nod of his head to Jack, hoping the man would just keep moving without stopping.

No such luck. "Seth! Finally out and about?" Jack stood over the table, grinning down at Kate. "And who do we have here? Hello, beautiful."

Later? Seth was going to stab the man. Repeatedly. Jack Roy was a born flirt and had the kind of face a lot of women went for. And now he was smiling down at Kate and she was blinking up at the man, stunned by the force of his smile.

"Jack," Seth said, hearing the tension in his voice but seemingly unable to sound any more relaxed, "this is Kate Burroughs, my real estate agent. Kate," he went on, mentally willing Jack to get the hint and leave, "this is Jack Roy, head painter at Crazy Horse."

"And a whole lot more," Jack murmured in a seductive voice that Seth had heard him use on every female he'd ever met.

Kate's cheeks colored again as she dropped her gaze to the table. Crap, this was terrible. Not only was Jack interrupting just as things had gotten interesting, now the man would probably call Dad up and ask if Billy knew Seth had been having dinner with a pretty real estate agent. How much had Jack caught? Had he seen Seth cup Kate's cheek? Or wipe away Kate's tears?

Damn it all. Seth pivoted and launched a careful kick in the direction of Jack's shins. The man flinched but, to his credit, didn't even let out a stream of obscenities.

Instead, he turned that smile up to full power. "You make sure this one treats you right," he said, a hint of steel behind his seductive voice as he nodded at Seth.

Kate's eyes widened in surprise. "Oh, no—we're just working together."

The quick defense pricked at Seth's pride, even if it was exactly what she should have said because it was the truth. "I'm buying a house," he added.

By God, if Jack made some sort of crack about how Seth was all grown up and a big boy now, the man's handsome nose would never look the same.

Jack's mouth opened and then he closed it. "Well, then," he said, notching a knowing eyebrow at Seth. Hopefully Kate couldn't see it. "I'll let you two get back to *business*." He reached down and appropriated one of Kate's hands, bowing over it. "Ms. Burroughs, it has been a true pleasure." Then the bastard kissed her knuckles.

A rumbling noise startled everyone at the table. It was only when both Kate and Jack turned to look at Seth that he realized the noise—a growl—was coming from him.

Jack's mouth curved into a knowing grin and Seth realized he'd walked right into Jack's trap. The jerk had intentionally provoked Seth with that kiss.

"Jack," Seth managed to get out without strangling the man.

"Seth—be good," Jack said with another wink before he finally, finally left.

Seth scowled at the man's back as he walked away. When he glanced back over at Kate, she was staring at him with what looked uncomfortably like confusion on her face.

Well, this evening was shot to hell. And he wasn't even sure what he'd wanted before Jack had interrupted.

This wasn't a date—Kate had said so herself. This was business.

This wasn't personal.

"Come on," Seth said, leaving a fifty on the table. "I think we're done here."

Eight

The ride back to the real estate office was tense. Or maybe that was just how Kate felt—because there was no missing the tension. Her dinner sat heavy in her stomach, and her head was a muddled mess. Her back hurt, her feet weren't any better and she was so tired she could barely see straight.

She just wanted to go home and go to bed and, inexplicably, she wanted to do so curled in Seth's arms. She wanted that *so* badly.

What kind of hormonal torture was this? There was no good reason why she should be craving Seth's arms around her, his chest pressed against her back. As fantasies went, it was downright boring.

Except if she went to sleep in his arms, then she'd wake up there and then…

No, *no*. She was not following that train of thought to its logical conclusion. Not a bit.

It wasn't that she'd been scared when that friend of his had shown up. The guy was obviously a smooth talker who considered himself God's gift to women—not that he'd done anything for her. Because he hadn't. She'd been able to empirically realize he was an attractive man but compared to Seth, he was like a cardboard cutout next to a real man.

Then there'd been that kiss on her hand. If Kate didn't know any better, she would've thought that kiss had been to intentionally provoke Seth. There hadn't been a single bit of heat to Jack's lips—but when Seth had growled?

That noise had shot right through Kate, primal and raw. God, it'd sounded so *good*. Almost like he'd wanted her and was more than willing to fight for her.

But to what end? She and Seth were not together and no one present was a caveman. In her experience, no one fought over her. Hell, Roger hadn't even bothered to be upset when she'd jilted him.

This was only the third time they'd ever met face-to-face. The first time, she had been a hysterical runaway bride. The second time, she'd been too stunned to put together two coherent sentences. And today…

Today, he'd told her he wanted to buy a much more expensive house—which came with a much bigger commission. He'd rubbed her back and bought her dinner.

She was not the kind of girl to rebound with the first hot guy she saw. Or the second. Or any guy. Kate Burroughs did not do anything so impulsive or crazy or…fun.

Right. That was final. No fun. She was not interested in Seth.

It didn't matter that he just kept right on drifting

through countless dreams, ones that always started with him riding up on his chopper before moving to him undressing her to hot, passionate lovemaking to…

Holding her while she slept. Making sure she felt safe.

Stupid hormones. She didn't want to do anything that would jeopardize their business relationship because she needed this business relationship more than she needed an attractive, wealthy man to rub her back.

They pulled up in front of the real estate office. Kate turned off the car but neither of them made a move to get out. Instead, they sat in silence and Kate had no idea if it was awkward or not.

"So," she finally began, unable to take the tension for another moment. "We looked at all the houses that were under two hundred and fifty thousand dollars. Do you want go up to three hundred thousand?" That was what most people did. They could handle increases of twenty-five to fifty thousand dollars at a time. And as much as she needed this commission, she didn't want to make this all about her.

But Seth wasn't most people. "I can't imagine there's a huge jump from what we saw today with a couple thousand dollars. Let's look in the three-fifty to five-hundred range."

She took a slow breath. The house on Bitter Root was four seventy-five. Would he like her favorite house or not? "Half a million is a lot of money, Seth. There's no need to buy more house than you'll use." Certainly not because of her. She didn't want to bankrupt the man just because he had a soft spot for…

Well, not for her. For pregnant women, maybe. But not for her.

He turned, facing her fully. There was something in his eyes—the same sort of almost possessive look he'd had when he growled earlier.

Heat flashed through her body as he stared at her. He'd looked earlier like he was willing to fight his friend over her. He looked very much the same now.

"We can't do this," she heard herself say before she completely lost her mind.

He lifted his eyebrows, and she immediately felt stupid. "Do what?" he asked, almost—but not quite—pulling off innocence.

"I'm not looking for a relationship." Well. So much for not making this awkward.

"Fair enough." He turned even more, resting one elbow on the dashboard and another against the back of the seat. "What are you looking for?"

Oh, hell. That was a question she most definitely hadn't seen coming. "I'm sorry?"

"You have to admit, Kate—there's something between us. I went to your office because I need to buy a house and an industrial property—but those weren't the only reasons." He leaned toward her—not close enough to touch her, but his gaze drifted over her and he inhaled deeply. "I couldn't stop thinking about you. I know that how we met wasn't exactly normal—"

Kate rolled her eyes. That was being generous.

"Look, I'm not in the market for a relationship, either," he went on, politely ignoring her unladylike response. "I don't plan on sticking around all the time. Settling down isn't in my blood."

Wasn't that what he'd basically said before? He was buying a house he only planned to live in for maybe six months out of the year? No, Seth Bolton wasn't the kind of guy who started playing house on a whim.

But still, hearing it baldly stated like that was physically painful, like someone was jabbing her hand with a pin. "What are you saying?"

"I need a house and you need a commission. That's all there has to be. But if you want something more..." His gaze darkened, and Kate swore it got ten degrees warmer in the car.

"More?" Her voice came out the barest of whispers.

She shouldn't be asking. She should, instead, get out of this car and thank him for his business and promise him that she would have a fresh slate of houses in a new price range that were sure to meet his needs by Saturday at 11:00 a.m. Their standing date.

"I think we want the same thing." His voice was low and serious, and another flash of heat ran through her body. Ironically, she shivered. How was he doing this to her? She was not sexy—not after being on her feet all day and mowing through that many fries. She was not desirable—her pants barely buttoned.

Yet here Seth sat, looking at her as if she were the ice cream and he couldn't wait to start licking. Her body felt warm and liquid, like she could melt right into him. "You're not looking for long-term. You don't want to be hurt again and you've got a baby on the way to think about. But it might do you good..." His voice trailed off as his gaze caressed her face.

"*What* might do me good?" She was powerless to do anything but ask that question, because it appeared that all common sense had abandoned her in the face of one hot, protective biker dude.

He didn't answer her for the longest second and

Kate thought she just might die on the spot. "Rebounds can be fun. Something short and sweet, no strings attached—something to help you get past those years lost to Roger. I think you deserve a little fun, Kate."

God, it sounded so good. So right. Because really—one conversation with Seth that didn't even involve touching, much less kissing, and she was already more turned on than she could remember being in years. Seth would be amazing. Simply amazing. Maybe the best she'd ever had, in her limited experience. And who knew what would happen after the baby came. She would be struggling to get through the long nights alone. Romance would be the last thing on her mind.

What if Seth were her last shot at romance—or even just good sex—for a long time? Years, even?

Was she willing to let go of that part of herself?

She wasn't, and she almost, almost said *yes* right then and there. Her mouth opened and the word was right on the tip of her tongue. *Yes*.

But she couldn't get it out because she wasn't the kind of person to willingly enter a sexual relationship just for the fun of it. Casual sex had never been casual. Not for her.

Still… "And you're fun?"

That smile—oh, she was not going to be strong enough. "I can take care of you, Kate. Even for a little while." His eyes darkened. "Just something to consider."

And the thing was, he seemed sincere about it. He wasn't boxing her in. He was focused on her, yes—but not intimidatingly so. "You're serious, are you?"

Please, let him be serious.

He nodded, the tip of his tongue touching his top lip. Jesus, she'd never seen anything so seductive. "You don't have to decide anything now. My offer's on the table. But promise me you'll think about it?"

She hated to ask this next question—but it was important she make a counteroffer. "And if I pass?" Because she needed the commissions he would bring in. She didn't want this to be some quid pro quo situation.

"Then you pass." He shrugged, as if rejecting his advances were no big deal. "Unlike some people, I know where the line is and I know not to cross it. I can keep business and pleasure separate."

Oh, that hurt. Because with Roger, they hadn't been separate. With Roger, she wasn't sure how much pleasure had been involved at all. The longer she was away from him—and her father—the more she was certain that Roger had only been with her because she came with the company.

Had there been any evidence to the contrary? No. There'd been no late-night calls, drunken or otherwise, professing that he really loved her and wanted her back. No daytime calls, either. No flowers. No big romantic gestures, like standing under her bedroom window and blasting their song until she realized she'd made a mistake.

Nothing. They didn't even have a song. When she'd asked what he wanted to play for their first dance, he'd shrugged.

And to think, she'd almost married *nothing*.

That did not mean that she wanted to jump into bed with Seth. It did mean, however, that the fact that he was making sense should be a source of concern.

So what if something short and sweet and fun sounded perfect? So what if it was Seth, who had made her feel safe from the very first moment she'd laid eyes on him? So what if the one man who seemingly gave a damn about her was the one offering to show her a good time—with no strings attached?

She had a baby on the way. There would always be strings attached.

"I can't," she said softly, unable to look at him when she said it. Because even if he was offering to make at least one of her fantasies come true, that wasn't her. Kate Burroughs wasn't that girl. She did what was expected of her and smiled and nodded and went along to get along. She did not have casual sex with a hot biker dude simply because it'd be fun and safe and so, *so* satisfying. That wasn't who she was.

Was it?

The silence in the car grew heavy and she didn't want to think about what would come next. Oh, she knew Seth wouldn't hurt her. Funny, how she trusted him with that. She simply didn't want the awkwardness. They'd laughed and joked and had an otherwise really lovely day together and she didn't want to ruin that.

"Then we won't. No harm, no foul." He didn't even sound upset by her refusal.

She peeked at him through her lashes. She didn't know what she'd been expecting, but that look bordering on concern wasn't it. Shouldn't he be mad? Insulted? Frustrated, at the very least?

Not concerned. Not for her. "And you're okay with it?"

He gave her a look as if she'd asked if he didn't like to kick puppies in his free time. "Why wouldn't I be? Besides…" he went on, leaning ever so slightly toward her. The tension between them tightened and she felt her own body move in his direction. “It’s a woman’s prerogative to change her mind.”

And with that parting shot, he was gone before she could blink, out of the car and around to the driver’s side and opening her door and—again—holding out a hand to her like he’d be honored if she joined him. “Otherwise,” he said when she put her hand in his, his strong fingers closing around her own, “I’ll see you at eleven next Saturday. We’ll take more breaks and I’ll buy you dinner again—no arguments, Kate,” he scolded, cutting her off before she could protest. “I’m not going to run you into the ground.”

And maybe it was the hormones or the exhaustion or the way he’d growled at his friend—or maybe it was the offer of something fun and easy—but whatever the reason, Kate didn’t let go of his hand when she had her feet underneath her, nor did she step away from him.

She’d never known anyone like Seth Bolton, and she might not be able to make sense of what was going on in his head—because, again, he was attracted to *her*? But she was flattered and touched and interested all the same.

She shouldn’t be, but she was.

Instead of putting distance between them, she held his hand and maybe even pulled on it a little, drawing him in closer. Not close enough to kiss, but close enough that she could feel the heat radiating off his chest, warming her on the chilly fall night.

“I’ll…” She shouldn’t say this but damn it, what the hell. “I’ll think about it.”

Seth’s fingers tightened around hers and he favored her with a smile so dazzling she almost had to sit down again. “Do that,” he said, his voice a caress on the wind.

And just when she thought he was going to lean in and kiss her, he instead took a step back. "Until next week, Kate."

He waited until she'd gotten the office door unlocked before firing up his motorcycle and riding off into the dim light.

Oh, sweet merciful heavens—she really was going to think about this. About Seth and all those dream fantasies that had kept her company for the last several weeks. About how she might not get another chance for a lover for years because once the baby came, she'd devote herself to her child.

Would she really let this golden opportunity pass her by? And if she did, would she spend the rest of her life kicking herself for letting Seth Bolton slip through her fingers?

Was she out of her mind?

Nine

So that was a *no*, then.

Seth took one look at Kate and sighed. She was wearing a black pantsuit with a white blouse that was buttoned up almost to her chin. Her glorious hair had been scraped back into a severe ponytail and there wasn't a smile to be seen anywhere despite the fact that it was another lovely late-October Saturday. She looked more like she was on her way to a funeral than a house tour.

And if that didn't make her position clear enough, there was no missing the way Kate's pretty mouth twisted into a scowl when Seth walked into Zanger Realty at ten fifty-eight in the morning.

Definitely a *no*.

He shouldn't be disappointed. This had been the most likely outcome, after all. There was no getting around the reality of the situation, and that reality was that Kate was expecting and she didn't want to get involved with anyone.

He should be relieved. Her personal life was a mess and only an idiot would put himself in the middle of that. Her rejection was going to save him a lot of trouble and not a little heartache.

And yet—relief was not the feeling that had his stomach plummeting. No, he was not disappointed. And if he were, it was about the fact that he was going to be missing out on some great casual sex. After all, he didn't have to worry about getting her pregnant, right?

But that didn't explain the weight of sadness that settled around his shoulders. He and Kate could've been great together, but now? They'd never know.

Still, he was a gentleman and a man of his word. He was not going to make this awkward, nor was he going to try to change her mind. He would not badger, nag or wheedle. He had no interest in being with a woman he had to wear down. He'd seen those kinds of guys in action in college and "pathetic desperation" didn't make anyone attractive. Good sex became great when everyone involved was equally enthusiastic about it.

So he straightened his shoulders and put on a friendly grin, even if it took effort to do so. "Good morning, Kate. What will we be looking at today?" Because the answer obviously wasn't each other.

Her scowl deepened as she stared at something on her desk. She looked positively insulted by his presence, which didn't make any sense. She hadn't even been insulted when he propositioned her. Shocked, maybe. Curious? Definitely. But not insulted. What the hell was going on?

"I have nine houses in your new price range on the schedule. We should get going."

The *no* couldn't have been louder if she'd shouted it. What a shame. "Nine sounds good," he said, striving his hardest for friendly. "Thirteen was too much last weekend." She still wasn't meeting his gaze, so he charged ahead. "I made dinner reservations at the Main Course for six thirty, but if you don't think we'll be done before then, I can change the time." She hadn't been comfortable at the diner—or at least, she'd been okay until Jack showed up.

Tonight would be different. They'd have a quiet dinner, just the two of them and a bunch of house listings. No interfering family friends, no distractions.

Although, given the body language she was putting off, maybe they could use a few distractions. Because even closed down, she still called to him on a fundamental level that had nothing to do with reason or logic.

He'd made his offer last week because he'd convinced himself that he could show her a good time, no strings attached. But today? When the answer was no?

He should be able to let it go. He'd asked, she'd said no, end of discussion.

But looking at her now, he wasn't sure his offer had been only about her. Because he still wanted her. Desperately.

She hadn't answered yet. "Kate? We're still on for dinner, right?" He expected any number of polite excuses—she'd had a long night, she had other plans, she would be too tired. She had an actual funeral, thereby justifying the outfit. Something.

So when she looked at him through her lashes and said, "That sounds nice," in a tone that stroked over his ears like a lover's kiss, he didn't know what to make of it. And when she shot him a nervous smile before dropping her gaze again, he had even less of an idea.

Because that wasn't a *no*. It sure as hell wasn't a *yes*, either.

What if he was looking at a *maybe*?

Five hours later, he had absolutely no idea what to make of Kate Burroughs. Through eight other houses, she'd kept her distance, never getting within two feet of him. Not like he was going to grab her, but still. She was definitely not close enough to touch. No accidentally brushing hands as they stood in a narrow hallway—of which there were several. No putting his hand on her lower back to guide her out of a room. No gentlemanly offers of his hand or his arm for her to lean against as they walked over uneven paver stones.

However, every single time he'd glanced at her, he'd caught her watching him. She always looked away quickly, as if she were going to pretend she hadn't been staring, but he could feel her gaze upon him. She'd also thawed—slowly at first, but she'd gotten noticeably warmer to him as the day had progressed. She'd left her scowl behind at the first house—a markedly more habitable dwelling than nearly anything they'd looked at the previous week. By the third house, her lips had gone from a tight line to a gentle smile and by the fifth house, she was laughing at his jokes again. By the seventh house, her eyes softened and she let her gaze linger upon him when he'd glance at her, like she didn't want to look away.

She was still absolutely captivating.

He had to play this cool. As much as he desperately

wanted to pull her into his arms and show her exactly how good they could be together, he didn't dare. She had to come to him, and besides—her decision was separate from their business dealings.

So he was doing his best not to think about anything other than real estate. It was a battle he wasn't necessarily winning, but he was trying.

"This isn't bad," he said, standing in the middle of a gleaming kitchen with a professional six-burner stove, a fridge with cabinet facings on the door and an island with a marble countertop. The whole thing was done in whites and grays with splashes of red and bright blue for accents. This was the last house of the day and they were on schedule, with a whole thirty-five minutes before their dinner reservations.

Kate snorted. "Four hundred and seventy-five thousand dollars and it's not *bad*?"

"Compared to what we looked at last week, it's amazing," he conceded.

He stood at the island, trying to get a sense for how the room flowed. And the fact that he was thinking about the flow of rooms was odd. He'd never considered work triangles and flow before. He and his mom had lived in a cramped two-room place before Billy Bolton had come into their lives, and then they'd moved into Billy's house and it'd been great simply because it was a real house with a room—and a bathroom—all his own.

The kid he'd been would take the first decent option he got. But he was a man of means now. He could afford to be picky.

He looked up at Kate, who was staring at the kitchen with open longing. Picky, indeed. "What do you think?"

"It's not going to be my house, Seth," she said in a quiet voice.

Something in her tone pulled at him. She sounded almost sad about that and he remembered what she'd said last week—she'd arranged for him to look at the least likely house first. This was the last house of the day, which meant she thought this was the best house they'd looked at yet.

"But you have a professional opinion, Kate. What do you think?" When she didn't answer right away, he added, "I'd appreciate it if you're honest."

About this kitchen, about the houses they looked at, about whether or not dinner was going to be painfully awkward.

About him. He wanted her to be honest about what she wanted from him. Just the commission or something else?

When she still didn't answer, Seth wished he could take it back. He never should've offered her a sexual relationship last week. He should've left it at flirting and making her smile, at making sure she was landing on her feet.

But then Jack had shown up and watching him hit on Kate had been more than Seth could take. She was *his*, not Jack's and not Roger's.

Except she wasn't. She wasn't a possession he could do with what he pleased. She was a complicated woman who had her own life to live.

"I'm just asking, Kate. Your opinion is important to me. Just tell me what you think. I've never done this before."

"You've never bought a house before?"

"That, either."

Her lips twisted to the side in a scowl that he now recognized as confusion. “You’ve never propositioned a pregnant older woman before?”

Finally, they were at the heart of the matter. “Oddly enough, no. There’s a first for everything, isn’t there?” He gave her a warm smile, hoping that would help.

He wasn’t sure it did. “But you’ve offered to have no-strings relationships with other women?”

He tried to process the line of thinking behind that question. How long had she been with Roger? Kate didn’t strike Seth as the kind of woman who’d had a lot of casual relationships. “I went to college.”

The scowl was back. But at least this time he’d earned it. He braced for her cutting rejoinder, but instead she squared her shoulders and said, “This is an amazing house,” in what he thought of as her real estate agent voice. “The master suite has that Jacuzzi bathtub and the office on the first floor has an amazing view. It sits on two acres so you don’t have any neighbors within immediate line of sight and although it only has a two-car garage, there’s more than enough room to expand or even build a separate workshop. The property is fenced so if you’re ever going to have a dog or children, there would be a huge backyard for them to play in.”

“It is a great house on paper,” he agreed. “But I can read. I want to know what you think of the house, Kate.”

“It was originally on the market nine months ago for five ninety-nine,” she went on, ignoring him. “But was overvalued and the market has been a little soft at this price range. The owners are probably desperate to sell, so we might be able to get them down to four-fifty.”

He might never figure this woman out, but he was

going to have a hell of a good time trying. "Kate." She swung around to look at him. "Do *you* like it?"

She blinked at him in confusion and he had to wonder, had anyone ever asked her what she liked before?

Then she exhaled heavily, looking defeated. He didn't like that look on her. "Roger and I..." she started, her voice trailing off. Then she tried again. "We'd already purchased a house when this came on the market and besides, it was out of our price range. But I've been through it several times now and..."

Her hand stroked over the marble countertop affectionately as she walked to the sink, making his gut tighten. He wanted her to touch him like that, to hear that longing in her voice when she talked to him.

Great. Now he was jealous of a house. Bad enough he was jealous of Jack, but at least that was another guy. The house was just a house.

She leaned against the sink and stared out the window into that big fenced backyard and damned if she didn't look like she belonged here. She loved this house and for some insane reason, he wanted to give it to her.

"The house just makes *sense*," she went on, a note of defeat in her voice that he didn't miss. "The way the rooms are arranged, the way everything works together—it's one of the best houses I've ever been in. Nothing to compromise on, nothing I'd want to change. I've always been able to see myself living here. It'd be a wonderful place to raise a family."

He understood what she was saying. She hadn't been able to afford it even when she'd had Roger's income to kick in and now? Even if the price could be negotiated down more, it'd still be beyond her. Instead, she was going to have to watch someone else buy her dream home.

Unless… "Question." She turned, her eyebrows raised. "We haven't started on the industrial properties for the museum. What happens if I buy a piece of property for, say, four million dollars? Will your commission be enough to buy this house?"

The color drained out of her face, which was not the reaction he'd been hoping to get. "Seth," she said softly, sounding even sadder—which had not been his goal. "You can't just snap your fingers and solve all of my problems. I got myself into my own mess and I am going to get myself out of it, too." She swallowed, her eyes huge. "I don't need you to save me."

"That's not what this is." But even as he said it, he wasn't entirely sure that was the truth. He didn't think about it in terms of saving her. He thought about it in terms of *helping*. Of course, why he felt this compulsion to help her was another question he didn't want to investigate too deeply right now.

"Then tell me what this is about. The truth, Seth."

The truth? Hell. The truth was he was worried about her. He couldn't stop fantasizing about her. He was glad she hadn't married Roger. He knew how hard single mothers had it and he didn't want it to be that hard for her. It shouldn't be that hard for anyone, but especially not for her.

He didn't say any of that. Instead, he closed the distance between them and cupped her face in his hands. "This," he said, lowering his lips to hers, "is the truth."

Then he kissed her.

Ten

Oh, God—Seth was kissing her. And somehow, it *was* the truth.

Because the truth was, she wanted him to kiss her and more than that, she wanted to kiss him back.

How had she thought that she could talk herself out of this need? God knew she'd tried. For a whole week, she'd diligently reasoned that it didn't make sense to fall into bed with Seth Bolton. It was a bad idea and the list of reasons why was long. Safer to keep their relationship strictly platonic.

In fact, she had gotten up this morning determined not to let things get to this point. But now that they were here—now that he was brushing his lips over hers, soft and gentle and asking for permission…

She sighed into his mouth and wrapped her arms around his waist. However many reasons there were not to do this, none of them trumped the simple fact that she *wanted* Seth. She wanted to hold on to this last chance to be Kate Burroughs before her identity was redefined by motherhood. She wanted her baby, but she didn't want to lose herself, either.

So she kissed him back. She opened her mouth for him and slid her tongue along the seam of his lips and thrilled at the groan of desire that rumbled out of his chest. She pressed her body to his and let the warmth of his solid muscles sink into her skin.

She stopped trying to fight this desire. She stopped trying to fight herself.

Seth was the one who broke the kiss. He pulled back and rested his forehead against hers, his chest rising and falling rapidly. "I shouldn't have kissed you," he said, his words coming out in a rush. "But I can't regret it."

This was it, her last chance to stop this madness before it consumed her.

Too damned bad she wanted to be consumed. "Yes, you should've."

He gave her a quizzical look. "Was I reading you wrong? I thought you weren't interested."

She had tried so hard not to be. "Seth, this is a bad idea." His face fell. "But that doesn't mean I'm not interested. I don't *want* to be interested in you. My life is complicated enough. But I can't help wanting you."

Dimly, she was aware that they were locked in an embrace inside a stranger's home. True, the home had been unoccupied for months. But ethically, she was pushing her luck. "We need to leave."

He nodded and stepped back, but he didn't let go of her. Instead, his arm slid down around her waist and he held her tight to his side. "Where do you want to go? Dinner or..."

She would need to eat—eventually. But she needed him more. "Or?"

He guided her toward the door. "What about your place?"

She hesitated. It was such a small apartment. She knew she shouldn't be embarrassed for him to see it—it was clean and neat. But after spending the day in some of the nicer homes in Rapid City, her apartment would look pathetic in comparison.

Besides, she didn't want Seth in her apartment because then she would have all these memories of him there. Every time she walked into her bedroom, she would remember him stretched out on her bed, the sheet around his hips and his chest bare. Every time she tried to fall asleep, his presence would keep her awake.

She needed to keep a little distance between the rest of her life and what was going to happen in the next few weeks. Because she couldn't imagine that this would last more than a few weeks.

Just long enough for her to taste true passion. Just enough memories to keep her going through what would be a few years of long days and sleepless nights. That's all she was doing with Seth—making memories.

"Your place?"

"I'm currently living in a hotel. But," he added, opening the door for her, "it has room service. If you're sure?"

Was she sure this was a good idea? No. She was pretty sure it wasn't.

But was she sure that Seth would take great care with her? That he would deliver on exactly what he had promised—something fun and satisfying, something to erase the lingering bad memories of Roger from her mind? Something *good*?

She leaned up on her tiptoes and brushed a kiss across his lips—a promise of more to come. "I'm sure. Are you?"

That smile—confident and cocky, sensual and heated—*that* was exactly what she was looking for. "You have no idea."

Twenty minutes later, Seth said, "We can order room service later," as he guided her into the room and kicked the door shut behind him.

Then she was sinking into his arms and wondering why, exactly, she'd fought against this so hard. It didn't mean anything. She was attracted to Seth and he was attracted to her, and she simply hadn't had enough fun in her life for so long that she almost couldn't remember what it felt like to enjoy herself.

Well, to hell with that. Because she was going to enjoy this time here, with this man. "Okay?" Seth asked again as his hands settled around her waist. They hadn't even gotten to the bed—he was still leaned against the door. But he wasn't going to let her go.

"Okay," she agreed, sliding her hands underneath his jacket and flattening her palms against his chest. It had been unseasonably warm today and he had on another Crazy Horse T-shirt. His body was hard and hot under her touch, and touch him she did.

He let her. He stayed still while she explored the planes of his chest. He didn't yank her clothing off, didn't try to skip the foreplay and get straight to the sex. He let her take her time and that felt important.

She didn't know how long they had together, but she didn't want to rush it.

"You never did tell me how old you are," she murmured as she pushed the jacket from his shoulders. He let go of her waist long enough for the leather to hit the floor and then she was studying his arms. She hadn't seen them before—the muscles that strained at the sleeves of his shirt, a tattoo visible on his right biceps. "Good Lord, Seth. Look at you."

"Twenty-five. And I'd rather look at you. Except… without these clothes." He peeled her black suit jacket off her shoulders. "Black and white are all wrong on you. You need bright, vibrant color, Kate. You're gorgeous in color."

She felt her cheeks get warm. "It was the only thing that fit," she admitted—and that was only because the pants had elastic in the back. Otherwise, she would've been showing houses in yoga pants.

"Ah. And here I thought you were sending me a message—hands off."

She could feel that her whole face had turned red and it only got worse as he reached for the buttons on her slacks. It wasn't like he hadn't undressed her before—he had. He had lifted her skirt and peeled off a petticoat and been within inches of her most personal areas. But it was different now. Her body was changing faster every single day. "I'm different. Since the last time we did this."

His mouth curved into a dangerous half grin. "We've done this before? I'm sure I would remember."

"You know what I mean," she said, whacking him on the side of the arm. "You have undressed me before. At least partially."

"Trust me, babe—I have not forgotten. I never will." He worked the zipper down and then slid his hands underneath the fabric, along her skin. "And this time, I'm not going to settle on 'partially.'"

She didn't have on a thong today, nor did she have on stockings and a garter. The best she could do was a pair of bikini-cut panties—white—with a little pink bow on the front and her new, very serviceable white bra. The underthings were innocent, almost—the most innocent thing about this particular situation, anyway.

She could feel the palm of his hand moving over the fabric of her panties and then lower, over her hips. The slacks gave way as he stroked down her skin. He followed the pants, falling to his knees before her as she revealed her skin and this time, she couldn't drop a skirt to hide.

This time, she didn't want to.

They felt like they were starting from the same spot—but it was different, too. She hadn't known anything about Seth the first time she'd balanced a hand on his shoulder so she could step free of extraneous fabric. She hadn't known if he was rich or poor, old or young. All she had known then was that she was safe with him.

She still was. "Tell me what you want," Seth said when she had stepped free of the slacks. He grabbed them and threw them out of the way, then began to slide her trouser socks off. "I want to give you what you need."

Her eyes fluttered shut and she tried to put words to what that was.

She wanted to be selfish. She didn't want to swallow down her disappointment in bed to protect anyone's feelings. She didn't want to accept mediocre sex because Roger was incapable of putting forth the effort to get better. She didn't want to settle because it kept the peace.

She needed to know what Kate Burroughs wanted. She needed to know that person was valuable and desirable and worth the risk.

She needed Seth to fight for her.

She needed to fight for herself.

"Anything," Seth said as her other sock and shoe were also tossed aside. He sat back on his heels and ran his hands up and down her bare legs, warming her skin. "Be honest, Kate."

"I don't want to regret this," she said, because that was the most honest thing she could think of. "I don't want to regret you."

"You won't. And I won't, either," he assured her. He leaned forward and pressed his lips against her thigh. "I had the most erotic dreams after the last time," he whispered against her skin as he kissed his way up her leg.

"I'm different now. Everything's changed." She felt huge and she knew she was only going to get bigger. Rationally, she knew it was because of the baby, but it was still hard to know that an ugly black suit was the only thing she could wear for her standing date with Seth Bolton.

She didn't feel ugly now, not as Seth moved to the other thigh and began to kiss and nip at her skin. She watched in fascination.

"You were gorgeous two months ago, but now?" Seth leaned back and began to undo the buttons on her shirt. He had amazingly long arms, powerful muscles. Everything about him was powerful and he was here with her. How did this make any sense?

"But now?" he said in such a sincere voice that even though it didn't make any sense, she had no choice but to believe him. He got the buttons undone, and she shrugged out of the shirt, letting it fall. "My God, Kate—*look* at you."

She was going to protest that there was nothing to look at—at least not anything good—but he sat forward and pressed a kiss right below her belly button. And then one below that. And then one even lower. What started out as a sweet, tender gesture rapidly became something else entirely.

"Seth," she said, her knees beginning to shake as his mouth moved over the thin cotton of her panties, coming ever closer to her sex.

"Tell me what you need, Kate," he said, bringing his hands up to cup her bottom—and bring her closer to his mouth. "Do you need this?"

He skimmed his teeth over her panties, pulling the fabric aside. She was so shaky that she had no choice but to bury her fingers in his thick black hair and hold on. He looked up at her and squeezed her bottom, a knowing smile tugging at the corner of his lips. "Come on, Kate—you have to tell me."

"Yes," she whispered. He was slow and methodical—and focused entirely on her. He wasn't keeping an eye on the clock or an ear on the game. He wasn't wishing he were anywhere else. She had his undivided attention and that, more than anything else, was what she needed right now.

That and his mouth on her. "More." It came out half an order and half a plea.

His grin sharpened. "Good girl. I want to hear what you like." Then he buried his face against her sex.

"Ohh..." That. Definitely *that.*

Somehow, he pivoted her so instead of her standing, she was leaning against a wall. He scooted her legs a little farther apart and pressed himself between them. He still gripped her bottom with one hand, but with the other, he reached around the front and pulled her innocent-looking white panties to the side. Not off—just to the side. "How about this? Do you need this?" he asked, pausing just long enough that she knew if she said no, he'd stop.

She didn't want him to stop. "I do," she said, her voice little more than an exhale.

He kissed the top of her thigh, teasing her. "Are you sure?"

For some reason, the question irritated her. She was tired of people not listening to her, tired of them assuming they knew best. She wanted Seth to make her feel gorgeous and sexy, she wanted the release of a good orgasm—but more than that, she wanted him to listen. She wanted to be heard.

She tugged on his hair—hard—pulling him back to where she needed him. "I said yes," she hissed, watching as his eyes fluttered shut and he inhaled her scent deeply. "And I meant it. I won't beg, Seth. You're going to give me what I want and that's final."

He moaned. He was on his knees in front of her, his face buried against her sex, and he *moaned.* It was a noise of pure want and it shot straight through her. And then he kissed her, right where she needed his mouth. His lips moved over that nub of skin and nerves and then it was her moaning as she held him to her. His tongue flicked out and traced a pattern on her skin, one that she would feel for the rest of her life.

He was marking her, and she was his to be marked.

As his mouth worked her body, the rest of the world fell away. She stopped worrying about her rounded tummy or her woeful closet. Commissions and tours and kitchens—they all fell away. Even the fantasy that had been Seth—him stripping her at the scenic overlook and instead of putting her on a motorcycle, doing this exact same thing—it fell away because that hadn't been real. It'd been a bedtime story she'd told herself, a lie to convince herself that she was still Kate Burroughs and that was good enough.

This? This was not a lie. She was Kate Burroughs and Seth wasn't some mysterious, handsome stranger, he was a man—a warm, solid, flesh-and-blood man—who wanted her. More than that, he was putting her first. Hell, she hadn't even gotten his shirt off. She wanted to see his body, to touch it and taste it.

She wanted him all for herself. Not for anyone else, not for a commission. She wanted Seth Bolton because he was a man she liked, a man who cared about what happened to her. A handsome, confident man.

A man who was very good with his mouth. There was something naughty about this. They hadn't made it to a bed—no one was naked. But there was something freeing about it, too.

"God, Kate—you taste so good," he murmured against her sensitized flesh, his words vibrating right through her. "Better than I imagined."

Well, they were being honest. "I dreamed of you doing this, too," she told him. The hand that was still on her bottom slipped underneath her panties so he could grip her harder. It wasn't enough. She heard herself say, "I need more, Seth."

The request shocked her. Had she ever said that before? If she had, she was pretty sure it hadn't gotten the desired result. When had she learned that, even in bed, she had to be quiet and go along to get along? Whose bright idea was that?

"Mmm, something more." He leaned back. The next thing Kate knew, her panties had been pulled down and Seth was back between her legs. This time, in addition to his mouth, his fingers began to work her. He stroked up and down and found that sensitive nub again, teasing it with his teeth as he slipped a finger inside her.

The relief was so intense that she could've cried. He thrust that finger into her in time with the movements of his tongue and his lips, and it was everything she'd ever wanted and never gotten.

Then, just when she was sure she couldn't take another moment, he added a second finger and she was lost.

Eleven

Kate's grip on his hair bordered on painful, but Seth wasn't about to do anything to stop the incoming wave of her orgasm. He could take a little pain for her.

She was so beautiful when she came. Her color was high and her eyes were glazed over with lust. And her body? Damn, her body. There was something so lush and gorgeous about her that even though he was inside her, he couldn't get enough. He had never been this hard for a woman, never this desperate.

"Seth—Seth!" she gasped as her body convulsed around him. He leaned in, putting just a little more pressure against the spot that drove her wild. The noise she made—he wanted to capture it in a kiss and hold it deep inside him, but he didn't dare let her go.

Her back arched off the wall and then the crisis passed and she slumped, her legs giving out. He managed to catch her before she toppled them both over. "I've got you, babe," he whispered against her breast as he studied her.

For a long few minutes, they stayed in this awkward pose, him on his knees, her half draped over him. She was breathing hard, and he wasn't much better off.

He needed to move. It was torture to sit on his heels in these boots, torture to keep these jeans buttoned. He needed to lay her out on the bed and show her *that* had just been a preview of what was to come.

But when he shifted to stand and sweep her into his arms, he realized there were tears running down her cheeks. "Kate?"

She blinked at him. "Seth…" she murmured, sounding almost as confused as she looked.

"Oh, God—I'm sorry," he said, scrambling to his feet and pulling her into his arms. He crushed her in a hug and then realized perhaps *crushing* was not the best option right now, so he shifted to make sure he was merely holding her firmly. "I'm sorry," he repeated.

"What? No—no, you don't understand." She sniffed and pulled away, scrubbing at her cheeks with the back of her hand. "That was amazing, Seth. I don't think… I'm sorry. I'm not upset. It's the hormones. I've never— This isn't— I…" She trailed off, looking, if possible, even more confused.

Oh, thank God. He hadn't hurt her, hadn't crossed the line—hadn't misread the situation. "So you're okay?"

She smiled—a watery smile, but a smile all the same. "Honestly, I'm not sure if I've ever been better. It was amazing. You," she said, poking him in the chest, "are amazing. And wearing far too many clothes."

"I can fix that." He grabbed the hem of his T-shirt, but she batted his hands away.

"I want to do it."

"Never let it be said that I don't give a woman what she wants." He let his hands fall to his sides as she began to tug at his T-shirt. She was in no hurry, her movements languid and relaxed. Her tears had dried and all that was left was that knowing smile, satisfied and ready for more. He'd put that smile on her face and by God, he'd leave another in its place.

She pulled his shirt over his head and let it fall to the side. "Good heavens, Seth—you're stunning."

She skimmed her hands over his chest, brushing his nipples and taking the measure of his waist. He fought to keep the groan from escaping. "I aim to please."

She paused at the button of his jeans and shot him a look. "What about you? What do you want?"

The word *everything* popped up in his head before he could think. But he didn't say that, not out loud. This was short-term, fun. No strings attached. He could have everything, for a limited time only.

For some reason, the thought made him sadder than he expected. He didn't expect it to upset him at all, frankly. He expected to get lucky and have a good time and call it a day. He didn't *want* anything more.

Kate began working at his button fly, drawing his attention back to her. She was simply the most beautiful woman he'd ever seen. He wanted to burn that ugly black suit and deliver Kate to his aunt Stella, the fashion designer. He wanted to wrap her in vibrant blues and golds and greens. He wanted to see Kate in all of her glory, instead of her beauty hidden.

He pulled the ponytail holder out of her hair and sank

his fingers into her locks. "Beautiful," he said as he arranged her silky hair around her shoulders.

She shoved his pants down and he kicked out of his boots. That left him in nothing but his boxer briefs—which were barely keeping his erection contained.

Kate straightened, a shy smile on her face. He knew she was no innocent, but there was still something unsure about her. Which she only reinforced when she asked, "Now what?"

He didn't particularly want to think about Roger Caputo right now, but again he had to wonder what the hell had been wrong with that man. Kate was a gorgeous, passionate woman and Roger had just let her go. Was he that damned blind that he couldn't see what was right in front of him?

If Kate were his, Seth would do everything in his power not just to keep her, but to keep her safe and whole and so blissfully happy that she never had to worry about anything.

Too damned bad she wasn't his.

"Bed," he said, having trouble thinking straight. He was personally familiar with the concept of lust—but this? This was different. More intense. He was *desperate* for her, and he had never been desperate before. Hard up, maybe. But not like this.

She ducked her head and turned toward the king-size bed. But Seth reached out and turned her back toward him. "Wait for me, babe," he murmured, drawing her in close so that he could feel her breasts pressed against his bare chest. He fisted his hand in her hair. Tilting her face to his, he brought his mouth down upon hers.

He kissed her with everything he had. She made a squeak of surprise but then she melted into him. She tasted so good—he couldn't get enough of her. And when her arms came around his waist and she slid her hands down to cup his ass, he got even harder.

He wanted to take his time with her—he *was* taking his time with her—but the intensity of his desire was blinding. He began to walk her back toward the bed, never taking his mouth from hers.

She came alive against him. He could almost see the moment when she forgot to be self-conscious and nervous. He could definitely taste the sweetness of that moment. He captured her little noises and need with his lips. He let go of her hair long enough to unfasten her bra and cast it aside, and then he had to look.

"Sweet Jesus, Kate," he groaned, cupping her breasts in his hands. They were full and heavy, her nipples a deep russet red. "Perfect," he said, brushing his thumbs back and forth over her tips and watching them tighten.

She gasped her arousal. "They're not usually that—oh, Seth," she moaned as he lowered his head to one and replaced his thumb with his tongue. "They got bigger. More—oh! More sensitive." Her hands found his hair and, just like she had held him to her sex before, she held him to her breast now.

The words were slow to penetrate the fog of desire in Seth's mind, but penetrate they did. More sensitive—that meant he needed to be gentle. It meant that if he played his cards right, he might be able to drive her to orgasm just by playing with her nipples alone.

The back of her legs hit the bed and she sat abruptly. Seth came off her breast with an audible *pop*. She blinked up at him, apparently surprised as to how she'd landed where she was. "Seth," she whispered. She stroked her hands down his chest, and his stomach—then she hooked her fingers into the waistband of his briefs and pulled.

They had all night. That was what Seth kept telling himself when his cock sprang free. He held his hands at his side, giving her the space to explore without making any demands. Because they had all night and he had nowhere he had to be tomorrow morning and by God, he was going to make this memorable for her.

"Wow," she said, tracing the tip of her finger along the side of his erection, making him quiver. "I had no idea." Seth was powerless to keep the growl inside.

Maybe he wouldn't despise Roger. True, the man had apparently never done anything good for Kate, but on the other hand, it was going to be easy—and enjoyable—to blow Kate's preconceived notions of sex and intimacy out of the water.

She wrapped her hand around his shaft and stroked once, twice—all while staring at him intently. "Is it okay if I do this?" she asked, stroking him again.

"God, yes." Why wouldn't it be?

"I just..." But she didn't finish the thought. Instead, she stroked him slowly, driving him past the point of thinking. And that was before she leaned forward and pressed her lips to his tip.

And suddenly it was too much. Before she could take him into her mouth, Seth grabbed her by the hair and pulled her away. "I can't— Kate," he said, not even able to get a coherent thought out. He leaned down and crushed his mouth over hers, desperate to be inside her. But at the very last second, his lone remaining functional brain cell kicked into gear—the condom. It wasn't like he could get her more pregnant—but safe sex was good sex. He forced himself to pull away from her and went to grab his jacket, fishing the condoms out.

When he turned back to the bed, Kate was leaning on her elbows, watching him intently. There was something so right about her, about them being here together. *Everything*, he thought, staring at her. She was everything.

He prowled across the hotel room, kneeling on the bed next to her. He was supposed to be saying things to her, he was pretty sure—sweet nothings about how gorgeous she was, how excited he was—how great he was going to be for her.

He had nothing. Not a damned thing. And when she reached out and gripped his erection again, the need to be buried inside her was overwhelming.

He rolled on the condom and fit himself between her legs. "Yeah?" he asked, dragging his erection against the folds of her flesh.

Her hips arched into him as her eyes fluttered. "Yes, please," she whispered, wrapping her arms around his neck and bringing him close so she could sear him with her lips.

"So polite." He was going to push her past that. He wanted her demanding and bossy, confident in her desires and in his ability to fulfill them.

He shifted and found her opening and then, as carefully as he could, he began to thrust. Her body was tight around his and the sensations—damn, the sensations. He'd always liked sex. Careful sex, of course. He wasn't going to get anyone pregnant and leave them high and dry. He was *not* that guy. But sex itself had always been fun.

This? Burying his body inside Kate's went far past fun, he realized as they fell into a rhythm. Being with

Kate wasn't a fun Saturday night. It was suddenly as vital to him as breathing.

She rose to meet him as he plunged into her again and again and he completely surrendered to her. Her hands gripped his shoulders, his arms. "Oh, God—Seth," she cried, her body tightening around his.

"Yeah, babe—yeah," he ground out, straining to keep his orgasm in check long enough. He wouldn't dare leave her unsatisfied. It simply wasn't polite.

She thrashed her head against the pillow and dug her fingernails into his back as her body gripped his with such strength that he couldn't hold anything back. He gave himself over to her and held on as she came.

He collapsed on top of her, both of them breathing hard for a few moments as his head cleared. This time, when he leaned back to withdraw, he was ready for the tears—because they were there again. She looked at him and smiled and then laughed and said, "It's good crying, I promise."

He was willing to take her at her word that this was a hormonal thing. "You never cried before?" he asked, getting rid of the condom and draping himself around her.

"No," she said, sounding tired and sated and happy. "Or laughed. But then, I don't ever remember having orgasms like that, either."

Roger was an idiot. A clueless idiot. "I am ever at your command, my lady."

She laughed again. "I think you were right."

He propped himself up on his elbow and began to trace her collarbone with his lips. "About what?"

She cupped her palm around his cheek and lifted

his face so he had to look at her. Her eyes sparkled. "I think you're going to be very good for me."

His chest puffed up with pride and he nipped at the space where her shoulder met her neck. "It was only the beginning, Kate. I can be even better for you than that in just a few minutes." He lowered his mouth to her breast again, but just then her stomach rumbled. He bit back his smile and leaned away, putting his hand on her stomach. If he didn't know she was pregnant, he wouldn't be able to tell. Soon, maybe. "Maybe we should have dinner first? I picked this hotel for the room service."

He would do anything for that smile of hers. Everything. "I'd like that."

Seth called in their orders while she got cleaned up in the bathroom. When she came back out wearing her boring white shirt again, he growled.

"I am not going to be naked when room service shows up, thank you very much. Besides," she went on as he stared at her legs, "you can always take it off again later."

"Woman," he groaned, falling back on the bed as if she'd shot him. "Come wait with me."

They curled up under the covers and turned on a game, although they didn't watch it. Seth was too busy touching her skin, massaging her shoulders, stroking her hair, to pay any attention to sports. By the time dinner showed up, he was more than half hard for her all over again.

And the whole time, he kept thinking that it was a damn shame that he had no plans to stay in Rapid City on a permanent basis. Though even if he were staying, he wouldn't want to keep this thing between them going. Kate didn't need a long-term relationship that was nothing more than casual sex. She needed a man who could settle down and stay in one place, someone who could be a good dad and shoulder his half of the load—if not more. She needed someone who would be there every night and every morning and that, sadly, was not Seth. He simply didn't have it in him.

He'd always been restless. Although his mom had never said so one way or the other, Seth attributed his wanderlust to his birth father. The man had disappeared before Seth had been born, never to be seen on the reservation again. Seth had no idea if his father was kind or hard, laughing or serious. All he had ever known about the man was that he left his girlfriend and his unborn child behind without a second look.

That was why Seth's new position at Crazy Horse Choppers fit him so well. He'd already spent a year in Los Angeles, hobnobbing with the rich, famous and the wished-they-were-famous. His uncle Bobby was always looking for the next big thing. Billy just wanted to build motorcycles. Ben kept an eye on the bottom line—but Bobby? Bobby wanted to take over the world, and he was more than willing to use Seth as a means to that end.

Seth was going to get this museum project started because he believed it would be both a great way to extend the Crazy Horse Choppers brand name and also expand their revenue streams. But beyond that, it would showcase the occasional mad genius that was the Boltons. And after that?

After that, Seth was looking toward the future. American-style motorcycles were beginning to take off in popularity in Asia. His uncles and his father—they were family men. All Boltons were. They loved their wives and were actively involved in their children's lives. It would be hard to ask them—even Bobby—to pack up and head to Shanghai for six months or so to open up the Asian market.

But Seth? He was unattached. No wife, no children. Just a restless wanderlust and an up-to-date passport.

That night, after he had pulled Kate on top of him and teased her breasts until she cried out with a shattering orgasm, he lay in the dark, listening to her breathe and feeling her warm body pressed against his. He decided he wouldn't tell her about the possibility of Asia. Not yet, anyway. It was still several months away, and he had to get the museum project going first.

Which meant he had several more months of nights like this.

Twelve

Just like it had every Saturday for the last three weeks, Kate's heart sped up when Seth Bolton walked into Zanger Realty. Today was no exception.

Rain had dampened his hair and a few stray drops clung to his eyelashes, and he was impossibly more handsome now than he'd ever been. When his gaze locked on hers from across the office, she could see how much he'd been waiting for this moment, too.

Because she had been waiting for *him*.

"Ms. Burroughs," he said, his voice going right through her.

"Good morning, Mr. Bolton." It was a little game they played, pretending to be professional when there might be someone else around, even though Harold Zanger rarely came into the office on Saturdays. She stood. "We have a busy day ahead of us—two industrial properties I think will work for you. And after that, are you ready to buy a house?"

He was buying the home on Bitter Root. Her house—although it wasn't hers. Soon, it would be his.

She'd always known she'd be sad when that house sold. But oddly, she was happy that if anyone else had to buy it, it was Seth. He'd take good care of it.

His eyes darkened as his gaze swept over her body. Because he was buying a house today, she had splurged on some new clothes that fit—she'd get her commission before the bills came due. The broomstick skirt with an elastic waist and the tunic top with a deep vee at the neck weren't outright maternity clothes, but she had read that it was a wise financial investment to buy regular clothing one size larger than she had been wearing because she would probably need them after she had the baby.

And although she knew this wasn't a committed relationship, she wanted to look her best for Seth. She couldn't do anything about her rapidly changing body—although Seth seemed to appreciate her new curves far more than she did—but by God she could at least put on flattering clothes. And lingerie. The new lacy black bra—yet another size up—and the matching panties made her feel like she could still be sexy.

Especially when Seth looked at her like that.

"I'm certainly looking forward to celebrating my new home," he said, his voice low. "You look *amazing* today, Kate."

She felt his words—and his desire—in her chest. Everywhere. A shiver went through her—the kind of shiver that promised better things to come. "I've always found home ownership to be *inspiring*." She couldn't wait until the ink was dry on the legal documents and the key to his new house was in his hands. Normally, she would buy clients a gift basket to welcome them to their new home—a candle, a few knickknacks that seemed to match the personalities of the buyers.

Today? She wanted to welcome him to his new home in ways that had nothing to do with candles.

His grin deepened and he took another step into the office, leaving wet footprints on the carpet behind him. "Incredibly inspiring," he agreed. "But assuming the rain moves off, we'll need to make a small side trip."

"Oh?"

His grin tightened and suddenly he looked nervous. "My sister's regular game got delayed because of the storm, but it's supposed to clear off soon. I promised I'd try to stop by. If they win today, they're in the championship."

"This is Julie, right?" They'd talked some about their families, but only enough to scratch the surface. What could she say about her parents? Her mother was a doormat and her father was a steamroller?

His family life seemed vastly more complicated. The man outright dismissed the notion of living in one place for more than six months at a time and yet he was the most devoted big brother she'd ever met. For a man who wasn't the least interested in setting down roots, he was perfectly happy to spend a crazy amount of money on a luxury home.

After a month of spending time with Seth, she was no closer to understanding him, really.

"Yeah. She and my cousins make up half the starting line. We won't have to stay for the whole game, but I do want to put in an appearance."

She was not looking for anything more permanent. She *wasn't*. She was appreciating this time with Seth as the gift it was. But still, his offer to include her in a family thing warmed her.

Wait a minute. "Will your parents be there?"

He dropped his gaze. "Yeah. The whole family will be."

Oh, dear. Of course, once she had figured out she would be spending time with Seth, she had looked up the reality show the Boltons had done a number of years ago—even catching glimpses of the teenage Seth working with his father.

Seth had been a cute boy on the verge of manhood then—but the Boltons? Billy was like an angry grizzly bear, Ben Bolton glowered sullenly anytime a camera was shoved in his face, and Bobby? Well, the last Bolton brother wasn't dangerous-looking like his brothers—but he was smooth and sharp and good on camera. And their father? He was the epitome of every tough old biker ever.

And Seth wanted her to meet these people?

"We don't have to," he said into the silence. "They can be overwhelming—trust me, I know."

It was tempting to say that they wouldn't have time for a side trip. Or to say she wasn't dressed for standing in a wet field. Or that she wasn't feeling up to it. All of those would be perfectly fine excuses to save her from meeting the Boltons en masse. Because meeting the whole family—that felt huge. Far too big for a casual relationship like the one she and Seth had.

But family was forever. Or, for a long time—until they disowned you, anyway. And she'd feel terrible if she caused any sort of trouble for him with his extended family just because she might be a little intimidated by a group of bikers. He was willing to go above and beyond for his family, and she couldn't fault him for that. If anything, she admired him all the more.

So despite her misgivings, she put on a smile and said, "We can do that. But we better get going if we want to have time."

When Seth opened her car door for her, she was past panic and straight over into stark terror. "You're not introducing me as your girlfriend," she told him, staring at his hand. "That's not what this is, right?"

He didn't answer for a long moment, and she suddenly didn't know how he'd answer that question.

Worse, she didn't know how she wanted him to answer that question.

"Right," he finally said, slow and serious. "You're my real estate agent."

Oh, this was a mistake. An epic, huge, grandiose mistake.

But she was going to make it anyway.

After he helped her from the car, they began the long trek to the playing field. Apparently showing up late meant that they got the worst parking spot. Although she'd worn boots to walk around the potential museum sites, she still had to hold her skirt by the hem to keep it from getting wet in the tall grass.

Which was fine because if she was holding her skirt, then she wasn't accidentally holding Seth's hand.

When they reached the playing field, Kate looked around. "Is that them?"

Most of the parents on the sidelines were regular-looking people sitting on folding chairs with coolers.

But at the end of the field, there was a group of big, burly men around a cluster of pickup trucks with the tailgates down. The trucks were massive and even at this distance, she could tell they were top-of-the-line.

And the Boltons were *loud*. Kate could hear them bellowing words of encouragement to the players on the field.

"That's them. Don't be intimidated. They're a lot nicer than they look. All bark, no bite—that sort of thing."

She shot him a look.

They paused at midfield, and Seth turned her toward the game. "We're rooting for the green team, the Mustangs. The forward? That's Julie. The right guard's Eliza and the left is Clara—my cousins. They're unbeatable." He said it with obvious pride when any other man his age might have been embarrassed or at least put out to have to give up part of his Saturday on a regular basis to watch little girls kick a ball around. But not him. He really did love his family.

The thought made Kate unexpectedly sad. She hadn't played soccer when she was young—but she'd had dance recitals and choir concerts, and had even acted in a few plays in high school. Her mom had come—but not her dad.

As they watched, Eliza passed the ball to Clara, who faked out a player on the other team and then kicked the ball to Julie, who bounced it off her chest and then kicked it in just past the goalie. The green team erupted into cheers—as did the parents on the sidelines. Especially the group of Boltons at the end of the field. Seth let out a tremendous whoop and the girls on the field pivoted as one and waved at him before their coach bellowed something and they all trotted off down the field.

"They seem pretty good," Kate said as they began to make their way toward his family—and her doom.

No, no—not her doom. Just a really awkward meeting with her not-boyfriend's parents. No need to panic.

"The Mustangs came in second in the championship last year. I think they're going to win it this year. Julie's unstoppable and Eliza is a monster on the field."

Kate kept an eye on the game. Julie and Eliza looked a great deal like each other but Clara? Kate had a feeling that if they all stood still next to each other, she'd be able to see the resemblance, but Clara was much lighter in coloring than the other two.

And then it was too late to turn back because the biggest of the three men stood up from the tailgate and bellowed, "Seth! About damn time. Where the hell have you been?"

Kate recognized him. It was Billy Bolton, the biggest and meanest-looking of the brothers. He was older than he'd been in the reality show, his grizzled beard shot with silver—but he was still a force to be reckoned with.

Then Billy's gaze landed on Kate and she froze like a deer in the headlights.

One of the women—petite and brown and who looked a great deal like Seth—put her hand on Billy's knee. "Language, honey."

A kid about eight or so looked up from the book he was reading. "Seth is here? Yeah!" He hopped up and gave Seth a high five and immediately began telling him about some complicated…card game? Kate couldn't tell.

A little girl, maybe five, squirmed out of Ben Bolton's arms and came charging up to Seth, who caught her easily. "Set!" she crowed. "Spin me!"

Kate's heart clenched at the sight of Seth making a

little girl squeal with joy while simultaneously carrying on a very important conversation with a kid. Of course he was great with kids. He was perfect, apparently.

And she was…not.

The woman who'd shushed Billy Bolton stood and made her way over to Kate and instantly, every hair on the back of Kate's neck stood up in warning. "Ignore my husband. Hi, I'm Jenny Bolton. And you are?"

"Kate." Kate swallowed, trying to remember who she was supposed to be right now. But that wasn't easy because every single pair of eyes at this tailgate party were now staring at her. Two other women, both about the same age as Jenny Bolton, closed ranks, standing behind Jenny. "Kate Burroughs," she finally remembered when the one woman with long, dark brown hair raised an eyebrow at her. "Of Zanger Realty. I'm Mr. Bolton's real estate agent."

Someone snorted, but Kate kept her focus on the women. Because it suddenly occurred to her—why had she been worried about the Bolton brothers?

She should have been worried about the Bolton *women*. Including but not limited to the three younger ones running up and down the field.

But maybe not the littlest one. Seth paused in spinning what Kate assumed was another cousin just long enough for the girl to grin at Kate and say, "Your skirt is pretty. Does it twirl?"

"I'm not sure," Kate answered honestly. "Twirling makes me dizzy." And God knew her sense of balance wasn't what it had once been.

"But that's the best part!" The girl giggled and then she and Seth were off again, making big, dizzying circles.

"Real estate?" Jenny's eyes narrowed as she took in

everything about Kate. The woman looked too much like Seth not to be his mother. The woman to Jenny's right was taller, more statuesque, perhaps a little lighter in coloring, but she bore a strong resemblance to Jenny. The woman to Jenny's left, however, had vivid blue eyes and an almost icy demeanor. To a woman, however, they were wearing stunning tops underneath their coats. Kate looked longingly at Jenny Bolton's soft peach sweater. She had a feeling that no matter how much her commission was, she wouldn't be able to afford a sweater like that. The same went for the diamonds in Jenny's ears and around her neck. And that had nothing on what the woman with blue eyes was wearing.

Kate refused to be intimidated by the unified wall of womanhood that was currently looking her up and down. Crap—could these experienced wives and mothers tell she was pregnant? Or were they just judging her by regular feminine standards?

"We were looking at an industrial property not far from here and had time to check in on the game before we signed papers on Mr. Bolton's house this afternoon." All of which was 100 percent the truth and had nothing to do with how good Seth was in bed.

After a moment's hesitation that spoke louder than any niceties could, Jenny said, "I see," in a tone that made it clear that she did—far too well.

Kate swallowed. This was not going well. Feeling desperate, she turned her attention to the rest of the group. "No need to get up," she said when it was obvious no one would, anyway. She gave a little wave. "It's a pleasure to meet you all. I enjoyed your show." Bobby Bolton, still as handsome as ever, grinned—but his brothers both groaned. Kate pressed on. "And

I'm excited to help your company move forward into its next venture." There. That was a perfectly professional thing to say.

No one reacted. "Kate's done an amazing job finding the right properties," Seth announced into the awkward silence.

She could feel her face heating up. Somehow, turning tomato red didn't seem to be the reasonable reaction here.

Then it only got worse because in the middle of that quiet lull, her stomach growled so loudly that it briefly drowned out the sounds of the game. "My apologies," Kate said hastily, wondering if a woman could actually die of embarrassment at a soccer game. "We haven't had time to grab lunch. We should go..."

But the words had no more gotten out of her mouth than the Bolton women descended upon her. "We have food," the paler one said in a surprising British accent. "I'm Stella—Bobby's wife. Clara's mother."

"Besides," the other added, "Connie won't turn loose of Seth for a good twenty minutes and Davey has to talk to someone about Pokémon—all the better if it isn't me. I'm Josey—Ben's wife. The rest of this brood is mine."

"You should sit," Jenny said, moving forward to put a hand on Kate's arm and leading her to a folding chair. "We have chicken or burgers."

And just like that, Kate wasn't on the outside anymore.

She had no idea if that was a good thing or not.

Thirteen

Dimly, Seth was aware that there was still a soccer match going on. But that wasn't the game he was playing right now.

"She's pretty," Bruce Bolton, Seth's grandpa, said. He turned his flinty eyes back to Seth. "What's she doing here with the likes of *you*?"

Seth tried to laugh that off. Over the years, he had learned to hold his own against the Bolton men. But that usually worked best when they'd chosen sides. The Boltons united was a fearsome sight to behold.

Like right now. The three brothers and their father were all staring at Seth, expecting a reasonable answer. It was at that moment that Seth realized he might have overplayed his hand. Time for some damage control. "Like I said, she's my real estate agent. I'm closing on my house this afternoon." They stared at him like he had lost his ever-loving mind.

"I wouldn't waste my time with a lovely lady like that on real estate," Bruce grumbled. Then he winked at Seth.

"The second site we looked at this morning seems like a good fit for the museum," Seth went on, desperate to keep the conversation away from how pretty Kate was. "It's halfway between the highway and the factory. It costs a little more up front, but the site's already been cleared."

If Seth had had any hope at all that talking shop would distract the Bolton men from the pretty real estate agent currently being coddled by the Bolton women, that hope died on the vine. "You be careful with her," his uncle Ben said.

"I am. I mean," Seth quickly corrected, "it's not like that. We're just working together."

His dad's glare hardened, and Bobby rolled his eyes in disbelief. Even Bruce looked like he wasn't going to buy that line. Seth wasn't a little kid anymore, but he began to sweat it. What if he couldn't convince them there was nothing unbecoming between him and Kate?

The Boltons were family men, and if they thought Seth was leading Kate along under false pretenses, Seth didn't want to even think what they might do. He wouldn't put a shotgun and a preacher past them, though.

But the moment the thought drifted through his brain, something weird happened. Instead of shuddering in horror at the thought, he could see Kate walking toward him, her belly rounded under a simple white dress—not that cupcake confection she'd been wearing the day he'd met her. A smile on her face as she came toward him…

He shook the thought from his head and glanced back over to where his mom and his aunts had surrounded Kate. Jenny had taken a seat next to Kate and appeared to be asking her a series of rapid-fire questions—about what, Seth was afraid to ask. Josey was piling a plate with food and Stella stood back a little ways, watching it all unfold. Kate glanced up and caught his eye. Her cheeks blushed a soft pink before she looked away.

"Yeah," Bobby said, chuckling. "*Just* working together. What did you say her name was?"

"Kate Burroughs."

"And she sells real estate?"

Seth nodded, feeling like he was sixteen and getting busted for staying out past curfew—again.

Bobby's grin turned sharp. "Wasn't there a wedding…?"

Of course Seth should've known that Bobby had his finger on the pulse of Rapid City gossip. "Yeah. I told you guys about that—I found the bride by the side of the road? That's her." He hadn't necessarily wanted to share that particular tidbit of information, but it was better to get out in front of this sort of thing.

Of course, being in front of anything with this crowd only guaranteed that he'd be run over. "You don't say," Ben said. *"Business."*

Honestly, Seth wasn't sure what this thing with Kate was anymore. It was, in fact, business. But it was also something casual and fun, a rebound to help Kate get back on her feet. And yet…

"Nothing but," he lied.

Not a single one of his male relatives bought that lie. Maybe because Seth didn't buy it himself.

Thankfully, something happened on the playing field

and for a moment, everyone's attention focused on the game. The Mustangs were up by three now, with fifteen minutes left in the game. The championship match seemed within their grasp.

He glanced at Kate again. Connie was practically in Kate's lap now, completely enamored of this fancy new person who wore pretty skirts. Kate leaned over, putting her at eye level with Connie. She had a big smile on her face and she clapped when Connie spun for her.

Something in his chest tightened. Kate was going to be an amazing mother. But he knew how hard it was to be a single parent. He didn't want that for her, damn it all. But aside from throwing two commissions her way, he didn't know how to help.

Kate caught his eye and gave Seth a tight smile. Then, as if by mutual agreement, they both looked away.

When Seth turned his attention back to his family, he found himself squarely in the crosshairs of his father. Billy threw an arm around Seth's shoulders and hauled him off to the side. "You're telling me," Billy began with no other introduction, "that you hired the runaway bride to be your real estate agent on purpose?"

Seth had had his disagreements with his adoptive father over the years. Billy was a hard man who did things his way. He wasn't afraid of a fight, either.

But for all that, he was a remarkably fair man. From the very beginning, he had treated Seth as if he were an equal. Seth wouldn't be half the man he was today if it weren't for his father. And he hated disappointing his father.

But he could tell that Billy was disappointed in him.

"She jilted her fiancé and he kept the house they had together. Her family didn't back her up and she had to quit their real estate office. I'm just helping her out. She needs the commissions."

All of which was true. Or at least, it had been a month ago. Now?

Billy gave him a hard look, one that had Seth standing up straighter. "Women are not to be trifled with, son."

"I am not trifling with her," he defended quickly. He'd made no promises to Kate beyond the next month or so. He was not leading her on with talks of love and marriage. There was no discussion of forever or happily-ever-after. No allusions to a future that existed past the new year. Ergo, it was not trifling.

"We're sending you to Shanghai," his father said in the kind of voice that Seth had seen make grown men damn near wet their pants with terror. "In the new year. Bobby thinks it could be six, eight months there, with a possibility of Mumbai afterward."

So it'd been decided? Good. Great. He loved it when a plan came together. So why was he filled with a crushing sort of disappointment? "And I'll be ready."

"Does she know that?"

"Of course she does. She knows my job is everything."

His father gave him a long look. "And yet you brought her to your sister's soccer game."

It was not a question. "I don't know how many times I have to say this," Seth ground out, pulling away from his father's embrace. "I'm not leading her on. We have a business relationship. We understand each other perfectly, damn it. And we were in the neighborhood."

Billy was not buying any of this. "If you get her pregnant," he said, as if he were Kate's father instead of Seth's, "your mother and I will expect you to do the right thing."

"I am not going to get her pregnant," Seth retorted. It was impossible to get her pregnant again. "Even if there was something going on between us—which there is not—I would never casually risk her health and well-being and you, of all men, should know that." For a moment, his dad looked almost chastised. Seth forced his shoulders to relax. "Now. Are you done threatening me so we can watch Julie play?"

He expected his father to glower or maybe even yell. So when Billy Bolton cracked a rare smile, Seth was completely caught off guard. "Make sure you're doing the right thing, son," he said, giving Seth a slap on the back that was hard enough to send Seth stumbling. Billy stepped around Seth and went to watch his daughter outplay the other team.

Seth glowered at his father's back. *Of course* he was doing the right thing. He was helping out a single soon-to-be mother. He was ensuring that she would have enough money to live on for the next year, if she wanted to. And he was helping her get over Roger. By the time Seth left for Shanghai, Kate would be financially secure and ready to move on with her life. Without him.

How was that not the right damn thing?

The garage doors shut behind them, sealing her and Seth off from the rest of the world. The afternoon had passed in a blur of legal documents and signatures, but the end result was now official—the home on Bitter Root was Seth's.

She wasn't going to be sad about that. She was just

going to be happy for him, and happy that he was willing to share this home with her, even for a little while.

He opened her car door and held out his hand, just like he always did. "I must say," he said, as she slipped her palm against his and let him help her from the car, "this has been one of the stranger days of my life."

"Buying a home is often very strange," she agreed. But that's not what made today strange for her.

The whole day had been a glimpse into a life she desperately wanted but would never get to have. This house was perfect for her and the family she was going to raise—but she couldn't afford it, not in this life or the next.

Just like Seth's family—aunts and uncles, grandparents and siblings, all coming together for something as mundane as a child's soccer game because they cared. They put family first.

Of course she knew that there were kind, loving, supportive families in the world. And hers was certainly not the worst, by far. But seeing the way that Seth's family had lined up to protect him from an outsider—her? And then there'd been that moment where, apparently by some unspoken agreement, she hadn't been on the outside looking in. She'd been made welcome and fed and, okay, so maybe his mom's questions about Seth's new house had really been thinly veiled questions about Seth and Kate's relationship. But there was no mistaking the fact that Seth's family would do anything for him—for any member of the Bolton family.

She wanted that unconditional love and support for her child. She wanted that for herself, but she was used to doing without.

Holding her hand, Seth unlocked the garage door. He

pulled her inside and then let go long enough to find a light switch. While he did so, she pushed aside her melancholy feelings. There was no point in moping over what she couldn't have. She needed to focus on what she did have—a gorgeous, caring, wealthy man who, for reasons she still didn't fully understand, was more than happy to give her almost everything she wanted.

"Welcome home, Mr. Bolton," she said when he found the light switch. He really was too handsome, she thought when he turned back to her. She tried to strike a sultry pose.

Seth's eyes darkened dangerously. "It's good to be home, Ms. Burroughs." He prowled toward her, the energy that made him so good in bed vibrating off him. "I feel like celebrating. How about you?" He paused, waiting for her answer.

"Yes." Because this was as good as it got. She could make love to Seth in his home and hold on to these happy memories through the long, lonely nights ahead.

He flattened her against the door with his body, hard and hot against hers. But even when he covered her mouth with his, taking and demanding—there was still a gentleness to him.

"Now, Seth," she whispered against his neck, grabbing the belt of his jeans. She didn't want to wait. She didn't want gentle. She just wanted this memory.

"Babe," he growled, and then he picked her up. She squeaked in alarm—she wasn't getting any lighter these days—but Seth cradled her to his chest as if it were the easiest thing in the world. Just like she had from the very beginning, she felt safe in his arms. She knew he wouldn't drop her.

"I apologize for the lack of furniture," he said as he carried her toward the kitchen.

"Don't," she said, throwing her arms around his neck and kissing his jaw. Tucking every contour of his face, every muscle in his neck, away into her memory. "Don't apologize for any of it."

He sat her on the island counter and kissed her again, harder this time. She managed to get his buckle undone and then he was shoving her flowing skirt up, pulling her panties down. "I need you so much, Kate."

"Yes," she hissed, shoving his pants out of the way. When was the last time anyone had needed her? Roger certainly hadn't. He'd barely even wanted her. Her parents had relied on her because she was cheap labor.

But who needed her because she was Kate?

No one. Just Seth.

They normally took their time with foreplay, but she didn't have the patience for it today and neither did he. He set himself against her and then, with one delicious thrust, buried himself deep inside. Moaning with pleasure, she fell back on her elbows as he grabbed her hips and slammed into her again and again.

She loved being with Seth, but this rawness, this need—this was what had been missing. She had thought he'd been holding himself back out of deference to her being pregnant. But today?

Today, he was like a man possessed. Seth pounded into her again and again, his fingertips gripping her hips with brute strength. Kate sprawled on top of the island, surrendering to him completely. Already, she could feel the orgasm spiraling up and up. Pulling her along until her back was arching and she was grabbing at his forearms, desperate for anything to hold on to. When her climax broke, it broke hard, wrenching a guttural cry from her lips. She didn't hold back, either.

She was Kate Burroughs and he needed her.

Seth flung back his head and made a sound that triggered another, smaller shock wave that left Kate completely boneless with satisfaction. He thrust one final time, the cords in his neck strained with the effort.

Then he fell forward, panting hard. She tangled her fingers in his hair and held him to her breast. They hadn't even gotten undressed on the way. It had been the most intense sex of her life, and she was glad it had been with him.

Seth withdrew and pulled her up, crushing her against his chest. Kate could feel the tears running down her face, but this time, it wasn't because the intensity of the orgasm had been overwhelming. She didn't even think it was the hormones, although they weren't helping.

This was supposed to be short-term. Fun. Seth had helped her secure her future. He made her feel desirable and beautiful even though her body was changing constantly. He'd introduced her to his family. And after all of that, he still made passionate love to her.

How was she supposed to let him go?

Fourteen

He could not wait for his bed to show up. An air mattress with two sleeping bags on it wasn't cutting it. Going back to the hotel would have been the smart thing to do. But he hadn't been able to wait to have Kate in this house with him and she was game, so an air mattress it was.

He wanted her in ways that didn't make a whole lot of sense. Which had to be why he was awake at some ungodly hour of the morning, trying to make sense of it all.

Thankfully, Kate was still asleep. She lay curled against his side, her burgeoning belly nestled on his hip, her leg thrown over his. Her breathing was deep and regular, and every so often, she'd twitch a little in her dreams. He hoped they were good dreams.

He gently stroked her hair and tried to think. In the midst of everything that had happened yesterday, Seth had almost overlooked one of the things his dad had said when he'd been telling Seth to man up.

They were sending him to Shanghai in a matter of months, then maybe to India. Which was great. Seth loved to travel. He liked to see the sights and try new foods and…

It wasn't like he had misled Kate. Part of their conversation about him buying a home had revolved around the fact that he was not going to live in it year-round. But he hadn't told her exactly what that entailed.

It was one thing to live in LA for a year. Sure, it took a little while to get from LA to Rapid City and back, but it was doable. Seth had made it home for birthdays and anniversaries and holidays with a few more frequent flyer miles under his belt and a growing distaste for airport coffee.

But Shanghai? Mumbai? Bangkok, maybe? Those weren't quick trips home.

It would be best for everyone, he reasoned, if the break was clean. He did not want to string Kate along. There was probably a great man out there who would appreciate everything she had to offer. Seth wouldn't stand in the way of that by giving her false hope that whenever he made it home, they could pick up where they left off.

Yes, a clean break was best. It just made sense.

Kate stirred against him. "Seth?" Her voice was heavy with sleep. "What's wrong?"

"Nothing," he told her, tightening his grip around her shoulders. "I'm just not used to the air mattress. Go back to sleep."

For a moment, he thought she was going to do just that. After all, he had run her all over God's green earth yesterday—industrial sites, soccer fields, soul-sucking house closings—not to mention several rounds of explosive sex. Plus, she was pregnant and he hadn't missed the yawns she'd hid behind her hands during the signings.

But then she put her palm on his chest and leaned up on her elbow. The room was too dark to see her face, but he knew she was staring down at him. "What aren't you telling me?"

I love you.

The words almost tumbled right off his tongue without his permission. He just managed to get his mouth closed around them before they complicated everything. Because if there was one way to make sure the break wasn't clean, it was those three little words.

"Seth?"

"I'm going to Shanghai," he told her, suddenly glad that they were having this conversation in the dark. He didn't want to see the hurt in her eyes. "My dad confirmed it yesterday at the soccer game."

The silence was heavy. "When?"

"After the holidays." He ran his hand up and down her back, willing her to lie back down. He didn't want to have this conversation about him leaving now. He didn't want to have it ever.

The realization was stunning. He loved her. When the hell had that happened?

"How long will you be gone?" Just because he couldn't see her face didn't mean he couldn't hear the sorrow in her voice. And that cut him deep.

"I'm not sure. At least six months. Probably a year."

"Oh."

Suddenly, he was talking. He couldn't let that one

single syllable be the end of this. He couldn't let this be the end.

"I knew this was a possibility, I just thought we might have a few more months. The Boltons are all family men," he explained. "Dad won't leave the shop, anyway. Bobby would go, but he doesn't like to be away from his wife and daughter very long and Stella doesn't like to take Clara out of school. Ben's a homebody and Josey wouldn't leave her school for that long," he explained, desperately trying to make her understand.

"So it has to be you?"

"It's a family business. They made me part of their family." When she didn't reply right away, he added, "I owe them, Kate. You don't know what it was like before they came into my life. Mom and I—we got by okay, but sometimes we were on welfare and in the winter, it got cold. She went to bed hungry so I'd have enough to eat, you know? She tried to hide it from me, always saying she'd eat after I went to bed, but I knew the truth. And I hated that she had to. I *hated* it."

His voice caught in his throat and it took a few moments before he could speak again. Kate didn't rush into the silence, though. She waited.

"I never wanted to see my mom suffer like that. And then, when Billy and Mom got together, that all went away like magic. Suddenly, we had plenty of food and I had my own room and clothes that fit—and I had a dad. I'd never had a dad before." He could still feel the sense of awe he'd felt in court, when the adoption had been finalized. The entire Bolton clan and almost half the reservation had shown up. "I had a *family*."

She sat up, although she didn't take her hand away from his chest. He clutched it, holding her palm over his heart. "I would never ask you to give up your family," she said solemnly. "Not for me."

He rested his hand on her stomach. She had hardly started to show, although now that he had been sleeping with her for a month, he could see the small changes in her body. He was going to give that up, too. He was going to leave before she got to the end of her pregnancy. He wasn't going to be there to see the baby born. He wouldn't see how her body changed with motherhood.

No, he knew that she would never ask. Because that wasn't who she was and that wasn't their deal.

"Kate," he said hoarsely, and then stopped because he couldn't be sure what he was going to say next.

She moved then, straddling him. The faintest glimmer of starlight came in through the bare windows—just enough that he could make out the generous swells of her breasts. His body responded immediately because he couldn't get enough of her.

He might never get enough of her.

She took him into her body and set a slow, steady pace that heated his blood all the same. Nothing stood between them now. "I will miss you," she whispered as he cupped her breasts and teased her nipples. She sank her hands into his hair and pulled him up. "God, how I will miss you."

She shuddered down on him, and he quit trying to fight it. He was lost to her.

What could he offer her? A nice house? Financial stability? Great sex, definitely.

But he couldn't offer her himself. He couldn't be there when she needed him. So instead of telling her that he loved her, that she was everything, he forced himself to say, "I will, too, babe," because it was the truth—just not the one he wanted it to be.

"So this is it, then?" Seth asked as he looked over Bobby Bolton's expansion plans for Shanghai.

"This is it," Bobby said, lounging in the chair in front of Seth's desk. "Setting up the showroom in Shanghai, training the staff, making sure everything goes smoothly for the Asia launch. In a perfect world, it'll take you six months."

"The world ain't perfect," Seth said, the sour feeling settling in his stomach. He didn't speak Chinese. He wasn't fluent in the local power structures. He needed to figure out his target market and the best way to reach them.

Even assuming he found the right bilingual staff who understood motorcycles, Seth was looking at a year in China.

He had jumped at the chance to go to LA for a year. He loved his family, but there was no getting around the fact that the Boltons could be overwhelming. And even then, Bobby had made a habit of stopping in every few months, unannounced, to see how things were going.

China was the ultimate fresh start. Seth should've been thrilled by this prospect.

"You know," Bobby said in a kind of voice that Seth had long since recognized as manipulative, "we could send someone else. I've made a few contacts..."

"What? No—I'm going. I'm a partner in this company. This is my job." He was a Bolton. He worked for the family business. He wasn't about to shirk his duties because he'd accidentally fallen in love with Kate.

The sour feeling in his stomach got more awful.

"The museum project is barely off the ground," Bobby went on, as if Seth hadn't spoken. "We still need to select the architect, finalize the design, and then there's the actual building to oversee."

"You're going to handle that." Of all the brothers, Bobby was the one who traveled the most—and that wasn't just because his wife was British. But the man practically turned into a homebody from September to May while Clara was in school.

Bobby stared at him flatly. Seth heard himself continue, "This was the deal, man. I promised to do this and I'm not going to go back on my promises to you guys. We're family." Bobby didn't respond, and an odd sort of dread churned around with the sourness. "Aren't we?"

"Have you ever spoken with your dad?" Bobby asked unexpectedly.

What the hell kind of question was that? "I talked to him this morning when I came into work. Why?"

"No, I mean your birth father. Have you ever talked to him?"

It shouldn't have hit Seth like a sledgehammer to the chest—but it did. "No. I don't even know who he was. All I know is that he left. Mom was pregnant and he left her alone."

He did not like the way Bobby was looking at him. The man was perhaps the most intelligent of the three brothers, but he hid it behind a veneer of playboy charm. There was no getting around the fact that Bobby played a long game. "She's pregnant, isn't she?"

The hits just kept on coming. "I'm not the father."

There was no need to ask who had figured it out. Kate had come to Julie's championship game—the Mustangs had easily won. And if no one had asked her if she was expecting, that was because her body made that question irrelevant. She was soft and round and glowing. Any idiot could see that she was with child—and his family was not full of idiots.

However, no one had asked. Kate's impending joy had been the elephant in the room that they had all avoided talking about at the game and ever since. Even Billy had skirted the subject, instead favoring Seth with hard looks that said more than words ever would.

Now Seth was going to leave Kate behind. Because his first priority was his family. Because that was what Boltons did. Family was first. Family was everything.

And Kate was…

He was going to be sick.

"I made a promise to you guys and to the company," Seth said slowly. "I haven't made any promises to anyone else." Which was true.

So why did saying it feel like a betrayal?

Because Kate was spending almost every night in Seth's bed and every morning in his arms. Because they ate dinner together and talked about their days.

Because he had asked her if she wanted him to go with her to her doctor's appointment where she found out she was having a girl. He'd discussed names with her. Because he had a diamond solitaire pendant with matching earrings already wrapped in silver-and-red paper with her name on it—his parting gift to her before he left.

Because, like an idiot, he had completely fallen in love with her. Deeply, irrevocably in love.

It didn't help that Bobby was still staring at him. Usually, you couldn't shut the man up. But today, he was acting more like Billy than ever. "Who else does she have? I did some digging, you know. Her ex-fiancé stayed with her parents' firm. An old friend had to give her a job. And then a certain knight in shining armor rode in and threw some big commissions her way. But if you leave, who else will she have?"

It was not uncommon for the Bolton brothers to come to blows. Bobby and Billy were like oil and water, and although Ben did his best to keep them from pummeling each other, Seth had seen a few noses get busted in his time.

Aside from that one incident before his parents had gotten married, Seth had never been a part of a family brawl. Mostly because he wasn't nearly as big as his dad and his uncles, but also it didn't seem right to take on the men who'd made a place for him.

But right now? Right now, he wanted to break Bobby's jaw. And maybe a few other bones, just for good measure. "If you're going to say something, just say it."

Bobby cracked that smooth grin of his. Seth wanted to push it in with his fist. "Wouldn't be surprised in the least if your aunts didn't descend upon that poor woman. Your mom, especially, wouldn't like the idea of Kate being all alone when she has that baby."

No, of course Mom wouldn't. Even though Seth was twenty-five years old now. Even though Mom had been married to Billy for almost eleven years, Jenny Bolton still ran an after-school support group for pregnant teenagers because she didn't want anyone to feel as alone as she had when she'd been pregnant with Seth.

"Are you done yet?" Seth ground out. "Because I don't know what you want me to do here, Bobby. You show up with a plan that will have me in Shanghai for almost a year and then simultaneously make me feel like crap for doing my job? Go to hell. And get out of my office." It felt damn good to be able to say that.

Bobby stood, in no hurry to go anywhere. He straightened his cuffs and popped his neck from side to side. "I'm not the one making you feel bad, kid." He headed for the door, but paused with his hand on the knob. "And we *are* family, Seth. Family is the most important thing we have." The words settled in the room like silt at the bottom of standing water.

Seth understood what Bobby was saying. His uncle had just been playing devil's advocate—but they still expected him to put the family first and do his best to open up the Asian market. "I understand."

He was definitely going to be sick.

Bobby gave him a measured look. "Do you?" And with that parting shot, he was gone.

Fifteen

"Katie, my girl," Harold Zanger said, striding out of his office and snapping his suspenders. "How are you getting on this fine day?"

Kate patted her ever-growing stomach. "Fine," she said with a smile as Harold beamed. She left out the part where she had to pee every seven minutes and her back hurt. According to the doctor, things were going perfectly. She only had another three months to go.

"Is that Mr. Bolton of yours going to be coming around?" Harold asked the question in a too-casual manner.

But Kate didn't miss the *yours* in that question. "I don't think it's physically possible for him to buy any more real estate," she said, dodging the question.

Seth was not hers. In fact, with Christmas weeks away, he was less hers every single day.

They hadn't talked about it, but she knew he was

leaving soon. And she knew it was selfish, but she didn't want him to go. The last three months with him had been the best three months of her life.

Harold gave her a kindly look. "He's done all right by you, hasn't he?"

Kate looked away. "He has. But then," she said, forcing a smile to her lips, "so have you."

Harold patted her on the shoulder. "You're a sweet girl, Katie. You deserve better." Tears stung in her eyes as Harold gave her shoulder a squeeze and then turned away, politely pretending she wasn't about to cry. "I'm off to show some houses today," he announced loudly, giving his suspenders another snap just for good measure. "You'll hold down the fort?"

"Of course," she said, smiling through it all.

Seth had done right by her. Thanks to the purchase of the house—which still had next to no furniture in it—and the industrial property, she was able to plan to take six months off with her little girl, whom she'd decided to name Madeleine.

More than that, he had given her back her sexuality. Kate hadn't even realized what she'd been missing until Seth had come into her life. But now? She wouldn't settle for anything less. He had built her up instead of wearing her down, and never again would she go along just to get along.

Seth was leaving and she was going to let him go. It would be selfish to hold him here, but God, she was going to miss the hell out of him.

She was lost in these thoughts and others—what should she get him for Christmas?—when the chimes over the door jingled. "It's a zinger of a day at Zanger, how may I..." She looked up to see a familiar figure standing in the doorway. Her stomach curdled because she recognized that man—and it wasn't Seth.

"Roger?" What the hell was he doing here?

He looked like hell. Oh, he still looked good. His hair was combed, his face cleanly shaven, his suit nicely pressed. But as he stepped into the office, Kate could see the shadows under his bloodshot eyes. He looked like he hadn't slept in a week, maybe longer. "Kate," he said, and then stopped when she stood up. His eyes widened. "God, you look so…"

She didn't know if it was anger or adrenaline—she hadn't seen him in months. Not since he'd agreed to pay child support but promised that he'd never have anything to do with her daughter. "Pregnant?" she finished before he could say something crass. "Yes. I'm pregnant. I told you that, remember?"

He didn't even have the decency to look ashamed at coming within a hairbreadth of insulting her. "Yeah, I know. I just didn't…" He waved a hand in her general direction.

She blinked at him. "If you're implying that I was lying about being pregnant—"

"No, no. I believe you. You just look…"

How had she ever thought she could love this man? It'd been a crappy lie that she had forced herself to buy into because, for some reason she still didn't understand, her dad liked this man. Maybe it was because Roger and her father were too much alike. And Kate did exactly what her mother had done—shut up and went along with what her father wanted.

Well, no more. Seth had spent months telling her how gorgeous she was, how beautiful she looked—even as she got huge. She was carrying Roger's daughter and all he could think about was that she'd gotten fat.

He could go to hell.

"Did you have a reason for being here or did you just feel like insulting the mother of your unborn child?"

Roger recoiled.

"And I swear to God, Roger, if you ask if I'm sure it's your child, I will not be held responsible for my actions."

"Jeez, Kate—calm down. I didn't come here to pick a fight."

When, in the history of womankind, had telling a woman to "calm down" ever worked? Because it sure as hell didn't now. "Then why are you here?"

He scrubbed at the back of his neck. "Listen, I've been thinking—that kid's not even born yet. You're not going to need any child support for what, another year or so?"

Good Lord, just when she thought it couldn't get any worse, it did. "What are you talking about?"

"I heard you had a few big sales," he went on, completely missing the horrified shock in her voice. "To Bolton, of all people. I would've thought he'd come to me if he needed something—we're friends."

Liar, Kate thought. She'd been spending nearly every waking moment with Seth for the last several months and not once had Roger made an effort to talk to either of them.

She didn't say that, though. Instead, she focused on what Roger was really saying. "Yes, I sold some property. I happen to be a real estate agent. What's it to you?"

"You don't have to get all upset," he said, his eyes

darting around the office. "I'm just saying, it would probably be best if we delayed the child support payments for a little while. That's all."

"Best for who?" Roger tried to smile, but it was more of a grimace. "Roger, what the hell is going on? I'm pregnant and you rolled in here to insult my appearance and try to get out of your financial obligations to a child you helped create?"

"Hey, I didn't ask you to get pregnant."

"News flash, I didn't ask to get pregnant. It was an accident, but if you're going to act like I did this all by myself, I'm going to have to explain some basic biology to you. What do you want?"

The silence was awkward, but she debated whether or not she needed backup. How fast could Seth get here?

"See," Roger began, and she heard the whine in his voice that made it clear that he hadn't gotten his way with something, "there were some investments that didn't pan out and business has been slow and..."

"And you're suddenly broke?" she supplied.

"*Broke* is a strong word. But there have been some cash flow difficulties."

She mentally translated those passive statements. Why hadn't she ever noticed that when Roger screwed up he never owned his mistakes? "You lost all your money, didn't you? What's the matter, my dad cut you off?"

That grimace again. Roger looked like a cornered animal trying to bluff its way out of a dangerous situation. "Look, are you going to help me out or not?"

The nerve of this man. And to think, she might've been stuck with him. "You want me to help you out by releasing you from your financial obligations to your own child for an indeterminate amount of time because you made some unwise investment choices and you don't have me to bail you out—am I getting all of this right?"

Finally, he looked ashamed of himself. As well he should. "I wouldn't put it quite like that. We could get married, you know."

She almost gagged. "No," she said with as much force as she could. "I don't have to take your crap, Roger. I don't love you. You never loved me. And if you try to bail on child support, I will sue you back to the Stone Age."

"Come on, Kate—"

"No," she repeated again. "You kept the house. You kept the wedding gifts. You went on the honeymoon without me. What do I get? Child support. I had to rely on a family friend to give me a job. You gave me nothing, Roger. You are legally obligated to provide for your child. And I will hold you to it. There's nothing else I want from you."

He jerked as if she had slapped him. "When did you get so bitchy?"

Oh, that just did it. "Get out. I'm not your doormat anymore."

"But—"

"Now," she repeated, putting as much menace as she could into her voice.

The jerk had the nerve to just stand there and stare, his mouth open in shock.

She was reaching for her phone when the door behind him jingled and suddenly, there was Seth Bolton, stepping around Roger and putting himself in between that jerk and Kate. "Roger," he said, his voice cool. He looked back at Kate. "Everything okay here?"

"Yes," Kate said before Roger could attempt to turn on the charm—not that Seth would fall for it. "Roger was just leaving, after renewing his commitment to paying child support." She left the *or else* hanging invisibly in the air.

Roger was an idiot, but not such a great idiot that he was going to argue with her in front of an audience. "We can talk later," he said in a conciliatory tone.

"No," she said, standing up as straight as her belly would allow. "We can't."

"Let me see you out," Seth said, almost—but not quite—sounding friendly. He crowded Roger toward the door and opened it, waiting.

Roger's shoulders slumped in defeat. He looked back at Kate and said, "You look great, you know."

There was a time when Kate would have clung to that halfhearted compliment as proof that Roger did care for her, that she was doing the right thing staying with him. Now?

Too little, too late. She did not return the compliment.

Roger opened his mouth as if he were going to say something else, but Seth cleared his throat. It was the most menacing sound Kate had heard come out of him yet.

Then the men were outside and Kate half wanted Seth to take a swing at Roger and half just wanted the idiot to go away.

She was going to have to take Roger to court—that much was obvious. Lawyers were going to be expensive, but she wasn't going to let him weasel his way out of this.

She sank down in her desk chair and dropped her head into her hands. He hadn't even asked if she was going to have a boy or girl. Why was she surprised? She wasn't, really. Of course Roger was going to disappoint her. He really didn't care. Not about the baby, not about her.

The door jingled again and there was Seth, shutting it firmly behind him. "He's gone," he said, looking at her with open concern. "Are you all right?"

Kate's throat was thick with emotion—damned hormones. "I stood up to him," she said around the lump in her throat. "He doesn't want to pay child support and I told him I'd sue him if I had to. God, what a hassle."

Seth grinned at that. He glanced back at Harold's dark office and then came around her desk, pulling her up into his arms. "You were amazing," he agreed. Rubbing her back in just the right place. "I wish I could've seen the whole thing."

She was crying—but she was also laughing. "Oh, you would've hit him. I would've liked to have seen that." Seth leaned back and stroked her tears away. She loved that her random bouts of hormones didn't freak him out. "I can't believe I almost married him."

He cradled her face. "I'm so glad you didn't."

Kate almost lost herself in the tenderness of the moment. No—she couldn't fall for Seth all over again. "Did he say anything to you outside?"

Seth snorted. "He seemed hurt that I hadn't used him for my real estate agent."

"Lord."

Seth hugged her tighter, and she sank into his

warmth. He was always here when she needed him, lending her his strength. Without him, she might have buckled and agreed to marry Roger. She might have let Roger out of his financial obligations.

She would've been miserable. But she wasn't. Upset, yes. Pregnant, definitely. But she'd refused to roll over to make someone else happy. Seth had shown her she could fight for what she wanted and for that, she would love him forever.

He stepped all the way around her and began to knead his thumbs into her lower back. God, it felt so good. "What are you doing here?"

"I needed to see you," he said, sending a thrill through her. Then, after a long pause while he worked on a particularly sore spot, he added, "We finalized the plan for the Shanghai showroom."

All of her good feelings disappeared in a heartbeat. Because this was it—the end. "Oh?" she got out in a strangled-sounding voice.

"Yeah." Kate couldn't tell if it was a consolation or not that he sounded almost as depressed as she felt. "Best-case scenario is Shanghai for six months, but it'll probably be closer to ten, maybe even twelve."

She shut her eyes, although that didn't change things. "That's great," she lied, because his job was important to him. His family was important to him, and she could not allow him to damage those relationships for her.

"Yeah," he said again, sounding positively morose about it. "It's going to be really exciting. I'll leave on the second."

They were down to days at this point. Sixteen days. And then he would be gone from her life and she would still be here, arguing with Roger and trying to do the best she could with what she had.

Suddenly, she couldn't bear it. She turned, throwing her arms around his neck. "I wish I could go with you."

His hands cradled her belly. "I couldn't ask it of you. I wish I could stay."

She shook her head against his shoulder. "I couldn't ask it of you, either."

He pulled a small box out of his pocket. "I got this for you."

She stared at the Christmas wrapping. She didn't want to open it—didn't want to accept the fact that the best thing that had ever happened to her was winding down to its natural conclusion. "Thank you. I haven't had time to get you a present yet."

"I don't…" He pulled her back into his arms and held her for a long moment. Then, almost by unspoken agreement, they both pulled back. Lingering would do no one any good. "Promise me," he said, taking her hands and staring down into her eyes. "Promise me you'll take care of yourself and Madeleine. Promise me you won't…" He swallowed, his eyes suspiciously bright. "Don't wait for me, Kate. There's a great guy out there who is going to be really lucky to have you and I don't want you to pass him up."

"You're being ridiculous," she said, hiccupping. She was almost seven months pregnant. The number of men who would look at her and see anything but baggage could probably be counted on one hand.

In fact, there might only be one of them. Standing right in front of her.

"If you need anything," he went on, ridiculous or

not, “you call my parents. My mom’s an expert about single moms with new babies. Okay?”

“Seth—”

“Promise me, Kate,” he insisted, squeezing her hands.

All good things came to an end. And that was what this was. The end. “I promise.”

She’d never realized how much that sounded like goodbye.

Sixteen

An odd sort of tension settled in and made itself comfortable between Seth and his family. Sure, they all opened presents together Christmas morning. But even Julie, who professed to still believing in Santa Claus, was giving him looks that he didn't want to think about. She was too much like their father sometimes, and he was in no mood to be judged by a ten-year-old.

His mom would look at him and sigh and damned if it didn't sound like disappointment. And his dad? The temperature dropped a solid ten degrees anytime he walked into the room.

No one spoke about it. No one asked about Kate. They barely talked about Shanghai. Just tension.

Just Seth slowly going insane. He hadn't seen her since that day in her office—the day he'd given her the necklace. She hadn't opened it. He almost called her

Christmas afternoon but he told himself he'd wanted a clean break and that it was for the best.

That didn't explain why he called Kate on New Year's Eve and asked her to come spend it with him. She must have been doing okay, because she refused and in a way, he was glad. He was flying out first thing on the second to LA and from there, to mainland China. If she came over for one last night, he honestly had no idea how he was going to leave.

He was miserable and pissy and worried sick about her being alone for Madeleine's birth. Even though he knew that if the shit hit the fan his family would step up and make sure Kate was taken care of, he still worried. What if Roger came back? What if she had to sue him for child support? What if there was a problem with Madeleine? Hell, what if there wasn't? He remembered how hard it'd been for everyone the first few months after Julie had been born. And Julie had had Mom, Dad and Seth to take care of her. How would Kate handle the sleepless nights and diapers and feedings by herself?

He did his best not to worry as he packed up his stuff. His dad took him to the airport. It was still pitch-black at five in the morning, but at least it was clear. Flying out of South Dakota in the middle of winter was always dicey.

True to form, they didn't talk. Billy just glowered, and Seth? He tried to focus on the future. He'd never been one to settle down. Wandering all over God's green earth was who he was. He knew it. Kate knew it. His family knew it.

At least, he thought they did. They got to the airport and Billy silently helped unload Seth's bags and Seth couldn't remember ever having been more miserable than he was right now because this felt wrong. Everything about it was wrong.

Panicking hard, Seth stood before the only man he'd ever called father. "I'm not Madeleine's father," he said, wishing he could take the words back even before he was done saying them.

It was not Dad's business—it was none of anyone's business. But he knew, deep down inside, that Billy Bolton was disappointed in him.

Billy jammed his hands on his hips and stared up at the midnight-black sky. "No, I didn't figure you were."

"I have to put the family first."

Once, long ago, Seth had punched this man in the face for daring to break up with his mom. It was the only time he'd ever struck Billy, and the man hadn't yelled or hit back. Instead, he'd looked at Seth with disappointment in his eyes—the same disappointment in his eyes right now. "Neither of them is family, but you already know that baby's name."

Seth's throat closed up. "You guys made me a Bolton. That wasn't something I took lightly. I'm not going to let you or the business down."

Seth hadn't realized he was staring at the sidewalk until Billy's massive hands settled on Seth's shoulders. "Son," he said, and it just about broke Seth's heart to hear that word spoken with so much sadness, "God knows I tried to do right by you and your mom. And God knows if it weren't for motorcycles, I'd either be dead or in jail."

"I know," Seth said, wishing for numbness because he couldn't take this. The business kept his father going and he couldn't turn his back on that.

Billy's grip on him tightened. "Look at me, Seth." Seth raised his head, swallowing back tears. "The business is important, but we could lose it tomorrow and it wouldn't change anything about you and me and our family. We will always be family because we chose you, and more important, you chose us." He gave Seth a little shake. "You don't have to prove a damned thing to me. You never did."

Then he pulled Seth into a mammoth bear hug before quickly shoving him away. "Write your mother," he called out as he got back into his truck and drove off.

Seth stood there for a moment in the freezing air, shaking.

He hadn't chosen the Boltons—his mom had. His aunt had—they'd both married brothers. He'd been part of the deal, but not as a voting member. He'd just…

He'd spent the last ten years of his life living and breathing motorcycles and the motorcycle business because when he welded a frame Billy approved of or pitched an idea Bobby got behind, it made Seth feel like he was part of something. Crazy Horse Choppers had given him a place. A purpose.

That was what mattered.

Wasn't it?

Not that anyone was buying real estate right now—no one really wanted to move on the second day of the year in the middle of winter—but Kate went to work anyway. She couldn't handle staying alone in her crappy apartment all day, staring at the lovely Christmas card her mother had sent.

She wore the stunning diamond pendant necklace and matching earrings Seth had bought for her. She wasn't an expert in diamonds, but she'd listened when the jewelry salespeople had talked cut and clarity and all that and she was wearing probably close to four carats of diamonds. It wasn't a stretch to say that she was wearing close to fifty thousand dollars' worth of jewelry—a fortune.

He'd spent that on her. It was a hell of a farewell gift and, if worse came to worst, it would take care of her and Madeleine for a long time.

But she couldn't bear the thought of selling Seth's gifts. She'd sold her engagement ring because she hadn't wanted to hang on to another reminder of Roger—and she'd needed the cash. But Seth's pendant?

She wore it on a long chain so it nestled next to her heart. It was the only way she could keep him close.

That, and being here at work. There were so many memories of Seth here. Hearing the door jingle and looking up to see Seth standing there, that grin on his face. She didn't want to entirely leave those memories right now, either. It was easier to pull those memories around her like a blanket at the office. She was even gladder that she'd never had him over to her apartment. It would've been too much.

She glanced at the clock—again—and slid the diamond along the chain. Seth should've landed in LA by now. He was probably holed up in a bar, waiting for his flight to China. Was he thinking of her? Was he wishing that she'd taken him up on his offer to ring in the New Year—just one more night together? She'd known she needed to say no to him, but now she wished she'd said yes. Because it already sucked, letting him go. What would one more night have hurt?

The baby fluttered in her stomach, and Kate put her

hand to where Madeleine was kicking. This was what she had to focus on now—impending motherhood. For all intents and purposes, she was all Madeleine had.

No, it wasn't exactly true. Seth had made her swear that if she needed any help, she'd contact his family. Part of Kate knew that wasn't a good idea because, while she genuinely liked his parents and his sister, that would presume a relationship that otherwise no longer existed.

On the other hand, it was clear from her mother's Christmas card that there wouldn't be a close relationship with her parents. And Kate was just coming to grips with the fact that she had a long, cold, dark three months of being extremely pregnant ahead of her.

It wouldn't be so bad if Madeleine were already here. The baby was going to take every little bit of energy Kate had—and probably some she didn't have. She wouldn't be able to dwell on Seth's absence once Madeleine arrived.

Kate tried diligently to focus on listings. The family she'd spoken to a few months ago was being relocated to Rapid City and anticipated moving by March. And since Kate had recently been in a vast majority of the homes currently on the market, she could with great confidence eliminate most of them.

That was what she was supposed to be thinking about. But even in that, her thoughts turned back to Seth. He'd purchased the house that she had long wanted—but refused to furnish it without her input. The house could be such a showplace, but right now, it was little more than an exaggerated bachelor pad, stacked with boxes that had been in storage. She hoped Seth would hire a good interior decorator when he came home and make something out of that house.

She was making another cup of tea in the small kitchen tucked behind Harold's office when the door jingled. "It's a zinger of a day here at Zanger," she called over her shoulder, pouring the hot water over the tea bag. Who knew? Someone had actually come looking for a house. It was a good thing she was here. "I'll be right with you."

She walked out into the main part of the office and then pulled up short so quickly that water splashed all over the place.

She was hallucinating, because it wasn't possible that Seth was here.

Then he smiled and she realized that no, she couldn't be imagining this. Seth Bolton himself stood in the doorway of the office.

He'd come for her.

He couldn't have come for her.

"Seth? What are you doing here?"

His smile faltered a little. "I've been thinking," he said, taking a hesitant step into the office.

"But... You are supposed to be on a plane? Or in LA by now. You're not supposed to be here."

"I couldn't leave," he said, his voice hoarse. "I couldn't leave you."

The room started to swim and the next thing she knew, she was in Seth's arms and he was lowering her down into her chair. "Breathe, babe," he said, kneeling in front of her and holding her hands.

"You're not supposed to give up your job with the company for me," she said, her voice cracking. "I would never ask you to put me before your family."

"You're not asking," he said, stroking his thumbs over the back of her hands. "Kate, I screwed up. I want to make it right and then, if you still want to be done, I'll go."

He'd come back for her. She didn't want him to leave again. She wasn't sure she was strong enough for that.

"We had an agreement," she said weakly. "Fun. No strings. You're not going to stay in Rapid City. That was the deal."

"I want to renegotiate the deal. I'm looking for something fun. Some strings attached. Slightly more permanently based in Rapid City. At least until Madeleine is old enough to travel."

At that moment, the baby chose to shift, sending flutters all over Kate's belly. Seth cupped her stomach and leaned down to kiss it through her clothes.

"You can't mean this," she said, giving up the fight against the tears. What was it about this man that always had her at her weakest?

He looked up at her, so handsome and perfect and *here*. "I never knew my father. He ran out on my mom before I was even born and I thought…I thought I was restless. That I needed to see the world—and that was because of him. But I don't think I'm restless. I just think I hadn't found a reason to stay in one place."

"Don't say that," she begged. "Don't break my heart, Seth. I can't take it."

"I couldn't take it, either—so I won't."

"I won't let you do this. I will not let you give up the family business for me. I'm not…"

His gaze sharpened. "You *are* worth it, Kate. And you know what? I'm a Bolton and if there's one thing I know about Boltons, it's that family is everything. Kate, you are *my* everything. What kind of man would I be if I didn't fight for you?"

She threw her arms around his neck and buried her face against his cheek. “No one has ever fought for me before,” she wept. “I just don’t want you to regret it.”

“Have a little faith in me,” he said, his voice shaking. “And have faith in yourself. Do you love me?”

“Of course I do,” she sobbed. “How could I not?”

“Then marry me, Kate. And not in some big lavish ceremony with a crazy dress that has petticoats and corsets and ruffles and strings. We can get married at the courthouse, for all I care. It’s not the wedding that counts—it’s you. You’re my everything, Kate, you and Madeleine. Let me be your family. It doesn’t mean I won’t do stupid things like nearly flying halfway across the world when I belong right here. That means I will fight for you, for us. Every day of my life, so help me God.”

“But your job…”

He leaned back and gave her a cocky look. “I’m a partner in the firm. It’s not like they can fire me. And besides, it’ll work out. It might be a little messy, but I’ll fight for what I want. I don’t have to prove myself to them. I just have to prove myself to you.” He swallowed. “If you’ll have me?”

“Yes,” she said, pulling him into a kiss. “God, yes, Seth. I couldn’t even think with you being gone.”

The baby shifted again, harder this time—demanding attention, no doubt. Kate gasped as Seth rubbed her belly. “I couldn’t miss this. She will always be my daughter, from the very first moment.”

This was everything she’d ever wanted. She wasn’t perfect, not by a long shot—but Seth understood who she was and loved her anyway. She cupped his cheek with her hand. “Seth?”

"Yeah?" He turned his head and pressed a kiss against her palm.

"You were right."

His eyes darkened as she ran her hands through his hair. "Oh? About what?"

"You're good for me," she replied, leaning forward to brush her lips against his. "Very, very good for me."

He grinned against her mouth. "Babe," he all but growled, pulling her into his embrace, "I'm just getting started."

Epilogue

"You don't think she'll run, do you?"

Seth shot Bobby a dirty look as the judge cleared his throat. "Shall we begin?"

Jack Roy began to strum his guitar as Julie walked into the judge's chambers, strewing rose petals before her. Davey walked next to his cousin, intensely focused on the rings he was carrying. Clara, Eliza and Connie giggled while their mothers shushed them.

Billy smacked Bobby on the arm and Ben made a noise of warning deep in his throat. Seth ignored them all because just then, Kate walked through the double doors, holding a sleeping Madeleine in her arms instead of a bouquet.

Seth's heart clenched at the sight of his family. Not that he hadn't seen them this morning—he'd gotten up with Madeleine at two so Kate could sleep.

But his aunt Stella had worked her magic, designing a simple cream wedding gown that clung to Kate's ample chest and flowed softly away from the waist. Compared to the monstrosity that Kate had almost gotten married in the first time, Seth was thrilled to realize this dress wouldn't require three lady's maids to remove.

Madeleine wore a similar outfit, although her fabric had been dyed with the faintest pink. Seth couldn't see his daughter's feet because the dress flowed well past Madeleine's legs.

"Beautiful," Billy whispered, sounding almost wheezy about it.

"Mine," Seth replied.

"I'm proud of you, son," Billy went on, his voice low enough that no one else could hear him. "I knew you'd do the right thing."

The last six months had been a whirlwind of change. Kate had moved into their home and Seth had given her free rein to decorate it as she saw fit. Madeleine had come two weeks early, healthy and beautiful. Seth had been with Kate for the entire twenty-two hours of labor.

He'd personally hired a man he'd worked with in LA who, it turned out, spoke semi-fluent Mandarin to spearhead the Shanghai showroom.

And Seth? He'd stayed in Rapid City, overseeing the museum expansion.

Expanding his family.

Today, not only would Kate become his wife, but Madeleine would legally be his daughter. He and Kate had debated getting hitched immediately—Seth's preference—but Kate had decided she wanted to wait until Madeleine could be a part of the ceremony.

Seth caught the eye of his future in-laws. Kate's dad was scowling, but he'd put on a boutonniere and he was here, so that was something. Kate's mom was dabbing at her eyes. Seth hoped that for Kate's sake, they could have a cordial relationship, if not a close one.

Then Seth turned his attention back to his bride.

The judge, it turned out, was an old riding buddy of Billy's. He'd been happy to combine a wedding and an adoption.

Kate made her way up to Seth and handed Madeleine off to Jenny. Then, before their families, God and the state of South Dakota, he married his bride and adopted his daughter.

He was a Bolton and this was his family. By God, he would do anything for them. They were the right thing. They always would be.

* * * * *

LITTLE SECRETS: THE BABY MERGER

YVONNE LINDSAY

This one is dedicated to my family,
each of whom hold a piece of my heart
in their hands and whose love and
support keep me going every day.

One

A flash of pale gold hair near the entrance caught Kirk's attention in the dimness of the bar. A woman came through the door, a tall, well-built man close behind her. She turned and said something, and the muscle looked like he was going to object, but then she spoke again—gesturing vaguely across the room—and he nodded and disappeared outside. Interesting, Kirk thought. Clearly the guy was an employee of some kind, perhaps a bodyguard, and he'd obviously been dismissed.

Kirk took a sip of his beer and watched the woman move through the area, searching for someone. There was an unconscious sensuality to the way she moved. Dressed down in a pair of slim-fitting trousers topped by a long-sleeved, loose tunic, she seemed to be trying to hide her tempting mix of curves and slenderness, but he saw enough to pique his interest. Most women hated it when they had well-rounded hips and a decent butt, and judging by the way she'd dressed to conceal, she was one of those women who wasn't a fan of her shape and form. But he was. In fact, he really liked her shape and form.

Who was she meeting here? A partner, he wondered, feeling a small prick of envy as his eyes skimmed her from head to foot. The weariness that had driven him here tonight in search of better company than employee files and financial forecasts slid away in increments as his eyes appreciatively roamed her body.

He knew the instant she saw the person she was looking for. Her features lit up, and she raised a hand in greeting, moving more quickly now toward her target. Kirk scanned ahead of her, feeling himself relax when he saw the couple who reached out to greet her affectionately. Not a partner, then, he thought with a smile and took a sip of the malty craft beer he'd ordered earlier.

He noticed one of her friends pass her a martini and pondered on the fact that they'd already ordered her drink for her. Obviously she was a reliable type, both punctual and predictable. Too bad those were not the traits of someone who might be interested in a short, intense fling, which was all he was in the market for. He had his life plan very firmly set out in front of him, and while his company's merger with Harrison Information Technology here in Bellevue, Washington, would definitely fast-track things, a committed relationship was still not in the cards for a long time. When he was ready, he'd tackle that step the way he did everything else, with a lot of research and dedication to getting it right the first time. Kirk Tanner did not make mistakes—and he definitely wasn't looking for love.

Kirk turned his attention away from the woman, but something about her kept tickling at the back of his mind. Something familiar that he couldn't quite place.

He looked across the room and studied her more closely, noting again the swath of pale gold hair that fell over her shoulders and just past her shoulder blades. Even from here he could see the kinks in her hair that told him she'd recently had it tied up in a tight ponytail. His fingers clenched around his glass, suddenly itching to push through the length of it, to see if it felt as silky soft as it looked.

As if she sensed his regard, the woman turned and glanced past him before returning her attention to her friends. This gave him the most direct view so far of her face—and yes, there was definitely something familiar about her. He'd certainly have remembered if he'd met her before but perhaps he'd seen her photograph somewhere.

Kirk searched his eidetic memory. Ah, yes, now he had it—Sally Harrison, the only child of Orson Harrison, the chairman of Harrison Information Technology. The very firm his own company was officially merging with at 3:00 p.m. tomorrow. The idea of a merger with Sally Harrison held distinct appeal, even though he knew she should be strictly off-limits.

Her personnel file had intrigued him, although the head shot attached to it had hardly done her justice. He scoured his memory for more details. Since high school she'd interned in every department of the head office of HIT. In fact, she probably knew more about how each sector of the company ran than her father did, and that was saying something. She'd graduated from MIT with a PhD in social and engineering systems. And yet, despite her experience and education and the fact she was the chairman's daughter, she'd apparently never aspired to anything higher than a mediocre middle-management position.

Granted, her department was a high performer and

several of her staff had been promoted, but why hadn't she moved ahead, too? Was she being very deliberately kept in place by her father or other senior staff? Was there something not noted in her file that made her unqualified or ill-suited for a more prominent position in the company?

And—the more compelling question—did she perhaps have sour grapes about her lack of advancement?

Her knowledge about the firm made her a prime candidate for the investigation her father had asked him to undertake as part of his staff evaluation during the merger.

Under the guise of seeing where staff cutbacks needed to be made, he was also tasked with investigating who could most likely be responsible for what could be unwitting or deliberate leaks to HIT's largest business rival. Orson suspected that the rival company, DuBecTec, was accumulating data to undermine his company with a view toward making a hostile takeover bid in the next few months. He had instructed Kirk to look at everyone on the payroll very thoroughly. Everyone including the very appealing Ms. Sally Harrison.

Kirk took another sip of his beer and watched her across the room. She'd barely sipped her drink yet but swirled the toothpick in her martini around and around. Just then, as he was watching, she removed the toothpick from her drink and, using her teeth and her tongue, drew the cocktail onion off the tip and crunched down. His entire body clenched on a surge of desire so intense he almost groaned out loud.

Sally Harrison was a very interesting subject indeed, he decided as he willed his body back under control. And before he left the bar tonight, he would definitely find a way to get to know her better.

* * *

Company merger. For the best.

Even though she was going through the motions, saying all the right things as her friends excitedly told her about their recent honeymoon, Sally couldn't stop thinking about her father's shocking announcement over dinner tonight. If she hadn't heard it straight from the horse's mouth, she would have struggled to believe it. She *still* struggled to believe it. And the fact that her father hadn't shared a moment of what had to have been an extensive forerunner to the merger with her raked across her emotions.

It was a harsh reminder that if she was the kind of person who actually stood *with* her father, versus sheltering behind him, she'd have been a part of the discussions. Not only that, if she'd been the kind of person she ought to be, confident and charismatic instead of shy and intense, this entire merger might not even have been necessary.

Her whole body trembled with a sense of failure. Oh, sure, logically she knew that her dad wouldn't have entered into this planned merger if it wasn't the best thing for Harrison IT and its thousand or so staff worldwide. And it wasn't as though he needed her input. As chairman of HIT, he held the reins very firmly in both hands, as he always had. But, until now, HIT had been the family firm, and darn it, she was his family. Or at least she was the last time she'd looked.

Of course, now the company would be rebranded—Harrison Tanner Tech. Clearly things were about to change on more than one level.

She could have predicted her father's response when she'd questioned the secrecy surrounding the merger.

"Nothing you need to worry about," he'd said, brushing her off in his usual brusque but loving way.

And she wasn't worried—not about the company, anyway. But she did have questions that he'd been very evasive about answering. Like, why this *particular* other company? What did it bring to HIT that the firm didn't have already? Why *this* man, whoever he was, who was being appointed vice president effective tomorrow? And why did her dad want her to be there during the video link when he and the new vice president of the newly branded Harrison Tanner Tech would make the merger announcement simultaneously to the whole staff? She couldn't think of anything she'd rather do less. Aside from the fact that she hated being in the public arena, how on earth would she look her colleagues in the eye afterward and possibly have to face their accusations that she'd known about this merger all along? Or worse, have to admit that she hadn't. Just the thought of it made her stomach flip uneasily.

Her father had always told her he worked hard so she didn't have to. She knew he worked hard. Too hard, if the recent tired and gray cast to his craggy features was anything to go by. It was another prod that she hadn't pulled her weight. Hadn't been the support he deserved and maybe even needed. Not that he'd ever say as much. He'd protected her all her life, which hadn't abated as she'd reached adulthood. To her shame, she'd let him.

Thing was, she *wanted* to work hard. She wanted to be a valued member of HIT and to be involved in the decision making. She wished she could shed the anxiety that led to her always hovering in the shadows and allowing others to run with her ideas and get the glory that came with those successes. Okay, so not every idea was wildly successful, but her phobia of speaking in groups had held her back, and she knew others had been promoted over her because of it. Her personality flaws meant she wasn't perceived to be as dynamic and forward thinking as people in upper management were expected to be.

When her crippling fear had surfaced after the death of her mom, and when years of therapy appeared to make no headway, her father had always reassured her that she was simply a late bloomer and she only needed time to come into her own. But she was twenty-eight now, and she still hadn't overcome her insecurities. She knew that was a continual, if quiet, disappointment to her father. While he'd never said as much, she knew he'd always hoped that she could overcome her phobia and stand at his side at HIT, and she'd wanted that, too. She'd thought he was still giving her time. She hadn't realized he'd given up on her. Not until today.

This latest development was the last straw. Her father had always included her in his planning for the firm, even implemented an idea or two of hers from time to time, but this he'd done completely without her.

The shock continued to reverberate through her. The writing was on the wall. She'd been left in the dark on this major decision—and in the dark was where she'd stay going forward unless she did something about it. She couldn't make excuses for herself anymore. She was a big girl now: It was past time that she stretched to her full potential. If she didn't, she'd be overlooked for the rest of her life, and she knew for sure that she didn't want that. Things had to change. She had to change. Now.

Gilda and Ron were still laughing and talking, sharing reminiscences as well as exchanging those little touches and private looks that close couples did all the time. It was sweet, but it compounded the sense of exclusion she felt at the same time. In her personal life as well as in the workplace, the people around her seemed to move forward easily, effortlessly, while she struggled with every step. She was happy for the others, truly—she was just sad for herself.

When they both looked at their watches and said they needed to be on their way, she didn't object. Instead she waved them off with a smile and stayed to finish her barely touched drink.

She should go home to her apartment, get an early night—prepare for the big announcement tomorrow. Should? It felt like all her life Sally had done what *should* be done. Like she'd spent her life striving to please others. But what about her? Change had to start from a point in time—why couldn't that change start now? Why couldn't she be bold? Accept new challenges?

"Ma'am? The gentleman over there asked me to bring you this."

A waitress put another Gibson on the table in front of her. Sally blinked in surprise before looking up at the girl.

"Gentleman?"

"Over there." The waitress gestured. "He's really hot."

"Are you sure it was for me?" she asked.

"He was quite specific. Did you want me to take it back?"

Did she? The frightened mouse inside her quivered and said, *oh, yes*. But wasn't that what she would have done normally? In fact, since she'd dismissed her personal security, wouldn't she normally have left with Gilda and Ron and shared a cab so she wouldn't be left on her own like this? Open to new experiences? Meeting new people? Flirting with a man?

Sally turned her head and met the gaze of the man in question. She'd noticed him before and rejected him as being way out of her league. *Hot* didn't even begin to describe him. He wore confidence as easily as he wore his dark suit and crisp, pale business shirt, top button undone. Sally felt every cell in her body jump to visceral attention as his eyes met hers. He nodded toward her, raised his glass in a silent toast, then smiled. The kind of smile that sizzled to the ends of her toes.

Be bold, a little voice whispered in the back of her mind. She turned her attention to the waitress and gave the girl a smile.

"Ma'am?"

"Leave it. Thank you. And please pass on my thanks."

"Oh, you can do that yourself. He's coming over."

Coming over? Sally's fight-or-flight reflexes asserted themselves in full screaming glory, shrieking, *take flight!* like a Klaxon blaring in the background.

"May I join you?" the man said smoothly, his hand hovering over the back of the chair Gilda had recently vacated.

"Certainly." Her pulse fluttered at her throat, but she managed to sound reasonably calm. She lifted her glass and tipped it toward him in a brief toast. "Thank you for the drink."

"You're welcome. You don't see many people drinking a Gibson these days. An old-fashioned drink for an old-fashioned girl?"

His voice was rich and deep and stroked her nerves like plush velvet on bare skin. And he certainly wasn't hard on the eyes, either. He filled his suit with broad shoulders, and the fine cotton of his shirt stretched across a chest that looked as though it had the kinds of peaks and valleys of toned muscle that a woman like her appreciated but oh so rarely got to indulge in. His face was slightly angular, his nose a straight blade, and his eyes—whatever color they were, something light, but it was hard to tell in here—looked directly at her. No shrinking violet, then. Not like her. His lips were gently curved. He didn't have the look of a man who smiled easily, and yet his smile didn't look fake. In fact, he actually looked genuinely amused but not in a superior way.

Not quite sure how to react, she looked down at her drink and forced a smile. "Something like that."

Sally looked up again in time to see him grin outright in response. Seeing his smile was like receiving an electric shock straight to her girlie parts. Wow. Shouldn't a man need a license to wield that much sex appeal?

"I'm Kirk, and you are?" He offered her his hand and quirked an eyebrow at her.

Sally's insides turned to molten liquid. Normally, she wouldn't give in to a drink and a slick delivery like the one he'd just pitched, but what the hell. She was fed up with being the good girl. The one who always did what was expected. The one who always deferred to others and never put herself forward or chased after what she wanted. If she wanted to make a stand in anything in her life, she was going to have to do things head-on rather than work quietly and happily in the background. Hadn't she just decided tonight to take charge of her life and her decisions? For once, she was going to do exactly what she wanted and damn the consequences.

She put out her hand to accept his. "I'm Sally. Next round is on me."

"Good to meet you, although I have to warn you, I don't usually let women buy me drinks."

Sally felt that old familiar clench in her gut when faced with conflict. The kind of thing that made her clam up, afraid to speak up for herself. It was one of her major failings—another thing she hid behind. But she'd told herself she wouldn't hide tonight. She pasted a stiff smile on her lips. Pushed herself to respond.

"Oh, really? Why is that?"

"I'm kind of old-fashioned, too."

She couldn't stifle the groan that escaped her. Despite being head of a leading IT corporation, her dad was also the epitome of old-fashioned. The very last thing Sally needed in her life was another man like that.

"But," he continued, still smiling, "in your case I might be prepared to make an exception."

Taken aback, she blurted, "In my case? Why?"

"Because I don't think you're just buying me a drink just so you can take advantage of my body."

She couldn't help it. She laughed out loud. Not a pretty, dainty little titter—a full-blown belly laugh.

"Does that happen often?" she asked.

"Now and again," he admitted.

"Trust me, you're quite safe with me," she reassured him.

"Really?"

Was it her imagination, or did he sound a little disappointed?

"Well, perhaps we should wait and see," she answered with a smile of her own and reached for her martini.

Two

How had it gone from a few drinks and dancing to this? Sally asked herself as they entered his apartment. Kirk threw his jacket over the back of a bland beige sofa. She got only the vaguest impression of his place—a generic replica of so many serviced apartments used by traveling business people with stock-standard wall decorations and furnishings. The only visible sign of human occupation was the dining table piled high with archive boxes and files.

That was all she noticed before his hands were lifting her hair from her nape and his lips pressed just there. She shivered at the contact. Kirk let her hair drop again and took her hand to lead her through to his bedroom. He turned to face her, and she trembled at the naked hunger reflected in his eyes.

Be bold, Sally reminded herself. *You wanted this. Take charge. Take what you want.*

She reached for his tie, pulling it loose, sliding it out from under his collar and letting it drop to the floor. Then she attacked his buttons, amazed that her fingers still had any dexterity at all given how her body all but vibrated with the fierceness of her longing for this man. A piece of her urged her to slow down, to take care, to reconsider, but she relegated that unwelcome advice to the very back of her mind. This was what she wanted, and she would darn well take it, and him, and revel in the process.

Kirk didn't remain passive. His large, warm hands stroked her through the fabric of her tunic, which, beneath his touch, felt like the sexiest thing she'd ever worn. She sighed out loud when she pushed his shirt free of his body and skimmed her hands over the breadth of his muscled shoulders, following the contours of his chest. While they'd danced, she'd been able to tell he was in shape, but, wow, this guy was *really* in shape. For a second she felt uncomfortable, ashamed of her own inadequacies—her small breasts, her wide hips, her heavy bottom. But then Kirk bent his head and nuzzled at the curve of her neck, and the sensation of his hot breath and his lips against her skin consigned all rational thought to obscurity.

For now everything was about his touch. She was vaguely aware of Kirk reaching for the zipper at the back of her tunic and sliding it down, then deftly removing her trousers, and felt again that prickle of insecurity as he eased the garment off her body, exposing her pretty lace bra and her all too practical full briefs.

She stifled a giggle. "Sorry, I wasn't quite expecting this outcome when I dressed for today."

"Never apologize," he ordered. His voice was deep and held a tiny tremor, which gave her an immense boost of confidence. “You’re beautiful. Perfect, in fact. And, for the record, I happen to find white cotton incredibly sexy.”

She looked at his face—studying it to see if he was serious or if he was simply saying what he thought she needed to hear—but there was an honesty there in his features that sent a new thrill through her. She bracketed his cheeks with her hands and pulled his face down to hers, kissing him with all that she had in her. With just a few well-chosen words, he’d made her feel valued, whether he knew it or not.

She couldn’t pinpoint the exact moment he unhooked her bra, but she would remember forever the first time his hands cupped her breasts. His touch was reverent but firm. His fingers, when they caressed her nipples, teasing but gentle. Unable to help herself, Sally arched her back, pressing herself against his palms, eager to feel more. She was no shrinking virgin, but she’d never experienced this kind of responsiveness before in her life. Right now she was lost in sensation and anticipation of his next move.

When he lowered his mouth to capture one taut nipple, she keened softly in response. Her legs felt like jelly, as if they could barely support her, and at her core her body had developed a deep, drawing ache of need.

“Perfect,” he whispered against her wet and sensitive bud, sending another shiver through her body that had nothing to do with cold and everything to do with an inferno of heat and desire.

Kirk’s hands were at her hips a moment later, easing her panties down over her thighs. She stepped out of them, for the first time in her adult life unembarrassed by her nakedness.

“It seems you have me at a slight disadvantage here,” she said with a teasing smile.

“I’m all for equal opportunity.” He smiled in return

and spread his hands wide so she could reach for his belt buckle.

She wasn't sure how he did it, but he managed to make shedding his shoes, socks, trousers and boxer briefs incredibly sexy. Or maybe it was just that she was so looking forward to seeing him naked, to having the opportunity to investigate every curve of muscle and every shadow beneath it, that every new inch of bared skin aroused her even more.

His skin peppered with goose bumps as she trailed her hand from his chest to his lower abdomen. His erection was full and heavy, jutting proudly from his body without apology or shame.

"You do that to me," he said as she eyed him.

Again he made her feel as though she was the strong, desirable one here. The one with all the authority and control. Without a second thought, she wrapped her fingers around his length, stroking him and marveling at the contradiction in impressions—of the heated satin softness of his skin and the steel-like hardness beneath it.

Somehow they maneuvered onto the bed. Again an exercise in elegance rather than the convoluted tangle of limbs she'd always experienced in the past. Sally had never known such synchronicity before. Exploring his body, listening to and watching his reactions as she did so, became the most natural thing in the world. Despite the sense of urgency that had gripped her at the bar, right now she wanted to take all the time in the world. Kirk, too, seemed content to go along for the ride, to allow her the time to find out exactly what wrung the greatest reactions from him, how to take him to the edge of madness and how to bring him slowly down again.

And then it was his turn. His hands were firm and sure as they stroked her, his fingers nimble and sweet as they tweaked and tugged and probed until she was shaking from head to foot. Wanting to demand he give her the release her body trembled for, yet wanting him to prolong this torturous pleasure at the same time. And all the while he murmured how beautiful she was. How perfect. It was the most empowering experience of her life.

When he finally sheathed himself and entered her body, it was sheer perfection. Her hips rose to greet him, and as he filled her she knew she'd never known anything quite this exquisite and might never know anything to match it again. Tonight was a gift. Something to be cherished. All of it—especially the way he made her feel so incredibly wanted when he groaned and gripped her hips as he sank fully within her.

"Don't. Move," he implored her as she tightened her inner muscles around him.

"What? Like this?" She tightened again and tilted her hips so he nestled just that little bit deeper.

"Exactly *not* like that."

She did it again, savoring the power his words had given her. Savoring, too, each and every sensation that rippled through her body at how deliciously he filled her. He growled, a deep, guttural resignation to her demands and began to withdraw. Then he surged against her. This time it was Sally who groaned in surrender. Her hands tightened on his shoulders, her short, practical nails embedded in his skin. She met him thrust for thrust, her tension coiling tighter and tighter, until she lost all sense of what was happening and felt her entire being let go in a maelstrom of pleasure so mind-blowing, so breathtaking she knew nothing in her life would ever be the same again.

As she lay there, heart still hammering a frantic beat, her nerve endings still tingling with the climax that had wrung her body out, she thought it such a shame that this was to be only a one-night stand. A woman could get used to this kind of lovemaking. But not a woman like her, she reminded herself sternly. She had a career path to follow. A life to build and a point to prove, to herself if to no one else. Throwing herself into another doomed attempt at building a satisfying relationship would only distract her from her goals. She had to take this rendezvous for what it was—a beautiful anomaly—and then thank the nice man for the lovely ending to the night before getting dressed and going home.

She couldn't quite bring herself to do it. To pull away and leave the welcoming warmth of his embrace, to end the age-old connection of their bodies. Kirk murmured something in her ear and rolled to one side, bringing her with him until she was half sprawled over his body. Oh, but he was magnificent, she though as she studied his upper torso. How lucky was she to have met him tonight? She lowered her head on his chest and listened to his heart rate as it changed from racing fast to a slower, more even beat. His breathing, too, changed, and his fingers stopped playing with her hair.

He was asleep. Five more minutes and it was time to go. Gently she extracted herself from his arms and tiptoed around the bedroom gathering up her things. A quick trip to the bathroom to tidy up and get dressed and she was out of here. No sticking around for embarrassment in the cold light of morning. No recriminations or awkwardness over breakfast.

She let herself out of the apartment and slipped her phone from her bag. She'd just opened an app to order a cab when her phone—put on silent when she'd gone out to meet her friends—lit up with an incoming call. She recognized the name on the screen immediately. Marilyn had been her father's PA since before she was born and had become a mother figure to Sally after her own mother's death. But it was late, after midnight. What on earth was Marilyn doing calling her now?

"Hello?" Sally answered as the elevator doors opened onto the lobby.

"Where are you?" Marilyn asked sharply. "I've been trying to call you for the past two hours."

There was a note to the older woman's voice that Sally had never heard her use before. She identified it immediately as fear and felt her stomach drop.

"What's wrong?" she asked, getting straight to the point.

"It's your father. He came back into his office tonight, and security found him while they were on their rounds. He's had a heart attack and he's at the hospital now. It's bad, Sally, really bad."

A whimper escaped her as she took a mental note of the details of which hospital he was at.

"Where are you?" Marilyn asked. "I'll send Benton with the car."

"No, it's okay. I'm not far from the hospital. I've got a cab coming already. Are you there now?"

"Of course," the PA answered. A note of vulnerability crept into her voice. "But they won't tell me anything because I'm not next of kin."

"I'll be there as soon as I can. I promise."

Waiting for the cab was the longest five minutes of her life, and as it pulled away from the curb, Sally wondered how life could turn on the dime like that. How, in one moment, everything could be perfect and exciting and new, and in the next all could be torn away.

She should never have left her father after dinner tonight, especially on the eve of something as big as tomorrow's merger announcement. But how was she to know he'd go back into the office and, of all things, have a heart attack? And why had the security guards called Marilyn instead of her? Surely she, as his daughter, should have been listed on the company register as his immediate next of kin? But then, he'd always sheltered and protected her, hadn't he?

She remembered how drawn he'd looked tonight. How she'd dismissed it so easily as nothing out of the ordinary. She hadn't even asked if he was feeling ill. Guilt assailed her. He hadn't wanted to worry her about the merger, so why would he worry her about not feeling well? Suddenly her decision to be bold and chase after her own pleasure without thinking of the consequences tonight seemed horribly pathetic and selfish. If she'd simply gone home after her friends had left the bar, she'd have gotten the call and been at the hospital hours ago. What if she arrived too late? She didn't know what she'd do if she lost her dad. He was her rock, her mainstay, her shelter.

"Hold on, Daddy," she whispered. "Please, hold on."

Always an early riser, Kirk woke as sunlight began to filter through the blinds, his body satiated like it had never been before. He took a moment to appreciate the feeling and decided he could definitely go for another round of that. He reached across his sheets for Sally's warm, recumbent form beside him and came up with empty space. When had she pulled away from him? It wasn't like him to sleep so deeply that he couldn't remember his bed partner leaving, but then again he'd all but lost consciousness after the force of passion they'd shared.

Maybe she was in the bathroom. He looked across the bed to where light should have gleamed around the bathroom door frame, but there was only darkness. He sat up and cast his gaze around the room looking for her clothes. They were gone, as was she.

It shouldn't have mattered—after all, he knew he'd see her again at the office, even if she wasn't aware of that little detail just yet. But there was something almost shameful in the way she'd slipped out of his room without saying goodbye. As if she was embarrassed by what they'd done or wanted to pretend it hadn't happened.

Well, maybe it hadn't been as good for her as it was for him. He shook his head and told himself not to be so ridiculous. He knew she'd been there with him, every step of the way. Sometimes leading, sometimes allowing herself to be led. In fact, just thinking about her reactions—the sweet sounds she'd made, the responsiveness of her body beneath his touch—brought his desire immediately to full, aching life again.

Kirk groaned and pushed back the covers, remembering he hadn't rid himself of the condom he'd miraculously had the presence of mind to slip on last night. The groan rapidly turned into a string of wild curses when he realized the condom wasn't intact. He went to the bathroom and took care of what was left of it.

Now wide awake, several scenarios ran through his head. Of course, she could be on the Pill. Goodness only knew he hadn't stopped to ask. He'd barely stopped to put on protection himself, for all the good it had done. Either way, he had to tell her, and soon. He wondered how that would go. It's not like he could wait for her dad to introduce them at the office and shake her hand and say, "Hi, about last night…the condom broke."

He heard his cell phone ringing from the sitting room and walked, naked, to retrieve it from his suit jacket. He recognized the number as Orson Harrison's private line and answered immediately, surprised to hear a woman's voice, though she quickly introduced herself as Marilyn, Orson's assistant, and explained the medical emergency from the night before. His blood ran cold as he heard the news.

"Assemble the board as quickly as you can," he instructed Harrison's PA. "I'll be there in twenty minutes."

Three

Kirk's head was still reeling. At the emergency board meeting, everyone had been shocked to hear the news of Orson's heart attack, but all had agreed that the company could show no weakness, especially when Orson's confidential report on his reasoning behind the merger had been presented to them. Therefore, they'd appointed Kirk interim chairman.

The new responsibility was a heavy weight on him, along with worry for Orson Harrison's health. And on top of all that, he still had to tell Sally about the possibility she might be pregnant. He closed his eyes for a brief moment. He'd been such a fool to allow desire to cloud his judgment. It was the kind of impulsive emotion and need-driven behavior he'd always sworn he'd never indulge in. And now look where it had landed him.

He was investigating her, just as he was investigating every staff member here—he never should have allowed sex to muddy the waters.

He had no doubt she wouldn't be happy to hear his news. Who would be, especially while her father's life hung in the balance? So far the hospital had released very little information—only that Orson was in critical condition. Even Marilyn, who'd known Orson for almost thirty years, had been trying on the phone all morning, and remained unable to get past the gatekeeper of patient details at the hospital. To be honest, Kirk had been surprised to see the woman at her desk this morning and he'd expressed as much. She'd curtly informed him that someone had to hold the place together in Orson's absence and had been ill-pleased when she'd been informed of his appointment as interim chairman.

Kirk flicked a glance at his watch. Perhaps she'd gotten ahold of Sally again by now. He hit the interoffice button to connect with the prickly PA.

"Any updates regarding Mr. Harrison?" he asked.

"No, sir." The woman's voice was clipped.

She'd made it quite clear that she wasn't happy about him using Orson's office—interim appointment or not. She was even less impressed when he'd ignored her protests and taken up residence. It made sense to him to stand at the helm right now, when he was supposed to be steering this particular ship. It would help the staff to see someone visibly taking charge. Well, the staff except for Marilyn.

"Thank you, Marilyn," Kirk replied, keeping his voice civil. "And Ms. Harrison? Has there been any communication with her yet?"

"I believe she's in the building but I haven't spoken to her myself, yet."

Kirk looked at his watch. Two thirty. They were going forward with the planned announcement of the merger—it was, after all, the only thing that would explain why

Kirk had taken temporary leadership—and the video link announcement was scheduled to commence at three sharp. Did Sally still plan to be there? He knew her father had wanted her by his side, but in light of recent events, he wouldn't blame her for skipping out. Coming into the office at all couldn't have been an easy decision to make with her father so desperately ill.

"Could you get a message to her and ask her to come to my office as soon as possible? I want to brief her before the video link."

"Certainly, sir."

Again there was that brief hesitation and slight distaste to her tone as she said the word *sir*. He'd already asked her to call him by his first name, but it seemed his request had been ignored. That, however, wasn't important to him right now. He had a far greater concern on his hands. Like, how the hell did he tell Sally about the condom?

It was only a few minutes before he heard women's voices outside the office door. The double doors began to swing open, and he heard Marilyn's voice call out in caution.

"Oh, but there's someone—"

And there she was. Sally Harrison appeared in the doorway, her head still turned to Marilyn, a reassuring smile on her face. A smile that froze then faded into an expression of shock when she saw him rise from behind her father's desk.

"K-Kirk?" she stammered.

Her face paled, highlighting the dark shadows of exhaustion and worry beneath her eyes that even makeup couldn't disguise. Kirk moved swiftly to her side, aware of Orson's PA coming up behind Sally. He gently guided Sally into a chair.

"A glass of water for Ms. Harrison, please, Marilyn," Kirk instructed the PA, who raced to do his bidding.

She was back in a moment, and Kirk took the glass from her before pressing it into Sally's shaking hand.

"Mr. Tanner, it's really too much to expect her to attend the video link," Marilyn began defensively. "She shouldn't have to—"

"It's entirely up to Ms. Harrison. Marilyn, perhaps you could get something for her to eat. I bet you haven't had anything today, have you?" he asked, looking at Sally directly.

Sally shook her head. "No. I couldn't bear to think about food."

She tried to take a sip of the water. Her hand was shaking so much Kirk wrapped his fingers around hers to steady her and keep her from spilling. She flinched at his touch, a reaction he was sure Marilyn hadn't missed.

"You need to eat something," he said. He turned to the PA. "Could you get a bowl of fruit from the executive kitchen for Ms. Harrison and perhaps some yogurt, as well?"

"Is that what *you* want, Sally?" Marilyn asked, moving to Sally's other side. "Perhaps you'd rather I stayed here with you while Mr. Tanner got you something to eat."

Kirk bit back a retort. He wasn't about to enter into a battle of wills with Marilyn here and now. And given the time constraints that now faced them, he wouldn't be able to have the discussion with Sally that they really needed to have. He studied her from the top of her golden head to her sensibly clad feet. Even in a demure pale blue suit and with her hair scraped back into a ponytail that gave him a headache just looking at how tightly it was bound, she still affected him.

Could she already be pregnant with his child? The thought came like a sucker punch straight to his gut.

"Good idea," he said, making a decision to leave their discussion until they could be guaranteed more privacy and uninterrupted time.

Of greater importance was letting Sally come to terms with his presence here—and the fact that he'd kept it from her last night. Once the shock wore off, he had no doubt matters between them would be less than cordial, especially once she discovered that he'd known exactly who she was all along.

Sally looked from him to Marilyn. "It-it's okay, Marilyn. You know what I like. Perhaps you could get it for me? I really am feeling quite weak."

"Of course you are," Marilyn said in a more placatory tone and patted Sally on the shoulder. "You've always had a delicate constitution. I'll be back in a moment."

Marilyn closed the door behind her with a sharp click, leaving Kirk in no doubt that even though Orson's PA had left the room to do his bidding, she certainly wasn't happy about it.

"Have another sip of water," he urged Sally.

He was relieved to see a little color coming back into her face.

"How is your dad doing?" he asked, determined to distract her until Marilyn's return.

She drew in another deep breath. "He's in an induced coma and they say he's stable—whatever that means. It's hard to see it as anything positive when he looks so awful and is totally nonresponsive." Her voice shook, but she kept going. "They're hoping to operate tomorrow. A quadruple bypass, apparently."

Kirk pressed a hand on her shoulder. "I know your dad. He's strong, he'll come through."

She looked up at him and he saw a flash of anger in her blue eyes.

"Just how well do you know my dad?"

Kirk felt a swell of discomfort, with just a tinge of rueful amusement. Trust Orson's daughter to cut straight to the chase. "I've known him most of my life, to be honest."

"And how is it I've never met you before last night?"

There was still a slight tremor to her voice, but he could see her getting stronger by the minute.

"Our parents were friends until my father died. After that my mom and I moved away. I was a kid at the time. There was no reason for you to know me before last night."

He kept it deliberately brief. There wasn't time for detail now.

"And now you're back." She fell silent a moment before flicking him another heated look. "You knew all along who I was, didn't you?"

Kirk clenched his jaw and nodded. He'd never been the kind of person who lived on regret, but right now, if he could have turned back the clock and done last night over again, he absolutely would have. Or would he? He doubted she'd have come home with him if she'd known he'd soon be her boss. Would he have missed the chance to lose himself in her arms the way he had? Never have known the perfect passion they'd experienced together? *Never had the broken condom*, the snarky voice in the back of his mind sharply reminded him. Okay, so he'd have skipped that part.

"I see." Sally swallowed another sip of water before speaking again. "She called you Mr. Tanner. That would be the Tanner in Harrison Tanner Tech? The new vice president?"

He nodded.

She pressed her lips together before speaking. "It seems you had me at a disadvantage right from the start. Which asks the question why you'd do something like that. Did it give you a kick to sleep with the chairman's oblivious daughter? Never mind—don't bother answering that."

Sally waved her hand as if to negate the words she'd just uttered.

"Look, can we talk about that later, over dinner?"

"I do not want to go out to dinner with you. In fact, I don't even want to be in the same room as you."

Her cheeks had flushed pink with fury. At least that was better than the waxen image she'd presented to him only a few moments ago.

Marilyn returned to the office and set a small tray on Sally's lap.

"There you are, my dear. Goodness knows, with your father so ill, the last thing we need is you collapsing, too. I've been telling your father for years now that he needs to slow down, but do you think he listens to me?" As if suddenly aware of the leaden atmosphere between Kirk and Sally, Marilyn straightened and gave Kirk a pointed glare. "Is there anything else…sir?"

"No, thank you, Marilyn. That will be all for now," Kirk replied. He flicked a quick look at his watch. "Eat up," he instructed Sally. "We have fifteen minutes."

"I don't feel like eat—"

"Please, Sally, at least try. It'll boost your blood sugar for now and hopefully tide you through the next few hours," Kirk said. "Whether you like it or not, we have to work together, today in particular. The last thing I want—and, as Marilyn already pointed out, the very last thing Harrison Tanner Tech needs—is you collapsing live on camera, especially during the merger announcement and even more so when news of your father's heart attack becomes public knowledge."

They locked gazes for what felt like a full minute before Sally acceded to his request and began to spoon up mouthfuls of the fruit.

"I still don't want to go out for dinner with you," she muttered between bites.

"We need to talk about last night, and we don't have time now."

"I don't particularly wish to discuss last night. In fact, I'd rather forget it ever happened."

Her words were cutting. Her anger and distrust right now felt like a palpable presence in the room. Such a contrast to the sweet openness she had shown him last night. And the tension between them was only going to get worse when she heard what he had to tell her. There was a knock at the door, and one of the communications team popped his head in.

"Ten minutes, Mr. Tanner! We need you miked and sound checked now."

"And me, too," Sally interjected in a shaking voice.

"Are you sure, Ms. Harrison?"

It wasn't Kirk's imagination—she paled again. But in true Harrison spirit, she placed her bowl on the desk in front of her and rose to her feet. She straightened her jacket and smoothed her hands over her rounded hips. Yes, there was still a tremor there.

"Absolutely certain. Let's get this over with," she said tightly.

"You don't have to speak. In fact, you don't have to do anything at all. I can handle the announcement."

"Really? Do you think that's a good idea given that people will be expecting to see my father? A man they know and *trust*—" she paused for emphasis "—and instead they're getting you?"

There was enough scorn in her voice to curdle milk.

"They can trust me," he said simply. "And so can you."

"You'll excuse me if I find that hard to believe."

Sally wished she hadn't eaten a thing. Right now she felt sick to her stomach. How dare Kirk have hidden his identity from her like that? What kind of a jerk was he? Was this some form of one-upmanship, lording his conquest over her before he'd even started here—making sure she knew exactly who was the top dog? And what if he tried to hold their one-night stand over her?

Sally stiffened her spine and looked him straight in the eyes. "In my father's absence, I would prefer to make the announcement regarding the merger. You can fill in the details afterward. It's what Dad would want."

The sick sensation in her stomach intensified at the thought of being the figurehead for making the company-wide statement. But she could do this. She had to do this, to save face if nothing else. Kirk looked at her for a few seconds then shrugged and reached across the desk to grab a sheaf of papers. He held them out to her.

"Here's the statement your father prepared yesterday. If you're sure you can handle it, I have no objection to you making the announcement and then I'll field any questions from the floor. After the Q and A from the video feed closes, we'll repeat the same again for the press announcement."

"Why will you be answering questions? Why not Silas Rogers, the CEO, or any of our other senior management?"

"Sally, your father and I have been working together

in the lead-up to this for several months now. No one else can give the answers I can. I'm the one who can carry out the plans your father and I made—that's why I've been appointed interim chairman. The board gave their approval at the meeting that was called this morning."

This morning. While she'd been at the hospital, out of her mind with worry over her father's condition. Her mind latched onto one part of what he'd said and yanked her out of her brief reverie.

"Several months?" Sally couldn't stop the outburst. "But I didn't hear about it until yesterday!"

"It was your father's decision to keep everything under wraps for as long as possible. Obviously he'd hoped to do the announcement with me today, present a united front and all that, but since he can't, we'll do the next best thing. Are you okay with that?"

Okay with it? No, she wasn't okay with it—any of it. But her dad had thought of everything, hadn't he? And none of it, except for a rushed dinner together last night, had included her.

"Sally?"

"Let me read the statement."

Sally scanned the double-spaced pages, hearing her father's voice in the back of her mind with every word she read. It wasn't right. He should be here to do this. This company was his pride and joy, built on his hard work, and he respected each and every one of his employees so very highly. Somehow she had to remember that in what she was about to do. Somehow she had to put aside her phobia and be the kind of person her father should have been able to rely on.

With every thought, she could feel her anxiety levels wind up several notches. *Be bold*, she told herself. *You can do this.* She drew in another deep breath then stood up and met Kirk's gaze.

"Right, let's go."

"Are you sure? You'll be okay?"

Blue-green eyes bored into hers, and she felt as though he could see through her bravado and her best intentions and all the way to the quivering jelly inside. He knew. Somehow, probably through her father, he knew about her glossophobia—the debilitating terror she experienced when faced with public speaking. Shame trickled down her spine, but she refused to back down.

"I'll be fine," she said, forcing a calm into her voice that she was far from feeling. "It's a video link, isn't it? Just us and a camera, right?"

"Look, Sally, you don't have to—"

She shook her head. "No, trust me, I really do."

He might not understand it, but this had become vital to her now. A method of proof that she was worthy. A way to show her father, when he was well enough to hear about it, that she had what it took and could be relied upon to step up.

Kirk gave her a small nod of acceptance. "Fine. Remember I'll be right beside you."

She'd been afraid he'd say that. But as they walked out of her dad's office and down the carpeted corridor toward the main conference room, she felt an unexpected sense of comfort in his nearness. She tried to push the sensation away. She didn't want to rely on this man. A man she knew intimately and yet not at all. *Don't think about last night! Don't think about the taste of him, the feel of him, the pleasure he gave you.*

She needn't have worried. Last night was the last thing on her mind as they entered the conference room and she was immediately confronted by the single lens of a camera pointing straight toward her. And beyond it was a bank of television screens on the large wall of the conference room—each screen filled with faces of the staff assembled at each of their offices. All of them staring straight at her.

Four

Kirk felt the shift in Sally's bearing the second they entered the conference room. He cast her a glance. She looked like she was on the verge of turning tail and running back down the corridor. She'd already come to a complete halt beside him, her eyes riveted on the live screens on the other side of the room, and he could see tiny beads of perspiration forming at her hairline and on her upper lip. And, dammit, she was trembling from head to foot.

"Sally?" he asked gently.

She swallowed and flicked her eyes in his direction. "I can do this," she said with all the grimness of a French aristocrat on her way to the guillotine.

Sally walked woodenly toward the podium set up in front of the camera. The sheaf of papers he'd given her earlier was clutched in one fist, and she made an effort to smooth them out as she placed them on the platform in front of her.

He had to give it to her. She wasn't backing down, even though she was obviously terrified. He wished she'd just give in and hand the papers back over to him. Making her go through this was akin to punching a puppy, and the idea made him sick to the stomach. Probably about as sick as she was feeling right now.

The camera operator gestured to Kirk to take the other seat and Kirk hastened to Sally's side. As he settled beside her, he could feel tension coming off her in waves. She'd grown even paler than when they'd arrived.

"Sally?" he asked again.

"Five minutes until we go live!" someone said from across the room. "Someone get mikes on them, please."

Kirk reached across and curved his hand around one of hers. "Let me do this. I've had time to prepare. You haven't."

He held his breath, waiting for her reply, but they were distracted by two sound technicians fitting them each with a lapel mike and doing a quick sound check.

"One minute, people."

Kirk squeezed her hand. "Sally, it's your call. No one expects this of you. Least of all your father—and especially given the circumstances."

"Don't you see," she whispered without looking at him. "That's exactly why I need to do it."

"Ten, nine, eight…"

"You only have to be here, Sally. That's more than enough given what you've been through."

"Live in three…" The technician silently counted down the last two numbers with his fingers.

Kirk waited for Sally to speak, but silence filled the air. Sally was looking past the winking red eye of the camera to the screens across the room, to the people of Harrison IT. Then, infinitesimally, she moved and slid the papers over to him. Taking it as his cue, Kirk pasted a smile on his face and introduced himself before he launched into the welcome Orson had prepared for his staff, together with a brief explanation that a medical event had precluded Orson from participating in the announcement.

Sally stood rigidly beside him throughout the explanation of the merger and the question-and-answer session that followed. The moment he signed off and the red light on the camera extinguished, Sally ripped off her microphone and headed for the door. He eventually caught up with her down the hallway.

"Leave me alone!" she cried as he reached for her hand and tugged her around to face him.

Kirk was horrified to see tears streaking her face.

"Sally, it's all right. You did great."

"Great? You call sitting there like a barrel of dead fish *great*? I couldn't even introduce you, which, in all honesty, was the very least I should have done given you are a total stranger to most of those people."

Distraction was what she needed right now.

"Dead fish? For the record, you look nothing like a barrel of anything, let alone dead fish."

She shook her head in frustration, but he was glad to see the tears had mostly stopped.

"Don't be so literal."

"I can't help it." He shrugged. "When I look at you, the last thing I picture is cold fish of any kind."

He lowered his voice deliberately and delighted in the flush of color that filled her cheeks, chasing away the lines of strain that had been so evident only seconds before.

"You're impossible," she muttered.

"Tell me how impossible over dinner after the press conference."

"No."

"Sally, we need to talk. About last night. About now."

He could see she wanted to argue the point with him, but he spied one of their media liaison staff coming down the corridor toward them. He was expected at the press conference right away.

"Please. Just dinner. Nothing else," he pressed.

He willed her to acquiesce to his suggestion. Not only did he need to talk to her about the broken condom, but he found himself wanting to get to know her better away from the confines of the office. He didn't realize he was holding his breath until she gave a sharp nod.

"Not dinner. But, yes, we can talk. I'm heading back to the hospital for a few hours first. I'll meet you later in my office. You can say what you have to say there."

It wasn't quite the acceptance he'd aimed for, but for now it would do. He watched her walk away and head to the elevators.

"Mr. Tanner, they're waiting for you downstairs in conference room three."

He reluctantly dragged his attention back to the job at hand. Unfortunately for him, Sally would have to wait.

It was late, and most of the staff had already headed home. The media session had run well over time, and afterward he'd been called into an impromptu meeting with the CEO and several others. The board might have agreed to appoint him interim chairman, but the executives still wanted to make it clear that they were the ones in charge. But he'd handled it knowing he had Orson's full support at his back, and that of the board of directors, too.

Now, he had a far more important task at hand. Kirk

loosened his tie and slid it out from beneath his collar as he approached Sally's office. He bunched the silk strip into his pocket and raised a hand to tap at her door. No response. He reached for the knob, turned it and let himself in.

The instant he saw her, motionless, with her head pillowed on her arms on the top of her desk, he felt a moment of sheer panic, but then reason overcame the reaction and he noted the steady breathing that made her shoulders rise and fall a little. She'd removed her jacket before sitting at her desk, and the sheer fabric of her blouse revealed a creamy lace camisole beneath it.

Desire hit him hard and deep, and his fingers curled into his palms, itching to relieve her of her blouse and to slide his hands over the enticement that was her lingerie. He doubted it was quite as silky soft as her skin, but wouldn't it be fun to find out?

No, he shouldn't go there again. Wouldn't. Whatever it was about Sally Harrison that drew him so strongly, he had to rein it back. Somehow. It would be a challenge when everything about her triggered his basest primal instincts, but—he reminded himself—didn't he thrive on challenges and defeating obstacles? He forced himself to ignore the sensations that sparked through his body and focused instead on the reality of the woman sleeping so soundly that she hadn't heard him knock or enter her office.

She had to be exhausted. She'd been through a hell of a lot in the past twenty-four hours. Any regular person would have struggled with the onslaught of emotions, let alone someone forced to be part of a video conference who suffered a phobia like hers. Orson had forewarned him that Sally experienced acute anxiety when it came to public speaking. He'd had no idea how severe it was or the toll it obviously took. Having seen her like that today went a long way toward explaining why she'd remained in a safe middle-management role at HIT rather than scaling the corporate ladder to be at her father's side.

He'd never before seen such despair on a person's face at the thought of talking in public and, he realized, he'd never before seen such bravery as she'd exhibited in pushing herself to try. Perhaps if she hadn't been so emotionally wrung out, she'd have been in a stronger position to attempt to conquer her demons today. But she hadn't and, from their conversation in the hall, he knew she saw that as a failure.

He made an involuntary sound of sympathy, and she shifted a little on the desk before starting awake and sitting upright in her chair.

"What time is it?" she demanded defensively, her voice thick with exhaustion. "How long have you been waiting?"

There was a faint crease on her cheek where she'd rested her face on the cuff of her sleeve. Oddly, it endeared her to him even more. This was a woman who needed a lot of protecting—he felt it to the soles of his feet. She was the antithesis of the kind of women he usually dated, and yet she'd somehow inveigled her way into a nook inside him that pulled on every impulse.

"Not long," he answered. "And it's late. I'm sorry, I got held up. How was your dad?"

"As well as can be expected. He's still stable and continues to be monitored, and they're confident he'll come through the surgery well tomorrow."

As well as can be expected. It was an awful phrase, he thought, remembering hearing the exact same words from the medical team who had looked after his mother after the first of the strokes that stole her from him.

Sally pushed up from her desk and stood to face Kirk. "But you didn't come here to talk about him, did you? What did you want to say to me?"

"I was hoping we could discuss it over dinner. I don't know about you, but I'm starving after today."

"I thought we were going to talk here," she hedged.

"Can't we kill two birds with one stone?"

"Look—" she sighed "—is this really necessary? There's no need to spend an hour making small talk over a meal before we get to the point. We're both adults, so surely we can continue to act as such. I'm quite happy to forget last night ever happened."

Kirk ignored the sting that came with her words. He couldn't forget last night even if he wanted to—especially not now. "And, as adults, we should be able to enjoy a meal together. Really, I could do with a decent bite to eat, and I'm sure you could, too."

She looked at him and for a moment he thought she'd refuse, but then she huffed out a breath of impatience.

"Fine. I'll let my security know I'm leaving with you."

Ah, that explained the muscle who'd accompanied her to the bar last night. "You have security with you whenever you're out?"

"One of the examples of Dad's overprotectiveness. When I was little and HIT was beginning to boom, there was a threat to kidnap me. Ever since he's insisted on me having a bodyguard. Trust me, it's not as glamorous as it sounds."

"It's hardly overprotective," Kirk commented as he helped Sally into her suit jacket. "Your father clearly takes your welfare seriously."

He felt a pang of regret as she buttoned up the front of her jacket, hiding the tempting glimpses of lace visible through her blouse.

"He likes to know I'm safe."

"I protect what's mine, too," Kirk replied firmly.

Sally raised her eyebrow. "Isn't that a little primitive?"

"Perhaps I should rephrase that. Like your father, I take my responsibilities *very* seriously."

"Well, considering you're standing in for my father at the moment, I guess I should find that heartening."

Kirk smiled. "I will always do my best by the company—for your dad's sake, if nothing else. You can be assured of that. He has my utmost respect."

"You say you've known him most of your life, and yet I had no idea he even knew you. No idea at all." For a second she looked upset, but then she pulled herself together. "Let me call Benton and then we can go."

He could see it really bothered her that her father hadn't shared anything about the merger until the ink was drying on the paperwork. But was that because she was disturbed her father had made those decisions without consulting her, or because she had something to hide? Kirk couldn't be absolutely sure either way.

She made the call, and in the next few minutes they were riding the elevator to the basement parking. Kirk led the way to his car—a late-model European SUV.

"You must be relieved for your dad. That he's stable, I mean."

"I'll be relieved when I know he's getting better again." She looked away, but he couldn't mistake the grief that crossed her face. "He was so gray when I left him this afternoon. So vulnerable. I've never seen him like that. Not even when Mom died. And he still has a major surgery to get through."

"Your father has more strength and determination than any man I've ever met, and he'll be receiving excellent care at the hospital. He'll come through this, Sally."

The words seemed to be what she needed to hear to pull herself together again. She looked up and gave him a weak smile. For a second he caught a glimpse of the woman he'd danced with last night, but then she was gone again. Kirk waited for Sally to settle in the passenger seat and buckle her seat belt before he closed her door and went around to the other side. She was still pale, but she appeared completely composed and in control. Not quite the woman he'd met last night, but not the woman caught in the grip of the anxiety attack from this afternoon, either.

He pulled out of the parking garage and headed down the road.

"Any preference for dinner?"

"Something fast and hot."

"Chinese okay, then?"

"Perfect."

A few blocks down, he pulled into the parking lot for a chain restaurant he knew always had good food.

"Looks like this is us."

He rushed around to her door and helped her from the car and they were seated immediately.

"A drink?" he asked Sally when the waiter came to bring their menus.

"Just water, thank you."

Probably a good idea for both of them, he thought, and gave his request for the same to the waiter. "Do you mind if I order for us?"

Sally shook her head, and he turned to the waiter and requested appetizers to be brought out to their table as soon as possible and ordered a couple of main entrées to share, as well.

Her lips pulled into a brief smile. "You really are hungry, aren't you?"

Sally slipped out of her jacket and put it on the seat

beside her. He looked at her across the table, noting again the imprint of her lacy camisole beneath her blouse. "You could say that," he replied with a wry grin.

Oh, yes, he was hungry for a lot of things, but only one of his desires would be satisfied by this meal tonight. To distract himself, he also shrugged off his jacket and undid the cuffs on his shirt and began to fold them back. He looked up and saw Sally's gaze riveted on his hands. Even in the dim light of the restaurant, he saw the rose pink stain that crept over her cheeks and her throat. Was she remembering exactly what parts of her body his hands had touched last night? Did she have any idea of how much he wanted to touch her again?

As if she sensed his gaze, she shook her head slightly and stared off into the distance, watching the other diners. Then, with a visible squaring of her shoulders, she returned her attention to him.

"Okay, so what was so important that you couldn't tell me at work?"

Kirk shifted in his chair. "It's about last night—" He paused, searching for the right words.

Sally felt her cheeks flush again. Did they really need to hash this all out? She'd much rather they just moved on.

"We covered this already," she interrupted. "Yes, it's awkward that we're working under the same umbrella after spending last night together. It happened, but it won't happen again. I'm sure we can be grown-up about it all and put it very firmly in the past. It doesn't have to affect our working relationship, such as it will be, and I'd prefer we just forget about it entirely."

She ran out of breath. Kirk eyed her from across the table.

"Are you quite finished?"

"Finished?"

"Your commendable little speech."

"Oh, that. Yes, I'm done."

"Great. I'd like to agree with you. However, we have a problem."

Sally looked at him in confusion. Did he think he couldn't work with her? She knew he'd mentioned redundancies in his announcement today. Surely he didn't mean to dismiss her from her job? Could he even do that? Was that what this dinner was about? Cold fingers of fear squeezed her throat shut.

"A problem?" she repeated.

"The condom broke."

Five

Of all the things he could have said, that was the last she'd expected. Sally felt the tension inside her coil up a few more notches. *The condom broke?* It kind of put her fear of redundancy in the shade, didn't it? She became aware that Kirk was watching her intently, waiting for her reaction. She forced herself into some semblance of composure. He'd seen her at her absolute worst already today—she couldn't afford to appear that weak to him again.

"Is that all?" She smiled tightly. "For a second there, I thought you were about to give me notice that you were terminating my job."

"You thought I was going to terminate you? Hell, no. But seriously, Sally—the condom. You have to let me know if—"

"You really have nothing to worry about," she interrupted him. She didn't want to hear him verbalize the words that were on the tip of his tongue. Didn't want to believe that pregnancy was a possibility, even though children were something she'd always desperately wanted. But not until it was the right time and, more importantly, with the right man. Certainly not with a man who would hide his identity and sleep with her while knowing exactly who she was.

"I'm on the Pill," she continued. "We're fine. Absolutely, totally and utterly fine."

"If you're sure?"

"One hundred and ten percent. Actually, no—just one hundred percent. One hundred and ten doesn't exist, really, does it? Percent meaning per hundred, right? So how can you have one hundred and ten hundredths?"

Darn, she was rambling. Nerves, combined with a healthy dose of anger, often did that to her in one-on-one conversation with people she didn't know well. It was a shame her phobia about public speaking didn't extend to rendering her mute in a situation like this, too. Kirk gave her a gentle half smile that made her stomach do a dizzy little flip, and beneath the lace cups of her bra she felt her breasts grow heavy and her nipples harden. Her body's helpless reaction to him served to stoke the fire of anger that simmered deep inside. He'd used her, she reminded himself.

"Okay then," he said with a gentle nod. "We're good. But if anything did happen, you'd let me know, right?"

"Of course," she answered blithely.

To her relief, the appetizers arrived and she helped herself to a lettuce wrap. She wasn't in the mood for small talk, and thankfully, now that Kirk had obviously gotten the business of the broken condom off his chest, he was far more invested in alleviating his hunger than indulging in idle chatter.

It didn't take long, though, before he steered conversation to work matters. It took a while to warm up to the discussion, and he seemed far more interested in asking questions than answering them, but overall she was surprised to find that Kirk agreed with and supported most of the principles she was passionate about for the company—especially her pet project of steering the head office at HIT, or HTT as it was now, toward more sustainable energy technologies and policies.

She wasn't certain if it was his skillful questioning or the energy burst she'd received from eating her first proper meal in twenty-four hours, but she found herself becoming quite animated as she delved deeper into her vision for the company.

"We could be leaders in this area if we do it right," she said passionately. "And with the correct systems set in place, we could take that platform to our clients, as well."

"Do it," Kirk said concisely.

"Do it?"

"Yeah. Draw up the proposal for me. I can already see how it would benefit us, but I'm not the only person you have to sell the idea to, right?"

This idea had been her baby from the outset, and she'd had a bit of pushback from a few of the senior managers when she'd floated it before. But getting the green light from Kirk was exciting, even if he was a low-down, deceitful piece of—

"I'll get onto it as soon as I can," she said. "I have most of the data assembled already."

"I look forward to seeing it," Kirk said. "Now, I think we've covered everything and it's probably time we headed home. You have an early start tomorrow, right?"

And just like that she hit the ground again. Her dad's surgery. How on earth could she have forgotten?

"Sally, don't feel bad. It's okay to escape now and then. Orson will come through this. You have to believe it."

Tears pricked her eyes, and she dragged her napkin to her lips in an attempt to hide their sudden quivering. After everything the last day had delivered, his unexpected compassion was just about her undoing. She blinked fiercely and put the napkin back down again.

"Thank you," she said. "Now, if you'll excuse me, I need to get a cab."

"No, I'll see you home. It's the least I can do."

She accepted his offer because she was absolutely too worn-out now to protest. She gave him her address and he smiled.

"Isn't that just a few blocks from the office?"

"It is. I like the building and it's close to Downtown Park when I need a blast of fresh air."

When they arrived at her apartment building, he rode the elevator with her to her floor.

"I'll be okay from here," she said as the elevator doors swooshed open.

"Let me see you to your door. It's what your guy—Benton?" he asked and waited for her nod before continuing "—would do, isn't it?"

She shrugged and walked down the hallway, hyperconscious of his presence beside her. Her hand shook as she attempted to put the key in the lock, and she almost groaned out loud at the clichéd moment when she dropped her keys and Kirk bent to retrieve them for her.

"Here, let me," he said.

Kirk suffered no such issues with his coordination, and he handed the keys back to her the moment the door was open. She looked up at him, all too aware of his strong presence beside her. Even though weariness tugged at every muscle in her body, she still felt that latent buzz of consciousness triggered by his nearness—and with it the tension that coiled tighter inside her with every moment they stood together. Suddenly all she could think about was the scent of him, the heat of his body, the sounds he'd made as she'd explored the expanse of his skin with her fingertips, her lips, her tongue.

She made a small sound and tried to cover it with a cough.

"You okay?" Kirk asked.

"I'm fine, thank you. And thanks for dinner, too."

"No problem."

Silence stretched out between them, and it seemed inevitable when Kirk lifted a hand to gently caress her face. The moment his fingers touched her skin, she was suffused with fire. *No*, she told herself frantically. She wasn't going down that road again. Not with him. She pulled back, and Kirk's hand fell to his side.

"Good night," she said as firmly as she could and stepped through the doorway.

"Good night, Sally. Sweet dreams."

She closed the door and leaned back against it, trying to will her racing heart back under control. One more second and she'd have asked him to stay. She squeezed her eyes shut tight, but it was no use. The image of him remained burned on her retinas.

Sally opened her eyes and went to her bathroom, stripping off her suit and throwing it in a hamper ready to send to the dry cleaner. She took a short, hot shower, wrapped herself up in her robe and went to her bedroom. Perched on her bed, she opened her handbag, pulling out the blister pack of contraceptives she carried everywhere with her.

She studied the pack, then flipped it over to check the days. Her chest tightened with anxiety the moment she realized that somewhere along the line she'd gotten out of sync. Probably around the time a couple of weeks ago when she'd traveled to the small European kingdom of Sylvain for the christening of the baby of her best friend from college. With the time zone changes and the busyness of travel and jet lag and then getting back to work, she'd slipped up. Normally, it wouldn't have been a problem—it wasn't as if she was wildly sexually active. But it certainly was a problem now.

She couldn't be pregnant. She simply couldn't. The chances were so slim as to be nearly nonexistent, weren't they? But the evidence of her inconsistency stared straight at her from the palm of her hand.

Sweet dreams, he'd said. How could she dream sweet dreams when every moment had just become a waking nightmare?

It had been four weeks since her father's surgery, and despite a minor post-op infection in a graft site on his leg, everything had gone well. He was home now, with a team of nurses stationed around the clock to ensure his convalescence continued to go smoothly. Sally bore his daily grumbles with good humor—especially when, as each bland meal at home was served to him, he called her to complain about the lack of salt and other condiments he'd grown used to.

She was too relieved he was still alive and getting well again to begrudge him his complaints. He still had a way to go with his recovery, despite how well he was doing, but it was ironic that each day he seemed to have more energy, while each day she had less.

She chalked it up to the hours she was working. After all, what with juggling expanding the proposal for sustainable strategies she'd discussed with Kirk the night before her father's operation and daily visits to her father on top of her usual duties here at the office, it was no wonder she was feeling more tired than usual.

She was no longer worried about the broken condom or the mix-up with her Pill. She knew people who'd tried for years to get pregnant. The odds of her having conceived after just that one encounter with Kirk…? No, she wasn't even going to think about that again. For her own peace of mind, a couple of weeks ago she'd taken a home test and it had showed negative—to her overwhelming relief. She was just tired. That was all. Things would settle down after the presentation, she told herself.

It had become vital to her to make her presentation better than her best effort. She had no room for error on this. There were plenty of people in the office who were on the fence about the whole concept of energy technology and sustainability in the workplace. All it would take was a slipup from her and a damning comment from the chief executive officer, Silas Rogers—who she knew already disagreed with her on principle—and no matter how much support she had from Kirk, the concept would be dead in the water.

It had been interesting these past couple of weeks, watching people react to Kirk being installed as interim chairman in her father's absence. There was a fair amount of wariness interspersed with the obvious suck-ups who wanted to ensure that their jobs would remain secure in the merger transition that would take place over the next twelve months. And maybe that was another reason she wanted to make this presentation flawless. If it went ahead, she'd be project manager, and her own position and those of her team would be secure, too. And maybe, just maybe, she'd be able to prove to herself and to her father that she had what it took.

Another week later and Sally was finally satisfied she had everything in place. She'd booked the conference room on the executive floor, she'd gone through her PowerPoint, tested transmitting it to her team's portable devices and rehearsed her part of the presentation until she could recite everything forward, backward and in Swahili. Okay, so maybe not in Swahili, but she knew her stuff and so did her team.

For all that they were an information technology company, there were several diehards among the senior management who still preferred a paper handout to reading a handheld screen. After today she hoped to change that. She was so excited about seeing her team put forward the full development of their ideas. It could mean such wonderful things for Harrison Tanner Tech long-term that she hadn't even had time to feel anxious about talking in front of a group. Granted, it wouldn't be a huge crowd and she knew every person who would be there, but that hadn't stopped her phobia from taking over before. This time, though, felt different. She felt as though she could really do this, and her veins fizzed with anticipation as opposed to the dread she usually felt.

Sally had taken extra care with her appearance that morning, choosing a dress she knew flattered her. Her hair was pulled back into its customary ponytail, and her makeup was perfectly understated. Kirk would be at the presentation. She felt a flush of color steal into her cheeks. She had barely seen him since the night they'd had dinner together, although they had spoken on the telephone. He'd said it was to check for updates on her father's recovery, but she had a suspicion that it had more to do with his concerns about their failed contraception. Her notion was backed up when the calls stopped after she'd told him about the home test result.

She knew Kirk had been in and out of meetings and had spent some time back in California, finalizing things for his move to Seattle. It had filtered through the grapevine—not without a few remarks, both envious and full of admiration—that he'd bought a lakefront property here in Bellevue. She'd been relieved that their paths hadn't had to cross.

A chime at her door told her that Benton was there to take her to work. As soon as she arrived in the HTT building, she went straight to the main conference room on the senior management floor. It was time to slay her demons. The last time she'd been here—for the video feed announcing the merger—she'd made a complete idiot of herself in front of Kirk, not to mention all the staff. She'd heard one or two comments, hastily hushed, as she'd gone by in the office. While some people knew she held her position here in her father's firm purely on merit, there were a handful, including the CEO, who made their thoughts on nepotism perfectly clear.

She had so much to prove today. Normally, such a realization would have been daunting, but right now she felt completely in control. Sally looked around the room and silently approved the layout that she'd requested together with the screen that had been set up in readiness. She did a quick run-through with her tablet. Everything was working perfectly. She had this.

Over the next thirty minutes, the chairs slowly filled up as senior managers made their way into the room. There was a hum of activity when Kirk arrived, and Sally found herself holding her breath in anticipation as he walked toward her to say hello.

Her nostrils flared slightly as he neared, the delicious scent of him sending a tingle through her body. A tingle she instantly did her best to quash.

"Good morning," she said, pulling together all the smoothness she could muster. "I hope your trip back to California was successful."

"It was, thank you." His eyes raked over her and her heart rate picked up a notch or two. "And you've been okay?"

"Just fine," she replied with a smile fixed to her face.

"Tanner, good to see you back."

Kirk turned to acknowledge Silas Rogers, who she knew couldn't wait to see her fail. He'd never liked her, and she could see that despite the congenial look pasted on the man's face, he resented Kirk's presence here, too. After all, he would have been the natural fill-in for her father during his illness and recovery had it not been for the board's appointment of Kirk.

Sally cast a glance at one of her team and gave them her signal to commence. She'd decided to keep her speaking role strictly limited to explaining the concept she wanted to see the company adopt in their head office and how it could be expanded over the next five years through all their branches. As soon as her second in charge, Nick, was finished with his spiel, she was ready to whirl into action.

A tricky little wave of nausea surged through her. Sally reached for her water glass and took a sip then breathed in deeply. Nick was beginning to wind up his introduction, and all eyes would soon be turning to her. Her armpits prickled with perspiration, and another wave of nausea swelled. Again she took a small sip of water then focused on her breathing. The sick feeling subsided. She let a sense of relief flow through her. She could do this.

"...and without further ado, here's our team leader, Sally Harrison, to fill you in on why we're all so excited about what this proposal will do for HTT now and in the future. Sally?"

She rose to her feet, tablet in hand, and started her spiel. If she kept her eyes fixed between the projector screen and her tablet, she could even pretend there were no other people in the room.

The first few minutes of her presentation went extremely well, as she explained why it was important for HTT to evaluate the energy technologies available to them, and the next stage started brilliantly as she showed how going paperless in the office was one small step on the ladder. She demonstrated how they'd implemented the change in her department alone, and the figures she quoted showed the significant savings this had brought—not to mention the diminished waste footprint left on the environment.

"So you can imagine the long-term impact this will have on an entire floor, the entire head office and especially each and every HTT office around the globe."

There was a general murmur of assent from about seventy percent of the assembly. Sally took another breath and continued with her presentation.

"Small, consistent changes made on a wide scale is what we need. Can you imagine how something as simple as replacing the current management motor fleet with hybrid vehicles and installing solar panels on the rooftop of the HTT building to feed energy back into the grid would reduce the company's carbon footprint? And while there would be some initial costs, in the end all these steps would significantly reduce our overall expenses."

She was heading into the homestretch when a vicious wash of dizziness struck, and she faltered in her speech and put a hand out to steady herself. Kirk spoke from his position a couple of yards away from her.

"Sally? Everything okay?"

She pulled her lips into a smile and made her eyes flare open wide. Anything to stop the influx of black dots that now danced across her vision. She'd had her share of panicked reactions to public speaking, but this was new...and a little frightening. What was wrong with her? And would she be able to hide it until the presentation was complete?

"I'm fine," she said, but her voice was weak.

She looked at the people sitting there, all of them with eyes trained on her. Saw the smirk on Silas Rogers's face. And then she did the unthinkable. While she stared directly into Kirk's face, her tablet fell and bounced on the carpet, and she followed it down, sliding to the floor in an ignominious and unconscious heap.

Six

Kirk acted on instinct. He scooped Sally into his arms.

"Finish the presentation," he instructed the nearest member of her team as concerned murmurs swirled around them. "She's counting on you."

Then, without wasting another second, he stalked out of the room and down the corridor to Orson's office.

"What's wrong with Sally?" Marilyn asked, rising to her feet as he came into the executive suite.

"She collapsed."

"We have a nurse on duty for the staff here. I'll call her."

"Yes, do that, thanks."

He laid Sally down on a couch. Thankfully she was beginning to regain consciousness.

"Wha—?"

"You fainted," Kirk filled in as she looked around her. "At least I think you fainted. I want you to go to the hospital for tests to make sure it's not anything serious."

Sally tried to struggle to an upright position. "Go to the hospital? Don't be ridiculous. I'll be fine. I need to get back in there. I have to finish what I started."

He could understand why she felt that way. A little research had revealed that Sally's fear of public speaking had held her back from advancing within the company, purely because she'd been unable to speak to any size group in a situation like the one today. That she'd done as well as she had this morning had surprised him. Even more surprising was how proud of her he'd felt while she was doing it.

If he hadn't been so focused on getting her out of the conference room, he would have stopped to wipe that ridiculous expression off Rogers's face. He made a mental note to have a word with the man about the aside he'd heard him make about Sally riding on others' coattails, implying that she was incapable of completing anything on her own. There was so much more to her than that narrow-minded stuffed shirt realized…so many depths to Sally Harrison that Kirk, in spite of himself, wanted to explore.

Over the past five weeks, he'd tried to tell himself that the crazy attraction between them was just that. A moment of craziness and nothing more. But seeing her this morning had brought his attraction to her back to the fore again. He'd resented having to turn and say hello to that pompous idiot Rogers when he'd finally gotten the chance to see her face-to-face again. Add to that the sheer panic that flew through him as she lost consciousness and hit the carpeted floor of the conference room, swiftly followed by the instinctive need to protect her, and he knew that the way he felt about Sally Harrison was more than crazy. It was downright certifiable.

A movement at the door alerted him to the arrival of the staff nurse, with Marilyn close on her heels.

"I have some water for her," Marilyn said, putting a fresh pitcher and a glass on the side table.

"Nothing by mouth until we know what we're dealing with," said the nurse firmly but with a friendly smile. "Now, Ms. Harrison, how about you tell me what happened?"

The woman efficiently unpacked the small bag she'd brought with her and put a blood pressure cuff on Sally's arm while taking her temperature with a digital ear thermometer. Sally briefly outlined how she'd felt in the moments before she fainted. Kirk could see she was embarrassed, but he wasn't taking any risks by letting her brush this off. A suspicion began to form in his mind.

"Blood pressure is a little low. Temperature is normal. So you say you felt some nausea before you collapsed?"

Sally flicked her eyes to Kirk and then back to the nurse. "Yes, just a little. It's not unusual for me to feel that way, especially when talking to a large group. I'm okay with my team, but this was an important presentation and, I guess, I may have let that get to me."

"You've fainted before while speaking?" Kirk asked before the nurse could ask the same question.

"Not exactly. Usually I just feel sick and freeze. Today was different. But then again, today I actually got through a lot of my presentation. I was doing okay up until that dizzy spell hit."

"You were doing great," Kirk reassured her. "And your team is well trained and will do a fabulous job going through the rest of it in your absence. Don't worry about it."

"But—" she began in protest.

"Sally, I know you want to blame this on your difficulties with speaking in public, but given the situation with your father's health I'm going to insist you still go to the hospital to rule anything else out. HTT cannot sustain any weakness in any department right now."

His voice was sharper than he'd intended, and he forced a smile to his lips to soften his words. Thing was, his statement was truer than she probably realized. HTT was vulnerable right now, in more ways than one. He'd received news today that another major contract had been lost to their main rival. It made him all the more determined to find the wretched mole who continued to undermine HTT's every potential new success.

Sally looked at him, and he watched as the light of defiance left her soft blue eyes. "Fine," she said through gritted teeth. "But I don't want to go to hospital. It'll take far too long. I agree to going to either an urgent care clinic or my own doctor and I'm coming back to work straight afterward."

"That will depend entirely on the outcome of your examination," he replied firmly.

She rolled her eyes at him, but he wasn't about to be swayed. If what he suspected was confirmed…? No, she'd said she'd taken a test. Said the results were negative. But home testing wasn't always a hundred percent accurate, was it?

He couldn't jump the gun. They'd wait until she'd seen a doctor, had some tests, then they'd deal with what came next.

The nurse agreed with Sally that a hospital visit wasn't necessary and, after a quick discussion, agreed Kirk should transport her to the nearest clinic. After their arrival there, nothing could dislodge Kirk from her side, and in the end it had been easier to simply allow him to be there in the treatment room with her, especially since she suspected he wouldn't trust her to deliver the results in full when she got them. That said, when the doctor returned after what felt like an interminable wait, to deliver the results of the first run of tests, she felt strangely relieved to have Kirk by her side.

"Okay, Ms. Harrison, you're a little anemic, but that's not unusual in your case. Overall you're in excellent health, and I'm going to discharge you. It's going to be important that you not skip meals and that you take some supplements to counter the anemia, and I want you to make sure that you get plenty of rest and fluids."

"Hold on," Sally said, putting up a hand. "Not unusual in my case? Why? I've never been anemic before. Yes, I've been busy lately and under a bit of stress, but why would that lead to anemia?"

"Did the nurse not let you know?"

"She hasn't been back. Let me know what?" Sally's voice rose in frustration, but Kirk had a feeling he knew exactly what the doctor was going to say.

"You're pregnant," the doctor said without preamble.

Bingo.

Kirk listened while Sally argued with the doctor, insisting that it couldn't be true, but apparently the proof was right there in the test results. Kirk said nothing, just let the news sink in. He'd been relieved when Sally had told him the home test had been negative. Hugely relieved. His life plan had been in the making from when he was in his early teens, and he'd seen no reason to ever veer from that. Marriage and children were far down the line in his ten-year plan. And yet...

He was going to be a daddy. The words resonated through his mind over and over. Together with the woman on the hospital bed, a woman he'd been completely unable to resist the night they'd met, he was going to be a parent. Sally, it seemed, was having an even harder time than him in accepting the news.

"I can't be pregnant," Sally said again, this time more adamantly than before. "It was only that one time."

"That's all it takes sometimes, I'm afraid. Perhaps I could refer you for some counseling?" the doctor said.

"I don't need counseling. I just don't see how this could have happened."

"Look, we'll deal with it together," Kirk hastened to reassure her.

"I guess we'll have to," she replied bitterly. "I didn't want this."

"I didn't plan for it, either," he agreed. "But now that we're faced with it, we can make plans."

And they *would* make plans. There was no way he was missing out on his child's life the way his father had missed out on his. His father's descent into drug addiction had seen him not only lose his position as the development manager for Harrison IT in its earliest incarnation, it had also resulted in Frank Tanner's death by suicide several years later—leaving his twelve-year-old son and his wife with more questions than answers and very little money to make ends meet. If it hadn't been for Orson Harrison's assistance, who knew where they'd have ended up?

No, his child would not go without—neither emotionally nor materially.

"Can I go back to work now?" Sally asked the doctor, interrupting Kirk's train of thought.

"Of course. Pregnancy isn't an illness, but I'd like you to reduce stress and get into a good routine ensuring you eat properly and regularly, take prenatal vitamins, and fit a little exercise into each day if you don't already."

"Surely you don't want to go back to work today," Kirk stepped in before Sally could respond. "Your body has had a shock. Take the day to recover fully."

She gave him a scathing look. "You heard the doctor. I'm pregnant, not sick. Besides, I need to get back to my team and find out the result of the Q and A after the presentation."

Kirk knew when to pick his battles, and this definitely wasn't one he'd be able to win. Better to give in gracefully rather than cause a scene in front of the medical center staff.

"Fine, we'll head back."

"Thank you."

Although she'd said the words with every nuance of good manners, he could sense the sarcasm beneath them. She was used to making her own decisions, and she wasn't going to accept him telling her what to do. He was going to have to become inventive if he was going to achieve his objectives with respect to being there for her and their baby. That was fine. He was nothing if not inventive.

They took a cab back to the office, barely speaking. Clearly Sally was still digesting the news about the baby, but this would be the last time she'd be doing any of it on her own—he'd make certain of that. Still, it wasn't the kind of discussion he wanted to have in the back of a cab, so he'd have to shelve it until they could be alone together again.

While he took care of paying the cab driver, Sally made her way into the building, and he managed to catch up with her by the elevators.

"In such a hurry to get back to work?"

"This is important to me, Kirk. It might have escaped your notice, but I'm the boss's daughter. As such, people either treat me as if I'm their best friend because they think being nice to me will advance their career, or I'm their archenemy because they think I'll run back to Dad and narc on them for any minor transgression—or you, now, since Dad's still recuperating. Many think I shouldn't be here at all. I have to work twice as hard and twice as long as anyone here for people to take me seriously, and all my hard work is probably ruined now thanks to fainting during the presentation today."

"I'm sure you're exaggerating."

"You think? Aside from my team and Marilyn, there are very few people here who believe I'm capable of doing the job I was hired to do. Yes, *hired*. I applied for that position just like anyone else, and that was after interning here during my summer and semester breaks as often as my father would let me."

"If it's all so hard, why bother? Why not go elsewhere? You are eminently employable. You have a sharp mind and great ideas. Any company would be lucky to have you," Kirk hastened to assure her.

He already knew a lot of what she'd just told him about her credentials and experience, but he'd had no idea that she was a pariah to so many, as well.

"Because my father started this business. It's in my blood, and as such I feel invested in it, too. And while I'll probably never be good enough to take over the company when he's ready to retire, like I always dreamed of when I was younger, the company and my father deserve my best—not some other nameless, faceless corporation."

The elevator doors opened onto Sally's floor, and she stepped out.

"Sally, wait. We need to talk about this."

"Thank you for your help today," she said, holding the elevator door open. "Call me and make an appointment if you want to talk. Right now it's—"

Her voice broke off, as if she couldn't even bring herself to discuss the child now growing in her belly.

"It's just too complicated," she continued, her cheeks flushing.

With that, she let the door close, and he caught a last glimpse of her walking away. Kirk wanted to refute her statement. It wasn't complicated as far as he was concerned. She was pregnant with his baby, and that meant they had a future together whether she realized it or not.

With the chemistry they shared, being together would be no hardship. But it seemed he had to convince her of that. He'd let her think she'd had the last word on the subject, that she had the upper hand. And then he'd try to change her mind.

Sally fielded the multitude of queries about her health in a convincing facade of good humor as her team gathered around her.

"I'm fine. I'd just been burning the candle at both ends and skipping a few too many meals. You know how important this project was to all of us. Everything else went on the back burner for me when it came to this. So, Nick, how did it go?"

"The presentation went really well. I'd say the majority of the managers there seemed very interested in exploring the concept further and starting to implement the changes. Everyone could see that it was a time-and money-saver in the long-term, even though initial outlay in replacing what we're already using, especially the motor fleet, will be costly."

There was something in Nick's tone that made Sally's stomach clench.

"And did they vote on implementation?"

Nick fell silent, and one of the other members of Sally's team filled the silence.

"Before they could vote, Mr. Rogers spoke up."

"I see." A ripple of frustration cascaded through her mind, but she couldn't let her people know how the news upset her. "I take it he's not a fan of the suggested changes, then?"

Her staff looked at her with the same disappointed expression she was certain was on her own face and, as a group, shook their heads. Some things just didn't bear saying out loud.

"So we need to work harder, then. Tackle this from another perspective."

"That won't be necessary."

Sally wheeled around to find Kirk standing behind her, fistfuls of takeout bags clutched in his hands. Couldn't he leave her alone for a second?

"And why not?" she challenged, ready to do battle.

"Because there's nothing wrong with the perspective you presented. Here," he said, putting the takeout bags on the meeting table in front of them. "I heard you guys haven't had a break for lunch yet, so it's on me. From what I saw you've put a great deal of planning into this project, and I'd like to see it developed further."

"And Silas Rogers?"

"Is not the chairman of HTT, nor is he interim chairman of HTT."

"He's still the CEO, and what he says carries weight," Sally argued.

"That's true," Kirk admitted and pulled up a chair to sit beside her. He ripped open a takeout bag and passed her a sub filled with salad fixings and well-done hot roast beef. "Eat, then we'll discuss this some more."

Sally bristled at his high-handedness, but her mouth began to water at the smell of the sub, and hunger won the war over pride. She reluctantly took it from him and sank her teeth into the fresh bread, groaning in appreciation as the flavors of the fillings burst on her tongue. She hadn't realized she was quite so hungry.

Next to her, she felt Kirk stiffen and shift in his chair. He tugged at the front of his trousers and pulled a napkin across his lap, but not before she saw evidence of a hint of arousal pressing against the fine Italian wool of his suit. Shock rippled through her, accompanied by a powerful wave of something else—desire. No, no, no. She wasn't going to go there again. No way. Never.

Even though she scolded herself soundly, she couldn't help the prickle of heat that crept through her, couldn't prevent the surge of sheer lust that forced her inner muscles to clench involuntarily. It was a turn-on to know that she was capable of arousing an attractive man without even trying. And while she had a whole list of problems with this particular man, there was no denying he was gorgeous—he had a body like a Greek god and he knew exactly how to use it. All of it. His mouth, his tongue, those hands and especially—

No! She squirmed in her seat.

"Is your lunch okay?" Kirk asked with a curious expression on his face.

"Great," she said, taking another bite, this time with less audible enthusiasm.

She'd have to eat more carefully in the future, she decided, if enjoying her sub had this effect on him. And if his reaction had the same domino effect on her. So she'd have to remember to control herself. That couldn't be too hard, could it? She had no plans to eat with him again after this, did she? In fact, she had no plans to spend any more time with him than their jobs absolutely required.

For some stupid reason, that thought caused a pang of something deep inside—something she didn't quite want to define. *He lied to you*, she reminded herself. By omission, yes, but keeping his true identity from her that night had been deliberate, and she still had no idea why he'd done it or what he'd hoped to gain by it. *So ask him*, the little voice at the back of her mind said pragmatically.

Maybe she would. But that would mean spending more time together, wouldn't it? Besides, referring to that night would bring back the memories of how she'd behaved so uncharacteristically. Of what they'd done—and of how it had made her feel.

Darn it! Maybe it was hormones, she thought. She'd never been the type to play sex kitten. In fact, she'd always been slightly embarrassed and a little uncomfortable when the girls around her in college, and even sometimes here in the office, ever discussed their sexual activities. But there was something about this guy that opened sensual floodgates she hadn't known existed. She'd always thought that maybe she was just slightly different from the other women she knew—less passionate, less sensual. But maybe she'd just been waiting for the right man to come along.

Except he wasn't the right man, was he? He was her boss. He was a sneak. And yet he was the best lover she was ever likely to have in her lifetime.

She sighed and put down her now empty wrapper. She'd been so caught up in her thoughts that she hadn't even realized she'd finished the sub.

For the next several hours, Kirk chaired a discussion between Sally and her team on the best way to begin implementing the proposal. By the end of the workday, she didn't know if she was energized because she was so excited about seeing her spark of an idea being set on the road to fruition or exhausted at the thought of all the work ahead. She did feel a deep sense of satisfaction, though, and she'd begun to see Kirk in a new light.

He had that rare talent of listening—and listening well—to what her team had to say. And when he injected his own thoughts and ideas, he was gracious about accepting criticism if those ideas were challenged. A part of her wished she'd never met him that night, that instead she'd had the chance of meeting him in the normal course of work and of seeing whether the attraction that crackled between them like static electricity might have grown naturally over time rather than exploding all at once in the accelerated fling they'd had.

But now they were linked by a baby. Her mouth turned dry as sawdust. While she wanted to have as little to do with Kirk as possible, she would never deny her child access to their father. The very thought was impossible to her, especially when her own relationship with her dad was such an integral part of who she was. But how could they coparent a child when there was still so much tension between them?

Maybe she was getting ahead of herself. She had plenty of time to think about all that. Plenty of time to work out adequate coping strategies and discuss this situation they had found themselves in like rational adults. People did that all the time, didn't they?

But did they spend half their time fighting a magnetic pull so strong she felt like a helpless tide being influenced by a supermoon? She didn't want to think about that right now. She'd have to put it on the back burner for as long as she could. But, judging by the quick glances flung her way by the man sitting next to her, that wouldn't be very long at all.

Seven

The meeting finished and Kirk hung back, talking to Nick, as Sally gathered her things together and stopped to give instructions to a handful of people. He liked watching her in action. Hell, he liked watching her, period. As if she sensed his perusal, she looked up and caught his eye. And, yes, there was that telltale flush of color on her cheeks. He was finding it more and more endearing each time he saw it.

Finally she was ready to leave, and he fell into step with her as she headed to the elevators.

"Feeling okay?"

She rolled her eyes. "I'm fine, seriously. There's nothing wrong with me."

"You're carrying my baby," he murmured close to her ear. "I think I'm entitled to be concerned."

She stiffened at his words. "So, what? You want to monitor me twenty-four-seven? Is that what it is?"

The idea had merit.

Sally huffed an impatient sigh. “Look, it’s still early, and I can assure you I will do whatever is in my power to stay healthy and to ensure that everything goes as it should.”

Somehow that didn’t satisfy him. For reasons even he didn’t understand, it just didn’t go far enough.

“I’m sure you will,” he agreed. “But you have to admit, sharing that responsibility has its advantages, too.”

“What do you mean?” she asked as they stepped into the empty elevator.

“I don’t know if you’ve been sick yet, but what if nausea does occur?”

“Then I’ll deal with it,” she said grimly and crossed her arms over her body. “I’m a big girl, Kirk. I’ve been looking after myself for a good many years now. I think I can cope with a pregnancy.”

“I’ve no doubt. But I’d really like to be a part of things. I know this news has come as a shock to both of us, but I’d like to think that together we can get through it. Look, can I see you home so we can talk about this in a more private setting?”

Sally rolled her eyes at him. “You’re not going to leave me alone until I agree, are you?”

He didn’t want to leave her alone at all. The thought came as a shock, but it felt right at the same time.

“I like to get my way,” he conceded. “But I’d feel happier if you conceded that this is something we should iron out sooner rather than later.”

“Oh, of course, your being happy is so very important,” she said with a touch of bitterness. “Okay, then. You can take me home. Benton will be waiting downstairs for me. I’ll have to let him know.”

It was a small victory, but Kirk was happy to take it.

Benton was waiting in the elevator lobby of the parking garage, and Kirk stepped forward to introduce himself. The man looked him over as if he was a potential threat before relaxing an increment when Sally stepped forward with an apologetic smile.

"I'm sorry I couldn't give you notice of this, Benton. Mr. Tanner and I need to extend our discussions, so he'll be taking me home this evening."

"Whatever you want, Ms. Harrison. I'll see you in the morning, then?"

"Yes, thank you."

Kirk walked Sally over to his SUV and helped her in.

When they arrived at her apartment building a few minutes later, he pulled into the parking space she indicated. They rode the elevator to the top floor, and he followed her into an elegant and well-proportioned apartment. While it was mostly decorated in neutral tones, an occasional pop of color drew his eye—a cushion here, a throw rug there. But overall there was very little to tell him about the woman who intrigued him far more than he wanted to admit.

He moved to the large windows that looked out in the direction of Lake Washington. It was growing dark, and across the lake he could make out the twinkle of lights around its rim. A sound from behind him made him turn. Sally had pulled the band from her hair and was tousling her fingers through the mass of spun gold. He liked this more relaxed version of her more than the buttoned-down woman who headed her social engineering department. On second thought, he liked the naked, warm and willing version from just over a month ago the best, but she'd made it quite clear they weren't going to go there again.

But it was oh so satisfying, he reminded himself. *And yet look at the trouble it has put us in*, he countered. Kirk slammed the door closed on his thoughts and looked at Sally more closely. Beneath her makeup he could still see the telltale signs of the stress she'd been under today. She had to be exhausted.

"Look, I won't take up a lot of your time. I know you need to get something to eat and then probably have an early night."

She barked a cynical laugh. "Are you my mother now?"

He gave her a half smile of apology. "I'm sorry, I guess I'm overcompensating."

"You think?" She moved toward the kitchen. "Did you want something to drink? I have beer, water, wine."

"A beer, thanks."

He watched as she poured the beer into a tall glass then opened a small bottle of sparkling water for herself. Of course she wouldn't be drinking alcohol. The realization hit him hard. She was going to have to make so many changes. So many adjustments. It was hardly fair, was it?

"Take a seat," she said, bringing their drinks through to the small sitting room.

Kirk sat at one end of the sofa, and Sally took the other end. Awkward silence stretched between them.

"You wanted to talk, didn't you? What about, exactly?" Sally asked.

"The baby, for a start. How do you feel about it?"

"Shocked, surprised. Scared."

"Yeah, me too. I hadn't planned on this at this stage of my life."

Sally sat a little more upright. "And just when had you planned it for?"

He couldn't tell if she was sniping at him or genuinely curious. He decided that honesty was probably the best policy right now.

"To be honest, I had hoped to start looking for a wife about five years from now and hopefully start a family a few years after that."

"Just like that?"

"Look, I know it sounds clinical, but I grew up with a lot of instability. Being able to make a plan and stick to it kept me anchored when things were tough at home, even when my dad was still alive." He didn't want to admit his father's weakness to her. He'd spent his entire adult life working hard to erase those memories, to overcome the hardships he and his mother had endured—and he'd succeeded. He wasn't about to be made to feel ashamed of that. Not by anyone.

Sally shrugged and took a sip of her water. "That makes sense, I guess. I'm sorry things were so hard for you."

"You know that saying about gaining strength through adversity? Well, I decided to adopt that a long time ago. And I've managed to achieve a lot of success by staying strong and keeping my focus on my goals. But now I need to reevaluate. This child we're having, I very much want to be a part of its life, Sally. I don't want to be a weekend father or an absentee parent. I want to be there, for everything."

"That could be difficult, considering we're not even a couple."

"But we could be. We already know we're compatible in the bedroom."

"Too compatible, it seems," she commented acerbically.

"Look, I never considered having a committed relationship or starting a family until I'd achieved my career goal targets because I never wanted a child of mine to miss out on anything—whether it be financially or emotionally. You want the same thing, right? For our child to have everything he or she needs to be happy, healthy and safe? Loving parents are part of that package. Perhaps we ought to consider being a couple."

"What, go steady, you mean?" she said with a gurgle of laughter.

"More than that. We should get married. Think about it—it makes perfect sense. This is only a one-bedroom apartment, right? Where would you put the baby when it's born? Have you even thought about that? And what about work? Do you plan to be a stay-at-home mom or continue with your career?"

Sally put her glass down very slowly. "Kirk, we only just found out about this pregnancy today. We have plenty of time ahead of us for decision making. Let's not be rash."

"Rash? I don't think so. It's logical."

"I'm sorry, but it isn't logical to me in the least. We hardly know each other, and I'm not sure that I want to be married to you. I'm certainly not going to make a decision like that on such short acquaintance."

Kirk fought back the arguments that sprang to the tip of his tongue. It was clear she was feeling more than a little overwhelmed by his suggestion, which was entirely understandable. She needed time to think, and so did he. If he was going to campaign successfully to win Sally's hand, he would have to go about it carefully.

"At least think about it," he urged. "And talk to me—seriously, anything. Any questions, any problems, bring them to me and we'll solve them together."

"Oh, I'll be thinking about it," she admitted with a rueful shake of her head. "I imagine I'll be thinking about little else. By the way, I don't want anyone else to know about this just yet."

He nodded. The only person he would have shared the news with would have been his mother, and with her gone he had no one else. No one else except the child now nestled inside the woman sitting opposite him. A feeling bloomed within his chest—pride tinged with a liberal dose of an emotion he'd had little enough experience with. Love. It was odd to think that he could love another being before it truly came into existence in the world, but he knew, without doubt, that he loved his child, and the intensity of the emotion shook him to his core.

Sally wasn't sure what was going through Kirk's mind, but if the determined look on his face was anything to go by, she was going to have some battles on her hands over the next few months. Probably over the next few years, she amended. He was a man used to having his way—it was inevitable that they were going to bump heads from time to time when it came to deciding what was best for the baby.

Her head swam. Discovering she was pregnant was shocking enough. Dealing with Kirk as her baby's father was another matter entirely—especially now that he seemed to believe they should get married.

Over the past couple of years, life had shown her that you had to reach for the things that mattered most to you. Had to fight for them. Her best friend from college, Angel, who'd turned out to be a secret European princess, had shown her how important it was to follow and fight for your dream.

Dissatisfied with a politically arranged betrothal based only on expedience with no affection attached, Angel—or, Princess Mila, as she'd been officially known—had broken with tradition and done everything in her power to ensure she won her betrothed's heart, even at the risk of losing him altogether.

Just weeks ago, they'd celebrated the christening of their first child, a little boy who would become crown prince of Sylvain—and to Sally's eyes, when she'd visited to attend the ceremony, neither Angel nor King Thierry had ever looked happier or more fulfilled.

She wanted that. She wanted a man who would look at her the way King Thierry looked at Angel. There was no doubt in the world that Angel was his queen in every sense of the word. While Sally had always hoped to be a mother someday, she'd intended to start that stage of her life by finding the right man to be a husband and father first. Had planned to bring her child into a home already filled with love and trust. How could she have any of that with Kirk? She didn't love him—she barely knew him. And trust? Not a chance. The only positive traits she could assign to him were his appearance, his bedroom skills and the fact that he seemed to be a very capable boss. *Her* boss, in fact. And that added another layer of complication.

Sally wanted a life that was lived with purpose. One that yielded great results for others as well as for herself. She wanted to make a difference, and she ached to fulfill her potential. It's what she'd spent at least eight years of her life studying for and even more time interning at Harrison IT for. And yet despite her dreams, she continued to remain in the background. Knowing she was being held back by her phobia was one thing, but having a baby added a whole other layer to things.

Kirk had spoken of his career plans, but what would this do to her long-term goals? No matter what anyone said, life was very different for a woman in the workplace. That glass ceiling was still well and truly in place, and there were few women in the upper echelons of management. She'd hoped that one day, if she could overcome her phobia, she might earn a position up there. That the people she worked with would respect that she'd climbed her way up that corporate ladder, striving as hard as the rest of them.

No one would take her seriously if she was married to the vice president. Any advancement in her career would be looked upon as being won because of who she was, not what she brought to the role.

"Look," she started. "I've got a lot to think about, and you're right—I'm tired and I need an early night. Would you go, please?"

"You promise me you'll have something to eat?"

She gave him an are-you-serious look.

"Okay, okay," he said, holding up one hand. "Don't shoot me for caring. You have no idea what it was like to watch you crumple like that this morning."

He made it sound like he actually cared.

"I will have something to eat."

"I cook a mean omelet. If you have eggs, I could make it for you."

Her mouth watered. "Fine," she said, making a sudden decision. "I'm going to grab a shower. I'm not sure what's in the fridge, but go knock yourself out."

Maybe once he fed her, he'd stop hovering over her like some overprotective parent. She stopped in her tracks. But that's exactly what he was—a parent—and so was she. She shook her head, went through to her bathroom and quickly stripped off her work clothes. She looked at herself in the mirror.

"Nothing to see here," she murmured out loud.

But her hand settled on her lower belly, and for a moment she stopped to think about the changes that were happening inside. Changes that would force her to make monumental adjustments in her life. For a moment it all seemed too much and far too hard. But she reminded herself of what Kirk had said about wanting to be there every step of the way. She wasn't in this alone. Not by any means.

Did she have the strength to embark on this journey with him?

By the time she stepped out of the shower and dressed in a pair of yoga pants and a long-sleeved T-shirt, she was no closer to reaching a decision. A delicious aroma wafted from her kitchen, and she followed the scent to see what Kirk was up to.

"Perfect timing," he said, folding an omelet in the pan and sliding it onto a plate that already had a generous helping of diced fried potatoes, bacon bits and onions on one side.

"I had all these ingredients?" she asked, sliding into a chair at the breakfast bar.

"You can do a lot with just a few key things. When I was growing up, I often helped my mom in the kitchen. She taught me a lot."

Sally felt a pang for the boy he must have been. Her own upbringing had been so vastly different. They'd always had staff, including a cook, and as far as Sally could recall, her mother had never so much as baked a cookie her entire privileged life.

Kirk reached for a jar of salsa and ladled a little across her omelet before putting her plate down in front of her with a flourish. "There, now eat up before it gets cold."

She forked up a bit of omelet and closed her eyes in bliss as delicate flavors of herbs and cheese burst on her tongue.

"This is so good," she said. "Thank you. I hope you made one for yourself, too."

"I can get something later."

"Oh, please, you've given me far more than I can eat. At least help me with what I have here."

"How about I whip up another omelet and you can give me some of your potatoes."

"That sounds like a good idea."

It felt oddly normal to watch Kirk working in her kitchen. He moved with an elegant grace and confidence that she found all too appealing. *He withheld his true identity*, she reminded herself. *And he slept with you knowing exactly who you were.*

And now they had made a baby.

She was going to have to press him for an explanation about that night, especially if they were going to move forward together and most especially if she was even going to begin to seriously consider his proposal. But not now. Not tonight. Right at this moment she was struggling to make sense of what her next step would be and how on earth she was ever going to be able to tell her father that she was expecting Kirk's child.

Kirk took over cleanup duties when they'd finished their impromptu meal. Sally was too tired to argue the point by then. The food had given her a boost, but right now her bed was calling. Once he'd finished, she walked Kirk to the door.

"Thank you for dinner," she said softly.

"I enjoyed it. I..." He paused a moment as if debating whether or not to say what was on the tip of his tongue. "I enjoy being with you."

Sally didn't quite know how to react. He was good company and she felt drawn to him in a variety of ways, but there was so much about him that she didn't know—

or trust. She reached for the door and opened it to let him out.

He was standing close, too close. The lure of his cologne mingled with the heat of his body and wrapped itself around her. She looked up at him and saw the way his pupils dilated as their gazes meshed. She wasn't sure who moved first, but one moment she was standing there with the door open, the next it was closed and her back was pressed against the wooden surface as his lips hungrily claimed hers.

Eight

She gave a small moan of surrender, and in the next moment he was lifting her as if she weighed nothing, the hard evidence of his arousal pressing against her sex, sending jolts of need through her body.

She wrapped her legs around his hips, pulling him tighter against her. His mouth was hungry and demanding, and she was equally voracious—meeting the questing probe of his tongue with her own, nipping at his lips. Through the cloud of need that gripped her, Sally became aware that she was no longer pressed against the door and Kirk was carrying her in the direction of her bedroom.

He lowered her to her bed and bent over her.

"I want to see you. All of you," he murmured even as he peppered small kisses along her jaw and down the column of her throat.

She was at a loss for words. One minute they'd been saying goodbye and the next, here they were, tugging each other's clothing off as if they couldn't bear to wait another second before they were skin to skin again. Right now, the only thing that mattered was losing herself in his touch, in the sensations that rippled through her body with his every caress.

"Your skin—it's as soft as I remember," he said reverently, stroking her underneath her top.

"You remember touching my skin?" she asked on a breathless laugh.

"Among other things."

"Tell me about those things," she implored him.

And he did, in clear and graphic detail. Following up every word with a stroke of his tongue on her heated flesh, with the heat of his mouth through her bra as he teased her tightly drawn nipples into aching buds of need, and with the tangle of his fingers as they stroked and coaxed the slick flesh at her core. Her first orgasm rocketed through her body, taking her completely by surprise, but he took his time over coaxing her body to her second.

She continued to shiver in aftershocks of delight beneath the onslaught of his mouth as he traced her every curve. And when his head settled between her thighs, she nearly lifted off the bed as he gently drew the swollen, sensitive bud of her clitoris against his tongue. Her second climax left her weak and trembling against the sheets, and when he shifted slightly to slide on a condom, she laughed.

"Locking the stable door after the horse has bolted?" she teased, reaching for him as he hovered over her again.

"You could say that. Maybe it's just taking longer for the news to sink in than I thought it would."

Whatever she'd been about to say in reply fled her mind as he nudged his blunt tip against her entrance and slid deep within her. She rocked against him, meeting his movements—at first slow and languid and then speeding up as demand rose within them both again. This time, when she came, he tipped over the edge with her, and she held his powerful body as paroxysms of pleasure rocked them both.

Minutes later, exhausted, she slipped into sleep, unaware of the man who now cradled her sweetly in his arms.

Kirk lay there waiting for his heart rate to resemble something close to normal. If he didn't take care, *he'd* be the one needing a bed in the cardiac care unit. The dark humor sobered him up immediately. This was Orson Harrison's daughter he was sleeping with. And while the man was recovering nicely from his heart attack, he still wasn't back at full strength. He still needed Kirk to carry the load of the company for him. Finding out about the baby had thrown Kirk for a loop, but he couldn't allow it to make him forget all his other responsibilities.

He allowed his fingertips to trace small circles on Sally's back as he listened to her deep gentle breathing. Somehow he had to disentangle himself from her warm, languid body and get dressed and get out of here. Put some distance between them so he could clear his head and do the job he was here to do.

While it was still possible that Sally was the leak that was passing information on to HTT's biggest competitor, he no longer wanted to believe that it could be her. Not the mother of his child. Not the daughter of the man he held in higher regard than any other man he'd ever known.

This pregnancy was a messy complication, but they'd work through it. Sally shifted against him, and Kirk found himself curving naturally to her. This wasn't the action of a man about to leave the woman lying next to him, he warned himself, and yet, try as he might, he couldn't find the impetus he needed to pull away. Perhaps just this once, he told himself, letting sleep tug him into its hold. It wasn't the cleverest thing in the world to remain in her bed, but for now it felt like the right thing.

It was still dark when he woke. Dawn wasn't far away. Beside him, Sally slept deeply, and he gently extricated himself from their intertwined limbs. His body protested, an early-morning erection telling him that leaving the bed was the last thing he should be thinking about. But he needed to get home to change before getting into the office for an early meeting. And he needed to examine his growing feelings for the woman still slumbering in the mussed-up sheets. He quickly and quietly dressed in his shirt and trousers and, carrying his jacket and shoes in one hand, he made to leave the room.

Something made him look back and take one more look at Sally as she lay there, the sheet halfway down and exposing her back and the curve of a perfectly formed breast. It took all his self-restraint not to drop his things where he stood and move to take her back in his arms.

Work, he told himself. *Think of work.* He wanted to be in full possession of all his faculties by the time he and Sally crossed paths in the office today. As he left her building and walked toward his car, he saw a town car creep into the visitor parking area. He recognized the man at the wheel as the bodyguard he'd met last night. It made him think. One of Sally's security team could just as likely be the leak he needed to find and eradicate from HTT. He knew how easy it was to conduct a business call in the back of a car without considering the ears of the person driving.

Benton got out of the vehicle and looked across to

where Kirk was parked. The man's eyes narrowed as he identified him. Taking the bull by the horns, Kirk walked toward him. He didn't want gossip about his relationship with Sally, such as it was, getting back to the office until she was ready for it to be made public.

"Good morning," he said to the bodyguard, extending a hand.

Benton's grasp was firm. Perhaps a little too firm, Kirk judged with an ironic lift of his brow.

"Morning, sir."

"I trust that Ms. Harrison's best interests are always at the forefront of your mind, Mr. Benton."

"Always, sir."

"Then I hope I can rely on you to keep the fact you saw me here this morning to yourself?"

The man hesitated a moment. "That depends, sir."

"On?"

"On whether or not *you* are in her best interests…sir."

Kirk nodded. "Fair comment. I will never do anything to hurt Ms. Harrison. You can rest assured on that score."

"Then we don't have anything to worry about, do we, sir?"

"No, we don't. Have a good day, Mr. Benton."

"Just Benton will do, sir."

Kirk nodded again and returned to his car. Somehow he didn't think that a bodyguard who took his duty to Sally so seriously could be a mole, but he'd have to check. Both Benton and whoever else ferried her about.

He looked up to Sally's apartment windows and saw the bedroom light come on. He needed to get going.

That evening, after work, Benton drew the car to a halt outside the front portico of her father's house. Sally thanked him and made her way to the door, where the housekeeper stood with a welcoming smile on her face.

"Good evening, Ms. Harrison. Mr. Harrison is in the library waiting for you."

"How is he today, Jennifer?"

"He's almost his old self, but we've had to remove all the saltshakers from the house."

Sally gave a rueful laugh. No matter what his cardiologist told him, her father still railed against his new dietary restrictions. "I'm so glad you have his best interests at heart. I don't know what we'd do without you all."

"It's our honor to work for Mr. Harrison. We're just glad he's recovering so well."

"Aren't we all?" Sally said with a heartfelt sigh.

She made her way to the library, where her father sat before an open fire nursing his one approved glass of red wine a day. He put down his drink when he saw her and rose to give her a welcoming hug. There was nothing quite like it in the world, Sally thought as she allowed her father's scents and strength to seep into her. And it still terrified her that she'd come so close to losing him.

"Hi, Dad. I hear you're giving the staff grief about your food again?" she said as they let each other go.

"Just keeping them on their toes," he said with a gruff laugh. "Can I pour you a glass of wine? This is a very nice pinot noir—you should try it."

"I—no, not today, thanks, Dad. I'll just stick with mineral water."

At some point she was going to have to tell her father why she wasn't drinking alcohol. She wasn't looking forward to the revelation, but she certainly wanted him to hear it from her before he had the chance to find out through anyone else. Especially after her fainting spell at work yesterday. Gosh, was it only yesterday? It already seemed a whole lot longer ago.

Her cheeks fired as she remembered exactly what had chased so much of yesterday's activity from her mind.

"Too hot in here?" her father asked, handing her a glass of water.

"No, no. It's fine. Lovely, in fact," she answered, flustered.

"Then what is it? What's bothering you?"

That was the trouble with being close to your parent, she admitted. They knew you too well and saw too much.

"A few things," she hedged.

"Is it work? I hear that Kirk has ruffled a few feathers. Glad to hear he's given your sustainability initiative the green light. It's about time we did more than just talk in circles about that."

He'd heard that already? Sally gave an internal groan. What else had he heard?

Knowing her father was expecting a reply, she managed to say, "Well, I always expected some pushback. You didn't seem so eager to embrace the idea, yourself."

"Couldn't be seen to be championing my own daughter, now could I. Had to make you work for what you wanted. I've always thought, if you're passionate enough about something, you'll make it work." Orson took a sip of his wine and put the glass back down beside him. "Now, tell me what you think about Kirk."

Sally felt the burn of embarrassment heat her from the inside out. Ah, yes, Kirk. That would be the man she'd slept with after turning down his proposal, after discovering she was pregnant with his baby. It sounded worse than the plot of a soap opera. She groaned to herself. Her father sat opposite her, clearly awaiting some kind of response from her.

"He seems to be very…focused."

Orson snorted. "He's good-looking, isn't he?"

"Dad!" she remonstrated.

"Focused." He snorted again. "The man looks as though he stepped off the front cover of *GQ* magazine, has a Mensa-rated IQ and you tell me he's *focused*. You're attracted to him, aren't you?"

"Dad, I don't think…" Sally let her voice trail off.

How did she tell him just how attractive she found Kirk? How he was so irresistible that the first night she saw him, she slept with him? That she'd done the same again last night?

Orson laughed. "I'm sorry, honey, can't help but tease you a little. You're so buttoned up these days. You can't blame your father for giving you a little prod. Besides, you can't argue the truth, can you?"

Sally chose to ignore his question and turned the conversation in another direction.

"Actually, now that you're better, could you please explain to me just why you brought him into Harrison IT? We were doing okay. We certainly didn't need to merge with anyone else, did we?"

And she certainly hadn't needed to *merge* with Kirk Tanner, but that hadn't stopped her from doing it again, that pesky little voice inconveniently reminded her.

Orson picked up his wineglass and swirled the ruby-colored liquid around the bowl, staring at it for a while before putting it back down.

"I guess, in part, you could call it guilt. Kirk's father, Frank, was my best friend in college. We started in business together. But what I didn't notice was that the man whose partying seemed harmless in college got in over his head when he partied hard in the real world, too. It got to the point where it took a lot of chemical help for him to get through the day. I didn't realize he was a drug addict until it was too late. By then he had a wife and son, and he was pretty resistant to help. Eventually he agreed to go to rehab, but he never got there. Instead he loaded up on drugs and took a dive off Deception Bridge."

He fell silent for a while, obviously lost in the pain of his memories. Eventually he drew in a deep breath and huffed it out again.

"I felt responsible. I should have been able to see the problem sooner, step in earlier, help him more."

"Dad, not everyone wants to be helped."

"I know that now, but back then I felt like it was all my fault. I did what I could to assist Sandy and Kirk when they relocated to California, and I set up a college fund for the boy. I've kept an eye on him. What he's done pleases me. I guess, in the grand scheme of things, you could say he's where he'd have been all along if things had gone differently with his father. Merging with Tanner Enterprises was a logical move—gives us both more strength in an ever more competitive market."

Even though he'd given her a backstory of sorts, Sally had a feeling he was still holding something back. As it was, she was still hurt he'd had such an influence in Kirk's life and yet never shared any of that information with her.

"Marilyn called me just before you arrived. She tells me that Kirk took you to the doctor yesterday, that you collapsed or something during your presentation. Honey, you have to stop pushing yourself. You may never get over that public speaking thing, and if so, that's fine. But, that aside, tell me—you're all right?"

His pale blue eyes, the mirror of her own, looked concerned. While he might not see fit to include her in his business plans, he was still and always would be her dad, and she knew he loved and cared for her.

"Everything's fine, Dad. Nothing to worry about."

He looked at her with a piercing gaze. "What are you not telling me?"

She gave a gentle laugh. "I could ask you the same thing. Like why had I never heard of Kirk before the merger announcement. Don't you think that's something you might have shared with me at some stage? You've treated him like an absentee son."

An awful thought occurred to her. Could Kirk be his son? But her father's perspicacity showed true to form.

"Don't be silly. You can turn that overactive imagination of yours off right now. There's no reason for the secrecy other than the fact that his mother wanted no reminders of her late husband or her life in Seattle in any way. While she reluctantly accepted financial help, that was where she drew the line. I had very little direct interaction with her or with Kirk. Your mother and I were friends with Sandy and Frank. We would have supported Sandy here, too, if she'd have let us."

Sally felt all the tension drain out of her in a sudden rush. Jennifer chose that minute to return to the library.

"Dinner is served in the small dining room, if you'd like to come through now."

Sally got up and tucked her arm in the crook of her dad's elbow, and together they walked to dinner.

"Dad, this place really is too big just for you. Have you ever thought of downsizing?"

"Why would I do that, honey? This house was your mother's pride and joy, and she loved every inch of it. She might not still be with us, but I feel her in every nook and cranny of the house and see her touch in every piece of furniture and art. Besides, I'd like to think that one day you might move back home and build your own family here."

Sally felt a clench in her chest. She should tell her dad about the baby, but how to bring it up? There was no way to dress up the fact that this child was the product of an unfortunate accident during a one-night stand. Granted, the man in question was already held in high regard by her father, but didn't that just complicate matters more?

Her father seated her at the table before taking his own place. Jennifer brought in the first course—smoked salmon fillets on a bed of lettuce and sliced avocado. Sally eyed the plate warily. She didn't know much yet about how to weather this pregnancy but she'd done a little research on foods she could and couldn't eat, and she knew that smoked or pickled fish was on the horribly extensive no list.

Orson noticed immediately that Sally only picked at the lettuce and avocado, pushing the salmon to the side of her plate.

"You're not going to eat that? I thought it was one of your favorites. You're not on some weird diet, or something, are you?"

She sighed. He was going to have to know sooner or later. "No, Dad. Not a diet. Actually, I have a bit of news for you."

"What's that? You're not going to tell me you're pregnant, are you?" He said it jokingly, but his face sobered when he saw Sally's expression.

"Well, that rather takes the wind out of my sails," she said softly.

"Really? You're making me a grandpa?" Orson's face lit up.

It wasn't the reaction she'd expected. After all, as far

as he knew, she wasn't even in a relationship with anyone, and he'd always made his thoughts on the challenges of sole parenthood quite clear. It was probably another reason why he'd supported Sandy Tanner and Kirk the way he had.

"Apparently," she admitted ruefully.

"Was that the reason for your fainting spell at work yesterday?"

She nodded.

"So you managed the speaking part okay?"

What was wrong with him? Why wasn't he demanding to know who the father of his grandchild was? She nodded again.

"That's great news, honey! And a baby, too."

He leaned back in his chair and smiled beatifically.

"You're not bothered by that, Dad?" Sally had to ask because his lack of questions was driving her crazy. She'd expected a full inquisition. Had mentally prepared for one all day, knowing she wouldn't keep this secret from her father for long.

"Bothered by the baby? No, why should I be?"

"But don't you want to know—"

Her father leaned toward her and patted her on the hand. "It's okay, honey, I know where babies come from these days. I expect you got tired of waiting for Mr. Right and decided to go with one of those designer baby outfits. Of course, I'm sorry you didn't feel as though you could discuss it with me first but—"

Sally had been in the process of taking a drink of water and all but snorted it out her nose.

"Dad!"

"Well, it's not as if you have a regular guy, is it? I'd hoped you might meet someone special when you were at college, like I did with your mom, but that's neither here nor there. Looks like you'll be moving home sooner rather than later, huh?" He rubbed his hands with glee.

"Why would I do that?"

"Well, you don't have room in that cute little apartment of yours, do you?"

Sally rolled her eyes. What was it with everyone lately that they wanted to make all her decisions for her? First Kirk, now her dad—didn't anyone think she was capable of looking after herself?

"There's plenty of time to think about that, Dad. Besides, I can always get a bigger place of my own."

"But why on earth would you need to when we have all the room in the world here?"

It was about then that Sally noticed another place setting at the table.

"Were you expecting someone else?" she asked.

Just then, the chime of the front door echoed through the house.

"He's late, but he called ahead and said not to hold dinner."

"He?"

She didn't have to wait long to find out who *he* was. Within about thirty seconds of the door chime sounding, Jennifer showed Kirk into the dining room. Great, just what she needed.

"Good to see you, Kirk!" Orson said effusively, standing to shake Kirk's hand. "About time there was someone here who can share a celebratory champagne toast with me. I'm going to be a grandpa! Isn't that great news?"

Kirk looked at Sally, and she suddenly understood the expression "deer caught in the headlights."

"Dad, you know you shouldn't have more than your one glass of red wine a day. Doctor's orders, remember?" she cautioned, desperate to shift focus to something other than her pregnancy, especially since she and Kirk had agreed to keep it quiet for now.

"Just a half a glass isn't going to kill me. This is cause for celebration, whether you know who the daddy is or not."

"Know who the father is?" Kirk asked with a pointed look in her direction.

"I know exactly who the father is," Sally felt compelled to say.

"You do? Is it someone I know?" Orson asked, looking from Sally to Kirk and back again as he began to sense the tension between them.

"It is," Kirk said firmly and straightened his shoulders. "It's me. I'm the father."

Nine

"I didn't even realize you two knew each other that well," Orson said, sinking back into his chair.

"We don't," Sally said bluntly.

Kirk wasn't too pleased about the older man's color. Obviously hearing that his new business partner was the father of his impending grandchild had come as something of a shock. Just then, Jennifer came bustling through the door, bringing a serving of the appetizer for Kirk. He took a seat at the empty place setting and waited as the silence lengthened in the room. A silence Orson eventually broke.

"So what now?" he asked, reaching for his glass of water. "Are you going to marry the girl?"

"I have asked her to marry me."

"And?" Orson demanded, color slowly returning to his cheeks.

"The girl said no," Sally said, her tone revealing her

annoyance at being discussed as if she was an accessory to the conversation.

"Why on earth did you say that?" Orson asked incredulously.

"It's still early," Kirk said smoothly. "We don't know each other that well yet, but I'd like to think that by the time the baby comes we'll be a great deal closer."

"You're obviously close enough to—"

"Dad—please! Can we not discuss this right now? We only found out yesterday ourselves, and we'd agreed to keep it quiet. I only told you because, well, you'd pretty much guessed already and I hate having secrets between us."

Kirk wasn't oblivious to Sally's silent censure toward her father. Those secrets included him, he had no doubt.

"It's only right that you told Orson," Kirk added.

"I don't need your approval, either," Sally said tightly.

"Now, honey, there's no need to be unpleasant," Orson interjected. "While I'm shocked, I have to admit that I'm relieved you have someone else in your corner. Becoming a parent is a big enough change in anyone's life. Doing it alone just makes things a whole lot harder than they need to be. What you need to realize is that you're more vulnerable now than you've probably ever been, and you have to make choices that are best for the baby, not just for yourself."

"I'm aware of that."

Kirk could see Sally didn't appreciate being talked down to. Orson apparently realized it, too.

"And now you're mad at me."

"Dad, I just wish you would let me be me sometimes. I'm a grown-up. I am capable of making decisions for myself."

Kirk had no doubt that last bit was directed at him, as well.

"Well, honey, I want you to think long and hard about the decisions you make now. I know your work is important to you. Mine always was to me, and over the years, I usually put it first. I have my regrets about that now."

"Regrets?" Sally asked, giving up all semblance of eating and pushing her plate to one side.

"Yes, I wasn't available enough to you while you were growing up, especially after your mother passed. I grew my business at the expense of my family, and while I can't turn back the clock on that, I can be there for you now. I hope you'll let me support you where I can."

Tears sprang to Sally's eyes, and Kirk felt something twist in his chest at being witness to this exchange between father and daughter. Far from offering his son this kind of support, Kirk's father hadn't even been able to hold himself together, gradually falling deeper and deeper into addiction. The memory and the scene before him only served to firm his resolve to be an active part of his child's life. No matter what transpired between him and Sally, he would be there for his son or daughter.

He hadn't managed to catch up with Sally in the office today. After returning to his new home before dawn and getting ready for work, he'd been caught up in meetings all day. One in particular had been distinctly disturbing, and it was part of the reason he'd agreed to come to dinner with Orson tonight.

It seemed Sally's project had been leaked to their main rival, who'd taken to the media already to advertise their willingness to implement sustainable workplaces throughout all DuBecTec offices, taking the thunder out of any similar announcements HTT might make in the future. Kirk's initial reaction had been to lay blame squarely with someone like Silas Rogers, who seemed to have some sort of grudge against Sally and might have taken action to keep her from getting credit for her ideas. But Kirk had enlisted the help of a forensic IT specialist, and it appeared that the information had been sent from Sally's own laptop.

The knowledge made him sick to his stomach. Not only because he'd spent last night with her, allowing his passion for her to overcome any sense of reason, but also because he realized he'd begun to develop feelings for Sally that went beyond the fact that he couldn't even be in the same room as her without wanting to touch her. Feelings that were now inextricably linked to the fact she was carrying his child—another complication he couldn't ignore.

His disappointment in discovering this proof that she'd been their leak all along was immeasurable. And, once the forensic specialist had found that link, it hadn't taken long for him to discover the others. All information going out had gone through Sally's device.

But mingled with his own feelings about the situation was the sadness of knowing Orson would be devastated. His own daughter behind the potential downfall of his pride and joy? They had to work fast to immobilize Sally and prevent her from doing any further damage. The fallout among her team would be another blow to the company. Those men and women would feel utterly cheated after all their hard work. Of course, HTT would carry on with implementing the plan—it made sense on so many levels Kirk was surprised it had taken this long. But they wouldn't be viewed as the leaders in their industry—they'd be the copycats. And that stuck in his craw like a particularly sharp fish bone.

He went through the motions with Orson, accepting a glass of champagne to toast the news of the baby, but his heart wasn't in the celebration and he could see Sally couldn't wait to be away from it, too. Dinner passed quickly, and Sally asked to be excused from sharing the dessert the housekeeper brought to the table—pleading weariness and the desire for an early night.

She'd blushed when she'd made her apologies. He knew exactly why she was so tired, but thankfully her father simply accepted her words at face value and, after exhorting Kirk to remain at the table, Orson saw his daughter to the front door, where her driver was waiting for her.

Kirk felt his stomach tie in knots as he considered what he was about to tell the older man on his return. There were many things the man needed to know—even if he wouldn't enjoy hearing any of them. Orson would be none too pleased to know that Kirk had deliberately hidden his identity from Sally that first night he'd met her, but Kirk knew he had to come clean and lay everything on the table—including the new evidence that had arisen today.

Last night had been one of the worst things he'd ever had to do in business. Seeing the devastation roll over Orson's face and knowing that he was the messenger responsible for putting it there hurt Kirk in ways he wouldn't have believed possible a few short years ago. But worse was yet to come. In light of the evidence, another special meeting of the board had been called this morning, and Orson had insisted on being in attendance.

Orson sat now at his desk and nodded to Kirk to make the phone call he was dreading.

He picked up the receiver and listened to the sound as

Sally's office phone rang at the other end. The moment she answered, he spoke.

"Sally, would you be so good as to come to the boardroom at ten this morning? And I think it would be best if you brought a support person with you."

"A support person?" she repeated down the line. "What on earth for?"

"Please, I'll explain everything when you get there but you will need an advocate."

"Kirk, I don't like the sound of this," she insisted. "What's going on?"

"You'll get everything laid out at 10:00 a.m. Please be prompt."

He hung up before she could say anything else. Across the desk, Orson looked deeply unhappy.

"I'd never have believed she could do something like this to me, or to the company. Why? Why would she do it?"

That was the big question plaguing Kirk, too. Sally stood to gain little from the internal sabotage that had taken place. If her goal was to cause the company to fail, then she hadn't been very successful. While the firm had taken a hit in terms of new client work, they continued to operate strongly with their existing clientele. But growth was key to any firm's success, and she'd stymied that with her interference. The subsequent weakness now made them a prime candidate for a takeover bid. Had she been bribed or blackmailed by one of their competitors? What was really going on here?

He and Orson assembled with the board in the meeting room at nine thirty, and Orson quickly acquainted the board with the information about the leaks he'd gathered in the lead-up to the merger. Kirk then went on to explain the investigation he'd undertaken and the evidence the IT specialist had uncovered—in the briefest and most succinct terms possible. No one looked happy at the outcome, and all concurred with Kirk's suggestion of dealing with the perpetrator pending a fuller investigation. When the knock came at the door to announce Sally's arrival, there was a collective shuffling of papers and clearing of throats.

She looked shocked as she saw the full board assembled there, her face paling and reminding Kirk all too well of how she'd reacted during the video conference the morning after Orson's heart attack.

"Dad? What are you doing here?" she said. "What's this all about?"

"Take a seat, Sally," Orson answered with a voice heavy with gravitas.

Kirk noted Orson's PA, Marilyn Boswell, come in behind Sally and gestured to the two women to take a seat at the table. He saw Sally's hand shake as she reached for the glass of water in front of her and forced himself to quash the compassion that rose within him. He'd slept with this woman. Celebrated intimacies with her. Made a baby with her. And now she was the enemy. You'd have thought his experiences with his father would have taught him how to handle this feeling of betrayal.

"Thank you for coming this morning, Ms. Harrison, Ms. Boswell," he said in welcome.

Marilyn stared back at him fiercely before flicking her gaze to Orson. Her expression softened immeasurably. "What's this all about, Orson? We weren't expecting you back yet. What's going on?"

Orson looked across the table at his daughter, a wealth of sadness in his eyes. Kirk wished it could have been anyone else but Sally doing this to him. The betrayal that one of his own staff had sold out to the opposition was bad enough, but that it was his daughter?

* * *

Sally clenched her hands together in her lap to stop them from shaking. She felt as though something truly dreadful was about to happen. Her father hadn't mentioned anything about this meeting last night, but then again, he had been a little distracted by her news. When Kirk had told her to come to a meeting this morning and bring an advocate, to say she'd been stunned would be an understatement. This was their usual protocol when someone was being brought into a disciplinary discussion or, worse, being notified of redundancy. Why would either of those situations apply to her?

What if she actually had to speak in front of these people? Already she could feel her throat closing up and the trickle of perspiration that ran down her spine. Next to her, Marilyn reached over and placed her hand over Sally's.

"Everything will be okay, don't you worry. Your father won't let anything happen to you," the older woman whispered reassuringly.

Sally couldn't respond. Already her mouth had dried and her throat choked. Kirk rose to his feet and began to speak. He was a commanding presence in the room and everyone gave him their full attention. Or maybe it was that none of them wanted to make eye contact with her. Not even her father. The remains of the breakfast she'd eaten so hastily at her desk this morning, in deference to the growing child inside her, threatened to make a comeback.

The only one paying attention to her was Kirk, who seemed to be addressing her directly as he gave what he described as a summary of the information he'd shared with the board before her arrival. She listened with half an ear as Kirk listed a series of HIT initiatives that had been leaked to another company before the merger with Tanner Enterprises and explained the assignment that Orson had given him when he'd agreed to the merger. The lost contracts weren't news to her. After all, she'd also been shocked at how they had happened.

"The only logical conclusion we could come to is that there was someone internally working against the company. After an investigation, we believe we know exactly who that person is."

Sally looked around the room. All eyes were on her now. Realization dawned. They thought she was the leak?

No!

Ten

"Are you suggesting it's me? That I'm behind all this?" The words felt like cotton wool in her mouth.

"Based on the evidence presented to us, yes. Would you like to respond to the allegation?" Kirk asked.

"Damn straight I would!" Anger seemed to overcome her fear of speaking in a group like this, and she shot to her feet. "How dare you accuse me of this? Dad? How could you believe him?"

"I'm sorry, honey. I didn't *want* to believe it, but the facts are all there. The information came from your laptop."

Sally felt the world tilt. Her laptop? The one she carried with her everywhere? The one with double password protection? She slowly sat back down, shaking her head.

"It wasn't me. Someone else must have accessed it."

"Are you saying you shared your passwords with someone else?" Kirk pressed.

"Of course I didn't. That's against company policy."

Giving access to her computer was almost as serious an offense as what they were accusing her of.

"I need a lawyer," she said, her voice starting to shake again as her rush of anger faded as quickly as it had happened and reality began to dawn. Whoever had framed her had done a thorough job. There was no way out of this without serious consequences.

"Yes, I believe you do," Kirk said firmly. "In the meantime, you will stand down from all duties and will forfeit all company property and passwords pending a full, externally run investigation."

"Stand down?"

"Standard operating procedure in a case like this," Marilyn said. "But don't worry. I'm sure everything will be just fine."

Sally begged to differ. Right now it seemed as though every facet of her life was in turmoil, and all of it tied back to the moment she'd met Kirk Tanner. Oh, yes, it was all too convenient, wasn't it? She remained seated at the table as one by one, the board members and her father and Marilyn left the room, leaving her alone with Kirk.

"This is all very convenient for you, isn't it?" she said bitterly when the last person closed the door behind them.

"Convenient?" He shook his head. "It's anything but."

"Tell me, then. When you met me that night at the club, did you already suspect me of this?"

She had to know, even though hearing the truth from his lips would cause no end of hurt.

"Everyone was under suspicion. But—"

"But nothing. I was under suspicion, and you seduced me, knowing who I was. Did you think I'd let something slip in the heat of the moment? If so, you were wasting your time. I'm innocent. Someone, or several someones, have set me up. I already told you that it was hard for me to prove myself here. Obviously that goes deeper than I thought if an employee is prepared to go to these lengths to discredit me."

"And if that is the case, the investigation will show it and you'll be reinstated. In the interim, there'll be an announcement that you're taking a short medical leave."

Sally barked a humorless laugh. "And doesn't that fall right into your hands."

"What do you mean?" Kirk paused in collecting the papers that had been in front of him on the table.

"You already made it clear you want to take care of me and support me while I'm carrying your baby, and I refused you. Is this your way of ensuring you get your way? You're already proving yourself to be the son my father never had. How much more are you going to strip from me before you're done?" She wished she could unsay the words she'd uttered, but maybe now that they were out, she could face the truth of them. The truth that she'd never been good enough, articulate enough, strong enough to be the person her father had truly needed.

To her horror, she burst into tears. Kirk rushed to her side, and she shoved him away from her.

"Don't touch me. Don't. Ever. Touch. Me. Again."

She clumsily swiped at the tears on her cheeks. Kirk withdrew, but she could see the concern painted clearly on his face.

"You didn't answer my question," she said, her voice shaking with the effort it took to bring herself under control. "You already admitted you slept with me that first time, knowing who I was. Did you think it was me from the start? Was that why you didn't disclose who you were when you first met me? Because you suspected me of being the person responsible for undermining HIT—was that why you slept with me?"

He didn't say anything, and she could see her words had found their mark. It was a cruel reality to have to face that she'd been a target all along. For information and nothing else.

A shudder racked her body. And to think she'd even begun to consider what it would be like to be married to him. To build a family home together. What kind of a fool was she?

One who learned from the past, that's who.

"Sally, that night wasn't what I expected—hell, *you* weren't what I expected—"

"No. Stop." She held up her hand. "Don't bother. I get it. If you hadn't wanted information out of me, we'd never have met until the merger announcement."

"I didn't fake my attraction to you, Sally. From the minute you walked in that bar, you had my attention. But, yes, I realized that I'd seen you before, and it didn't take me long to figure out it was from the files your father had supplied me. I'd been going through all the staff profiles, trying to get a sense of the people I would be dealing with and, to be honest, trying to see who might have the means and a reason to be supplying our rival with sensitive information."

"Did my father suspect me?"

"No, he didn't, but he had to include you in the profiles because not to do so would be seen as showing bias. You understand that, don't you?"

She sighed heavily. "And now you think I'm it. So what now? You get security to escort me to my office to empty my drawers and then march me out of the building?"

"That won't be necessary."

She felt a glimmer of hope that she wasn't to be treated like a criminal, but then he continued.

"Marilyn will be instructed to remove your personal items from your office. As to the rest, including all your electronics and your cell phone, they'll be retained as part of the investigation."

Even though she knew she was innocent, the very thought of what was happening made her feel dirty somehow. Tainted. Would she ever be able to return and hold her head up high? Would her colleagues be able to look at her the same way? Trust her? Oh, sure. She knew that they were being told she was going on medical leave, but they were clever people. Her taking time off hard on the heels of the announcement by a competitor of an identical project to the one they'd touted to the senior management only two days ago? They'd put two and two together and links would be made.

She was ruined. Everything she'd yearned for, trained for and dreamed of had been torn from her by a traitor in this very building. She had to find some way to prove her innocence. Maybe then she could redeem herself in her father's eyes and in those of her peers.

"I see," she said with all the dignity she could muster. "Tell me, Kirk. Was I worth it?"

"Worth it?"

"The sacrifice of sleeping with me? Taking one for the team."

Before he could answer, she slammed her cell phone on the table in front of her, swept out of the boardroom and headed for the elevators. She pressed the down button and prayed for the swift arrival of a car to get her out of here. All her life she'd wanted to prove herself here—to be a valued member of the team—and now she was a pariah. She couldn't even begin to parse through her grief. And her dad? She'd seen the look on his face, seen the disappointment, the accusations, the questions. She hoped he would believe in her innocence once they'd had a chance to talk, but since Kirk so obviously already had her father's ear, what hope did she have of him believing her over Kirk?

The elevator in front of her pinged open, and she stepped into the car and hit the button for the lobby level. The doors began to slide closed but jerked back as a suited arm stopped them from closing. Kirk, of course.

"What? Did you forget to frisk me before I leave the building?" she baited him as he faced her and the doors closed behind him.

"Don't take this out on me, Sally. You know everything we've asked of you is standard practice while the investigation is being conducted."

"Don't be so pompous. You've lied to me from the moment you met me. Why not try being honest for a change?"

"You want honest?" he said tightly. "I'll give you honest. You caught my eye the second you arrived in the bar that night. I didn't recognize you immediately, but I couldn't take my eyes off you."

She snorted inelegantly. "I may be a little naive from time to time, but don't expect me to believe you on that one. There were any number of women, far more beautiful than me, in the bar that night."

"And yet I only had eyes for you."

The look she gave him was skeptical. "A little clichéd, wouldn't you say?"

"Sally, stop trying to put up walls between us."

"Me?" She was incredulous now. "You're the one accusing me of corporate espionage!"

"Look, I feel sick to my stomach about this entire situation. We have to investigate further and we have to be seen to be dealing with this in the correct manner. I don't want to believe you're the culprit, but the evidence is too strong to suggest otherwise."

"How sweet of you to say so," she replied in a tone that made it quite clear she thought it anything but.

Sally held herself rigid as the doors opened to reveal the lobby. She had to get out of here. Out of the elevator, out of the building and out of Kirk's sphere. She started to walk, barely conscious of Kirk walking beside her.

"Sally!" he called as she strode out the front doors and onto the sidewalk.

She stopped and turned around. "You have no power over me out here. I'm just a regular person on the street right now. Remember? I don't answer to you or to anyone else."

"Where's Benton?"

"Right now, I don't know and I don't care. Maybe the decision has been made that I don't need a bodyguard anymore. I'd say my commercial value has dropped given this morning's revelations, wouldn't you? Don't worry your handsome little head about it."

Kirk took a step forward and took her by the arm. "You're still carrying my baby," he said coldly. "I have a duty to care for my child."

She closed her eyes briefly. Of course. The baby. There was always something or someone else that would take precedence over her, wasn't there. She opened her eyes and stared at his hand on her arm then up at his face. He wasn't holding her firmly, but he wasn't letting go, either. It drove it home to her that the life she thought she'd had was not her own. Never had been and likely now never would be.

Sally looked very deliberately down at his hand and then up to his face. He let her go. Turning on her heel, she walked briskly away from him and headed for home.

* * *

She'd been stuck at home for a week. The weather, in true Seattle fashion, had been gloomy and cold. Thanksgiving was only a week away, and Sally was finding it darn hard to be thankful for anything right now. The lawyer she'd spoken to had told her there was little they could do until charges were officially brought against her, if that indeed happened. In the meantime, she'd had dinner with her father a couple of times but the atmosphere between them was strained, to say the least. The good news was that he'd recovered enough to begin working again. He was doing half days at the office three times a week, and she had a suspicion he was also working a little from home. Not surprising, since his work had been his key focus all his life.

Medically he was hitting all his markers, and his cardiologist was pleased with his recovery. For that, at least, she was grateful.

Sally had caught up with her leisure reading and, wrapped up warm, had gone for several walks in the park over the past few days, but she itched to be able to use her mind to do more. Being inactive didn't suit her at all. And, all the time, it bugged her that whoever was truly behind the leaks from the office continued to work there. Obviously lying low for now.

She had spent a lot of her walking time thinking about the situation and what she could do to prove her innocence. Since her own access to the internet had been restricted by the confiscation of her equipment, she decided that she would have to use public means to conduct her own investigation. And that investigation would start with Kirk Tanner.

Last night she'd booked time for a computer at the Bellevue Library and when the cab dropped her off at the building this morning, she felt a frisson of excitement for the first time in days. She had a maximum session length of only two hours. She'd have to work fast.

Sally had always loved research and delving deeper into problems. Now she had something she really needed to get her teeth into. She started with Kirk. After all, wasn't he the epicenter of the quake that had shaken her life off its foundations?

It didn't take too much digging before she began to bring up information that related to Kirk's family. Thanks to the digitization of the local papers, there was plenty of information readily available about Frank Tanner, starting with a photo and article of him and her dad excitedly announcing their start-up IT company.

She stared at the photo of the younger version of her dad and a man who looked a lot like Kirk. The men's pride in their achievement was almost palpable. Sally sent the article to the printer and moved on to the next news story. This one was a lot less joyful. It described the arrest of a man under the influence of substances after police had been called to a domestic violence incident. The man was Frank Tanner.

A chill shivered down her spine as she read the brief report of his court appearance. A few years later there was another report—again with substance abuse, again with domestic violence. And then, finally, a brief report of Frank Tanner's death from a fall from Deception Bridge. The autopsy had reported that he had enough drugs in his system to cause multiple organ failure, even if the fall hadn't killed him.

Sally looked at the first picture she'd printed. Frank and her father had been so young then, so full of hopes and dreams for their future. Sally felt a pang of sympathy for Kirk, wondering what it must have been like for him to watch his home disintegrate, and at the same time grateful that she'd never have to truly know. Her father might have been focused on business, but at least he never raised a hand to anyone or ever let his family go without.

Discovering more details about Kirk's father's past went a long way toward explaining why his mother had been so determined to leave the area and make a new life for herself and her son in California. Sally could understand why Kirk was so driven, why he had a plan that he lived and worked by. His youth must have been so unsettled.

Her time was running out on the computer, so she quickly collated her printed pages and shoved them in her tote to read further at home. She knew her father had provided financial help to the Tanner family, including the fund that had seen Kirk through college. But was there more? Had Kirk somehow believed he had a rightful place at HIT? Had it been him who approached her father about merging their two companies? Had he possibly engineered a risk of potential takeover of her father's company to create an opening for himself where he felt he should have been all along?

Sally called her father that night and asked if she could come and visit with him over the weekend. When she arrived, he was still a little reserved with her, but as they sat together in front of the fireplace in his library, she decided to go at this situation head-on.

"Dad, do you really believe I'm responsible for the leaks at HTT?"

He looked at her as if he was shocked she would ask him such a thing. "I'd like to think not, honey. After all, why would you do such a thing? But Marilyn said you were frustrated at work, even though I never saw any evidence to support that. I always thought you'd bring any problems to me if you had them. It leaves me asking myself what you would hope to gain from such a thing."

Sally was a little taken aback. Marilyn had been telling her dad she wasn't happy at work? Sure, she'd often told the PA that she wanted to climb further up the corporate ladder, that it had been her goal to support her father in any way that she could. But she'd never expressed dissatisfaction to the extent that anyone could say she wasn't happy.

"Obviously I have nothing to gain," she said. "It wasn't me. I want you to believe that."

"And I want to believe it, too. However, what I think isn't the key here. We have to prove, beyond a shadow of a doubt, that it isn't you, don't we?"

She was heartened by his use of the term *we*, rather than the singular *you*.

"Tell me about the early days, Dad. About when you and Frank Tanner set HIT up. They must have been exciting times, yes?"

A gentle smile curved her father's lips. "They were very exciting times. The beginning of the boom times in information technology, and we were full of ideas and passion. Those were good years—challenging and exciting, difficult at times, but good nonetheless."

He fell silent and she knew he was thinking about his business partner's death.

"I learned a bit more about Frank Tanner's addiction, Dad. Why do you think he fell victim to it?"

Her father knotted his hands together and sighed heavily. "I don't really know. In college he was always the party guy, but he was so brilliant that it didn't hold him back. He never struggled to keep his grades up and always skated through exams without needing to crack open a reference book. I envied that about him. Everything I did, I did through sheer hard work."

Sally nodded. She was much the same.

Her father continued, "I guess he always put more pressure on himself to be more and do more than any other person. It was as if he was constantly trying to prove himself. Constantly striving for more and better than he'd done before. Money was tight for all of us when we started up, and we worked long hours. Frank even more than me. I guess he started depending on the drugs to keep himself sharp through the all-nighters. I could never figure out how he did it, but when I stop and look back, I realize he had to have been using something to boost himself.

"Anyway, by the time I realized he was dangerously hooked on drugs, it was too late. Not long after that, he was dead. As his friend I should have seen it, should have questioned him more closely. I should have recognized that he needed help, especially when things at home weren't so good between him and his wife."

"She always dropped the abuse charges, didn't she? Maybe, deep down, she still loved him and still hoped that he could change."

Orson looked at her. "I might have known you'd find that horrible history out."

"What can I say? I'm methodical, like my dad."

He gave her a smile, and he looked at her warmly. She'd missed this expression in his eyes since Kirk's accusations.

"What happened to Frank wasn't your fault, Dad," she said with deep conviction. "He was on a road to self-destruction long before you guys set up in business together. Even if you'd have noticed back then, do you honestly think you could have made a big difference? He had to want to change. If he couldn't do that for his family, he wouldn't have done it for you."

Her words were blunt, but they had the weight of truth behind them. She hoped her father would see that.

"I guess I know that deep down, but I still feel the loss of his friendship. When he died I had to help Sandy. She was a wreck, though she tried to hold it together for Kirk's sake. He was twelve when his dad died, a difficult age for a boy even without the additional test of having an addicted parent. I discussed it with your mother, who agreed we had to do whatever we could to help Sandy and Kirk start fresh. So we did."

Sally looked at her father. Going over the past like this obviously caused him pain, but she wasn't sorry she'd asked. She needed to understand the whole situation. She'd also hoped that perhaps learning more about the history of HIT might give her more insight into who was trying to hurt the company now. It distressed her that her father may still consider that she might be responsible for the leaks from HTT. Until she could remove every element of doubt, there would always be a question in his eyes whenever he looked at her. She couldn't live with that for the rest of her life.

"Dad, when did you begin to suspect there was a problem with information security at work?"

Orson looked a little uncomfortable and shifted in his chair. "It's been happening for about a year," he finally admitted.

Sally looked up in shock. About a year? That coincided with her appointment as head of her department.

Her father continued. "I did what I could but kept hitting blank walls when it came to trying to figure out who was behind it. That's when I turned to Kirk."

"Why him?" *Why not share your worries with me?* The silent plea echoed in her mind.

"I guess you're upset I never mentioned anything about him to you before," Orson commented with his usual acuity.

"Of course I am. I won't lie to you, Dad. It really hurt to discover him behind your desk the morning after your heart attack, especially after you'd presented me with the done deal at dinner the night before with no warning or prior notice."

"Well, in my defense, I did plan to be there with him. I didn't plan for my ticker to act up the way it did."

Sally got up from her chair and walked over to the fire, putting her hands out in front of her and letting the heat of the flames warm her skin.

"Why did you never tell me about your involvement with Kirk and his mom?"

"It wasn't something you needed to know," he said bluntly.

She thought about it awhile and was forced to concede he was probably right, except for one small fact—that he'd decided to bring Kirk in as his equal the moment the firm had been weakened. She decided to take a different tack with her questioning.

"Why do you think that someone has been sharing our details?"

Her father's response was heated. "Why does anyone do it? For money, of course. Why else would anyone betray the firm they work for? Someone has put their personal greed ahead of the needs of the company. Corporate espionage is a dreadful thing, and it creates weaknesses that allow others to gain leverage when it comes to hostile takeovers."

"Is that what was happening to us?"

Orson looked nonplussed for a moment, as if he'd let out more than he ought to have. Eventually he nodded.

"So there's been a threat of takeover," Sally mused out loud. "How do you know it wasn't Kirk behind it all along? Maybe he set it all up so he could come in as a white knight and suggest a merger."

"Kirk?" Her father sounded incredulous. "No. He'd never stoop that low. He's the kind of man who would come at a thing head-on. No subterfuge about that guy."

Wasn't there? Hadn't he withheld his identity from her the night they'd first met? It hurt and angered Sally, too, to realize that while her father refused to consider Kirk a suspect, he'd had no trouble believing it could be her.

"Besides, it was me that approached him from the get-go. I've kept an eye on him and his achievements ever since he and his mother left Seattle. I may have put him through college, but it's because of his own abilities that he's been able to really do something with his life. From the outset it was clear that he had his father's brilliance, but beyond that he had the sense to apply it where it would do him the most good. He had all of his father's best attributes, and none of the bad.

"To be totally honest with you, Sally, HIT needed Tanner Enterprises far more than the other way around. I was up front with him from the start. It was a risky move for Kirk to agree to the merger, but I needed him."

Sally could hear the honesty in her father's words, but that didn't stop the emptiness that echoed behind her breastbone that told her that no matter how bold she thought she could be, she would never be the kind of person who had the drive and hunger for success that Kirk so obviously had. If she had, wouldn't she have found a way to push past her phobia instead of hiding behind it?

She couldn't hold herself back any longer. She had to prove her innocence of the accusations leveled against her. And soon.

Eleven

Over the next couple of days, Sally spent hours trying to figure out who could be responsible for the leak. She covered her dining table with sheet after sheet of paper, many of them taped together with lines drawn between names and dates and points of data. On another sheet she wrote the lists of names and what people might stand to gain by such a thing.

After all her years at HIT, from intern to paid employee, she had gotten to know a great many of the staff within the various departments. She knew that because of the positive working environment and the benefits offered by the firm, staff retention was very high. She could understand the idea of a disgruntled employee wanting to punish their employer, but how could that apply here? Despite all the time she spent poring over everything, she still couldn't reach a solid conclusion.

Her days began to stretch out before her with boring

regularity, and even a visit to her ob-gyn couldn't give her the lift she needed. Kirk had accompanied her, and the atmosphere between them had been strained. His presence at the appointment was just another confirmation of her links to a man who neither trusted her nor could be trusted. And yet, every time she thought of him, she still felt that tingle of desire ripple through her body.

A week after Thanksgiving, which she'd spent with her dad and Marilyn, she was struggling with a knitting pattern she'd decided to teach herself when the intercom from downstairs buzzed. She looked up in surprise, dropping yet another darn stitch from the apparently easy baby blanket she was attempting, at the sound. She certainly hadn't been expecting anyone, and when she heard Kirk's voice on the speaker she was unable to stop the rush of heat that flooded her body. Flustered and certainly not dressed for any kind of company, an imp of perversity wanted her to tell him to leave without hearing what he had to say, but she sucked in a deep breath and told him to come on up.

In the seconds she had to spare before he arrived, she dashed into the bathroom and quickly brushed her hair, tied it back into a ponytail and smoothed a little tinted moisturizer onto her face.

"There, that's better than a moment ago," she told her reflection. "Shame you don't have time to do anything about the clothes."

Still, what was she worried about? This couldn't be a social call. A dread sense of foreboding in the pit of her stomach told her that this had to relate to her suspension.

Despite the fact she was expecting him, his sharp knock at her door made her jump.

"Just breathe," she admonished herself as she went to let him in.

She hadn't been prepared for the visceral shock of actually seeing him again. Dressed in sartorial corporate elegance, he filled the doorway with his presence, making her all too aware of the yoga pants, sweatshirt and slippers that had virtually become her uniform over the past couple of weeks. But it wasn't so much the way he was dressed that struck her—it was the hungry expression in his eyes as they roamed her from head to foot before coming back to settle on her face again.

"Hello," she said, annoyed to hear her voice break on the simple two-syllable word.

"You're looking well," Kirk replied. "May I come in?"

"Oh, of course," she answered, stepping aside to let him in the apartment.

As he moved past her, she tried to hold her breath. Tried not to inhale the scent that was so fundamentally his. Tried and failed miserably. Whatever cologne it was that he wore, it had to be heavily laden with pheromones, she decided as she closed the door and fought to bring herself under some semblance of control. Either that or she was simply helplessly, hopelessly, under his spell.

Maybe it was the latter, she pondered glumly as she offered him something to drink. Wouldn't that be just her luck.

"Coffee would be great, thanks."

"Take a seat. I'll only be a minute."

He sat down on the sofa where she'd been attempting to knit just a few minutes ago, and she saw him lean forward to pick up the printed pattern for the baby blanket.

"Nesting?" he commented, sounding amused as he picked up her knitting and tried to make sense of the jumble of yarn, comparing it to the picture in his other hand.

"Something like that. I needed to do something to

keep me busy," she said a little defensively. "It's my first attempt."

It wasn't, in truth her first attempt at this blanket. In fact it was about her twelfth, but the project was very much her first foray into the craft of knitting, and as she ripped her successive attempts out yet again and rewound the yarn, she found herself missing her mother more and more. Her mom had loved to knit.

"You're braver than me," he said simply as he put everything back on the coffee table.

Sally made herself a cup of herbal tea and brought it through to the living room with Kirk's coffee. She put the mug down on a coaster in front of him then took a seat opposite, not trusting herself to sit too near. Maybe with a little distance between them she could ignore the way her body reacted to his presence and maybe her nostrils could take a break from wanting to drown in that scent that was so specifically him.

"Why are you here?" she asked bluntly, cupping her mug between her hands.

"I wanted to deliver you the news myself," Kirk said, giving her a penetrating look.

"News?"

"You've been exonerated of any wrongdoing."

Even though she knew all along that she was innocent, Sally couldn't hold back the tidal wave of relief that now threatened to swamp her. Her hands shook and hot tea spilled over her fingers as she leaned forward to put her mug on the table. Kirk jumped straight to his feet, a pristine white handkerchief in his hand, and he moved swiftly to mop her fingers dry.

She thrilled to his touch but fought back the sensation that unfurled through her as his strong, warm hands cupped hers. She tugged her hands free and swiftly stood, walking away to create some distance between them.

"I can't say I'm surprised," she said, fighting to make her voice sound firm when she was feeling anything but. "I told you it wasn't me."

"Your father told me the same thing," he said smoothly.

Sally briefly savored the evidence that her father had supported her in this after all. "But you still felt there was room for doubt?"

Kirk ignored her question. "The forensic investigation of your devices showed that a false trail had been set up to look as though the data had been sent from your computer. At this stage, they still haven't been able to ascertain exactly who created that path. Obviously it was someone with a very strong knowledge of computer technology."

"Which, considering we're an information technology company, narrows it down to maybe ninety percent of the workforce at HTT," she said in a withering tone. "Do you plan to suspend everyone until you've figured out who it is?"

"That would be counterproductive," Kirk responded with a wry grin. "As I'm sure you know."

She looked at him, wishing that seeing him again didn't make her feel this way. Wishing even harder that none of this awfulness of suspicion and doubt lay between them and they could actually explore what it would be like to be a couple without any of the stigma that the investigation had left hanging like a dark cloud around her.

"I'm free to return to my work?" she asked.

"Tomorrow, if that's what you want."

"Of course that's what I want. I have a lot to catch up on."

"I thought you might say that." He reached into the

laptop bag he'd brought and fished out her computer, her tablet and her smartphone. "Here, you'll need these."

She all but dived in to take them from him. She flicked on her phone and groaned out loud at the number of missed calls and the notification that her voice mail was full. It was going to take her hours to sift through everything. Still, at least she had her devices back.

She put her things on the table and looked Kirk in the eye. "Are you satisfied with the outcome? With my being cleared of involvement?"

He sighed deeply. "More than you probably realize, yes."

"I'm glad. I would hate to think you still suspected me."

He looked at her again. "Why is that, Sally?"

"Because, despite everything, we still are going to have to raise a child together."

Was it her imagination, or was there a shaft of disappointment visible in his aqua-colored gaze?

"I would like to think that we can handle this thing between us with civility, if nothing else," she continued.

"Civility." He nodded. "When I look at you, civility is the farthest thing from my mind."

His voice dropped a level, and Sally felt the intensity of his words as if they were a physical touch. She fought for control again, determined not to allow herself to fall victim to her confused feelings for this man.

"My father told me about your dad and why he asked you to join forces with him. What he couldn't tell me is why you agreed."

Here it was, his opportunity to begin to mend fences with Sally. It had been such a relief when she'd been cleared of wrongdoing that he had come straight here tonight instead of calling her into the office in the morning. His motives hadn't been entirely altruistic. He'd missed her and ached to see her again. He'd spent every day wondering what she'd be doing, how she was feeling and hoping like hell she was looking after herself properly.

She deserved his honesty now more than ever before.

"I had several reasons," he said carefully, looking directly into Sally's eyes. "One of which was the fact that I had always held your father in very high esteem. He owed my mother and me nothing, but when my dad died your father helped Mom and me get a fresh start—away from the memories that made my mom so miserable, away from the shame that she carried in her heart that she couldn't help her husband or prevent him from killing himself."

He looked at Sally, searching for recrimination or disgust in her eyes. Instead he only saw compassion. It gave him a ridiculous sense of hope. He took another deep breath.

"That sense of helplessness was one I struggled with, too. You see, the whole time I'd been growing up, it was with a kind of barter system where I'd convince myself that if I kept my room clean and tidy, my mom wouldn't cry that day or my dad wouldn't fly off into one of his temper rants. Or I'd convince myself that if I did well at school and got good grades, my dad would smile and play ball outside with me rather than lie on his bed shaking.

"It became vital to me to control everything around me, to do whatever it took to coax a smile from my mother's face, to keep my father calm when he was at home, to deflect the attention of the neighbors on the nights when everything turned to shit. And then to act like nothing had happened each time the police came and took Dad away. I learned that if you wanted things a particular way, you had to do certain things in repayment—that you had to earn any good thing that you wanted in your life. And yet, with your father, he didn't expect anything in return for aiding my mother and me. He just wanted to help."

Kirk looked at Sally, wondering if she could even begin to understand the depth of his gratitude to Orson for all he'd done.

"Dad has always had a compassionate heart," she replied. "I think it's helped him do so well, but he tempers it with drive and determination. He doesn't suffer fools gladly, and he won't tolerate injustice or laziness."

"Exactly. I actually used HIT as my business study in college—I guess you could say my family connection led me to being a little obsessed with understanding everything my father had been a part of before it all went so wrong. Through that, I grew even more respect for your father. In fact, I modeled my own business structure on what he'd done—and I modeled myself on how he's lived. When he approached me and asked me if I'd consider merging Tanner Enterprises with HIT, I could see more than one benefit for both of us. Structurally, it was a solid, sensible decision that would benefit both companies. But personally…he said he needed me, and I finally had a way to pay him back for all the good he'd done for Mom and me over the years."

Sally looked at him, her eyes glistening with emotion. "Kirk, I'm so sorry your childhood was so awful. I wish it could have been different for you."

"I don't. Not anymore. It helped to shape me into the man I am now—it helped me know exactly what I want from life and where I want to be."

"Ah, yes," she said with a soft smile. "Your plan."

"Hey, don't laugh. Everyone needs a plan, right?"

Sharing this with Sally felt right. He felt as if a weight had lifted from him.

"So, what happens to HTT from here?" she asked. "Now that you know I'm not the leak?"

"We keep investigating," he answered in a matter-of-fact tone. "And we will find the perpetrator. It's a deliberate criminal act, and they must be held to account."

"And what happens now with *us*?" she asked unsteadily.

"What do you want to happen?"

"Kirk, I don't know how to cope with this. I don't know who I am with you." She felt lost, afraid to speak of her feelings, but she forced the words out. "You made me believe things about myself that first night we were together that gave me confidence and strength. When I found out who you were, all that confidence in myself shattered and made me doubt my attractiveness and appeal all over again.

"You see, I may have grown up with more than you did, and certainly without the uncertainty you had when your father was alive, but because of who I am and who my father is, there have always been expectations on me. Expectations I haven't always been able to fulfill. You've seen the worst of it, the fear of public speaking—"

"But you've made inroads on that, Sally. I saw you at that sustainability presentation. You were totally in control."

She smiled. "Well, not *totally* in control, but better than in the past, I'll accept that. Until I fainted, anyway."

"But even that wasn't you. It was your pregnancy, not your fear."

She nodded again. "Even so, I ended up delivering what everyone there expected me to deliver. Failure. It's something I've made rather a fine art of since my mother's funeral. I had written a poem for her. All I had to do was read it, but I couldn't. I choked. I couldn't even tell my mom goodbye the way I wanted to. Now, whenever I get up to speak to a group of more than two or three people, I'm back there in the chapel, standing there in front of all those expectant faces—disappointing all those people and failing my mother's memory."

Her voice choked up, and tears spilled on her cheeks. "Even remembering it—" She shook her head helplessly. "It feels like it was yesterday. It never goes away."

Kirk was at a loss. He knew from Orson that Sally had had professional counseling to help her deal with her phobia—and that it had been unsuccessful. He reached for her hands, holding them firmly in his and drawing her to him until she was nestled against his chest. He felt her body shudder as a sob escaped from her rigid frame. He put his arms around her and stroked her back slowly, offering her comfort when words failed him. He felt her draw in a deep breath and then another.

"I've failed my dad, too. And that's the worst of it. I wanted to be his trusted, dependable right-hand man more than anything in my life. I pushed myself in college, I interned at HIT—I did everything I could to be an asset to him, rather than another disappointment. Oh, don't get me wrong, he's never made me feel as if I've let him down. In fact, I don't think he ever expected me to join him in the upper echelon at HIT. Sometimes I think nothing would have made him happier than if I'd just stayed at home and taken on my mother's old positions on the boards of the charities she supported. He's always told me he will support me in whatever I decide to do. But I wanted to support him, too."

"He values your input, Sally. Never think for a minute that he doesn't."

"But he doesn't turn to me. I'm not there for him the way I should be. At least not in his mind. When push came to shove and the company needed help, he turned to you."

Again, Kirk was lost for words. There really was nothing he could say in response to what was an absolute truth. Sally's father loved her. But he didn't see her as the strong, capable woman she truly was—the woman hidden behind her fears and insecurities. Somehow, he had to help Sally fight past her demons, to achieve the goals she'd set herself. He, more than anyone, understood how important those personal goals were.

Sally tried to pull away, and he reluctantly let her go. She sat up and dashed her hands over her cheeks, wiping away the remnants of her tears and visibly pulling herself together the way he had no doubt she'd done many times before.

"Listen to me blubbering on. It must be pregnancy hormones," she justified with a weak smile. "I hear they wreak havoc on a woman."

"Hey, you can blubber on me any time you need to," he said. "Sally, I don't want you to ever feel you're alone in any of this."

"This? The pregnancy or the fact that you suspected me of being the company mole?"

She said the words with flippancy, but he clearly heard the hurt beneath them.

"It's little excuse, but I had to follow procedure when the evidence pointed to you. I already knew you couldn't possibly be the leak."

"Well, it certainly didn't feel like you were sure I was innocent at the time."

"I'm sorry," he said frankly. "I'm sorry I wasn't honest with you when we met, and I'm sorry I put you through these past few weeks alone. I know it's little consolation, but I was massively relieved when it was proven, without doubt, that you were in the clear. It was also vital to the integrity of the investigation that we be seen to follow all the right procedures."

He winced. The words coming from his mouth were so formal, so precise and correct. They weren't the words he wanted to say at all. He wanted to tell her how much he'd missed her, ached for her—how much he wanted to hold her and show her how he felt about her.

"You're right, it is little consolation, but I'll take it. Which brings me back to my earlier question—where do we go from here?"

He knew exactly where he wanted to go. Right into her arms. For now, he hoped actions would speak louder than words. He reached a finger to her cheek and traced the curve of it.

"I know where I'd like us to go," he said softly.

Her pupils dilated. He leaned forward. Her lips parted, and her eyelids fluttered closed as he sought her mouth with his own. When their lips connected, he felt his body clench on a wave of need so strong it made him groan out loud. Sally's hands were at his shoulders, then her fingers were in his hair, holding him close as he deepened their kiss—as his tongue swept across her lips and he tasted her. Every nerve, every cell in his body leaped to demanding life, and he swept his hands beneath her sweatshirt, skimming over her smooth skin, relishing the feel of her. Wanting more, wanting her.

She arched toward him, and he tore his lips from hers to trace the line of her jaw with small kisses, then down the cord of her throat. He felt her shiver in response, felt her fingers tighten. He pushed the fabric of her top up, exposing her lace-clad breasts to his gaze. With one hand, he slipped one breast from its restraint. Her nipple was already a taut pink peak. He bent his head and caught the sensitive flesh between his lips, flicking the underside with his tongue and coaxing sweet sounds from her that drove him mad with need.

Kirk scooped her up into his arms and walked with her to the bedroom. After that, time blurred but sensation didn't as they rediscovered the physical joy they promised each other, and when pleasure peaked, it was the most natural thing in the world to fall asleep locked in each other's arms.

"Marry me."

Sally barely had her eyes open, and those two little words were echoing in her head.

"What?" Her voice was still thick with sleep.

"Marry me."

"Good morning to you, too," she said, rolling out of the bed and grabbing her robe from the back of a chair.

"I mean it, Sally. You can move in with me now—my house is huge and designed for a family. If you don't like it, I'll buy something else. We can create the nursery together. Plan for the future together. Travel to work together. It makes perfect sense."

Did it? Shouldn't a declaration of love come with a proposal of marriage? Shouldn't it sound better than being just the right thing to do?

"I'll think about it. I…I'm not sure I'm ready for marriage."

"Hey," he said, pushing up to a sitting position—and Sally had to avoid looking at him as the sheet dropped to just below his waist. "I didn't think I was ready, either, but we can make it work. We have a lot going for us."

"In bed, maybe," she admitted, tying the belt on her robe tightly at her waist. "But we still hardly know each other."

"We can learn about one another better if we're living together."

"You're persistent, aren't you," she said with an evasive laugh. "I need time. We don't have to rush. I said I'd think about it, and I will."

Kirk rose from the bed, the sheet falling away to expose his nakedness as he walked toward her and lifted her chin with one finger. His lips were persuasive as he kissed her, coaxing hers to open so he could explore her mouth more intimately.

"I'll be waiting for your answer," he said, his voice—and a very specific part of his anatomy—heavy with desire. "Shall I wash your back in the shower?"

And just like that she was putty in his hands. Hands that were already at the sash of her robe, undoing the knot and pushing the silk from her shoulders. Hands that roamed her body, cupping her breasts and tweaking at her nipples until they were tight points that sent shivers through her body as his palms skimmed their hardness. Hands that moved lower and pressed against the other nub of sensitive flesh at the apex of her thighs until she was quivering with need.

Needless to say, they barely made it into work on time. Even though her hair was pulled back into its usual ponytail, it was still damp. Sally hoped no one would notice and jump to the right conclusion, especially as she and Kirk had been seen together.

As she walked through her floor, she was welcomed back by several members of her team, who appeared genuinely concerned for her. It was gratifying. She was a part of this, a part of these people and what they did here. But she wanted more than that. She wanted more, period. She wanted a sense of certainty that she was working to her full potential, that she was achieving something worthwhile for herself, on her own merits.

If she agreed to marry Kirk, wouldn't she simply be absorbed into the life he'd created for himself? How would she maintain her hard fought for identity? How could she expect her colleagues to treat her as an equal rather than as someone they had to watch themselves around? And then there was her goal of moving up the professional ladder. Who would believe she earned a promotion when she had things nicely sewn up between her father and Kirk?

On a more personal level, Kirk had admitted modeling himself on her father, both professionally and personally. She already had one overprotective father in her life—she didn't need another person sheltering her constantly. When—if, she corrected herself firmly—she married, she wanted to be treated as an equal by her partner.

Kirk had already made it more than clear that he wanted to be her protector and provider. That sounded to her as if what she brought into a marriage didn't even rate a consideration on his revised grand plan. And, when it came to working together, based on Kirk's standing within HTT and his grasp of what the company offered and how they could remain current and relevant into the future, his knowledge and experience far exceeded her own.

Doubts flew at her from all directions. Maybe she never really would be any better than who she'd always been—the woman on the eighth floor who stayed in the background and allowed others to get the credit for her ideas.

Over the course of the day, as she caught herself back up on her projects, she found her mind wandering backward and forward until she was almost dizzy with it all.

As she sat down in her office to the lunch Kirk had packed for her before they'd hurriedly left her apartment, she forced herself to reevaluate her goals. After a great deal of deliberation, she had to recognize that, no matter what, she wanted to be a part of Harrison Tanner Tech now and in the future.

When Benton took her home that Friday evening, she was still in turmoil. Over the weekend, she spent time making a list of all the reasons why it would be good to marry Kirk Then, she made a list of why it wouldn't work.

"No matter which way you look at it, great sex does not equate to a great marriage," she said out loud once she was done. "And great sex does not equate to lifelong happiness, either."

By the time she went to bed on Sunday evening, she felt sure she'd reached her decision. Now it was just a matter of telling Kirk.

Twelve

Kirk had been in the office since five this morning. Staying one step ahead of the mole was a challenge he enjoyed getting his teeth into. The only thing he'd enjoy more would be unmasking the traitor and seeing them punished to the fullest extent of the law.

In the meantime, the company was running smoothly and the merger activities were fully on track. This week was shaping up well, and he was relieved that Orson would be back in the office full-time starting today. The man's recovery had been steady, and he'd been itching to get back to his desk full-time.

Kirk paused for a moment and considered the talk he'd had with Orson last night. Orson had continued to express his approval of Kirk marrying Sally. He was old-fashioned enough to want to see his grandchild born in wedlock, but he'd cautioned Kirk that while Sally appeared to be soft and gentle, she had a core of steel and a determined independence that didn't waver once she had her mind made up on anything.

He was heartened her father saw that in her but wondered if Orson had ever expressed any admiration for those traits to Sally's face. It might have gone some way toward helping her beyond her phobia if she realized that her father wasn't waiting for her to fail in everything she did—he was actually waiting for her to succeed. Of course, maybe she knew that all along. Maybe that was, in itself, as much of a yoke around her slender shoulders as anything else.

He felt a buzz of excitement at the idea of being married to Sally, of being a couple. Of waking to her each morning, of spending free time together and looking forward to the birth of their child. His son or daughter's life would be so vastly different from his own. And his wife wouldn't experience any of the suffering his father had put his mother through. Sally would never have to fear a fist raised against her in frustration or anger, and his child would grow up secure in the knowledge that their father was there for them every step of the way. There'd be no trade-off. No coercion. There would be love and stability and all the things Kirk had dreamed of as he'd made his plans for his future all those years ago.

A sound at his door made him look up. As if thinking about Sally had caused her to materialize, there she was. Kirk felt a now-familiar buzz of excitement as he saw her standing there. He'd seen Sally wear many different faces and in today's choice of a black tailored pantsuit with a pale gray patterned blouse underneath, she looked very serious indeed. As he rose and walked around his desk to greet her, he wondered if she wore one of those slinky camisoles beneath the blouse. His hands itched to find out.

"Good morning," he said, bending to kiss her.

She accepted his greeting but withdrew from his embrace quickly.

"Kirk, have you got some time to talk?" she said without preamble.

"Sure, for you, always."

He gestured for her to take a seat and he took the guest chair angled next to hers. As he did so, he studied her face carefully—searching for any telltale signs of tiredness or strain. She was a hard worker, harder than many here, and she needed reminders every now and then to put her needs before the needs of the company.

"I missed you over the weekend," he said.

She'd made it clear to him on Friday that she'd wanted space—time to think about them—so he'd given it to her. Now he wondered if that had been the right move. Her expression was hard to read as she looked up at him, the pupils in her eyes flaring briefly at his words. Did her body clench on a tug of desire the way his did right now? Had she spent the weekend reliving their lovemaking on Thursday night? She averted her gaze and shifted in her seat.

"What did you need to talk about?" he coaxed.

"I've reached a decision about your proposal."

He felt a burst of anticipation. "When can we start making plans?"

"I don't want to marry you."

What? "I see," he said slowly.

But he didn't see at all. When they'd come to the office together on Friday morning, it had felt so right, so natural. As if they'd been together forever and would be in the future, too. He searched her face for some indication of what she was thinking and watched as she moistened her lips and swallowed a couple of times, as if her mouth was suddenly dry. He got up and poured a glass of water from the decanter on his desk and passed it to her.

"Thank you," she said, taking a brief sip and putting the glass back down on his desk. "I didn't see the point in keeping you waiting on my answer. So, if there's nothing else we need to discuss, I'll get to work."

She got up from the chair and started for the door.

"Hold on a minute."

She froze midturn. "Yes?"

"I thought we were a little closer than that. Can you at least tell me why? Are you sure you've thought this through?"

"Since the first time you asked me, I've thought of little else. We don't live in the Dark Ages. Having a baby together is not enough reason to marry. We can coparent just as effectively while living our separate lives. I don't see why this—" her hand settled briefly on her lower belly "—should change anything."

Her voice grew tighter with each word. If he didn't know better, he'd have thought she was on the verge of a full-blown panic attack. But didn't that only happen when she had to speak to a group? Unless, of course, she was so emotionally wrought by the idea of turning him down that she was working herself up.

"Take a breath, Sally," he urged her.

"I'm fine," she said testily. "I'm perfectly capable of looking after myself. Look, I knew it wouldn't be easy to tell you my decision, and I suspected you wouldn't be happy about it. I just would like you to respect my choice and let us move on."

"You're right, I'm not happy about it," he said, trying to rein in his frustration and disappointment. "I didn't just ask you to marry me for convenience's sake, or because of how things look. I want to be a daily, active part of my son or daughter's life. I want to ensure that he or she doesn't miss out on the bond between father and child the way I missed out with my own father."

She closed her eyes briefly, and he saw her chest rise and fall on a deep breath. When she spoke, she sounded calm, but he could see the tension in her eyes and etched around her mouth.

"We can work to make sure that our kid knows we're always going to both be there for them. But that doesn't mean we have to get married or even live together—a shared custody arrangement will work perfectly well in our situation, just as it does for people all over the world. Seriously, Kirk, being married is no guarantee of a happy home when the two people involved don't love one another—it isn't even a guarantee when they do!"

Her voice rose on the last sentence, and he watched as she visibly paused to drag in a breath and assume a calmer attitude. "Look, I understand how you feel, but remember, you are not your father. You're not a drug addict. You're not going to let down this child, or any other child you might have in the future. It's not in your nature. I believe you'll be a good father, and I'm happy for you to be fully involved in your child's life. I just don't want to marry you. Please, will you respect my decision?"

There was a quiver in her voice that betrayed her rigid posture. If he was a lesser type of man, he'd push her now, try to persuade her otherwise. Use all the ammunition he could think of to try to get her to change her mind. But despite the desire to do so, he realized that if he pushed her too hard, he'd probably only succeed in pushing her away for good. He clenched his hands and then forced himself to relax, unfurling his fingers one by one. Decent men didn't give in to emotion like this. Decent men didn't bully or threaten so they could get their way.

"I do respect your decision," Kirk said heavily. "But I would beg you not to close the door on the idea entirely. Please allow me the opportunity to try to get you to change your mind."

"No. Please don't." Her voice was firm again and she was very much back in control. "In fact, I think it would be best if we confine our interactions to work-related matters only."

"You can't be serious. What about the baby?"

He couldn't help himself. The words just escaped. Was she truly closing the door on everything between them? Everything they'd shared?

"I will keep you apprised of my ob-gyn appointments and of course you can come along with me to those, but everything else—" she waved her hands in front of her "—stops now."

Kirk felt a muscle working at the side of his jaw, and he slowly counted to ten, forcing himself to relax. Then he nodded.

"If that's what you want."

"It is. Thank you."

He stood there, overwhelmed by disappointment and frustration as she walked away. This wasn't how he'd imagined this panning out at all. Sometimes, it seemed that no matter how well you planned things, it all just fell apart anyway.

By the time she got home, Sally couldn't remember how she'd gotten through her workday. From the moment she'd left Kirk's office, it seemed that everyone had wanted a piece of her and her time. The first of the new hybrid cars for the fleet were ready for pickup, and she'd had to coordinate the coverage with the managers involved and the PR team so when the next company newsletter went out it did so with the appropriate fanfare. There had been no point in making a media announcement. Not when DuBecTec had already stolen the wind from their sails.

Sally slumped down on her sofa, weariness pulling at every part of her body. All she wanted to do right now was take a nap. In fact, a nap sounded like a great idea, she decided as she swung her feet up onto the sofa and leaned back against the pillows she had stacked at one end. She'd no sooner closed her eyes than her cell phone rang. With a groan she struggled upright and dug her phone out of her handbag.

Kirk's number showed across her screen. She debated rejecting the call but then sighed and accepted it.

"Hello?"

"I just wanted to give you a heads-up. The media have gotten wind of the fact that you're pregnant, and that it's my baby."

All weariness fled in an instant. "What? How? Who?"

"That's what I'm going to find out," he said grimly. "But I wanted you to be prepared."

"But we agreed not to tell anyone. I'm not even showing yet. How could something like this have happened?"

Was this some ploy of Kirk's to try to get her to agree to marry him after all?

"The only other person we told is your father and I doubt he's responsible, but you can rest assured that I will be asking him."

With a promise to get back to her the moment he had any further news, and an admonition to screen her phone calls to avoid being badgered by the tabloid press, he severed the call.

Sally stood where she was, trapped in her worst nightmare. Now it didn't matter what she did anymore. Everyone at work would know. There'd be sly looks and innuendo and, no doubt, outright questions, as well. She'd hoped to have time to manage the situation. After all, she was still getting used to the whole idea herself.

Over the last few weeks, whoever it was that had been leaking information had held back. Oh, sure, the company had still faced some media criticism. There'd been the occasional aspersion about her father's illness in the media—the rhetorical questions about whether or not HTT's dynamic leader would remain as much of a power broker as he'd been in the past—but with Kirk's strong hand at the tiller and his no-nonsense leadership style while her father returned to full strength, those questions had faded as quickly as they'd arisen. But this was a personal attack against her and against her right to privacy. She felt violated and sick to her stomach.

She had to do something. But what? Attempting to discover who their problem was by using logic hadn't worked. So what did that leave? Her mind reached for something that she felt she should know, but everything came up blank.

Her landline began to ring. No one she knew actually used it. Even her dad used her cell number. She took a look at the caller ID but didn't recognize the number and switched the phone through to her voice mail.

Sally went to take a shower and change for an early night. She was no sooner out of the bathroom than the doorman buzzed from downstairs. Apparently there was a TV crew from a local morning show wanting to speak to her. Sally shook her head in disbelief. Aside from the time when she'd almost been kidnapped as a child, she'd only rarely been deemed newsworthy. After all, it was hardly as if she held the same kind of profile as her friend Angel, and Orson had actively avoided letting his family be exposed to the limelight of what he called pseudo celebrity. "I'd rather our family be judged on our achievements and what we do for others than by whose clothes we wear or what we were seen doing," he always said.

With a few tersely chosen words, Sally asked the doorman to ensure that she wasn't disturbed by the TV team or by anyone else not on her visitor list. She walked over to her windows and looked down at the parking lot. A second TV crew pulled into the lot. The onslaught had begun.

Thirteen

Thankfully, by the next morning, the gossip news focus had moved to the latest public celebrity meltdown and Sally's pregnancy had been relegated to a footnote. That said, when she was ready to leave her apartment for work, she discovered there were two bodyguards assigned to her—one to remain with the car at all times, the other to escort her inside and ensure she wasn't harassed by anyone. She was surprised to learn that the additional man had been ordered by Kirk, but she wasn't about to complain. She had no wish to discover that her car had been bugged or to be ambushed by anyone with a microphone.

She had planned to have lunch with Marilyn today and was looking forward to catching up with her. Everyone had been working so hard lately that it felt like forever since they'd had a good talk. The morning went by quickly, and the photo shoot for the new cars and their assigned drivers went according to plan. Sally was beginning to feel like she had a handle on things. At one o'clock she went down to the lobby to wait for Marilyn, who was just a few minutes late.

Sally kissed the older woman on the cheek and gave her a warm smile when she arrived. Shadowed by Sally's bodyguard, they walked a block to their favorite Italian restaurant for lunch and were shown to their regular table.

"So, tell me," Sally asked after the waiter had poured their water and given them menus to peruse. "How are things in the ivory tower?"

Marilyn smiled a little at the moniker given to the executive floor at the top of the building. "Busy. Mr. Tanner has yet to appoint a PA of his own, which doubles my workload."

"Have you asked for an assistant? I'm sure Dad—"

"Oh, I don't want to worry your father about something as ridiculous as that. I do work a few extra hours now, but it's nothing I can't handle. I guess I should consider myself lucky. At an age when most of my peers are settling down and enjoying their grandchildren, at least I still have a rewarding career."

Did Sally imagine it, but was there a tinge of regret, or possibly even envy, in Marilyn's tone?

"I'm sure Dad wouldn't see it as a worry, Marilyn—you know you can talk to him about anything. After all, you've worked for him for how long now?"

Marilyn's face softened. "Thirty years next week."

"Wow, that's got to be some kind of record."

"Your father and I are the only original staff left. I keep telling him it's time to pass the reins on to someone else. For him to slow down and actually enjoy the rest of his life. For us both to retire." Her mouth firmed into a straight line, and her eyes grew hard. "But you know your father—work comes first, last and always with him. I would have thought with this latest business with the leaks to competitors, and then with his heart attack, that he would have learned his lesson about slowing down—but oh, no. Not him."

It was the first time Sally had heard bitterness in the other woman's voice when talking about Orson, and it came as surprise. Normally Marilyn would stand no criticism of her boss from anyone. To hear it from her own lips was definitely something new. Maybe it was just the extra workload she had now, supporting two senior managers, that had put Marilyn in a sour mood. Even so, Sally felt she needed to defend her father.

"He's always tried to make time for family—and HIT has always been his other baby. I don't think you should be too harsh on him."

"You know I care about your father. I only want what's best for him. It would be nice if he'd just stop focusing on work with that tunnel vision of his and look around him once in a while. Anyway, that brings me to something that's been bothering me awhile. When were you going to tell me about the baby, Sally?"

Sally swallowed uncomfortably. "I didn't want to make a fuss at work, Marilyn. I'm sure you understand why, especially given how hard I've had to work to earn any respect there."

"But I'm not just *anyone*, am I? I thought we were closer than that."

"And we are," Sally hastened to reassure her. Marilyn looked truly upset that she hadn't been told, and, in hindsight, perhaps Sally should have included her in the news, but she'd had her reasons for wanting privacy, and they hadn't changed. "I'm really sorry, Marilyn. I don't know what else to say."

The older woman sniffed and reached in her handbag for a tissue and dabbed at her nose. "Apology accepted.

Now, what are you having today? Your usual chicken fettuccine?"

Sally hesitated before closing her menu. "Yes, I think so."

Marilyn placed their orders and the food was delivered soon after, but Sally found herself just toying with her fork and pushing pasta from one side of her plate to the other. It wasn't that she wasn't hungry, but she was still unsettled by how Marilyn had spoken about Orson. She'd never heard the other woman make a criticism of her father before. Ever. To hear it now had struck a discordant note, and it got her to wondering.

Marilyn was privy to pretty much everything that went over Orson's desk. Given her current disenchantment, could she be the leak Kirk and Orson were looking for? She was the last person anyone would suspect, given her long service and well-documented loyalty to Orson. Was it even possible that she'd do something so potentially damaging to the company? How on earth would she benefit from something like that?

The questions continued to play in the back of Sally's mind over the next day and a half until she couldn't keep her concerns to herself any longer. She had to talk to someone about it. She called her dad at home and asked if she could come over.

Jennifer let her in the door as she arrived.

"Dad in the library?" Sally asked as she stepped inside.

"Where else is he at this time of evening?" the housekeeper answered with a smile. "Mr. Tanner is with him."

Sally hesitated midstep. Her dad hadn't mentioned anything about Kirk being over when she'd called. Maybe he hadn't wanted to put her off coming. She'd already told him that she wasn't planning to see any more of Kirk outside the office and that she'd turned down his proposal. Her father had expressed his disappointment, stating that he firmly believed a child's parents ought to be married. Without pointing out the obvious—that his stance on the matter was archaic at best—Sally had made her feelings on the subject completely clear, and he'd eventually agreed to abide by her wishes.

She'd barely seen Kirk in the office over the past few days. And she'd kept telling herself that was just the way she liked it. Regrettably, her self begged to differ. The thought of seeing him now made her pulse flutter and her skin feel hypersensitive beneath her clothes. *You can do this*, she told herself. She could talk to him and her father in a perfectly rational and businesslike manner without allowing her body's urges to overtake her reason.

"Thanks," she said to the housekeeper. "I'll let myself in."

"Can I get you something?"

"No, I'll be fine, thank you."

The idea of eating held no appeal. She already felt sick to her stomach over what she suspected. Maybe she was completely off track with it, but what if she wasn't? It would be good to have the benefit of someone else's opinion.

Her father and Kirk rose from the wing chairs by the fireplace as she entered the library. She crossed the room and kissed her father, nodding only briefly to Kirk.

"It was an unexpected, but lovely surprise to get your call this evening," Orson said when they'd all settled down again.

"It may not be so lovely when you hear what I came to say," Sally replied, smoothing her skirt over her thighs.

She stopped the instant she realized that the movement had attracted Kirk's attention. Her gaze flicked up to his face, and she saw the flare of lust in his eyes before he masked it. Lust was all very well and good, she told herself, but it wasn't love, and unless he could offer her that as well, she had to hold firm.

"That sounds ominous," Kirk observed.

"I could be completely wrong, but I think I might have uncovered the leak."

Both men sat upright, all semblance of relaxation gone in an instant.

"Who?"

"You have?"

Their responses tumbled over each other, and Sally put her hand up and looked directly at her father.

"Dad, you're not going to want to believe this, but I think Marilyn is behind it all."

"Marilyn? What? She's worked for me since before you were born. Heck, I've known her longer than I even knew your mother."

A shaft of understanding pierced Sally's mind. Was that an explanation for Marilyn's behavior? She'd said she cared for him, but was she in love with Orson? Had she been all along? Was that why she wanted him to slow down?

"Think about it, Dad. Who else had access to the information that's been spread? Even the news of the baby. No one else aside from the three of us knew at HTT. Unless you told Marilyn."

Orson shifted uncomfortably in his chair and puffed out his cheeks. "Well, I might have told her that I was looking forward to being a grandfather. She may have put two and two together from that. And as for linking you and Kirk together, she's very astute, and someone would have to be deaf, dumb and blind not to see the way you two look at each other."

Sally stiffened in shock. They would? She looked over

to Kirk, who appeared equally shocked. He rubbed a hand over his face and leaned forward, elbows on knees.

"Sally, what brought you to this conclusion?"

Of course he wanted proof. As would she in the same position, but somehow it rankled that he was the one asking her, not her father.

"It was a few of the things she said to me over lunch the other day." Sally repeated them for the men. "There was a tone to her voice, a hardness that I hadn't heard in her before. She sounded really fed up. Bitter. Angry. Plus, she was the one to cast doubt on me, telling Dad that I told her I was frustrated with my job—which is not true."

"We'll have to interview her," Kirk said to Orson. "Test the waters without making an outright accusation. We'll need to be careful. We don't want her suing us for defamation."

"Oh, Marilyn wouldn't do that," Orson protested.

"If she's behind the leak of information, then she's already shown she's willing to hurt the company. I tell you what. I'll do a little investigating of my own. Have my forensic specialist delve a little deeper. If she is responsible, she's very, very good at hiding it. It might not be so easy to prove."

Sally fidgeted in her chair. She felt terrible for believing that the culprit could be Marilyn, but if she was their leak, she had to be stopped before she did irreparable damage to the company. Each information release had undermined HTT's integrity just that little bit more. The loss of new business had been felt, and if existing clients began to doubt the safety of their information and started to withdraw from HTT, it wouldn't take long before the company truly began to crumble.

"Should I tell her to take some days off?" Orson asked

Kirk. "She's due for some time, and she's been working long hours lately."

"No, I think that would tip her off that we suspect her. Better to just keep things going as normal."

After a brief discussion about their plan of attack, Sally stood to leave.

"It's late and I'm tired. I'll be heading home unless there's anything else you need me for?"

Kirk stood, too. "I'll take you home. It's time I headed off, too."

"That's not necessary. I have my driver and my guard."

"Please, I'd like to talk."

"I'll tell Jennifer to let your men go," Orson said, getting up and going to the door. "And I'll see you two at work."

He was gone, leaving them alone together. Sally bristled at Kirk's nearness. She grabbed her handbag and headed toward the door, but Kirk beat her to it, holding the door open for her as she went through.

The scent of him tantalized and teased her. Reminding her of what she was missing out on, of what was right there, hers for the taking if she wanted it.

And she did want him. But what she really wanted was more than he seemed willing to give. Love, forever, the whole bundle. And he hadn't offered her that.

"Sally, slow down a sec," Kirk called as she strode out down the corridor to the front door.

He drew level with her, and she gave him a querying look.

"In such a hurry?" he teased, taking her by the arm and making her slow to his more leisurely step.

"I am, actually. I wasn't lying when I said I was tired. I really need to get home."

Kirk looked at her more carefully. In the subdued lighting in the library he'd only seen how beautiful she was, but here, in the main entrance, he became aware of the shadows under her eyes and the strain around her mouth. It brought his protective instincts to the fore and made his gut clench in concern.

"Is everything okay with you, the baby?" he asked.

He'd been so frustrated by her refusal to consider their marriage that in all honesty he'd been avoiding her these past couple of days. Part of him hoped that absence might make her more willing to reconsider his proposal, while another, less calculating part was learning to deal with not getting his own way. It wasn't something he'd had to do often in adulthood, and he found he didn't like it now any more than he had back when he was a powerless child. But he couldn't force Sally to accede to his suggestion, and she had made it very clear that she wouldn't be coaxed, either. Which was all the more frustrating.

Kirk escorted her down the front stairs of the house and held the door to his car open for her. She stopped in her tracks.

"This isn't your usual SUV, is it?"

"Nope. This one's a hybrid."

She turned and looked at him. "Really?"

"How can I expect everyone else to follow your sustainability proposal if I'm not doing it myself?"

He closed the door as she settled in her seat and resisted the urge to punch the air in triumph—he definitely hadn't missed that look of approval on her face. Score one for him, he thought with a private smile as he walked around the back of the vehicle and to his door. As he got in and secured his seat belt, Sally spoke again.

"And the other managers?"

"As their leases come due on their existing vehicles, even good old Silas will be going hybrid or full electric."

"Seriously?"

"No point in being halfhearted about it, is there?"

"And you approach everything in your life full-out like that?"

He caught her eye and hesitated a few seconds before answering. "When I'm permitted."

She looked away.

"Are you sure you're okay? Not overdoing things?" he asked.

"I'm fine. Did you get my schedule of prenatal visits?"

He nodded. He hated this skirting around the subject he really wanted to discuss, so he took the bull by the horns.

"Sally, I wish you'd change your mind about us marrying. I can promise you my full commitment to making it work. To being a good husband and father."

She shook her head slightly. "I thought we agreed to leave this subject where we finished it."

"Actually, no. *You* said the subject was closed. But *I'm* still very open to negotiation." He started the car and put it in gear, driving smoothly up the driveway and through the automatic gates that swung open as he approached. "I miss what we had."

She stiffened beside him. "What we had was a few brief and highly charged sexual encounters. Nothing more than that."

"Really? Is that how you see it? You know more about my background than any other woman I ever dated."

She snorted. "If they know less than me, then I'm sorry for them. I don't even know what your favorite color is. What kind of food you like. Your favorite drink. Your favorite author. We don't know one another at all."

"Blue, Italian, beer and J. K. Rowling."

"Kirk, it's not enough. And not knowing you isn't the only thing. I don't want to marry you. Please respect that."

Silence fell between them. And then Sally giggled.

"What?" he asked, not feeling at all like laughing given her very solid rejection.

"J. K. Rowling? Really?"

He shrugged. "What's wrong with a little fantasy in a man's life? I've done reality every day for thirty-four years. When I read I like to escape into someone else's world."

Sally fell silent again. When he pulled into the parking area at her apartment, she sighed heavily.

"I apologize for laughing. I didn't mean to poke fun at you—it just seems so incongruous. You strike me as more the type to enjoy self-help books, or male action adventure."

"I read those, too. You asked for my favorite author." He shrugged. "I told you."

He got down from the car and opened her door for her before escorting her up to her apartment. She opened the door and turned to him.

"Thank you for driving me home. I'm sorry if I disappointed you again. Good night."

And before he could reply, she was inside her apartment and the door was firmly closed behind her.

Kirk stood there a full minute before spinning on his heel and heading for the elevator. She might think she'd had the last word on the subject of their marriage, but one thing she hadn't yet learned was that, for him, disappointment only served to whet his determination and appetite for success. One way or another, he'd figure out how to break her walls down. He had to, because somewhere along the line she'd become less of a challenge and more of a necessity in his life.

Fourteen

Sally tried to give Marilyn a breezy smile as she arrived at her father's office. She'd never make it as a spy, she told herself. It was all she could do not to break down and beg Marilyn to explain why she'd done it. It had taken a week, but Kirk's specialists had found a trail, well hidden, of the information Marilyn had misused. She and Marilyn had been called to a meeting with Orson and Kirk to discuss what was going to happen next. Sally knew Kirk wanted to press criminal charges, and he had every right to, but she honestly hoped it wouldn't go that far.

"I don't know what this is about, do you?" Marilyn asked her as she quickly smoothed her always immaculate hair and reapplied her lipstick.

"No," Sally lied, not very convincingly. "Have you heard anything?"

"Not me," Marilyn said with pursed lips and a shake of her head. "But then, since Kirk Tanner has come on the scene, I'm the last to find out about anything, even your pregnancy."

Sally stiffened at the veiled snipe and watched as Marilyn fussed and primped in preparation for the meeting. She wondered again how it had come to this. The woman had been a maternal figure to her for as long as she could remember. It was one thing to betray the company, but the betrayal of Orson and his family went far deeper than that. What on earth had driven her from faithful employee to vindictive one?

Marilyn snapped her compact closed and returned it to her handbag, which she locked in the bottom drawer of her desk.

"Right, we'd better go in, then," she said, standing and squaring her shoulders as if she was preparing to face a firing squad. "Ironic, isn't it? That I was your support person not so long ago and now you're mine?"

Sally could only nod and follow Marilyn into her dad's office. Her eyes went first to Kirk, who wore an expression she'd never seen on his face before and, to be honest, hoped never to see again. Anger simmered behind his startling blue eyes, and his lips were drawn in a thin, straight line of disapproval. Orson, too, looked anything but his usual self. The second she saw him, Marilyn rushed forward.

"Orson, are you all right? You look unwell. Are you sure you should be here today? I told you you've come back to work too soon."

Orson stepped back from her. "Marilyn, please. Don't fuss—I'm absolutely fine. Take a seat."

"But surely we can put this off until some other time. You probably should be resting."

"Please, sit!" he said bluntly.

Marilyn looked affronted at his tone, her gaze sliding

from Orson to Kirk and back again before she sniffed to show her disapproval and finally did as Orson had asked. Sally sat in a chair next to her, perched on the edge of her seat. She knotted her fingers together in her lap and kept her gaze fixed on the floor. Orson resumed his position behind his desk and Kirk drew up another chair next to Marilyn and turned slightly to face her.

Once everyone was settled, Orson began.

"We have had some…difficulties…in the past year with losing business to DuBecTec. At first I thought it was just their good luck, especially with their strengths in networking systems, but as it happened more often, I began to suspect that we had a traitor in our midst here who was feeding information about our prospective clients to our competition."

Sally flicked a look at Marilyn, who shifted in her seat but kept her silence. The tension became so thick you could cut it with a knife.

"And it seems that the traitor was quite happy to set Sally up to take the fall for their insidious and, quite frankly, illegal behavior. I could have forgiven a lot, but I cannot, ever, forgive that."

Sally was shocked to hear the break in her father's voice. She hadn't expected him to bring the suspicions of her own conduct into the equation, but to hear him stand up for her like that came as something of a surprise. He'd barely mentioned the accusations against her when she'd returned to work, but now she could see a cold fury simmering beneath his professional facade. She began to feel some sympathy for Marilyn, but that was soon dashed as the older woman began to speak.

"But Sally was cleared, wasn't she? Of course she was. She had nothing to do with it, I knew that all along and so should you!" Marilyn protested.

"That's right, she had nothing to do with it," Kirk said, rising from his chair and moving to stand beside Orson's desk. "But the strain *you* put her under by planting evidence against her was inexcusable."

"What? Wait. Me?" Marilyn's voice rose in incredulity.

"We have proof, Marilyn. We know who our culprit is," Orson said heavily. "What we don't know is…why?"

"I don't know what you're talking about," Marilyn insisted, but her face had paled and small beads of perspiration had formed on her upper lip. She looked toward Sally. "Tell them, my dear. Tell them I could never be involved in something like that. I love this company and I love your fa—"

Her voice cut off before she finished her sentence, as if she'd suddenly realized she'd revealed too much. She slumped back in her chair, her gaze shifting from Orson to Kirk and then Sally before settling back on Orson.

"I have loved you for thirty years, Orson Harrison. And this is how you treat me?"

Orson, too, had paled. "This is about your behavior—not mine," he said gruffly. "And you know there has only ever been one woman for me."

Marilyn laughed, a brittle, bitter sound. "Well, I was good enough for you once, wasn't I?"

"I told you then and I'll tell you now, it was a wretched mistake. I was a grieving man reaching out for comfort, and I never should have put you in that position."

Sally looked at her father in shock. He'd had an affair with Marilyn after her mother's death? How on earth had they continued to work together for so long after that? Had Marilyn's unrequited love been what kept her, day in and day out, at her desk in the hope that one day

Orson Harrison would change his mind? Sally swallowed against the lump that had solidified in her throat.

All her life Marilyn had been there. With no mother to turn to, Marilyn had been the one to explain about the things girls needed to know about their bodies, to talk about what was right and wrong when it came to boys, to take her shopping for her first bra. To dry her tears when her best friend from elementary school moved away or when a high school crush broke her heart.

At every major turning point in her life, Marilyn had been the female perspective she'd needed. Now she was learning that Marilyn had loved Orson for all those years. And yet, despite all of that, despite all those years, she'd been quite happy to let Sally take blame for something she herself had done—even knowing how much that stigma would hurt Sally and Orson.

"I can't believe you were going to let me take the fall for this, Marilyn."

"Oh, please. As if it would have been an issue for you. Your father would never press charges against you. And besides, it's not as if you need the work. You were born with a silver spoon in your mouth. No, it would all have been neatly swept under the carpet and maybe, just maybe, the shock would have been enough for Orson to finally see *me* again. Do you know why he never took our affair any further? Because of you. Because he didn't want you to feel he was replacing your mother. After you freaked out at the funeral, he realized how weak you were. How needy you'd become. So he put me on the back burner."

Orson rose to his feet. "That's not true!"

Marilyn also stood. "Isn't it? It certainly felt like that to me. Do you realize what I've given up for you? Everything, that's what. My youth. My hopes. My dreams for a family of my own. But you didn't care. And when I thought you might finally be coming around, that with the right encouragement you might step away from the business and maybe actually look at retirement with me still there by your side, what do you do? You merge with *him*! The son of the man who almost destroyed this company just as it was getting off the ground!"

She pointed a finger sharply in the air in Kirk's direction. "Even after your heart attack you kept working, when a rational man would have given up. Don't you see? I did all that for you, for us! Can't you understand what it was like for me? How I was looking down the barrel of retirement alone? I gave my life for you, Orson. And in return you gave me nothing."

Kirk stepped forward. "I think you've said enough, Marilyn. You are hereby relieved of your duties at Harrison Tanner Tech. I'm calling security to come and hold you until the police can be called so we can press charges."

"No, wait," Orson said, looking a lot older than he had only short moments ago. "This is my fault."

"Dad, no. It's not," Sally cried, pushing upright out of her chair.

"Honey, I'm man enough to admit my mistakes. I shouldn't have turned to Marilyn for comfort, but I made a much bigger error when I expected there not to be any repercussions. Marilyn, I'm sorry. I should have taken better care of you at the time. I should have found you employment elsewhere instead of continuing to take your loyalty to me for granted."

"Orson, she betrayed everyone here with her actions. She could have destroyed everything," Kirk argued, his hands clenched futilely at his sides.

"But we stopped her in time, didn't we? I don't want

to press charges." Marilyn gasped in shock, and Orson fixed his gaze on her. "Even though they are warranted. What you did threatened not only my family but the families of all the staff here. It was unforgivable."

"I did it for you," Marilyn repeated brokenly.

"No." He shook his head sadly. "You did it for you. But I will right my wrong." He mentioned a sum of money that made even Sally's eyebrows rise a little. "I will offer you that severance on the condition that you leave Washington, never come back and never contact me again. The legal department will draw up a nondisclosure agreement. Upon signing, you will agree to say absolutely nothing about what transpired during any of your time working here. You will never share information about the company, me or my family ever again. Do you understand me?"

Marilyn sank back in her chair and nodded weakly. "You're sending me away?"

"I'm giving you a chance to make a new life, Marilyn. The choice is yours. Take it and rebuild, or stay and face the consequences of what you've done."

Not surprisingly, Marilyn accepted his offer with the scrap of dignity she had left. As she turned to leave the room, she looked at Sally.

"You think it's all about work and making a name for yourself here, but it's not. One day you'll be just like me. Alone."

Sally stood to face her. "No, I won't be like you, Marilyn, because I could never do what you've done to hurt the people who've always supported you."

Kirk escorted Marilyn from the office and requested security to accompany her from the building once she'd removed her personal effects. Anger still roiled through him, unresolved. He didn't agree with Orson's offer, didn't trust Marilyn as far as he could kick her, but he had to abide by the older man's dictates.

Marilyn looked broken as she moved about the outer office, packing her personal mementos. All the fight and fire gone, every one of her years etched deeply into the lines on her face.

So much damage, so much risk—and all for unrequited love? It wasn't as if she'd even done it out of spite or greed. She'd done it to try to force the man she loved to notice her—to stop being the work-driven tycoon he'd always been.

And wasn't he just like that, too? Hadn't he modeled himself on Orson Harrison his whole adult life? Didn't he aspire to enjoy the same success Orson had? But at what cost? After Marilyn had been escorted away, Kirk sighed heavily and returned to Orson's office, his thoughts still whirling. He'd asked Sally to marry him, more than once, without stopping to consider what he was offering her. Oh, sure, he said he wanted to be a hands-on parent—there for his child every step of the way. But had he even once stopped to consider Sally's feelings?

What about *her* needs, her dreams for the future? Had he ever asked her about what she wanted? No, it had all been about him. Him and his desire to be everything his father wasn't. The realization was an unpleasant one.

He'd never considered himself a selfish man—he'd always bestowed that honor on his father, who always put his needs and addictions first. But looking at himself right now, Kirk found his actions wanting. He needed to change. He needed to be a man worthy of a woman like Sally Harrison if he was ever going to win her.

Kirk closed Orson's office door behind him and sat heavily in the chair Marilyn had vacated.

"She's gone?" Orson asked.

He still looked drawn, but beneath his pallor Kirk detected the steely determination that had made Orson the successful man he was. On the other side of the desk, Sally looked shaken, as well, but he saw the same strength in her. He wondered if either father or daughter realized how alike they truly were.

"Yes," Kirk answered. "The legal department is standing by for your instructions."

"Good, good. I'll get to that next. Have you two got a few minutes? We need to talk."

"I'm okay for a while," Sally said. "But if you'd rather, Dad, we can do this later. I know you're upset. I'm pretty stunned myself. I trusted her all my life."

"And I trusted her with mine. It's taught me a painful but valuable lesson. My own lapse in judgment in having that brief affair with Marilyn led her to nurse false hopes that there could one day be more between us. For myself, all I ever felt after that encounter was guilt and disappointment in myself. I guess that's one of the reasons I kept her on here. I felt I needed to make it up to her that I couldn't offer her more." He sighed and shifted a set of papers on the desk in front of him.

"Looking back won't change anything, but we can look forward, and my heart attack was a long overdue wake-up call. I've been reevaluating things, and I believe I am ready to step back and relinquish many of my responsibilities here. I want to be able to enjoy the rest of my life, enjoy my grandchild when he or she comes along. I want to take time to focus on what really matters before it's all taken from me."

"Dad, are you sure? Medically there's no reason—"

"No, medically there is no reason for me not to stay in this saddle for a good many more years yet. The thing is,

I don't want to anymore. And I'm starting to think I don't need to. The company will be in fine hands even if I step back, and you…I suppose part of the reason I stayed was because I felt the need to look out for you. I turned to Marilyn for advice about you once your mother passed away, especially when it became apparent that you were struggling with your phobia. When Marilyn told me not to push you, I didn't. In fact, I didn't ever encourage you to reach your full potential, did I? I could have done a better job in teaching you to reach past your fears, but I deferred to what I believed was her better judgment instead of listening to my own heart as your father. And despite all that, you strove for excellence anyway. Look at you now—head of your own department here and motivating the entire firm to embrace sustainability. You've achieved that by your own hard work, not from any handout from me.

"I know it hasn't been easy for you here. I've heard the rumors that you only got your position because you're my daughter. Despite—or maybe because of—my doing my best to protect you, there are others who've made things difficult for you. And still, you've never quit, never given up."

"I get that from you, Dad. When it comes to tenacity, you're king, right?" Sally smiled, and Kirk felt his gut twist at the bittersweet expression on her face.

Sally's father's words echoed in his head. He'd been just the same, just as determined to try to shelter and protect Sally—to make her decisions for her rather than trust her to make her own. To be her own person.

"I'm very proud of you, Sally, I want you to know that. I'm not just proud of you, the woman, I'm incredibly proud of what you have achieved here. If you were anyone else, I would have been fast-tracking you on a development program—pushing you up through the ranks to senior management. But I obviously had my own prejudices when it came to my daughter in the workplace. So, I want to ask you a question. Do you want to take on the additional training and responsibilities that come with escalating your seniority in the company?"

"It's what I've always wanted," Sally said in a strong voice.

Her blue eyes glowed with excitement, and Kirk began to see the woman she truly was. Not just the beautiful blonde who'd turned his head in a bar one night. Not just the lover who'd tipped his world upside down. And not the woman who now carried his child. Instead he saw who she should have been all along. A strong, intelligent individual who deserved to shine.

"But what about my phobia?" she asked. "Won't that be a problem?"

"We will find a way to work around it. You're getting better—I'm told your sustainability presentation was going very well until you fainted." Orson's tone was teasing and indulgent. "Right, that's decided then. Kirk, she's going to need support from you in this. Can I rely on you to be there for her?"

"If it's what Sally wants, then I will be there for her every way she needs me," Kirk said in a steady voice.

"Good," Orson replied. "Now, if you'd give Sally and me a moment or two alone? Then perhaps you and I can meet over lunch to iron out a few changes."

"Sure." Kirk got up to leave and paused at Sally's side. He resisted the urge to lay a hand on her shoulder. It wasn't what he'd do with any other colleague, and his desire to touch her would have to be firmly kept in rein from now on. "I'll call you this afternoon to schedule some time to discuss your plan going forward, okay?"

"Thank you," she said with an inclination of her head. "I'll look forward to it."

And yet, as Kirk left the office, he had the distinct impression she looked forward to anything but.

He'd created that resistance between them with his behavior from the very first moment he'd met her. He had a lot of work to do if he hoped to build their relationship to any kind of level where she would let him back in again.

Fifteen

Sally watched her father reorder the papers on his desk again. Clearly, he was uncomfortable with what he was about to say to her. Never hugely demonstrative, to hear him offer the words of pride he'd given her today had been a golden moment for her. For the first time since that awful moment at her mother's funeral when she'd frozen in front of all the mourners, she felt as though she had his attention for all the right reasons.

Orson cleared his throat. "Sally, are you sure you want to follow this leadership track?"

"As I said, Dad, it's what I've always wanted. I just never thought you believed in me enough to suggest it, to be honest."

Sally cringed inwardly at her words. She'd never had this kind of discussion with her father before, but obviously the time for openness between them was long overdue. They'd each always done what was expected of them, without a thought for what either of them really wanted. Orson was right—it was time for change.

"Hmm." Her father nodded, then looked up and pinned her with a look. "What are you going to do about your feelings for Kirk?"

"My what?"

"Don't play coy with me, my girl. It's no use denying it. I might not have been the best father in the world, but I know my daughter. You love him, don't you?"

Sally sat frozen in her chair. She'd pigeonholed her feelings for Kirk as inconvenient at best, especially when it was clear he didn't love her. But had her developing love for Kirk been so painfully obvious? Her father continued.

"I guess what I really want to know is, are you going to act on those feelings, or are you going to let the opportunity for a long and happy married life slide by you because you're too afraid to speak up for what you really want?"

"I'm not afraid. I know what I want, and it begins and ends with this company," she said bravely.

"Are you sure about that? Your mother and I didn't have long enough together. There isn't a day that goes by that I don't think of her and miss her with an ache that never fades. Work gives me something to do—but it's no substitute for her. Don't be like me, honey. Please. You and my grandbaby deserve more than that."

Sally looked at her father in surprise. Were those tears shimmering in his eyes? Surely not. But then, he'd changed since his heart attack. He'd obviously spent time reevaluating his life and found it wanting. He was right, though. She had to give her own and the baby's future careful thought. Obviously she wouldn't block Kirk's access to his child, but marriage? She still wanted to hold out for what she believed marriage to be—a deep commitment to blend the lives of two people who would love each other until their dying breath, and beyond.

She chose her words very carefully. "I have given it a lot of thought, and I reached my decision. I would ask that you respect my choice. I want more than just a marriage and security. Between the trust fund Mom left me and my salary, I'm in the fortunate enough position that I certainly don't need a partner for financial security—even with the baby. But if I'm to consider marrying anyone, I need to be certain that they can provide what I need on an emotional level, and right now I don't think he can."

Orson slumped in his chair, disappointment and acceptance chasing across his features.

"Thank you for being honest with me about how you feel, Dad," Sally continued. "It means more to me than you probably realize to know you care. And I'm sorry it isn't what you wanted to hear, but this is my life and I have to take care of me, too, not just the baby."

She rose and went around to him and wrapped her arms about his shoulders. "I love you, Dad."

"I love you, too, honey."

Sally went back downstairs to her department and shut herself in her office, but she couldn't concentrate on the work in front of her. Her mind was whirling with everything that had happened today. So much to take in. But if her father and Marilyn's example had taught her anything, it was that she shouldn't settle for a relationship that was anything less than what she truly wanted.

She wanted more than just to settle for the sensible option. More for her baby, more for herself. And one day maybe she could have that. Working her way up the ladder, taking more responsibility here at work was all she'd ever wanted careerwise, and now, finally, she was on track to attain that. If she found a truly fulfilling love, then she'd embrace it. If not, she'd be fine without it. She didn't doubt for a minute that she'd be able to balance motherhood and work. Of course it wouldn't be easy, but women around the world combined successful, high-octane careers with parenting. She would make adjustments and she'd cope.

And, with that, Sally was finally completely satisfied with her decision. She would not compromise. She would not marry without a reciprocated love. Despite their chemistry, she and Kirk both deserved more out of a relationship than that. They would successfully co-parent, the way countless others had before them. And even if seeing him every day—being mentored by him—would likely be absolute physical and emotional torture, she would do it rather than compromise on her values.

You couldn't make someone love you—Marilyn was proof of that. All the wishing, hoping or pushing couldn't do it. And living with unrequited love was equivalent to a lifelong sentence of unhappiness.

If she was certain of anything, it was that she deserved so much more than that.

Kirk kept his distance from Sally even though it killed him. Orson had cut his hours back to two and a half days a week, which put a great deal more responsibility on Kirk's plate. Thankfully, he'd been able to hire a new PA, and the woman was a marvel at organization. She also had the uncanny ability to anticipate his needs, which made his life roll a great deal more smoothly.

Without being obvious, Kirk kept a close eye on Sally. She'd quickly settled into a pattern, attending the leadership program mentoring sessions with regularity. Judging by the standard of work she was returning to him, she was spending a lot of hours outside the office on the tasks assigned to her. He was surprised at her tenacity, but then again, didn't her résumé reflect that she'd been tenacious all her life?

She was doing excellent work with the sustainability rollout. It was also being implemented in the other branches of HTT, which meant some travel time for her, both by air and road. He'd heard she was slowly overcoming her speaking issues, too. Granted, the groups she was dealing with were all smaller than here at the head office, but Nick had reported back regularly that she was doing better with each presentation.

He hated it when she was away and had recruited Nick to ensure that she ate regularly and well. The other man had been surprised but had taken it in stride. It meant that when Kirk made his nightly calls to her while Sally traveled, he didn't have to come across like a drill sergeant checking she was taking her vitamins and supplements and getting enough sleep.

Christmas had come and gone. Sally was sixteen weeks pregnant now and had the cutest baby bump. Kirk had bookmarked a website on his laptop that showed him the stages of pregnancy, and he marveled every day at the changes that were happening in Sally's body. The realization that it was his child growing inside her still took his breath away. Their latest prenatal appointment, where they'd heard the baby's heartbeat, had made the pregnancy overwhelmingly and incredibly real and had left him feeling oddly emotional.

He looked at his watch. She should be back home from her New York presentation by now. Her flight had been due in about ninety minutes ago. Would she object to him making a check-in call? Too bad if she did. Suddenly he had the overwhelming urge to hear her voice.

Except when he dialed her apartment, there was no reply. That was odd. He called her cell phone and got an automated message saying her phone was off or out of range. A sick feeling crept through him. He wasn't one to jump to conclusions, but something didn't feel right.

Kirk was just about to call Nick's cell phone when his screen lit up with an incoming call. It was Orson.

"Kirk, it's Sally. She's been taken to the hospital."

A shaft of dread sliced through him, stealing his breath and making his heart hammer in his chest.

"What is it, what's wrong? Is it the baby?"

"I'm not sure, and she's not answering her phone. I just got out of a meeting to find that she'd left me a message saying she'd landed but that her leg was sore and swollen and that Benton was taking her to the hospital to be checked out. A swollen leg after flying, that's not good, is it?"

It wasn't good, not under any circumstances. Along with learning about the growth of the baby, Kirk had been driving himself crazy reading about risks in pregnancy, and he knew that a swollen leg could be indicative of a blood clot.

"Where do they have her?"

"She didn't say. She told me not to worry, but it's kind of difficult not to when you love someone, right?"

Orson's question reverberated through Kirk's mind. Was that what this sudden abject fear was? Love?

"Leave it with me, Orson. I'll see what I can find out and let you know the minute I hear anything."

"Good, thanks. And if she calls me, I'll be sure to tell you."

Kirk called Nick's phone and finally got hold of him, except the man could offer him no help. Sally had apparently been fine when he'd left her at the airport with

Benton. Kirk hung up as quickly as he could and called the bodyguard, who was in the ER waiting room at the hospital. The moment Kirk had the details and had shared them with Orson, he was in his car and on his way to the hospital.

He released Benton to go home as soon as he arrived, promising to let the man know Sally's prognosis the moment he heard anything. Then began the struggle to get some information on Sally's condition. But it appeared that no amount of coercion, charm or outright badgering would budge the staff. And so began the longest two hours of his life.

This was far worse than when his mother had died. By the time her cancer had been diagnosed, it had been too late for treatment and they'd had a few months to come to terms with things—as much as anyone came to terms with impending death. But he'd known and understood every step of her journey. Had made it his business to. This, though—it was out of his control, and he found he didn't like it one bit.

Fear for the baby was one thing, but a possible blood clot was a serious business and could potentially put Sally's life at risk. The very idea of losing her terrified him. He'd agreed to abide by her wish not to marry, as much as he'd hated it, but right now he wished he had pushed her harder to accept him. Then he'd have the right to know what was happening, how she was.

He got up and began to pace, but the ER was a busy place and there was hardly enough room for anything, so he found a spot against the wall and stared at the double doors leading to the treatment area and waited. And, as the hands on the clock on the wall ticked interminably by, he couldn't help remembering what Orson had said.

She told me not to worry, but it's kind of difficult not to when you love someone, right?

Love. He'd never imagined he'd ever know what true, romantic love was. He'd seen what love had done for his mother and how her affection for his father had slowly been crushed out of her until all that was left was sadness and despair. When he'd created his life plan, he'd known he was prepared to settle for respect and affection in marriage without the soaring highs or devastating lows that so many people experienced on the road to happily-ever-after. He didn't have time for that, didn't need it, didn't want it.

And yet, he wanted Sally. Wanted everything to do with her—to be by her side, to guide her and see her reach her career goals, to watch her become a mother and to traverse the minefields of parenthood together. But most of all, he finally realized, he wanted to love her. He wanted the right to be the one she turned to in times of trouble or in times of joy. He wanted to be the one to fill her heart with happiness, to take her problems and make them go away. He wanted to laugh with her, live with her and love her forever.

Kirk realized he was shaking. The yearning inside him had grown so strong, so overwhelming that tears now pricked at the back of his eyes. He hadn't cried since his mother passed, and then only in the privacy of his own home. But this—it was raw, it was real and he'd never felt so damned helpless in his entire life.

A movement behind the doors caught his attention and he saw Sally being wheeled out by an orderly—a fistful of papers in her hand and a tired smile on her face. A smile that faded away in surprise when she saw him striding toward her.

"Kirk? What are you doing here?"

"I'm here for *you*, Sally," he said, and he'd never meant anything more seriously in his life.

Unfortunately the ER waiting room was not the place for the discussion they desperately needed to have.

She looked a little disconcerted but then nodded. "I'm fine—honestly. I've been cleared to go home."

"Everything's okay?"

"Yes. It was just an overreaction on Benton's part. I mentioned my leg was a bit achy and swollen when he met me at SeaTac, and he insisted on bringing me straight here."

"I'm giving him a bonus. That's exactly what he should have done. You didn't give him grief about that, did you?" he asked as they walked toward the exit.

"I was going to, but then I thought about the traveling I've been doing lately and, to be totally honest, I got scared about what it could have been and was only too happy for someone else to make the decisions for me. But why are you here?"

"Orson called me. He got your message, which was pretty scant on details and left us both worried."

"I should call him," she answered, reaching in her bag for her phone, which she turned on. "Oh, I've got missed calls. Dad—" she scrolled through the list "—and you."

"We were concerned."

Those three words didn't even go halfway to explaining how worried he'd been. They reached the parking area and Kirk helped her into the car and waited, not bothering to start the car yet, as she called her dad to reassure him that everything was okay.

"No, no, I'm fine. I don't need to come to your place. Everything checked out normal—just a bit of fluid retention. No, Dad, it's really nothing to worry about. They did scans and everything."

Eventually she hung up and sighed heavily.

"Tired?" Kirk asked.

"Worn-out."

"Let me take you home. You're sure you don't want to go to your father's? Or my place?"

"What part of 'I'm fine' don't you men seem to understand? Look—" she yanked her discharge papers from her bag and shook them at him "—everything is normal."

But there was a wobble to her voice that struck Kirk straight to his heart. She'd been afraid and alone. He didn't stop to think twice. He simply reached out his arms and closed them around her, pulling her toward him. In the confines of the car it was a challenge to offer her the comfort he knew she needed, but he did his best.

At first she stiffened and began to pull away, but then she sagged into him and he felt her arms reach around his waist.

"I'm so glad you're okay, Sally. Quite frankly, I was terrified for you. I never want to feel that afraid again."

She sniffed, and he loosened his hold so he could grab a bunch of tissues from the glove box. She took them from him and wiped her eyes and blew her nose.

"Thanks. Can we go home now?"

"Sure."

He waited for her to buckle her seat belt before doing the same, and then he drove to her apartment. Once there, he followed her inside.

"Sit down," he instructed. "I'll make you a hot drink."

It was a measure of how tired she was that she didn't protest, just merely offered her thanks. Kirk quickly brewed a cup of chamomile tea and brought it to her. The china cup and saucer felt incongruously delicate in his large hand, a simile for the delicacy of their relationship and how he could all too easily damage it if he didn't use care, he realized.

He sat down with her as she sipped her tea, and when she was finished he put an arm around her, encouraging her to snuggle against him and relax. She felt so right in his arms. Sexual attraction aside, there was something incredibly satisfying about just being with her. And that was a crucial part of getting to know one another that they'd skipped. Maybe if he'd been more restrained, had shown more of his interest in getting to know all of her and not just her body, they'd have stood a better chance.

But now he had something to fight for. He knew, without any doubt, that he'd fallen crazy in love with this incredible, strong woman. He just hadn't let himself see that his feelings went deeper than physical appeal. Hadn't wanted the mess and the clutter in his emotional life that he knew being in love could bring. Today had taught him that he'd been so very wrong.

"Sally?" he asked, wondering if she'd fallen asleep.

"Hmm?" she answered.

"Could I stay tonight?"

She shuffled away from him, and he felt the loss as if a piece of him had been sliced away.

"Stay? Here?"

"I can sleep on the couch. I don't expect…I just need to know you're going to be okay and to be on hand to get you anything you need."

When she started to protest, he put up a hand.

"Seriously, I know you're worn-out with the visit to New York and flying home and having been to the hospital. And if I left you here alone, I wouldn't sleep a wink—I'd be up all night, worrying about you. Let me help you, for both our sakes, okay?"

She stared at him, her blue eyes underlined by shadows of weariness that made him want to do nothing more than swoop her up into his arms and take her to her bed and insist she stay there for the next week. But he didn't even have the right to suggest it.

"Okay, if that's what you want."

"Thank you."

"But why, Kirk? You know I'm okay, don't you? I don't need to be monitored or anything."

"I know. *I* just need to be sure. Today scared me more than I thought it was possible to be. It brought a few truths home to roost."

Sally raised her brows. "Oh?"

"It made me take a good long hard look at myself. At what I want. I meant what I said at the hospital. I'm here for you. And I really wish I had the right to be here for you on a permanent basis."

She sighed and looked away. "Kirk, we've discussed this. I told you I don't want to marry you."

"I know. I've been an idiot. You were right to turn down what I was offering. I thought that all it would take was for us to agree to be a couple, but today taught me that there's so much more than that. Yes, I wanted the dream—the beautiful wife, the perfect child, the career every man envies. But I wasn't prepared to work hard enough for any of that. I wasn't prepared to make myself vulnerable or even admit that I needed anyone else to achieve my goals. To be totally honest, I was prepared to accept something that would look more like a business partnership than a marriage, and it absolutely shames me to admit it."

Sally frowned, looking uncertain. "What are you saying?"

"I'm saying that I didn't believe you needed love, real love, to make a successful marriage. But now I know that for a marriage to really mean something, the people have to truly mean something to each other."

She nodded slowly. "That's my understanding of it, too. I won't settle for less."

"Me either. Standing there in that ER waiting room, knowing I had no right to be there with you, no right to support you the way you deserve to be supported—" His voice cracked, and he rubbed a hand across his face. "Sally, it was the toughest thing I've ever done in my life, and it made me realize something very important."

"And that is?"

"That I love you. I'm not a man who is big on expressing my feelings, but please believe me when I say that today was hell on earth for me. You mean more to me than any person I've ever known. I want to spend the rest of my life proving that to you, if you'll let me."

"And the baby?"

"And the baby, too, of course. But no matter what, I love you—and whether you agree to marry me or not, I always will."

Sally's eyes washed with tears and she looked away. For a moment he thought she was going to turn him down, but then she looked back at him and a tentative smile began to pull at her lips.

"Always?" she asked, her smile broadening.

"Forever. I mean it."

"And I'll continue in the leadership program at work?"

"Of course. You're a valuable member of the team, why wouldn't I want you there?"

"Forever, you say?"

He nodded, holding his breath.

"I couldn't accept your proposal without love, Kirk. My parents had a short but loving marriage. No one deserves less than that. Even you."

He looked at her in confusion. Was she turning him down again? Was she saying she couldn't love him? It would kill a piece of him to accept her decision, but he'd do it if that was what made her happy.

Sally reached out and took his hands in hers. "Thank you for opening up your heart to me tonight. I needed to hear it—needed to know that you had it in you to feel as deeply for me as I feel for you, because I love you, too."

Kirk sucked air into his lungs, barely able to believe the words she'd just said.

"Thank you," he said on a whoosh of air. "You have no idea how happy that makes me."

She nodded and leaned in until her lips were just a whisper away from his. "Me too," she answered before kissing him. She drew away far too quickly and smiled. "There's just one thing I need to ask of you."

"Anything," he hastened to say. "Name it and I'll move heaven and earth to make sure it's yours."

She shrugged and gave him another of those beautiful sweet smiles. "You probably don't have to go that far," she teased.

"What do you want from me?" he asked.

"Will you marry me?"

"I absolutely will," he said and bent to kiss her again.

When they drew apart, Kirk looked at Sally, stunned by the gift she'd bestowed on him. "You won't regret it. I promise to spend the rest of my life making sure you don't."

"As I will, too," she answered solemnly.

For a moment they simply sat there and drank in each other's presence, but then Kirk looked around them. "So, about me sleeping on the couch…"

Sally laughed out loud, a full-throttle belly laugh that immediately had Kirk responding in kind.

"I think we can forget the couch tonight, don't you?" she said, getting to her feet and offering him her hand.

And, as Kirk walked with Sally into her bedroom, he knew that he was the luckiest man on earth. Lucky to have learned the truth about love before it was too late. Lucky to have a child on the way. And most of all, lucky to have this woman in his life.

* * * * *